JOAN NORLEV TAYLOR is a New Zealander of Anglo-Danish heritage currently living in Wivenhoe, England. Her writing has been published in the UK, USA, Australia and New Zealand. In addition to novels and poetry, she has written a narrative history of the travels of Elizabethan merchant adventurer Henry Timberlake (*The Englishman, the Moor and the Holy City*, 2006) and edited and annotated a 19th-century Danish memoir (*Cecilie Hertz, Livserindringer: Memories of My Life*, 2009). She also writes academic non-fiction in her specialist fields of ancient religion, history and archaeology. Having taught at Waikato University in the departments of History and Religious Studies, she now works at King's College, London.

By *the same author*

FICTION

Conversations with Mr. Prain (New York: Melville House, 2006; reissued with a new cover and reading group questions, 2011).

kissing Bowie (London: Seventh Rainbow, 2013).

NAPOLEON'S

*W*ILLOW

JOAN NORLEV TAYLOR

RSVP

First published in New Zealand by RSVP Publishing Company Limited
PO Box 93 Oneroa
Waiheke Island
Auckland 1081
www.rsvppublishing.co.nz

Napoleon's Willow
ISBN 978-0-9876587-8-4

Cover Design by Jane Dixon-Smith
Edited and typeset by Stephen Picard
Set in 11pt Palatino
Printed in New Zealand by Wickliffe New Zealand Limited

National Library of New Zealand Cataloguing-in-Publication Data

Taylor, Joan E. Norlev
Napoleon's Willow : a story of Akaroa / Joan Norlev Taylor.
ISBN 978-0-9876587-8-4
I. Title.
NZ823.3—dc 23

Visit www.rsvppublishing.co.nz for more information about all our books.

for Aroha

and dedicated to the memory of my father,
Robert Taylor

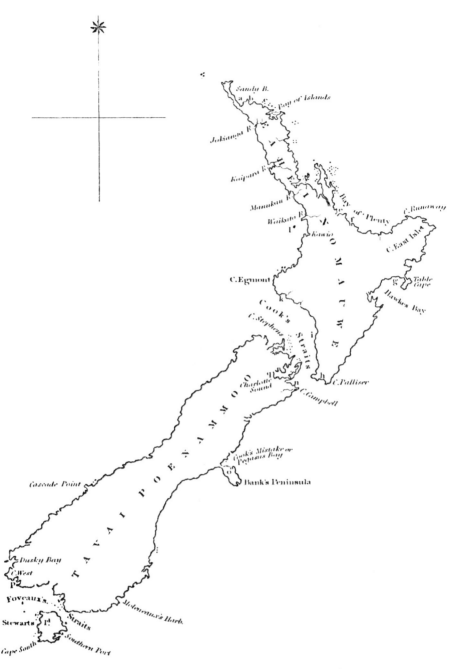

Sandy B.

Bay of Islands

Jokianga R.

Kaipara R.

Manukau R.

Waikato R.

Kawia

Bay of Plenty

C.Runaway

C.East Isle

C.Egmont

Table Cape

Hawkes Bay

Cook's

C.Stephens

Straits

Charlotte Sound

C.Palliser

C.Campbell

Cook's Mistake or Pegasus Bay

Cascade Point

Bank's Peninsula

Dusky Bay

C.West

Foveaux's

Moleneux's Harb.

Stewarts Id.

Straits

Cape South

Southern Port

EAHEINOMAUWE

TAVAI POENAMMOO

NEW ZEALAND.

Geographical Miles

Contents

A Glossary of Maori Words

atua – god(s)
hapū – wider family, clan
iwi - tribe
kahikatea - white pine, *Dacrycarpus dacrydioides*
kainga or *kaika* – village
kākā - forest parrot, *Nestor meridionalis*
karakia – ritual chants, blessings
kumara – sweet potato
mana - prestige, authority, status, spiritual power
matai – black pine
mātua – parents
moko - tattoo
pā – fortified village
Pākehā – European (origins of the word are obscure)
paua – shell fish
pūhā – a type of sowthistle, *Sonchus kirkii*
pipi – cockle
rangatiratanga – chiefly authority
tamariki – grandchildren.
Tāne – god/guardian of the forests
Tangaroa – god/guardian of the seas and oceans
tangata whenua – people of the land
tapu – restricted
tī-kōuka - cabbage tree, *Cordyline australis*
Tinirau – god/guardian of sea creatures
tipuna – grandfathers
toetoe – a type of tall grass, *Austroderia*
toheroa – shell fish
tohunga – expert, healer, sage
totara – tree
urupā – burial ground
wairua – spirit, soul
waka – canoe
weka – woodhen, *Gallirallus australis*
whānau – family

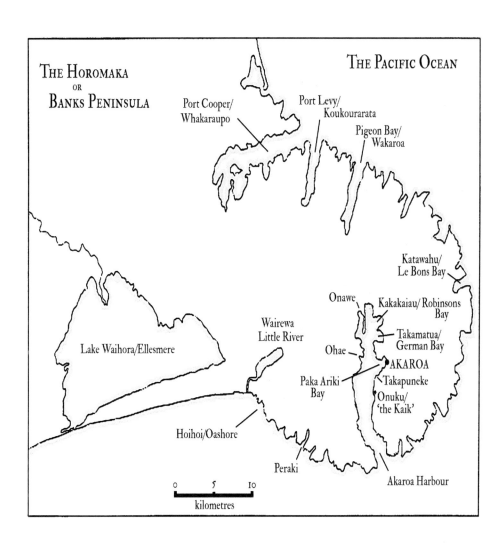

THE HOROMAKA
OR
BANKS PENINSULA

THE PACIFIC OCEAN

Port Cooper/
Whakaraupo

Port Levy/
Koukourarata

Pigeon Bay/
Wakaroa

Katawahu/
Le Bons Bay

Onawe

Kakakaiau/ Robinsons
Bay

Wairewa
Little River

Takamatua/
German Bay

Lake Waihora/Ellesmere

Ohae

AKAROA

Paka Ariki
Bay

Takapuneke

Onuku/
'the Kaik'

Hoihoi/Oashore

Peraki

Akaroa Harbour

0   5   10
kilometres

1
St. Helena

He was looking for a tree in the middle of an island, in the middle of an ocean. He climbed upwards, faltering as the earth lurched. He cursed himself for losing his balance. He'd need to find his land legs after so long on the waves. He'd need to find his land sight, because everything seemed strange now that he was accustomed to the ship and the swaying seas.

He stopped for a moment and observed the steep cliffs, as sharp as a saw. How this landscape must have cut the soul of the Emperor Napoleon, exiled by the cruel victors after Waterloo, imprisoned here on St. Helena: the remotest island on earth.

It was September, 1837. The lone walker was in his late twenties, of average height, well-built and strong, with heavy eyelids and thin dark hair. François Lelièvre – dressed as a crewman – was a blacksmith from Normandy, hired to serve on board the French whaler, the *Nil*.

It was his ship of exile. He was destined to roam, he believed, since the failed Bonapartist uprising of the year before. France had rejected him, and so he would be a homeless wanderer, with only the hope of visiting this one place in all the world where he could find a brief moment of rest.

He had to go on. The first mate would start wondering where he was.

François Lelièvre planted each foot firmly on the ground and quickened his pace. At the top of the next hill he picked seeds of aloes and wild geraniums and stuffed them in his pocket. After rounding a bend, he walked past a residence bleakly named 'The Briars'. A Union Jack was flapping at the top of a high pole.

He strode even faster, until at last he paused again and turned to look down at the ships anchored at harbour, and the bleached houses of Jamestown. The settlement seemed now to be just a cluster of paper cuttings stashed in a huge grey fold of rock far below. How could people live here?

Panting, François now shook off his sailor's jacket and tied it around his waist. He pulled his black cap down tightly on his head so that the blustering air wouldn't whip it away.

It was quiet; no birds were singing. The wind pulled at his shirt and tugged at his trousers, like the fingers of a port whore. He drank from a water bottle.

He looked ahead again to a tribe of goats on the green grass and beyond to the mountain top, where clouds lay like a pile of carded wool. He gazed down at a dazzling view of the southern coast laced with thin white waves. There was nothing to this island.

Going on, he took a path away from the main track and scampered along a meandering route down into a small, woody valley. He was following directions given to him at the alehouse, and everything was as expected.

A paradise. He entered another world. There was birdsong and the sense of a tiny forest.

As he descended he looked at a stream formed by a natural spring, an area of grass and wild flowers, and several weeping willows, framed by a fence. As if to welcome him, the sun came out and shone down, like a man with a gaslight showing him a sacred grotto, and he paused, a little shy. Delicately, he opened the gate, and paced forwards.

The grave of Emperor Napoleon lay not far from the stream, behind a plain iron railing, with his name on a concrete slab: 'Napoleon Bonaparte'.

François felt a rising tightness, and dropped to his knees. How could they do this? How could they not return his body to the French people, to lie in French earth?

He could not help himself and began to cry. But as he wept he found his anger turning to awe. To think that Napoleon himself lay beneath! Here he was, kneeling next to the emperor.

Over the grave hung the largest of the weeping willows, brushing its branches on the iron railings. He knew what had been said, that it was under this very tree that the emperor used to sit in his terrible solitude – writing, remembering. A rustling breeze blew the leaves of this and other willows edging the stream, making their boughs sway like skirts, and the water pattered like dancing feet on an earth floor. Such natural motion surrounded a point of utter immovability: that concrete slab, a coffin. Here they'd buried him, in this place where Napoleon had spent his lonely days.

And then the stab of a voice.

"Oy, Frenchie. Come 'ere alone, did ya?"

François jumped to his feet and spun around to face the English-speaker, alarmed and embarrassed at being seen at such a time of emotion, and fearful he would be arrested as an unauthorised intruder. He did not understand a word. The Captain of the *Nil* was an American, Gilbert Smith, but the shipboard language was French. The only English words François knew from the Captain were his curses.

The British soldier was a hard-eyed, swaggering youngster, dressed in that red uniform with the white cross that always made François think of shooting practice. This soldier was clearly returning from his duty of patrolling around the valley. Ever since the burial of Napoleon here, in May, 1821, the place had been visited by travellers en route to the South Seas, drawn by the grave of the dead emperor and the power of the willow, all wanting a memento to take away with them. The guard looked derisively at this new pilgrim, and held his rifle fast.

François took off his cap and greeted this guard formally in his most polite French, meaning: "Good day, sir. Excuse me, but I am a blacksmith from Normandy, on board a whaler, the *Nil*, which lies now at anchor. I come to visit the grave of our Emperor Napoleon. I understood that this was permitted. Many of my companions on board wish to make the same journey, tomorrow, only I came as soon as I could, for I am a blacksmith, as I said, without so many duties."

The guard whistled through his teeth to hear this barrage of French, and looked around. "*Seul?*" he said.

Alone? Or did he mean to say *saule* - willow? François hesitated.

"*Vous tout seul?*" said the guard, loudly and emphatically, or rather: Voo toot sul. The English made the French language into bricks. You are alone?

"*Oui.*," he replied. I am alone, he thought. That was his manner of living, always. He was never one of a crowd. He was silent when others would speak. He kept his thoughts to himself.

13

"*Seul*," repeated the guard, nodding, grinning, as if pleased that he had him completely at his mercy. Then he pointed to the willow that hung its branches low over the grave of Napoleon and made a slashing motion with his hand. "No chopping off pieces. *Ne pas couper.*" He shook his head.

François could see now that the willow had been cut back in many places, as people had taken bits of it away.

"Napoleon's willow," said the guard, continuing in English. "Know the story, don't you, Frenchie? Your Boney got a bit soft in the head out here and spent his days under this tree. He asked to be buried here, and we buried him here. So his corpse feeds the tree now, and look! Half of it has been taken away by the likes of you, as if you fancy a part a' the bones of Bonaparte. Ha!"

François looked at the guard's mouth moving, waiting for a word he could understand. Bonaparte. Ha.

"But... you've got to understand... the Governor thinks it's a right how d'ya do to see you frogs taking your relics. On an island named after St. Helena, at that, our English St. Helena who found the True Cross in Jerusalem! Governor thinks it's a blimmin' irony. Everyone knows what your bleeding emperor thought of religion... fucking atheist. It's not like this tree's the True Cross, is it, Frenchie? Boney's not Jesus Christ! 'A practice to be discouraged,' says the Governor. Now I know you don't understand a word I'm saying, you stupid French bastard, but let me give you a clue."

François, not comprehending the insults, could still tell by the manner of the guard that his words were full of derision. Then the guard shook a money pouch hanging on his belt and pointed again to the tree. François understood.

"Just between you and me, Frenchie, we could come to an arrangement."

As if he would pay this English idiot any money for a slip or two of the tree.

So, he played a trick. The guard wanted to know if he was alone. It was just his word of assurance that had confirmed it. Alone, he was at the soldier's mercy. But how would he cope with a throng?

He glanced away, up the track into the distance, and shouted, "Pierre, Henri, Charles... *venez voir!*" Come and see.

The guard twisted round.

"Bastard... you said you're alone."

"*Venez voir. Le saule de Napoleon!*" Come and see, the willow of Napoleon!

"Who's that up there?"

The trees up along the path shivered and groaned, like people weary from a long climb, conspiring with François to give the impression of intruders hiding behind their branches, to give voice to imaginary companions. You could almost hear their footsteps in the skitting leaves, in the pittering of water.

"Pierre, Henri, Charles! *La tombe est ici! Venez vite!*"

"Shut your fucking mouth!"

"*Allez les chercher.*" Go and look for them, said François to the soldier, "*C'est votre travail pour trouver les intrus.*" It's your job to find intruders.

The guard peered vainly at the track.

And then François shouted again, "*Venez vite, regardez l'arrogance du rosbif qui pue la merde anglais collé sur son cul.*" Come here, boys, and look at the arrogant meathead who stinks of the English shit stuck on his arse!

The guard ran towards the track and gazed up, straining to see the figures of three further French mariners arriving in the valley, and in an instant François Lelièvre whisked out his knife and swiftly cut two slips from the hanging willow. He turned and stabbed the blade into a long ridge of the bark, and pulled down, hard, ripping a piece away with dexterity, catching a shower of fragments in his hand. And then he ran. He did not look back to see the furious face of the guard.

A sound – a crack, something like thunder. A ping on a rock somewhere behind him.

As he heard the gunshot, François was running away, over the fence, through the stream, not knowing where he was running, just away, following the obscuring bodies of trees, listening to the shouted curses of the guard growing dimmer: words which he finally recognised from the Captain's language.

Like a hare, he could spring quickly out of sight. He went up, up, around, scrambling off, sure he could find his way back to the town even with a detour around the whole island. There was no danger of getting lost. St. Helena's Island was a tiny little rock, this place they had imprisoned Napoleon, after he'd surrendered in good faith when everyone knew he could have escaped from Aix. A hundred fishermen would have conveyed him to safety.

Such betrayal. Napoleon gave himself up to the English believing they would treat him honourably, as honourably as the emperor would have treated a defeated Nelson. Instead, he was conveyed to this prison and left to die. How could they have done this to him, the cowards? What were they so afraid of, to maroon the emperor on this miserable place, as if he was some monster they had to humiliate and kill slowly, by the torture of endless loneliness?

So François ran, up and up, with the trees hissing above him. There was no more gunfire. The curses stopped. The guard, perhaps, had no enthusiasm for a chase, only for an easy coin.

He slowed a little, and went on until at last he reached a barren plateau, high and windy, where there was a low, rambling house and farm buildings. He stood completely still then, breathing hard, amazed at what he was now seeing. *"Mon Dieu!"* François gasped, knowing at once that he'd found his way to Longwood, the place Napoleon spent most of his exile. When not with his willow, it was here that the emperor had sat, thought, read, written, and made his garden. He dug this very soil!

This was the place where the great man had died, sixteen years earlier! François remembered hearing the news from his mother, as she came back into the yard from the meadows, with her baskets full of wild, medicinal herbs. Her face was fierce. "They have killed him at last, the lion Napoleon, in their tiny cage. Never trust the English."

François inhaled deeply to get his breath, and looked back to where he'd come. Had he lost the guard? What should he do? There would be more of the English here – more guards perhaps? He glanced all around, listening intently, and quickly went to the walls, as if he might blend in with the white, painted boards. There was no sound of any human being. There were no dogs. The windows were shut up. The garden was overgrown.

Was the area deserted? Stealthily, he rounded the large wooden buildings until he came to the front entrance, which stuck out like a peninsula from the house. He walked up the steps under the middle of three arches formed by trellis work and paused, listening, on the veranda. Silence. No one was about. Eerily, the right-hand double door was standing a little ajar, and he pushed it open.

He walked forward into a large, dark entrance hall, on floorboards that squeaked as if in surprise, and saw in the corner of his sight the black flash of mice scurrying to hiding places. The hall was completely empty. There were no pictures on walls, or furniture, or rugs to make it look more homely. Slowly, quietly, he kept going, gazing around. Most of the shutters were closed, and small, cut-out circles let in light, like the moon shining through a cloud. There were two sad old flags – one French, one British – crossed over a fireplace, and some rags in a corner. Bits of wallpaper had been torn off the walls, and even wood from the skirting boards had been taken.

Then he reached another large room, and here he stood still, his heart pounding in his throat. He was clutching the willow cuttings and the bits of bark to his chest in a clenched hand.

He realised he was not entirely alone. At the far end of the room, there was Napoleon.

The bust of the emperor, laurel-crowned, was placed on a wooden stand near an unshuttered window: a bare room, with this one ornament, situated where Napoleon breathed his last.

François now inched forwards, one tender step at a time, and neared the effigy as if it were in some way alive. Before it, he paused.

That noble face! He looked at the blank eyes, the curve of the nose, the short hair. This is what he looked like. An image captured from a moment of life. This was how his mouth was formed. These were his ears.

Without thinking further, Francois released his fist from his chest, and held up the willow slips and tree bark in front of the emperor, as if in offering.

The wind gusted, and swung the front door of the house shut with a bang. François jumped, and heard from another room further inside the voice of a woman waking and yawning, and apparently talking to a cat or child, but such was François' sense of wonder at being in this place he was unsure whether or not he'd heard a ghost. The yawn, the whispering, filled him with dread. He felt the spirit of Napoleon here, as if it wandered up and down from the willow to the house, vagrantly, waiting to go home to France, unable to rest in peace. 'Everything for the French people,' his spirit seemed to say.

'Do not forget.'

But France herself had rejected him!

'Take me away with you,' his spirit demanded. 'Take me away.'

How, how?

The wind clattered a shutter, and shuddered the house. François felt suddenly caught by the walls, the windows, ceiling, floor. He had to go! This was a place of entrapment.

"Your willow will grow again in new soil," he said to Napoleon, as he stepped back. "It will grow, and your soul will have rest."

Then François ran, out through the front door of Longwood, leaving the sleepy woman to wonder at the sound of a voice, and footsteps, as the cat jumped from her lap.

François ran all the way to the corkscrew bends of the carriage slope along the eastern side of Jamestown Valley. He hurtled himself down the eight kilometres from Longwood to the cramped streets of the little town, far below.

By nightfall, he was back at the ship, exhausted, still clutching his willow slips and bark. The next day the ship sailed, for the sake of a fair wind, and none of the other mariners on board had a chance to disturb the soldier who guarded Napoleon's grave. This was François' moment, only his.

François kept the cuttings with their ends stuck in a potato in a tin hanging beside his hammock. The bark he put with the aloes and geranium seeds in a special painted box his mother had given him before the voyage, which held many dried roots and herbs, and some other seeds. She was a midwife, after all, and knew about such things. Onwards, went the ship, to the rich whaling waters of New Zealand.

2
Wivenhoe

In September, 1837, a young woman was weeping under a willow tree as the sun lowered. The branches hung around her like a ragged curtain of luminous green. The birds of the valley woodland twittered, and a busy stream tinkled at the bottom of a bank.

Held in this gentle lap of uncultivated land, Marianne sobbed hard, relieved to have the privacy to grieve. Here she did not have to keep things to herself. She could be hammered by tears, so that all of the sadness was broken up inside her where it lodged like a cold, hard slab. It was necessary to cry it out until there was nothing left but emptiness. She stopped, thinking she'd reached that point of cleansing, only to find new influxes of thoughts and memories filling her mind and heart.

"Oh God," she said aloud. It was like being sick.

She'd trusted him; that was the pathetic part. It wasn't as if she didn't know that seducers could say sweet words to a girl to woo them, without good intentions. This was a cheap tale of female folly. Everyone knew certain men could behave that way, to have their way, to march over all the inhibitions and constraints that made a good girl do the right thing. One moment you were the nice young lady; the next minute you were a trollop, simply on the basis of your response to what certain men were prone to do.

That was it: certain men. The behaviour of men who 'deflowered' some girl was discussed at the port all the time, but it was just not the kind of behaviour she'd associated with James. He was as pure as light, unable to do anything wrong. He could not be one of that devious category, or so she'd thought. He was not some dark-eyed rake in a high hat, smoothing his moustache, planting compliments and insinuations. That was not James.

James was a gentleman. He'd taken her out walking, because he loved to breathe the healing fresh air after his long residence in London; the doctors had ordered it. And the two of them on their walks had simply talked of everything in the world, and laughed, and spun around each other in a whirl of delight. He'd spoken so fulsomely of nature, and of love, and of everything that was ideal, beautiful and sweet. He'd read her poetry, sitting on the beach overlooking Fingringhoe, watching the redshanks and curlews.

How could James, of all people, be a seducer? How could James do this to her? Everything about him was warm and mild: his fair wavy hair, his shining blue eyes, the elegant clothes he wore, silk shirts, silk handkerchiefs, perfect nails. His heart was surely good. He was staying with Mr William Brummell, a much respected man, though not a kindly one. After all, Mr Brummel had taken poor destitute Susannah Brewer – with three small children and a dying husband – to court for stealing his turnips in the icy starvation of her winter, and she had to spend a week in gaol.

It was as if James had suddenly transformed into another person; there was a weird changeling in his place. This new James Placard would utter words such as: "I have to go back to London, Marianne, now my health is improved. Don't you see... we are free creatures of the spring and the summer, whose love withers in the coming autumnal chills. We are children of nature, this countryside and river, not the city. We are butterflies, whose dance is short." That could have been poetry, or something much rehearsed. But then it was followed by cruelty: "No one in London could accept our love. You must have known that there was never going to be a lasting commitment between someone like me and someone like you. Oh, your face! Don't you understand? My course is in the city and there are rules I cannot transgress... or else I'd be an outcast forever."

Marianne shook her head. If only Uncle had warned her! He'd met James at the funeral of Mr Ridge, father of the doctor who supervised James' care, with the church bell clunking idly, and Uncle had been given some chance to appraise James through conversation. He'd said afterwards only the merest word about "Londoners" being rather frequently in Wivenhoe ever since the experiment with the baths, after which Wivenhoe had become known among a certain part of society as a pleasant village charged with sea air, well-situated for constitutional walks and recuperation, and then he'd added that "Charlie Barrell's daughter went and married a London gent." So she'd interpreted that as hopeful approval. She'd hoped that one day she might be mentioned in the same way by others coming in to St. Mary's churchyard.

Oh folly: there were a hundred silly stories like hers. Uncle had thought she might, surely, marry James. She was, after all, courted by quite a handful of shipbuilding apprentices, especially Bill Sainty, who'd brought her tulips and Dutch cheese, and seemed truly crestfallen that first day as she'd sauntered off with James along the river. It was just that, ever since she'd gained some independence in her role as a schoolmistress, she'd felt she could do rather better in life than have the future a man such as Bill Sainty could give her. A few years ago she could have had her pick of ropers, sailmakers, coopers, blacksmiths and fishermen, but now they seemed ignorant and small-minded.

She needed a husband who could discuss remarkable things in the *Times*, the newspaper which arrived handed down through the town to Uncle's circle of friends. She relished all the stories of new discoveries in Africa, or the Pacific Ocean, and strange tales. The world was so diverse and extraordinary; she couldn't be with someone who only thought about building ships. She was thinking of perhaps a schoolmaster, or even someone in a commercial office: a man with some education and a wide view. She did not aspire to social status; she aspired to having a husband she would truly respect as a wife ought to, whose education and knowledge were better than hers. Yet she knew her place was nowhere as high as those who were invited to Wivenhoe Hall, the manor on the hill, sitting there as if it were a throne everyone couldn't help but look up to.

James had arrived and she'd almost tumbled over his bags on the quay as they were unloaded from the London ship. She hadn't been looking where she was going, hurrying back from buying oysters for Uncle's birthday, blinded by the April wind. That was their first occasion for laughter and conversation. She'd accepted the invitation to walks and picnics with the cursory approval of Uncle, whose mind was far more on ship-building and his friends than on the vulnerabilities of his niece. A lifelong bachelor with interests only in masculine matters, he'd noted that her age – twenty-three – made her ripe for marriage. She'd convinced him that no one could be better as a husband than a 'London gent' whose clothing, speech and polite demeanour appeared to indicate someone of a far better class than would normally take an interest in a schoolmistress living in a fishing port of less than two thousand people, where someone of good status was anyone not a smuggler (and most of the sailors were also at times smugglers) or an illegal liquor seller.

Oh Uncle. The shame! People would talk about her! They were probably talking about her already, but she'd been in such a bubble of romance she hadn't thought about it. What would they say now? Marianne knew people thought of her as something of an anomaly, having been brought up from the age of twelve by Uncle. They'd never really liked her mother, a French seamstress from La Rochelle, and she knew they'd bristled to hear the French language spoken between mother and daughter in public. French was the language of her home, her first tongue; even her father had learnt it. But the fear of the French was still strong. Uncle had done the best he could, once she was orphaned, to make sure he honed the mind of his ward with his own knowledge. He was a keen letter-writer, active in the anti-slavery movement, successful in aiding abolition, and was now concerned with the education of women. He sent her to the Wivenhoe 'British School', where she'd been a "bright little button" who had made him smile.

Marianne cried another stream of tears. Uncle had been so proud of her; doing well at school and becoming a proper English schoolmistress, with an income of her own. He'd been so pleased, after all those years of kindness, to see her well set up, either as an independent woman, or as a catch for someone who deserved a hard-working, unpretentious young wife with excellent skills.

And what had she done to repay him? She'd trusted James Placard, who'd said that in this new age love was more important than the old strictures of society. They had to throw off the constraints of the world and be free, like the natives of faraway lands, natural in the sheer innocence of their romance. And she'd wanted that. She'd found inside herself an eagerness for touching and closeness, skin on skin, fed by his words of love and the way his fingers explored her. He'd conquered bit by bit parts of her that even she barely saw. She could write poetry about this! Everything was extreme, romantic, carefree: a world of true adventure where true life was – raw life.

She'd believed him that pregnancy could only occur after full intercourse. She'd remained 'a virgin', or so she thought, and there was no one to ask for confirmation of such a delicate matter, no books to consult on this subject in the school library, nothing but James' word for it. They had come here to this willow tree in the valley woodland by the stream, relying on its distance from the village, its wildness and its obscuring leaves. They'd made this place their secret. Her best yellow, flowery dress she'd kept on, only releasing buttons, loosing petticoats and underclothing.

She leaned back on the hard bark he'd pressed her up against.

The willow tree, by the stream, was a tomb now. The memories were a corpse. She grieved at the sepulchre of the love that had died. James had turned dull and dim when some letter came from London and he'd felt bound to leave. Already she'd wondered about the lateness of her monthly bleeding, but she'd said nothing to him, fearing a blight on their final days. What she'd been waiting for, as the hours went by – she cried more to think of it – was that question.

She'd believed that any moment, after all that had passed between them, he would ask her to marry him. She'd dreamt it over a hundred times. He'd always said that once his cough had gone he would return to London – that was always clear. But she'd trusted that he would realise when that terrible moment came that he couldn't live without her. So then – given his wonderful passion for the new poetry – he would announce that social status was nothing to him when nature told him to love, and he would bring her to London as his proper wife. He would rise in the legal profession and she would be his loyal supporter and confidante, running his home, raising his children, in perfect happiness.

So those hours had closed around her like a suffocating pillow. Her words were stifled. Her heart was extinguished. His words, his expression, were devoid of warmth.

"Oh my God!" she cried aloud again. How could she have been so stupid? Wasn't this a story told over and over? How many women throughout time had been in this same wretched position? Men could do what they liked, but women were held inside a veil of sexual virtue. How many stupid girls had suffered the same ridiculous fantasies? He hadn't even made promises. She'd trusted without there being any cause to trust, simply because she loved him. She thought he was good.

"God help me!"

But what was she supposed to do now that he'd actually board-ed that new steamship with his cabin ticket, a smile and a wave? She would be expelled from the school.

She placed her hand on her belly. In truth, even with the corset it felt different: hard, solid, where once she could have pushed it softly like a down cushion. There was nothing to see on the outside; her belly kept its composure as she did. But inside there was – she knew – a little creature growing. A little piece of James!

Sobs and sobs. She had to return to the village. The sun would be going down beyond the river and it was not easy walking back in the dark along the muddy edge of Vine Farm. She'd said she was going there for eggs, butter and black pudding, and she'd already completed that task before veering off to the valley, to the stream, to the willow.

She had to go back to Uncle. He'd want his supper.

Swallowing hard, she wiped water off her cheeks and nose with her sleeve. There was only one simple solution. She would quickly make Bill Sainty live up to his name and be her salvation: she would finally be interested in his affections, go down the same road as with James, and then if she indicated she might be with child he would marry her in a jot. Her life would be as a shipwright's wife, once he ascended to his full ambition, and that would suffice. At any rate it was survival, when there was nothing else to live for.

Picking up her wicker basket, she tied her hat on again, sniffing and breathing deeply, in and out. So it would be. Bill Sainty.

Quickly, she climbed up the bank to the open meadows, where black-faced sheep were nibbling grass while the light held, and she marched stolidly off southwards to where the village roofs were em-broidered with summer smoke from stove fires. The warm tones of the day were fading, yet there were great orange and yellow swathes of clouds high above on the pale sky giving strong colour. The wind-mill was not turning today; the air was so still.

Now hugging the valley she walked on through the farmlands, avoiding the main roads into the village. She strode the mile back along the verge of fields and then crossed the stream at a makeshift bridge to climb up along the eastern edge of the great ballast pit, keeping to the path along the ridge. There she stopped, and looked beyond the stubbly barley field to the distant silvery river, fading in the smudge of dusk, to a high-masted brig anchored there. She scanned the range from Alresford to Mersea Island, and thought of the sea, lying as a vast blanket behind. A well-formed 'V' of honking geese flew across the sloping pastures, heading towards the water like a noisy arrow firing in the direction of her gaze. It seemed to be an invitation.

There is another option, thought Marianne.

The brig. Where was it going? It was one of the bigger vessels to come up the Colne, perhaps loading with ballast, so it was not destined simply for London, Gainsborough or Hull. It was a ship bound for Ostend or beyond: Holland, Norway, France, Spain, Portugal. Where else?

Would they take a passenger? Should she escape?

What was she thinking? There was really only one alternative, and Bill Sainty wasn't a bad lad.

But could she fall into Bill's arms with her heart injured, her mind such a ragbag, her nerves like a frayed carpet?

No, she had to think of her child. This little being had surely taken root inside her. She had to protect it, come what may. There had to be safety: a home, a livelihood, a good name.

She walked again, solemn, down the gravel path past Ballast Quay House, until she descended to the straight-backed homes of captains on Anglesea Road, and there saw the figure of the gaoled turnip thief, Susannah Brewer, with her three children, the older boy barefoot. Susannah was just being turned away from Captain Pigott's front door by an irate maid. "You don't come here knocking again, Mrs Brewer. You been here quite enough already of late. We don't have no shoes for you today nor next week nor next month neither. You be gone."

Susannah, holding the youngest in her arms, wore a threadbare green dress and grey shawl. She was thinner now. Marianne had known her at school, as one of the older girls who had flair and diligence. She'd married her handsome sweetheart, Eddie Brewer, and had three children in quick succession, but even before the third one was born she'd changed, lost herself to worry. Eddie had been a good cooper, but he'd contracted an illness that wasted him away. He'd lost his strength and his ability to work, and so he lost the wages his family depended on. His feet swelled up, and then his knees, with the dropsy, so that he couldn't walk. He was short of breath, slowing down day by day until all he could do was lie on the floor under blankets that never warmed him. He was like a living corpse, people said, until he died. Soon after, Susannah had her term in gaol. Then she was a widow in a cellar in Hog Lane, with three children and no man to support her, living on the charity of the churches and the town, which only stretched so far.

"Susannah," said Marianne, hailing her old schoolmate anxiously.

"Ah, Marianne, fancy coming by you here. You been up Ballast Quay way?"

It was impossible not to notice that Susannah's eyes lighted on her basket, with its farm-fresh bundles. Susannah's concern was generally with procuring food. She'd managed to find some work mending sailor's clothing, but her pay never stretched very far. The two older children were often seen gleaning spilt coal from the river bank and salt marshes.

Marianne hardly thought twice before reaching into the basket and pulling out the black pudding. She'd explain to Uncle, make him an omelette and pay for it herself. She'd been doing quite well with her savings, even after board being paid. She looked down at the round faces of the children, William and Lily, coal-stained, but rosy-cheeked and brown from the summer sun. "Just needs a loaf of bread to go with it and it'll be a meal for days," said Marianne.

"Ah my, ah my," said Susannah, taken aback by the generosity. "No, no, I can just take a l'il piece, or you'll have no supper for yourself."

Supper was the last thing she felt like, Marianne thought. In fact, thinking of black pudding made her feel queasy. She handed over the lot with insistence. "It's for you and the children. We're not all fortunate in this life."

Susannah took it with an expression of gratefulness and pain, as her sooted children smiled. Marianne thought Susannah might weep, but she seemed to tuck away her emotions sharply.

Then Susannah looked back at her, and she became curious. "You be all right there, Marianne?" Could she see there was something wrong? "You quite well?"

"Well enough, Susannah. Now you take care of yourself," she

said, primping herself up with schoolmistress airs and her best vowels. This was not the time to speak of herself, and this was not the right person to speak with. In fact, there was no one to talk to at all. She strode off towards the Yachtsman's Arms, by the spring at the bottom of the hill, where there were tall, well-built men drinking in the doorway.

"You'll be in my prayers," said Susannah, after her.

Marianne coughed slightly. Prayers! Was God listening? How often had she prayed for James' question! Was she being punished for loving and trusting a man she believed was an angel? How could innocence be repaid with such harsh treatment? Where was the grace of God when it came to Susannah? If there was no mercy for her, then why would there be for anyone else? God did not care. In fact, there might as well be no God at all.

She glanced at the entrance to the public house without thinking. One of the sailors, a rather handsome, tall and rugged man leaning in the open doorway, made a whistle through his teeth, and said: "A toast to your beauty, my princess. And you'd be the prettiest girl in the whole of New South Wales if you sailed away with me."

She knew to ignore such drunken comments from sailors, and marched on.

New South Wales, she noted, nevertheless. Perhaps he was an ex-convict. Though – come to think of it – she'd heard talk of there being quite a city being built up now in Sydney Town. The *Times* had an article about it. There were immigrants establishing trades and farms. People made their fortunes. It was truly a new world.

"Tim Blake, of the *Albatross*, moored in the Colne, if you change your mind," the sailor continued.

Marianne stopped, stock still by the splashing spring and torrent of the brook, as she found herself unable to walk forward or backwards. She was like a pulley that had been jammed. That brig anchored on the river was bound for Sydney?

No, keep walking, she thought. But her feet would not move.

She was just a typical fallen woman in a typical moral tale; a mere silly girl with romantic thoughts, stuck with her lot. What if she broke free? What if her story was something completely different, not what you would expect? There were tales sailors told of women pirates and adventurers, stories beyond a novelist's wildest imaginings. What if she bolted, right now? She could be the horse that jumped over the gate.

Think! They might well need schoolmistresses there in Sydney. Perhaps it was better to stay an independent woman in this world, a confirmed spinster even if no longer a maiden, with her own independent wage, rather than trust to the care of a husband who might sicken or die.

She could pay for her passage, like others she'd known who'd gone to Quebec or Jamaica from the port. Sailors like that one in the doorway could say a saucy word, but as a paying passenger she'd not be trifled with, being under the Captain's protection, even as a solitary woman. And in six months she would be topsy-turvy, away from her former life and the agony of her loss, walking into one of those articles in the *Times*: articles built for men. What about women?

In New South Wales there would be nothing to remind her of James: no Colne birds, no willow trees. It would be alien, with endless possibilities. She could pretend anything on the other side of the world, in that new land. She could say she was a widow like Susannah Brewer, with a child. Who was to know?

She'd miss Uncle and the children at school. Everyone else she could leave without sorrow. Perhaps the poetry James had recited had taught her something: she could have freedom.

New South Wales. It was either that or Bill Sainty, and a life that was really no safety at all, with a man she didn't love.

This was no ordinary day, no ordinary decision. This was utter madness when there was no other course. This was like throwing herself into the water to see where the current would take her. She'd died today, seeing James off on that steamship to London. Marianne Brooke no longer existed.

She then turned around to the doorway caller and looked him straight in the eye.

3
Akaroa

After they passed around the Cape of Good Hope the sailors on the *Nil* talked more and more of their destination, and, from what they said, François Lelièvre formed a strong idea of New Zealand. Spacious, isolated, secretive, the land was split into three islands: the flatter, warmer Northern Island, the large Middle Island with an uncharted interior of Alps, and a small, chilly Southern Island. The forest that covered this place was beautiful and terrifying, for it was divided between native tribes the sailors could praise for their dignity and generosity in one breath and curse for their atrocities in battle in another. While there were small missionary and whaling stations, the only significant European settlements were far in the north, where the British dominated thanks to their rule in New South Wales, across the Tasman Sea. In this strange land, at every turn there seemed to be stories of exotic surprises: great flashing rivers on wide beds of grey pebbles, hot bubbling mud, weird birds, geysers, fjords, mountains lost in clouds, sparkling, black sand beaches.

For some forty years American and European whaling ships had made the long journey south, as the supply of whales in northern seas had dwindled, and now the trade in the Pacific was booming. Whales of all kinds, who came to the islands to calve, were a resource that seemed inexhaustible. There were sixty French ships alone in New Zealand waters, and everywhere there were men intent on fortune. They could be away from home for as long as four years, searching for their prey, but it was worth it, since crews would get a share of the total profits. It was a wide open market in the Pacific, with few European colonies proper and, therefore, no customs duties.

François looked at whales as a wonder, as both monsters of the deep and magnificent resources on which the world turned: gold made flesh. Whale oil lit street lamps in the growing cities, factories and homes of Europe and America. One whale's spermaceti could light a town; it was a necessity for civilisation. The crew of the *Nil* had seen whales everywhere in the distance, and managed to harpoon a small baleen that – once hauled on board – had the decks so slippery in blood and the oil from the fatty meat that you had to hold on tight to the railings to walk on it. The ship became a great floating abattoir, with all men engaged in cutting, boiling up the blubber in try-pots, pouring the oil into barrels. These whalers were strong men, their work being hauling, cutting, mauling flesh.

But François was not particularly strong. He was nervous about many things, and, even when swaying asleep in his hammock, he was bothered in dreams by the New Zealanders. He'd seen pictures of these natives of the land and they looked to him like demons. Horrific stories were told of what they did to their foes, such as eating them.

Nevertheless, some New Zealanders worked now as whalers, or crewmen. At the whaling stations European men could trade with the New Zealanders, swapping muskets, blankets, powder and alcohol for potatoes, pigs and women. Sometimes sailors would desert, and be discovered years later living with a New Zealand tribe, the father of five children. François found these stories disturbing: that European – especially French – men could betray civilisation, especially France, and cohabit with 'savages'.

Most European whalers had no wish to settle among the New Zealanders, but thought – in the main – of an easier world waiting for them at home, once they had money. The hard life would pay off and they would make enough to live well, escaping drowning in their own poverty by drowning the mammals of the water.

There were no New Zealanders on the *Nil*, only the men from France and the American Captain. They had become a village unto themselves, a floating encampment in which everyone had their place, their special task, and every interaction carried the weight of lead. François could not say he was fond of shipboard life. He'd gone to sea after the failed Bonapartist revolt in 1836 because he was dispirited and felt hunted and exiled, and because he could at least sell his services as a blacksmith to these whaling ships, which needed sound tools for the sailors to go about their work. Iron-working was always required and he had his own area below decks for his trade, with a furnace and his tools: a dirty, cramped room, hot and stinking, where he was always afraid of setting the ship alight by stray sparks. Here he would dream one day of owning a bit of land which he could farm with his own hands. Here he would dream of being clean, well-fed, breathing fresh air, with a wife beside him and a cluster of healthy children.

The men saw him as a bit of a loner. He was not a whaler, or a sailor, just an artisan, and he did not have so much to say unless anyone mentioned Napoleon. He did not join in with shipboard pranks, drinking and humour, or the unending rivalries. He seemed too serious and detached. The others left him alone.

*

At last, they reached Banks Peninsula. It protruded fifty kilometres from the eastern side of the Middle Island of New Zealand, like a gigantic green thumb pressing into the Pacific Ocean. The *Nil* sailed through the narrow mouth of Akaroa – 'long harbour' in the language of the people of this land. Sheltered, calm and deep, it was perfect for shipping. A legacy of lava and pumice, ash and fire was written in the sharp cliffs that edged the water, before they were engulfed by a primeval forest of trees that no European, apart from Latin-minded botanists, had named.

There, in May, 1838, they anchored off Paka Ariki Bay, surrounded by high, wooded hills, so far inside Akaroa Harbour that François could believe they were on a lake rather than in water connected to the open sea. The harbour mouth was no longer visible, as if the hills had drawn a curtain, and they were in the middle of a stage viewed by an audience of stately trees and the skewed tops of mountains.

Pulling his courage together, François asked Captain Smith for permission to go ashore, to set up his equipment and furnace in a place where he did not have to worry about sparks. He was granted his request, on condition that he would go back to the ship to sleep. When he went ashore the next day, he took with him his two slips of Napoleon's willow, thinking that he would explore a little and plant these willows somewhere. They couldn't live on potatoes forever, though they were doing well, with bright light-green leaves and white roots. Surely, this was a land that was rich, watered and fertile, where the willows could grow. He would fulfil his promise to plant them in new soil, and Napoleon's spirit would live in this place. They would be a sign to Frenchmen coming to these shores. Frenchmen would know where they came from.

But that afternoon one of the crew said that when François returned to the ship that night he would slit his throat.

This announcement did not take place out of the blue. There was a surly hard-drinking group who did not much care for François. They did not like his detachment, and thought he was secretive. They didn't know what he was hiding, but they didn't like it. After a night of gambling there had been some money that had gone missing, and François was considered to be the most likely thief, even while the Captain's investigations were proceeding in a different direction.

So that afternoon François found himself surrounded by a gang of foul-teethed men, who folded their powerful arms around him, and stared down their noses as he sat with his anvil and hammers. He looked at them and asked them what tools they wanted him to mend. They grimaced and spat.

"How long have you been thieving, François? Think you can run away from us here?"

François looked up at them, one by one, and dropped his hammer. He tried to indicate his innocence. "Me? If you believe I stole anything, then you should produce the evidence for your accusation. We operate here according to French law." François then turned away, and swung his hammer down hard, banging out his heart-drumming fear by a fierce pounding. He was a weakling to them, even if surrounded by fire.

The gang leader, nicknamed Clou, suddenly grabbed him around the neck from behind, and said: "We've searched through your stuff on board, but you've got it here, haven't you, you fucking thief."

François closed his eyes, and held his breath, thinking of his treasure there: his mother's painted box where he kept herbs. But he should show no worry. The shaved man let him go, but pulled him to his feet.

They then searched him, using the opportunity to manhandle and push him around. They emptied all his tools on the ground and kicked him. Then Clou picked up a red-hot poker and held it in front of François' eyeballs. François listened with disgusted terror to each word coming out of the man's unwholesome mouth. "I tell you, François, you lying piece of shit, that when you return to the ship tonight I'll slit your throat."

Then the poker was dropped with a clang on the other tools.

The gang swaggered off in the direction of the native village, Onuku.

François stood there a long time, breathing sharply, trembling, looking after them.

*

François did not take long to think things through. This incident of threatening behaviour could be reported to Captain Smith, and the perpetrators would be whipped – if the Captain believed him. But why should he be believed? And a lashed man could still cut his throat, having more reason than ever to want to kill him.

He could run. But punishment for desertion was severe: a man would be lashed when he was found, and search parties were always sent out.

Better to have a lashing when eventually they tracked him down than risk returning to the ship, he reasoned. If he could stall for a few days, then the true thief could be found and his assailant might change his mind, though, admittedly, jumping ship would not look good in terms of proving his own innocence. He could keep quiet about the manhandling and threats once he was no longer the suspect, and that would surely count in his favour with his accusers. They would see him lashed, and they would spare his life.

He'd seen those hard-drinking men with sharp knives in their hands, cutting through the whale flesh, covered in blood. They butchered whales for a living. It was nothing to them to butcher him too. He felt his neck. They would all stick together, so the Captain would not know which one of them had done it.

There was no point in seeking justice now. There had been a rumour that a sailor – old Martin – had had his throat cut and been thrown overboard in the South Atlantic. He'd simply disappeared. But he was always a bit crazy, being the kind to talk to things not there, so you could believe that he'd jumped. The testimony of witnesses said he'd been sleep-walking. But the witnesses, in retrospect, were members of the hard-drinking gang.

So then, when no one was looking, François picked up a few things, including his willow slips, and ran.

He went directly inland to where the land was covered with low bush, and followed a little stream for about half a kilometre. It reminded him of the brook he'd walked beside on St. Helena's, as if this one might also lead him somewhere extraordinary, to a shrine, and to a magical house on a hill. But here there was nothing but the thickening forest, where ferns caught his feet and a dipping bird with a fanned tail laughed like a child. At a small clearing he paused, and ate some ship's biscuit. He filled up his water canister from the stream and drank. He splashed himself with the cold water. Then he looked at his willow slips, and around at the ground. The soil was moist, loamy. Surely a willow would grow well here.

Walking away from the stream up the slope a short distance, he dug a hole with a stick and carefully placed a sprig from Napoleon's willow into it. He built up soil all around and looked at it there, poking out of the ground with enthusiastic green frailty, surrounded by the strange trees of this strange land.

Would Napoleon's spirit grow here?

He waited a little, listening to the weird calls of birds, observing the bird's laughing dance nearby, and the rustlings and cracklings of the forest. Then, fearing someone might have seen him go inland up the stream, he went north, into the hills, and lost himself in the heavy, alien forest. Darkness came, and cold. The month of May brought chill air and damp in this upside-down country.

All night, François Lelièvre crouched in the icy bush, hiding, afraid of returning to the ship. He made a bed for himself out of dry leaves in the hollow of a tree, but he did not sleep. Long, cold hours passed until sharp daylight cut through the canopy of ferns and leaves and ripped up the night all around. He got up then and kept walking until he came out to a bay, further along to the west from where the *Nil* was anchored.

There was no one about. Beside another small stream he planted the second willow cutting, and then he sat down there, ate the remainder of his ship's biscuit and tried to work out what he should do. Where could he run to? Should he just keep going further towards the heart of this land? There was supposed to be a station at

a bay on the other side of the hills to the west, where he could rein-
vent himself and no one would know which ship he came from. But
how could he get to it? He grew weary. The sun grew warmer in the
strong, blue sheet of sky, and he lay back on wild grasses, exhausted.

He knew he should keep going, further away from the shore.
Just a moment of rest. He felt the motionlessness of the earth, after
the ship's lulling turns, and yet his head and body seemed to be
rocking, side to side, despite the embrace of this still earth, despite
the constancy of the pure, cloudless sky. He seemed to be like a baby
in the cradle, swung, quietened, into sleep.

In a moment he was listening to his own mother, the midwife,
soothing. In his dream there was a young woman, moaning, and his
mother did what she always did and placed herbs around the birth-
ing bed, made the woman drink the draught for women in labour,
and sung a song. But in this dream he felt a terrible sense of threat,
and his mother started speaking gibberish, and wiped his face with
a wet towel.

He felt a breeze. The words were real words. He was hearing
them as he lay on the ground. This was the air and the smell of the
earth, and this was the sound of someone speaking, and more – a
monstrous slobbering on his cheeks!

With a terrible start, François opened his eyes to find himself
staring directly into a tattooed face of a brown-skinned man who
was accompanied by a brown, panting dog now sniffing him all over.

"Ah, *mon Dieu!*" François cried, terrified. He pointed randomly
out to sea, and scuttled sideways like a crab, closely followed by the
dog who was investigating his entire history by smell. From bad to
worse – he'd run into the arms of a cannibal!

"*E Wiwi*," said the New Zealander. A Frenchman. He continued
in French. "So you are from the *Nil?*"

Hearing his own tongue coming from the mouth of a horrify-
ing, powerfully-built savage, as he appeared to him, François stared,
astonished. Was he still dreaming? He looked at the man's clothing:
a jacket that looked as if it came from a French sailor, and trousers
alike. He had a greenstone pendant hanging from his ear, and long
black hair tied back into a knot on his head. Over his shoulder hung
two dead wood pigeons. His thick-soled feet were bare. What kind
of being was this?

35

"I do know Captain Gilbert Smith," continued the New Zea-lander. "For many years I worked on the French ships along these coasts." He looked momentarily sombre, and then glared intently at François. "But why are you here alone? Have you deserted?"

François tried to think. It was the most bizarre thing he'd ever experienced, to discover his language on the lips of this being, as if a bear were speaking, like in an old folk tale. What could he say back? How could he make a break for it and run? There was no possibility of distracting the man, who stared him in the eyes, in confrontation, his curving tattoos making his gaze seem all the more fierce. In the face of such scrutiny, François simply told the truth. "If I return to the ship, I will be killed. There are cut-throats there. They believe I've stolen something, but I am innocent."

At this, however, the New Zealander seemed amused. "You are a deserter, because you are afraid. But now you meet me, and I frighten you even more than those men!"

The man sat down, seemingly nonchalant, beside François and looked towards the water. He slipped off the pigeons from his shoulder and pulled out from a small flax-woven bag a bulbous root, which he then began to eat. After a long time chewing, he added, "Explain to me why you put this plant from your land in the earth of my land."

François looked at the small, pathetic sprig of willow and felt his spirit was the same. Was planting offensive?

"I grow my vegetables behind, over there," said the New Zea-lander, gesturing. "We have told your people many times that when you see our vegetables growing, this is our land. Your people look for houses, and you think that if there are not houses, or enclosures, or the animals you have, then the land is open to you. But this land is closed to you, all the land here, unless you enter as our guests. Captain Smith understands this. To him and to his ship we have of-fered welcome. We give you what you need in exchange for what we need, but you must not take without asking. This is the agreement we have made with you, the French, not the English, in this place."

François half-wanted to qualify that Captain Smith was an American, even though the ship was French, but that would have required an explanation of why Americans and French were linked by a bond of revolution, and there was a much more important thing to say, for the New Zealander's words struck him as remarkable. "Why the French, and not the English?" he asked.

"We understand the difference here between these two tribes of your lands. The English betrayed us here. The English hid our enemies in a ship that came to destroy us." Then the New Zealander stood up, walked away, and gestured to the distance, saying many things in his own tongue, angry and mournful, as if speaking sadly to ghosts. He slapped himself sharply on the arms, and then was silent. François looked on, no longer so afraid now, until, finally, the New Zealander turned back to him, and said, "You see the land there behind me that looks like a small island?"

François nodded. It must be a tiny peninsula, he thought.

"This is Onawe. In this place was a *pā*. You see all these bays, all these hills. Once we were numerous here. There were many of our boats on the water. We sold flax to the people of the ships. You could see our cultivations and smell our cooking on the wind. Not any more. Our enemies learnt that we prospered." The man called his dog back from burrowing into François' pockets after crumbs of biscuit. "Six years ago the English Captain Stewart brought them here secretly on his ship. We trusted the English ships when they came to trade. That day, the ship held a secret cargo of warriors, led by Te Rauparaha, with English muskets and English bullets. They came to Takapuneke – over there behind you – and killed hundreds. I was not here. I was on the whaler, the *Loup*. I returned, and my people were dead. My father was dead. Two years later, Te Rauparaha, drunk on the blood of warriors from Kaiapoi, returned. My people thought they were safe in the *pā* of Onawe, defended by trenches and muskets. I was again away, on the *Ajax*. My wife and my children were in the *pā*."

The New Zealander made noises and spoke again in his own language, mourning, for some minutes, looking to Onawe. François was intrigued by the pain on his face; clearly he had feelings of deep grief, and such grief seemed to make him more human. More significantly, perhaps he was losing interest in him, and would let him go. But then, suddenly, he turned around with wide eyes, and demanded sternly: "You will tell me why you placed this plant in the earth." There was nothing to be done but explain. So François reluctantly told the story of Napoleon's willow that grew on the island of St.

Helena, and how he'd cut some sprigs from the tree, two of them, and planted them in the land here, because of Napoleon's spirit. Whether this strange being from New Zealand would have any inkling of understanding, he did not know. He felt a sad weariness, now, rather than fear. He was going to die, like the dead pigeons that lay beside him, and he was oozing truth.

The New Zealander was not placated. "You planted the spirit of Napoleon here without asking permission of the spirits of the forest?" he said with defiance. "You planted without asking permission from the people? You did not come to me, Manako-uri, who is called Matthieu Le Bon." His brown eyes were staring, angry.

Matthieu Le Bon. Matthew the Good. He did not seem like this. François cringed, ready for a blow. He'd thought of the land as open, free, wild, belonging to no one but simple savages who would not notice a couple of trees. It was not as if he'd cleared a part of the forest and built a house. Had he committed some grave insult to this native who spoke the French tongue, who seemed to possess some stock of authority? His mouth went dry. "It felt to me the right place. I did not mean any harm."

"You make a claim?"

"No, no, I don't claim anything here."

"This is a tree, not eaten for food?"

"No, not for food."

Manako-uri was thoughtful, and then looked around. The dog, who had roamed near some bushes, scampered back and sniffed the Frenchman again with new familiarity. "But why does the spirit of Napoleon want to be here, in this place?"

"I don't know. It just felt that it was the right time to plant this tree."

Tree. It looked more like a piece of green hair.

The New Zealander remained thoughtful. "I have heard your people speak of Napoleon. He was a great warrior?"

"Yes." François looked up. How could he explain? The truth again? "Napoleon... had a better way for our people, for all the people of Europe, and for the world, not just for France. Some people have great power and riches, and grow fat, and others are very poor and powerless, and die of hunger. In France we tried to fight off the oppression of the rich and powerful, and the ways of injustice, to bring new laws and equality, but it has been a struggle, with much… loss of life. Napoleon wanted to see a world where there was liberty, equality, brotherhood for everyone, and he would fight for it with the sword, for a noble purpose. He was an ordinary soldier, one of us, but he became emperor… a chief of chiefs. He was our emperor. He was us. His power was our power. He conquered many places and removed the old kings, but of course the English resisted and attacked us. The English believe in the rule of kings, or queens, like their young Victoria. Many Frenchmen now still hold Napoleon's dream, but today our government is stupid, and afraid."

"You condemn your new chiefs for being afraid?" This man, Manako-uri, called Matthieu Le Bon, looked with scepticism at François. "I do not understand all these things you say. Your lands are strange to me. But… the chief Napoleon, was defeated by the English, yes?"

"Yes. But he was tricked."

"*Nē*?" Manako-uri pondered and looked away to the distance again. A breeze blew around and scuttled leaves. François felt that he was waiting for the judgement of a magistrate. This alien place. This alien. Why had he run here? Here he was, a stone rolling down a hillside, finally stopped under the naked heel of a savage.

"Perhaps the land called you," said Manako-uri, finally, with consternation. "Perhaps the pieces of the tree you have planted need to be planted here. Sometimes the spirits and the trees have their own purposes. The proof will be if the shoots grow. If they do not grow, then the spirit of Napoleon has no place among us, and you have angered Tāne."

François nodded, sensing that Tāne, whoever he was, should not be angered.

"So, we will see if this tree grows, and also the other. For now, we leave them, and I will take you back to Captain Smith to be punished as a deserter and to confront your enemies, because, of course, a man must not be guided on his journey by fear."

*

Lash. The sheer shock of pain. This is what it is. This is it.

The whip struck François' back hard, sharp, with a great slap.

He recoiled, only to tear his wrists, tied tightly with rope between the foredeck railings. Men watched in silence. The theatre of justice would play itself out.

There were no extenuating circumstances in the case of desertion. Either you had deserted or you hadn't, and François' case was simple. He hadn't returned to the ship when expected. Yet, before that, it had been reported to the heavy figure of Captain Smith that François' belongings had been scattered, and his painted box full of dried plants had been tipped out and broken. The Captain had put two and two together and decided that he must have been intimidated, accused of theft. The Captain's searches had already found the missing money, in the kitchen, secreted away by an assistant cook. The mystery had been solved, the culprit immediately punished.

Lash. The same ugly flash of pain. The tickle of trickling blood.

A Captain was required at all times to show strict discipline, or else there could be mutiny. There were no allowances, for softness could lead to more trouble. The men had to know that to abandon the ship was a very serious matter. They couldn't lose manpower. Everyone on board had a role to play; each one of them was a valuable resource. Who would replace the blacksmith here?

Lash. François gasped for air. He was being ripped open! Oh no! This was unbearable. He would cry out loud. He would lose control over his bowels.

His mind went back to his return to face these consequences. Manako-uri had brought him back on his canoe, where the dog had known to lie down, quiet, and they had paddled in silence to the ship, a floating piece of France, cut out from a picture from another world and stuck on to this backdrop of bright blue, placid sea and green forest. The bare masts had stuck up high into the air, a cluster of trunks from the other side of the world, stripped, straight and firm, hanging with thin ropes and all the metal parts he laboured to maintain. The trees on land, rich in leaves and crowded, had watched impassively.

Lash. The crack of the whip. The pain deep in the flesh, flicking out to his arms, ribs, buttocks, calves.

He'd known this would happen. As he'd stepped up to the deck, Captain Smith had greeted his capturer warmly, as an old friend whom he called 'Matthieu'. He'd shaken hands with him and patted him on the shoulder – this to a native – and met François with grave disappointment. "François... I gave you my trust."

"He was afraid," the New Zealander had said.

"I didn't steal the money," he'd said.

"The thief has been caught," the Captain had said, "so why did you run away?"

Lash. François whimpered, bit his lip hard, and his arms started to shake, his knees tremble. He would collapse. He would soil himself. He would show himself to be no man at all!

His mind kept leaving, rewalking the road to this Golgotha. Matthieu had defended him. "He needs to speak to you in private. There is a greater threat than his desertion in your ship." This Matthieu had said to the Captain.

François, Captain Smith and Matthieu had gone below to the Captain's cabin, where he'd made his confession, as if to a priest, but this confession was also an accusation. Men of the ship had made a false charge and threatened him with summary execution, undermining the authority of the Captain, which was mutinous treachery. Only the Captain could organise investigations and punish. Only the Captain held the absolute power of life and death, and could examine the scales of justice.

Lash. But this time the whip did not land on François' back, but on that of another. Clou's shaved head went white with pain. His strong arms tensed. He uttered a cry.

François was untied and made to watch what took place, in accordance with the rules of French ships. He saw the punishment of men who rejected a Captain's authority and took the law into their own hands.

*

Later François was offered rum and given leave to tidy his kit below. He went down to his hammock on the second deck and found his few possessions cast around. His bag itself was sliced wide like a carcass, with all the entrails spilt. The painted box his mother had given him lay in several pieces, and the precious herbs and roots and seeds – and willow bark – were strewn over the boards, some lost to cracks and holes. Gingerly, he put the pieces of the box together and tied it. He picked up what remained and gathered them in a rag, though his hands were unsteady; his back was a thorn bush of pain that shot down his arms even to his fingers.

"I am to be your guard."

François started at the voice, having heard no footsteps, to see Matthieu squatting nearby, watching him picking up tiny seeds.

He did not feel like speaking anymore. He turned to his task, concentrating.

"You can leave the ship and live on the shore. You can do your work there and I will build you a *whare* where you will live. I have made an agreement with the Captain. He has given me three sacks of seed potatoes. It is my job now, François Lelièvre, to make you safe on the land where you have my permission to stay. You will not run away."

He knows my name, thought François. My name has come from the mouth of such a being as this. He didn't know whether to thank him or curse him. He kept picking up small bits of bark.

"These plants are powerful?" asked Matthieu, after some minutes.

François leaned back on his knees and looked down sadly at the broken box, and what was left of the contents. "My mother knows about these things. She's a midwife." A *sage-femme*, 'wise-woman'.

"My father was a *tohunga*, and also knew about such things," said Matthieu, solemnly. "But the plants that cure the *Pākehā* sickness, we do not know."

The two men looked at each other then with understanding. Both knew that true knowledge of the powers of plants was a secret knowledge, passed on from an adept parent to a chosen child. In this recognition, there was no difference between the New Zealander and the Frenchman. From that moment, they forgave each other.

*

François Lelièvre lived in a well-built hut, a *whare*, in Paka Ariki Bay, up the hill from the stream where he planted the first willow. There he learnt many things from Manako-uri, called Matthieu Le Bon, about the planting of *kūmara* and other vegetables in the ways of his ancestors, and about how to treat the soil, how to hunt and fish, but he did not learn about the powers of the plants in this land. Tāne, he was told, was the god of the forest, and unless he knew how to honour him, nothing would be granted. It remained to be seen whether Tāne accepted his trees. François planted no seeds of his own.

Matthieu observed the skills of François with interest: how iron melted in fire and how it could be reshaped into a different form. Matthieu had seen this before on the ships he'd worked on, but that metal could be both liquid and solid with a change of heat – like ice or fat – fascinated him. François showed him how to mend broken implements of all kinds, and was impressed by how quickly he learnt. Out of iron fragments, Matthieu made small blades useful for surgical operations, and needles for sewing up broken skin.

Matthieu lived in Onuku, not far away to the south, but he and his people could encamp in many places. At night François sometimes listened to strange sounds carried on the breeze: rhythmic, chanted, mournful, a music of flutes, castanets, shakers, voices, loud and throbbing. At first it scared François because this eerie music felt like dark magic, but as time went by it soothed him, like his mother's songs, and lulled him to sleep.

He visited Onuku with Matthieu and traded some of his less important tools for trinkets they made, and food. He learnt what he could of the language of these people. He found the children – a couple of whom had lighter faces – quick to smile, as if there was always a joke lying behind the surface of the world, but the people of the village were too often burying corpses in the hillside, and too often there were women wailing.

François learnt about the native people of New Zealand, whom he soon no longer thought of as savages. He learnt that the New Zealanders looked with amazement at the hunger of the people from far away, the *Pākehā*, the 'pale ones', who came and slaughtered the seals and whales with a technology and efficiency that made the killing of great battles seem tame. The New Zealanders were cautious, negotiating their way through the strange manners of these foreigners intent on plundering the realm of Tangaroa, the god of the ocean, secretly making propitiation to Tinirau, protector of fishes and whales, for the violations.

In the days before the coming of the *Pākehā*, the god Tinirau would give a whale, or a dolphin, or a seal, for a feast, and for the intricate carving of bones, but now it seemed that the *Pākehā* took without permission, mighty in their great ships and with huge harpoons, and just as the creatures of the sea surrendered to this onslaught so they had felt the stings of unknown spirits brought with the white-skinned people, spirits that killed children, the old people, the frail, whole villages, with fierce brutality, sending them to their long sleep in fiery sweats, or bloodied coughing fits, or with eruptions of lesions and swellings that no herb could assuage nor *karakia* soften.

For over forty years, since the first coming of the *Pākehā* to kill the whales, the people of the land had suffered from these calamities, and whole *hapū* had gone, their villages abandoned, with survivors working at the whaling stations or joining other clans, and it seemed to some that the gods of the *Pākehā* were much stronger than the gods of the land and that to co-operate was better than fighting, when these gods could kill by stealth in the night, not by sending warriors. By this co-operation, assuagement, the foreign gods could yet withdraw the spirits of death from the people. These are things that Matthieu Le Bon said to François. This was one reason that Matthieu had gone to work on the whaling ships.

François lived in the *whare* all the while the *Nil* was based in Akaroa Harbour, and avoided going with the ship during its forays out to the bays where the whales came to calve. He stayed until August 3, 1838, and then joined the ship as it left, with little confidence that he would not be murdered en route home. He watched the two sprigs of Napoleon's willow till his departure, and both of these survived the winter.

Matthieu gave his word he would neither water nor destroy the growing willows, but would rather see whether Tāne accepted or rejected this intrusion. In order to protect them from human harm he made the willows restricted, or that is how he explained it to François. There was a secret ceremony. "Napoleon's willow in my land is *tapu*," said Matthieu Le Bon, after this ceremony had taken place. François did not himself see Matthieu weave the spell that made the tree protected, but he understood that this is what he'd done. Afterwards, François saw that there were poles painted red-ochre hammered into the ground by the tiny willows. The son of a *tohunga*, Matthieu Le Bon appeared to be something of a *tohunga* himself, an expert in mysteries and arts no others would know.

On the day of departure, François gave his word that he would return, and parted with a heavy sorrow in his gut for the New Zealander who had become his friend. Matthieu pressed his nose to the sharp nose of the Frenchman, inhaling his breath, and then let him go.

4

The Albatross

Marianne had long heard talk of great sea voyages. Niece of a dedicated shipwright and daughter of a captain, who'd even been at the Battle of Trafalgar, she knew so many tales of sea life that there was little she did not expect on board the *Albatross*, a privately-chartered trading vessel registered in Sydney Town, now loaded with goods for the colony. She knew about the illnesses, the terrible food, the chances of death, the abuses, the smells, the cockroaches, the noise. She knew, as a female passenger, it would be much like sitting in gaol, an endlessly moving cell, for month after month, except when she went out to make herself useful laundering and sewing for the passengers or shipmen, or playing nurse, or dining with Captain Wright, who had her and the two other passengers at his table. Her small wooden cabin on the port side consisted of a narrow bed, a cabinet beside it which had to always be locked or else things would fall out, and a space for her trunk beside the foot of the bed. Through the port-hole she could look up from her needlework and stare at the ever-changing shape and colour of the waves. She'd never realised before what variety there was in the patterns of the ocean.

She knew there would be a great deal of time for thinking, and that everything on board would become of immense significance. In the first weeks she thought endlessly about James and their time together, until it felt that every possible thought and memory had been exhausted, returned to over and over, and wept about again and again. Then these gave way to all kinds of other memories: childhood, the school, her friends, her foes. She thought about her poor father, lost at sea en route to Norway, and her mother then wasting away until she died, yearning for one more sight of France. She wept at everything, even happy memories, grieving an entire life that had gone: mourning at the grave of her own self.

She turned over her last days with Uncle. The recollections of explaining to him the reason why she wished to take her father's inheritance and her own savings, and pay for a passage to New South Wales and a future life on the other side of the world, kept her awake for many nights. She recognised that it had helped her at the time that part of her heart was dead. She'd been able to speak as if she'd thought everything through quite carefully. But on board the *Albatross*, as she lurched from seasickness to the sickness of her condition, her mind exposed all the emotions she should have had on leaving, throwing them in her face like a bucket of mud. That terrible evening under the willow! Uncle had wondered at her lateness, but he'd seemed content with anything she'd served him for supper. She'd made her announcement by stating that from henceforth he would need to hire a housekeeper, because she needed to go away. She'd been thinking for some time about the fact that the colonies needed schoolteachers and skilled workers – a *Times* article had noted this four months earlier. Now, there was a brig anchored – the *Albatross* – bound for Sydney Town. She'd had a quick word with a certain Tim Blake, who turned out to be First Mate. He'd been very polite and answered her questions plainly. Would Uncle permit her to travel?

Uncle was a gentle, imperturbable man, as a rule, but he'd grown very sombre, and then he'd said she was very much like her father. He would not clip the wings of one who longed to fly, and she was old enough to make adult decisions. But he also cautioned her against rash convictions in an hour of emotion, and for talking to strange men outside a public house.

She'd told him then – because she couldn't bear to leave Uncle under the cloud of a lie – about everything that had passed between her and James Placard. He hadn't been even a bit surprised. He'd known, he'd said, because "of the kind of young man James Placard is", and because "that is the way of men", but Uncle had always thought James would do the decent thing if she'd been left with child. Marianne had then confessed her belief that she was indeed expecting, but stressed that it was completely irrelevant. She would not force James to be locked together with her if that was not his wish. At that, Uncle had got up and gone outside in their little garden for a few minutes. When he'd returned, his eyes were moist. He'd been deeply shaken. "Truly Marianne, you're very much the daughter of my brother," he'd said, and embraced her tightly. "But how can you ever be safe? How can your child be safe?"

"You must release me to find my own safety, after what I've done. If I stayed here, I would be buried alive with shame, and bring it upon you as well. This way, I will be reborn somewhere far away. My child will be safe there, and so will I."

She could hardly believe she'd said such things.

Captain Wright, an older man at the end of his career who looked rather like an owl, had a special private discussion with Uncle. Marianne suspected that Uncle had paid him something extra to ensure his special care of her, because he was attentive, and knowing. Tim Blake seemed knowing too, though he kept his distance. She'd made it quite clear that her response to his call was not out of interest in him, but in the *Albatross*.

Three days later she'd sailed out past Mersea Island to the Colne River mouth, southwards down the Essex Coast and up the Thames to the cacophonous India Docks in the chaos of London, where the two other paying passengers had come on board: Dr William Kingsley – brought out by a charitable organisation for the sake of better medical services for the colony's small hospital in Sydney – and Mr Arnold Hart, a commercial trader who had chartered the ship to take his goods for sale in Sydney Town. These two passengers, the Captain, and Tim Blake became her world. She liked them all. Dr Kingsley had a quick wit, and Mr Hart was full of interesting stories of trading in distant lands. The Captain was dignified and kindly. Tim Blake was a sharp card player with a glint in his eye, though he kept to himself. They were all clever, in very different ways, and knowledgeable. She felt immediately, in their company, that she'd made the right decision, no matter what, no matter how deep her misery.

For some time she was mysterious with them, and stated that she was going to be a schoolmistress in Sydney Town, leaving the other passengers to suppose she was attached to a mission. Her work in the dissenting Congregationalist school in Wivenhoe would have been quite a perfect training for an evangelical young woman set on providing services at a mission school for young girls. Mr Hart and Dr Kingsley were not themselves particularly religious, but they couldn't have been more courteous to her in view of her 'courageous act of service' in going to Sydney Town.

As a pious young woman, as they saw her, it seemed that both (widowed) Mr Hart and (unwed) Dr Kingsley were quite taken with her, which caused minor incidents of competition. However, during the second month at sea they appeared to realise that she was swelling in her belly – after all, she'd had to let out her dresses twice – and they were then divided in their manners of reacting. The doctor became detached, professional and concerned, but assumed an air of disapproval and disappointment. The trader became aloof. The Captain remained considerate and cheerful, but he was always busy and preoccupied. It was Tim Blake who was more attentive than ever.

She knew it was time to talk. She told her story with absolute openness on the fortieth night they were at sea, at the Captain's table, with Tim there too, since he made up the four men at cards. African air blew in from the open windows as the sun went down into the shimmering tropical sea and painted the cabin with red, like the shame that seemed now to rest upon her.

She'd decided that she would not lie about her circumstances when the time came, as a kind of closed experiment with these men in a ship. She would not say she was a young widow. She would not say she'd been violated. She would not say she was looking for a husband, or appear to be looking. She would simply be fallen. If they had feelings for her, she wanted them to show their true colours.

The story was told baldly with no emotion, and then she went to her little cabin and lay awake for hours listening to the pillowed voices next door as the four men talked, gambled and drank as usual, but with little laughter.

The next day, there was concerned caution in the doctor's manner, a clear coldness from the trader, and the Captain was busy with matters to do with the stores. But Tim Blake caught up on her way to the main decks with a bucket of soapy washing water to tell her that half of the population of Sydney were the children of fallen women.

"Don't you worry, Marianne. My sister was knocked up by some bloke from Parramatta and had a proposal of marriage for every second week she showed. But that's the thing about Sydney... there are about five men to one woman, so my sister was saved even though everyone knew the story. She got married to the seventh one that asked."

Marianne put down her bucket. She liked Tim Blake. In body he was as strong as a stone bridge, but his heart was soft. "Tim, I could have stayed in Wivenhoe if all I'd thought of was catching a man to marry and give my child a father. But I know what would happen. There'd be another seven children and all I'd ever do is what every woman does: work all the day and half the night looking after the children, running the household, doing all the tasks of the home, making sure my husband can earn the family wages, labouring for more money for the family. Can't a woman make her way on her own in Sydney without a man?"

"No." He shook his head. "Too dangerous. So, I think you'd be best off marrying me."

Marianne couldn't help letting out a guffaw. This was a proposal. "You've been waiting for this moment, haven't you, ever since you called to me in Wivenhoe?"

"I know how to hold my tongue." Tim smiled a little.

Marianne shook her head. Then she grew serious. "Look, if I married you, Tim, and then you died, and I had three children, and – " The image of Susannah Brewer came to her.

"There'd be another man, in Sydney. There'll always be another man in Sydney."

Marianne folded her arms. "I don't want a husband, and I don't want another child. Can't I get a girl to help me at home, and earn my own living running a school? I'd hire a guard and be safe."

Tim grimaced. "Ah, maybe, but... it would be... a waste."

"A waste?"

Tim looked sheepish. "A woman like you... I tell you, no one would leave you alone. Why not let a husband look after you?"

Marianne frowned. This was an interesting experiment, all things considered, but underneath it there was a painful truth. It wasn't just that she'd lost James. She'd lost a faith, not a religious faith, but one that she was supposed to have had innately as a woman: a trust that a man would look after her. It was not just born of a broken heart. When her father had never come back from the journey to Norway, and no one knew what had happened to the ship, her mother had managed as a seamstress and she'd sat up with her late into the night sewing fine work, at the age of ten. But women earned a fraction of what men could earn, no matter how hard they laboured, and they'd had Uncle aiding them. Had there been more mouths to feed than hers, and no Uncle, then what would have happened? What would have happened when her mother was ill? A schoolmistress income was by no means anything like a man's wage, but it was something. Why should she hand over the money to any husband, as was required? She didn't need to be looked after.

She looked at Tim Blake and the simple earnestness in his expression. He was at least a man of the world, who'd seen things, and clearly had intelligence with matters of cards, navigation and the various technologies of the ship. But she didn't have any strong feelings for him, other than affectionate liking. She doubted she'd ever have any feelings for any man ever again; the whole store of a lifetime of love had been cast away at James, and there was nothing left for anyone else. What could she say?

"Just tell me that in your new world I can be my own woman, and that my bastard child will not be an outcast."

Tim groaned a little and shook his head. "It's a hard country."

Marianne's resolve felt frail. Indeed, what did she know of life there? What kind of life had she chosen? The Captain and Tim had told many tales, but how would it really be? Men talked of opportunities to earn ten times what they might earn in England; but what was life like for women? Her mind suddenly lurched back to the alternative she'd left behind: to pretend to Bill Sainty, to pretend the child was his, to have an ordinary life in Wivenhoe.

"I know you don't love me and you don't want to trust any man," continued Tim, "because of that fine gent who did this to you. And you could do better than me, given your learning and your looks. But you won't get anyone like me, Marianne, who'd let you be like you want. If you don't want any more children, then there are ways... I mean... there are things you do and you don't do." He looked away awkwardly. "If you want to be a schoolmistress, then be one as a married woman and even keep your own pay. I'm not looking for seven children. I'm not wanting an Eve to be my helpmeet. When I saw you walking past with a face as sad as the gallows ... well, I don't go calling to every pretty girl that passes me by."

At this statement Marianne felt a peculiar stirring inside, as if something had been dislodged. She realised that plain-speaking Tim Blake was the very opposite of James Placard. James would have considered him uncouth. This was a man who would not lie to her.

"If you don't want a wife who's a mother and a housekeeper, as a helpmeet like Eve, then what do you want a wife for?" she asked, curiously. "You sailors don't lack women when you go into port. Your wages pay for as many as take your fancy."

Tim Blake laughed. "Ah, that's right, spoken like a captain's daughter." He looked at her with amusement and she struggled not to smile.

"So tell me," she said.

He quietened himself and spoke softly, close to her cheek. "Because... I reckon... I'd look after you, and the child, and we'd set up a house and be a... family. I'll be a captain myself in another voyage or two. You know... I can be at sea for a year. But I want to be able to come home."

Marianne was touched by his words, spoken with honesty and feeling. Tough Tim Blake wanted a home. How fundamental. Everyone needed one somewhere, even a sailor. She knew from past conversations that Tim had sailed since he was twelve years old, when his own parents had long been dead, and he and his sister had been sleeping on the floor of the tiny wooden house belonging to his older brother. He would be as accommodating to her wishes as he could, as long as she'd make him a home.

My, she thought, perhaps this was a kind of destiny. Her passion for James, her calamity, was all necessary to bring her here. This was where she was supposed to be, with a man who'd be a captain like her father. Perhaps he was the right man to make a home with.

Her breath caught. She felt the corners of her mouth flutter.

"I'll think about it," she said, stuffing away her feelings and picking up the bucket.

In five days, they were wed.

*

Tall Tim Blake was in many ways far too big for Marianne's cabin, so she often bedded with him in his First Mate quarters, while retaining her own space for daytime leisure. He had a private cabin himself since there were few passengers – next door to the Captain's, off the navigation room. She hardly dared think what the Captain, who had married them, would hear, but Tim Blake was a man who certainly knew his way around a woman's body, and managed to elicit from her what James Placard had never succeeded in doing, she realised, being intent only on his own pleasure. She couldn't help making noises, or even saying things, which afterwards she reflected might have been uttered rather more loudly than she'd realised at the time.

Given her condition, there was no need for Tim to engage in intimate practices designed to forestall pregnancy, and he seemed to wish only to see her beside herself. He relished the shape of her in her ripe state. She felt like a delicious fruit he was enjoying to the maximum. And she enjoyed him. She liked the curves of his muscles, and the inked patterns etched into his thighs, made by a native of the Navigator Islands. They were dark, swirling, like a dense forest all over his loins, like the forest of sensation she lost herself inside. She liked it that these tattoos, being covered by his breeches in public, were drawings only for her view.

With her marriage, various changes in her happened simultaneously: she did not lie awake remembering the past and she felt relaxed and refreshed during the days. Captain Wright seemed rather pleased with the way things had "all fallen into place" as he put it, and commended Tim Blake as a very fine seaman. "It's a damned good turn to see you smiling, Marianne. I'll be sure to post my own letter to your uncle when we next call at port." For the Captain, it was also some relief, surely, since in his view he'd passed the promised care of Marianne to another.

She was smiling, that was true. She felt quite absurdly happy. Tim laboured diligently and commandingly on the ship, of course, but it was not endless drudgery. The shifts incumbent upon him allowed odd times of privacy; day could be as night, and night as day, since the ship had to be sailed as well through darkness as through light. The strange shipboard life was perfect for getting very closely acquainted with him, with time seized not only for intimacy but for a kind of childlike play. Tim Blake could make her laugh with his wry observations of things: the doctor's fussy habits or the trader's mannerisms. With him as her husband she felt confident to range around the ship, and she could spend more time up on deck, watching the great sails, and the sea-birds when they appeared. She got to know the sailors and their ways. Dr Kingsley and Mr Hart became themselves again, and treated her with respect, though not without an occasional wink to each other.

She soon felt she did indeed love the manly Tim Blake as much as she'd loved the romantic James Placard, though this also frightened her. How fickle! One moment she'd thought she could never love again, and the next here she was with a brand new husband, thrilled by his loving, eager for the next moment of privacy.

No matter what she now felt, she was firm in her resolve for a greater independence in New South Wales than she would ever have at home. Perhaps it was a perversity, but she must be the one to make up her own mind for herself. She would manage to teach and raise the child and be a woman with her own money.

Then there was the storm.

They were off the Cape of Good Hope and it was nearly night when the wind rose all of a sudden and the black clouds gathered before them. Great curtains of rain were dragging over the sea ahead. She was ordered by Tim to go to her cabin and stay there till he came for her.

As if passing through some invisible line from one ocean to the next, the ship bent down into troughs of water and rose sharply up at the peaks, askew and vulnerable, as things not tied down slid across the floor and fell from ledges below decks. She heard Tim blasting the boy on the lookout. The Captain shouted. Men were furling sails high in the air. Marianne got to her room with difficulty, pushed to the left and to the right by the bending of the ship, and managed to shut the door only to find that the port-hole latch was loose and the window was banging backwards and forwards, opening and closing. She tried to secure it, but the latch kept slipping. Then as they dipped to the starboard side a wave like a monster rose up and crashed against the hull, sending Marianne back against the door, throwing cold sea water through the port-hole into her cabin, soaking everything.

As the ship turned again she flung herself to the port-hole and finally clipped it tightly shut.

Her cabinet, which was fixed to the floor, stayed firm, but her trunk shifted backwards and forwards clunking dangerously. Sodden, she sat on the wet floor gripping hold of the side of the bed as the ship went down and up, turned to one side, and then the other. Her head was dizzy. It was noisy with the wind, the sea, the rain pounding, and the creaking and groaning of the ship as if it were in pain. Diabolical sounds! She heard shouting and fretted for Tim's safety. She felt sick, and feverish.

Soon she was in complete darkness with only the noise and the terrible motion of the tossed ship all around her, as she gripped the side of the bed and tried not to be flung one way or another. It was impossible to think of lighting a candle. She thought only of holding on, over an hour, and another hour.

And then somewhere in the midst of this she realised there was another sensation: it was warmth, over her legs, in her groin – and then there was pain, a dragging, deep pain within her.

"OH MY GOD, HELP ME!" she shouted, in horror, as the ship seemed to be breaking apart around her and the child seemed to be breaking apart within her. Her world was chaos everywhere outside and inside, complete darkness and isolation. She screamed, as a final cramping pain came again deep inside, and again as another wave pushed the ship hard. At that, she lost her tight hold, banging her head and shoulder as she hit the side of the door.

*

Marianne dreamt of willows. She was in a glade of them, surrounded, but they were not benign. These trees were creatures of grizzled trunks and green matted hair. They moved and swayed in a fixed dance, blown not by wind but by some inner evil. She had to pass through the willows that surrounded her, and find her precious love.

Who was it? Where was he? Where was she?

She thought she saw Uncle for a moment.

"Uncle!" she cried out. "I'm here! Look, it's me, Marianne. Uncle! I'm so sorry! I want to come home!"

But then there were different voices.

Marianne heard her husband Tim Blake saying "thank you". He commented that they had to be grateful there was a good doctor on board to help.

She opened her eyes and recognised the ship's infirmary. The bright sun was shining on great dusty ribbons through the port-holes and an open door. The ship was moving gently. There was Tim, sitting on the end of the bed, looking as if he'd been in a fight, with a swollen red forehead and eye, a cut lip and his ripped clothes splattered with blood. There was Dr Kingsley, who was also unchar-acteristically dishevelled, though not bloodied, putting his equip-ment away in a black case. There were a couple of the sailors, who looked as battle-injured as Tim.

"She's awake," one of them said.

Marianne wanted to sit up and ask for water, but even the slightest movement was painful. Dr Kingsley quickly plumped up a down pillow and placed it cautiously behind her head, and she was able to drink then what Tim offered in a canister.

She had a strong sense of the dream, of the demonic threat of willows.

Dr Kingsley spoke as if it was his duty as the professional. "You miscarried during the storm. We found you unconscious on the floor of your cabin." He glanced away then, as if remembering the ghastliness they'd found.

"You were mighty tossed, Marianne. You're battered and bruised," said Tim, sorrowfully. "We were all night keeping the ship afloat, but she's been damaged, and we lost Harry, Seth and Maggs overboard."

He looked exhausted and sad, and his voice cracked as he spoke. He said nothing more, offering her water again. She swal-lowed, bit by bit, and lay back as nausea rushed upon her. Her head hurt. It came back to her: the terror of the storm, the wave washing through the port-hole, her tight gripping on to the bed, the warmth between her legs. So she'd lost the child, that bit of James that had sprung inside her. It was all gone now. She felt such a mixture of things then, at once relief and grief together, turning around in an inner storm of sickness. She looked to Tim's injured face and hands. She couldn't speak, but knew what he was thinking and wanted to say it too: it is better this way. But instead there were only tears, warm like the sensation of the night, trickling down her cheeks.

And so it was that repairs were made, to both ship and crew. They healed, and the voyage on to Australia passed without further calamity. The newly-weds settled to a more controlled liaison, after the losses and the damages. The ship sailed on.

5
Le Havre

In the autumn of 1839, François Lelièvre couldn't say he was glad to be home. He'd thought he would feel so relieved to return after his hard travels that he would never want to set sail again. But in France once more, he remembered very well why he'd left in the first place. France was not the way it should be, after all the struggles of the Revolution and the wars. Everything was sliding into the old.

The voyage back had seemed to go on forever. He'd become inured to the roughness of the whalers, and the harsh life, and even less inclined to conversation. He could go for weeks saying, "Yes, sir," and "No, sir" and nothing else. After they'd left Akaroa Harbour they'd spent months, till March, 1839, bay whaling in more southerly parts of the Middle Island. The whalers were hungry for maximum profits. Able seamen would be paid a two-hundredth share of these, so no one wanted to leave until every centimetre of space in the hold was filled with barrels of booty.

The first thing he'd done when he left the ship at Normandy was return to his tiny home village of Beslon in Normandy to visit his family, most especially his mother and his brother who lived in the old farmhouse with his wife and children. He'd given his mother some of the bark from Napoleon's willow out of the repaired painted box and waited for commendation. Outside the door, while she pulled feathers out of a hen, he'd told her the whole story of his visit to the island of St. Helena, and his planting of the trees in New Zealand, and she'd not said a word. It had made her go quiet for an entire afternoon, and then in the evening she'd simply said, "The willow belongs in France, not on the other side of the world."

It had disappointed him and he'd not stayed long. He packed her comment away inside himself like the pain of his lashes, which he did not tell her about. At any rate, he needed to get work.

But, at the Normandy port of Le Havre, getting work was difficult, owing to the competition and the economic depression.

The summer had been soft and beautiful, but he couldn't see how he could make a living. None of the blacksmiths he knew had enough work, despite the many ships at port. He could go and work on building the railways, but that kind of dismal hard labour did not seem preferable to a life at sea. Day after day, he loitered around the harbour trying to ply his trade, freelance, with all his heavy equipment. He'd shoe a horse, mend a wheel, create a new blade or two. That was all. At nights he would dream he was in his *whare* again, listening to strange birdsong and the New Zealanders making peculiar music. He longed for the peace of Paka Ariki Bay, and walks through the bush with Matthieu Le Bon, hunting, learning bush lore and the 'Zealand' speech, as they called it. He missed Matthieu, who was someone he could actually count as a friend. It seemed odd to him now that once he'd been so frightened of him and of his people. In fact, he saw attributes of their ways that were superior: a certain comradeship and communality that surely had been the aspiration of the French nationalists.

What would happen now, to France? What would happen to him? When should he return to New Zealand to see if the willows had grown? He just had to wait.

He began to feel like an audience to life, a detached spectator who looked at actors reciting their lines and playing their parts as if he did not exist.

His despondency and indecision continued until one day as he drank at one of the crowded old port bars, late in the autumn, a remarkable thing happened. He found himself, listening in to a very interesting conversation taking place right behind him.

"Very hush-hush," a man was saying loudly, clearly after too much wine. "We sail for New Zealand as soon as the ship is ready. If you know of anyone of discretion willing to serve on board, or anyone wishing to put himself forward as a colonist, you must tell me his name."

Colonist?

"The British must not learn of this venture. It's not only under the Nanto-Bordelaise Company, but under the auspices of King Louis-Philippe himself, you understand, as I told you. I've promised his majesty, and Duke Decazes. This is the most important foreign enterprise the king has ever taken, not that I do it for *him*. Not at all.

I do it for the hope of the Republic! This land I've bought will be just the start. We have a mandate to buy as much land as possible, as soon as we can, and also to 'spread the Catholic religion' as they ask," he laughed derisively, "only for reason that... if the New Zealanders become Catholic then they will become French."

François could hardly believe it. They had land? This man behind him was leading a colonisation project for France?

How had this happened? Was it the willow tree, working its magic? A portion of France would grow in New Zealand? François could barely stay upright on his stool. His hands began to shake uncontrollably. This was the most extraordinary thing that had ever happened to him, that he was placed back to back to a man speaking of these things!

François Lelièvre did not think any further. Immediately he spun around, stood up and presented himself to a small group of strange faces. "Excuse me, sirs, but I could not help overhearing. I understand that this a private meeting? But my name is François Lelièvre and I've served on the whaler, the *Nil*, as a blacksmith. I know well shipboard life, and I know New Zealand. I know what grows. I know which wood is good for building. If you need a blacksmith on board ship, or an ordinary sailor, then I'm your man."

The man who had been speaking looked at this interloper sternly and stood up. François stared at a short, solidly-built man in his early thirties, with a pock-marked face and wide-spaced teeth. He was not attractive; he was as rough as an old dog.

"I remember... the *Nil*, sailing under Captain Smith?"

"Yes, sir." François stared in amazement that he knew his ship.

"Langlois, Captain of the *Cachelot*," said the man, introducing himself, shaking François' hand. "We were in Port Cooper when you were in the harbour of Akaroa."

François had indeed heard talk of Langlois and the *Cachelot*. Captain Jean François Langlois was said to be as resilient as Lelièvre's anvil, having spent seven years as a sailor, harpooner and officer before receiving his first command of a ship. He was a child of the new France that had been forged by the Revolution: literate, businesslike, pragmatic and feisty. And it was also said that he could drink anyone under the table.

Unless you went by ship or boat, Port Cooper was a long walk overland from Paka Ariki Bay, on a difficult track that wound up the high bush hills over thirty kilometres. Men went there for grog and gambling, but then he'd never had much interest in such things. This was Langlois' world.

Langlois shook the hand of the blacksmith for some time with much solemnity, mixed with wonder and genuine pleasure. He turned then to his companions, and said, "Can you believe it? I swear I've not staged this incident. This meeting is purely by chance." The six young men at the table looked curious and mystified. Langlois turned back to François, and announced. "You have the opportunity to be part the first French colony of New Zealand in the very place your ship anchored in Akaroa Harbour. Congratulations. Sit down."

François pulled his stool to the table and sat down with his jaw open. This was a complete miracle! He had to ask, "How could this happen?"

There followed a monologue by Captain Langlois, in which he told an astonishing tale, recounting what had taken place in New Zealand, and France.

In Port Cooper, in August of the previous year, 1838, amazingly just one day before the *Nil* sailed out of Akaroa Harbour, Captain Langlois had watched as eleven notable local chiefs, many of whom had worked on whalers, carefully drew a cross or their *moko* – their facial tattoo design – on a sheet of paper, whereby they passed over the whole of Banks Peninsula. For this land, totalling approximately three hundred thousand acres, the chiefs received one hundred and fifty francs in goods, with a remainder of eight hundred and fifty francs' worth of goods to be paid in due course. The down-payment in fact had consisted of twelve oilskin hats, a woollen coat, a pistol, six pairs of trousers, two red woollen shirts and a couple of pairs of shoes. The rest of the payment would be paid when possession was taken up. As a celebration following the signing, wine had been poured out for all. A round of toasts were offered to the health of everyone, and to the health of King Louis-Philippe.

François' heart sank down. He found his expression becoming a little fixed as this story was recounted, and he was quite tempted to interrupt with questions, though he was too nervous to do so. He found it very hard to believe that the New Zealanders, with their particular belief that the forests and the land belonged to the god Tāne, would in any way 'sell' the huge entirety of Banks Peninsula to any Europeans.

François wanted to ask Langlois if he was sure that the chiefs understood that they were selling. He'd learnt from observing the villagers in Onuku how the people discussed things: all the time, despite the authority of the chiefs, with the women having as strong opinions as the men. Chiefs acted with due recognition of these opinions, and you had to know too which chief had authority over which stretch of land. The chiefs were not lords with the power to sell unilaterally tribal land won generations before by the whole tribe, in war and in blood. Furthermore, after defending their land so fiercely against the incursions of another tribe from the north, led by Te Rauparaha, why on earth would the New Zealanders of Banks Peninsula give it away to Langlois for this paltry compensation?

Clearly there must have been interpreters, but François knew well from the sailors and whalers of the *Nil* that Port Cooper was largely a place where deals were such that even transactions between two Frenchmen, speaking the same language, could end in a brawl. The wine mentioned at the end was perhaps a key to the puzzle.

Matthieu Le Bon for one had not been party to this agreement. He had been in Onuku. He was not a chief, but surely he was a man necessary for a land sale.

But Captain Langlois continued with his monologue without François' concerns puncturing the great bubble of glory he was blowing. He said that, with this document, he saw the foundation of a French colony in the Pacific, in the heart of the whaling waters. This would be an instrument of France's prosperity. France would now be perfectly positioned for the exploitation of the riches of the sea, and it would check any avarice of the British.

In New Zealand, the British were one thousand kilometres away from Akaroa, after all, cosy in the warm climate of the Bay of Islands, Kaitaia and the Hokianga in the north of the Northern Island. Let them stay there, under the supposed authority of 'British Resident' James Busby, installed under the authority of the New South Wales administration to act as policeman over the band of British and Australians settled in Kororareka. That town was a civilisation of scum: former convicts, ex-whalers, men on the run, thieves and prostitutes. Let the British have Kororareka and the Bay of Islands, unless the Americans hoisted their flag there first as they were trying to do. Banks Peninsula was cold, but uncorrupted and rich. Let the British keep their corner; France would have the larger island.

There were loud toasts to France at this point, and the captain answered questions. "How did you convince the king?" asked a red-haired youth.

Langlois told his story, trying to mute his voice. He recounted a meeting. In July, 1839, he was back in Paris. In the entrance lobby of a grand mansion, he had stepped up to greet one of the most esteemed men of France: Élie, Duke Decazes et de Glücksberg, former Prime Minister and now Grand Referendary of the Chamber of Peers. Langlois was extremely proud of catching the interest of such a man, and even prouder of what followed.

Langlois had produced his contract, with the inked markings, and presented his proposal. He – as owner of Banks Peninsula – would hand over the land to a company. This could be a commercial operation. There would need to be a group of financial backers, high placed in society, to fund a venture of colonisation in the heart of the lucrative whaling waters, with the approval and sponsorship of the French Government.

Astoundingly, their meeting had been concluded with a handshake of trusting solidarity, and been followed by a flurry of letters and meetings. Duke Decazes was more than a little interested in this project. A week later, he was speaking to the King.

François shifted uncomfortably. Like Langlois, he had little love for the monarch. King Louis-Philippe was renowned as a rather weak man, and more than slightly unsure of his position. Since the bomb exploded in an attempt on his life in 1835, it was known that Louis-Philippe had become particularly cautious of inciting violent acts on his person. He was not prone to bold strategies.

And yet, King Louis-Philippe himself had been convinced. Why? The reasons were simple. Unless France acted quickly to take some initiative in New Zealand, the islands would rapidly go the way of New South Wales. The British would colonise and charge customs duties on all French shipping. They had little right at the moment, on the basis of a few hundred settlers in the northern tip of the islands. If the French, however, quickly established a colony, then France could claim the Middle Island and found a naval base in the southern Pacific. The British should not have a monopoly on whaling here.

After false starts, frantic discussions, letters, meetings and decisions had resulted in the formation of the Nanto-Bordelaise Company. The French Government and the company together would provide transport, food, tools, materials, weapons and thirteen months of rations for sixty colonists – initially – to found a settlement to be named after the king himself: Port Louis-Philippe. The company had bought the land of Banks Peninsula from Captain Langlois and paid him in shares. He was confident on a good return.

Having told this story, Langlois then waited for everyone to respond. There were hearty congratulations.

François was not quite sure what to say. Was this the spirit of Napoleon? The name Port Louis-Philippe was repellent.

But Langlois was very proud of his achievements. The French Navy had given the Nanto-Bordelaise Company a five-hundred and fifty-tonne transport ship, almost brand new, named the *Mahé*, which was renamed the *Comte de Paris* after the grandson of King Louis-Philippe. Its keel was plated with copper and bronze and its main mast measured twenty-two and a half metres. He would be sailing her to New Zealand as captain, in January, from the naval port of Rochefort.

No matter what the circumstances, or the details of the transactions, François felt as though the spirit of Napoleon had to be at work for this chance meeting to have taken place at all. Now he had an opportunity to return to Akaroa Harbour. It was a miracle.

Was it the right thing to do? The sign would be that if one of the cuttings of Napoleon's willow still grew, then he knew he would stay. No one could say that New Zealand was like France, and yet it could be forged perhaps into a new form: a France even better than the one he left behind, a new Republic. That is – if the land sale was truly a sale.

Captain Langlois produced a piece of paper then, with some names, and put it on the bench in front of François. "You can sign here, and be counted as a colonist."

At this, François flinched. To colonise meant to trust in the King, and the Nanto-Bordelaise Company. He was not sure of the deed signed in Port Cooper. And he had to see about the willow trees.

François wondered then – had the chiefs in Port Cooper done this for fear of the British? Were they sealing an alliance with the French, by some kind of treaty of protection? How had they understood what they had done? Only Matthieu could explain.

No, he couldn't be a colonist after all. For the meantime he would be better off getting on the ship's crew. The ship and the colony would need a blacksmith. Then he would get a wage at least for his pains. He could make his way into the colony in time, but only if the willows grew. Would his little *whare* – built with instructions and help from Matthieu Le Bon – be the founding structure? Everything depended on what happened to the cuttings from Napoleon's willow.

François pushed the paper away, anxiously. "Take me as a blacksmith and I will work for you, Captain Langlois, but I will not work for the so-called king, Louis-Philippe. The Revolution did not take place so that he could rule France."

For a moment, Captain Langlois looked baffled. Everyone fell silent. But then Langlois leaned back and burst out laughing. This laughter went on for an unusually long time, until he went and slapped François very hard on the back, on his lash scars, and said, "Spoken as a true Frenchman! You're a man with your own mind, François Lelièvre. You will be our blacksmith."

6
Sydney Town

Marianne and Tim Blake arrived in Sydney Town on March 14, 1838, to find a great welcoming party on the quay and a small band piping a tune and banging drums. Once a ship was spotted coming in to the harbour the news soon went out, and it was always exciting when a brig like the *Albatross*, full of supplies and traders' goods, came into port. It was a celebration, and they were prepared for it, with everyone dressed in their finest, and smiling.

Sydney Town was a revelation to Marianne. As they came into the port it seemed huge, so much bigger than she expected, spread out along the shore, with a centre of fine stone buildings and very wide streets: a real little city much bigger than Colchester, with an impressive harbour full of tall ships. The convicts, once released, had clearly been busy; no wonder so few of them chose to return to England. No wonder there were more colonists coming. Despite being only early spring, the strange trees were verdant green or grey-green everywhere, and the sun was shining brighter than on midsummer's day in Essex. The seagulls were larger and differently marked, and above in the air a flock of black swans flew to some inland water.

Tim rented a well-built wooden cottage on Hunter Street, and they had social events in which he caught up with his family and friends. They hired a young black girl, Flora, to help in the house with cooking and cleaning. She was the younger sister of a 'blackfella' that Tim counted as a friend from childhood, Billy Muster. He continually came to call, and had a meal sitting with them at the table, though he ate with his hands. He also brought gifts of bizarre creatures that he'd hunted and killed. It was Flora who dealt with these. Sometimes Billy and Tim would speak together in the language of Billy's people; Marianne tried to learn a little from Flora, but its complexities were trying and Flora always ended up suppressing a giggle.

Marianne also learnt that Tim was, in his attitude to Billy, an oddity. One night Billy came to the house with his face and body torn and bloodied, and was tended by Marianne and weeping Flora, for many hours.

When Marianne told Tim about this, he was knowing and circumspect. "It's not the first time he's been thrashed. He was given a hiding even as a child, after we'd been playing together. They came and burnt his camp. I could do damn-all about it on my bloody own. I thought he'd lost an eye. One of his brothers was left lame."

Tim told her about how it was when his parents had died when he was just five-years-old, how his brother had to look after the two younger siblings, him and his sister, and how they used to play with the blackfellas up the creek, which is how he learnt a bit of the language spoken by the Cadigal people and others round about. Some rival kids with their fathers came and 'taught the blacks a lesson'. It didn't stop his friendship with Billy Muster, and the two of them eventually learnt to round sheep together, before Tim took to sea. Billy was known as one of the best musterers in Botany Bay, but in Sydney they just saw him as a thieving nigger, and there were plenty of types in town who wouldn't suffer any of the blacks to appear on the streets.

"But this was their home before we came," said Tim, thoughtfully. "It's not like they're all the same and they can move inland... those people out back are like the French are to us... speak a different language, different ways. It's like we took their country. No bloody wonder they're swigging grog."

Tim himself, as the kind of powerful man he was as an adult, wouldn't let any gang 'beat the shit' out of the blackfellas, who mainly lived down at Circular Quay and worked on the wharves. So Marianne was taught by Tim a way of being with the people who were aboriginal to the continent of Australia that was different to the way of some others she met in Sydney. In shops and markets, banks and post offices, she heard it said that the blackfellas were stupid, yet wily; they were lazy and unreliable, and would go off for days doing their own hunting or fishing; they were ignorant and dirty; they were dangerous, and should be 'cleared'.

There were various 'hidings' meted out to them. In June there was a massacre near Myall Creek Station in the north. Reports came in of the murderers using the most barbaric forms of death imaginable. Governor George Gipps ordered an investigation, but there were some people in Sydney who claimed that the men who did this were heroes leading the vanguard, doing a job that had to be done, because the blacks had to be exterminated, like rats on a ship, for the health of the colony.

Marianne, for her part, made a friend in Flora. They could have a laugh about little mistakes and misfortunes. Flora laughed at the absurdity of things. But there were some things they couldn't laugh about, like when someone threw a dead rat on the front porch with a tag around its neck reading 'blak bitsh'.

But, despite such incidents, Tim and Marianne's life settled, as Tim served on ships local to New South Wales and went only as far afield as Hobart Town in Van Dieman's Land. He passed his exams and became a captain, sailing first the schooner *Alfie*. Marianne set up a small school for girls in their front room, gaining clients from well-to-do immigrants by advertising herself as teaching not only the basic skills of education (reading, writing and arithmetic), and of course needlework, but also French. By October, 1838, she had a group of seven girls, aged from eight to twelve, who were keen and delightful, and she felt she couldn't be more content. She also acquired certain ladies for adult French conversation. As they had agreed, Marianne and Tim kept an unusual system of separate finances, with Marianne keeping part of her earnings from tuitions in her own tins. And, also as they had agreed, they practiced methods, in terms of marital acts, that forestalled pregnancy.

This was how it was for seven good months until October, 1838, when an influenza epidemic struck Sydney Town. With more and more ships bringing in colonists, the spread of disease was hard to control. North Head, which was occupied by dispossessed aboriginals, was made into a quarantine station, but it was too late to stop the latest contagion.

Marianne heard of many children's deaths, which made her count her blessings, as they say, namely one: she had the thought that even if the child that had expelled itself in her cabin all those months ago had lived, the chances were that it may well have died now. She watched anxiously as her young pupils, one by one, contracted the illness, and spent at least two weeks absent. A bright fourteen-year-old named Betty Wand went to the hospital, since her malady had turned to rheumatic fever.

Somehow she did not expect her strong husband, Tim Blake, to fall prey to this disease. On October 21, 1838, he was just back from another voyage, this time of ten days, to Hobart. He was full of enthusiasm about what he'd heard from sailors who told him of New Zealand: great forests, rich earth, water, and the possibilities for new enterprises. He'd known about the whaling and sealing, but now there was real talk of settlement, with a good part of the north under New South Wales. He showed Marianne some paper bank notes he'd saved and kept hidden in the bottom of a carpet bag, which had a false base. He had seven pounds and ten shillings; enough to buy land and build a house. But in the midst of his hopes and dreams the sickness infected him. It was like some virulent fungus destroying the trunk of an oak tree, to see a man like Tim Blake have to lie ill all day on his bed, too weak to move, dependent on Marianne and Flora.

After a few days all he did was lie flat, sweating, shivering, rasping and coughing, as his temperature soared. He slept fitfully, plagued by terrors. Marianne and Flora changed the sheets as often as they could, and tried to get water inside him, mint tea, or even a little chicken broth, but often it came out, his stomach expelling every attempt they made to sustain him. Marianne hoped for some improvement with every morning, but the illness was set on staying. She kept a steady chain of cold compresses going, filling muslins with wheat, soaking them in cold water, applying them all over his skin, but nothing took the heat out of his body.

On the tenth day Flora herself went sadly back to her stricken camp outside the town, with a raised temperature, headache and sore throat, and Marianne was left alone. She knew the risk of dehydration now was great. Tim had hardly eaten anything for a long time, and even sipping water was difficult for him. His body seemed to be contracting, becoming older and frailer, as its vital juices were squeezed out. She could feel his bones more, and his heart was beating like a drumroll.

In the morning of October 31, Tim Blake became delirious, as dreams and reality could no longer be distinguished. He was back on the *Albatross*, fighting the storm, "Maggs is overboard!" he kept shouting. "There's nothing to be done! Keep her steady!" He thrashed about, reliving his actions on that night, rolling up sails, pulling ropes, running about. He was hurling himself out of bed.

Marianne had to heave him up and in, fighting with some spirit of the past that had him possessed. Then Tim went into fits, his body jerking violently, his grunts like a stricken animal. She didn't know what to do as a jolt hit through his body, flicking back his head and knocking his skull against the bedpost, so that blood came pouring out all over the white sheets.

Three hours on, as the fits progressed, Marianne was beside herself. There was no one to turn to; everyone was caught by the same disease. The undertakers were coming up Hunter Street every third day. It felt as if she did not need so much a physician, but an exorcist. She prayed. Despite her weak religious beliefs, she begged God for an angel of mercy. She prayed in French, as her mother had taught her, to Our Lady, in the Catholic way. An hour or so on, Tim Blake became calm, breathing scarcely. He was like the ship when they had gone through the hellish storm: broken, still afloat.

Marianne wept, not knowing whether to send thanks to Heaven, or not. Late in the afternoon she heard a rattle outside and thought it must be the undertakers asking whether she needed their services. Distraught, she went to the front porch and found Billy Muster with a horse and cart. "We take him to hospital," said Billy. "Flora told me. She's sick now. Everybody's sick."

The two of them went through to the bedroom, and together they carried Tim out in a blanket and laid him in the cart. After securing the house, Marianne climbed up. The wooden cart reeked of sheep. She placed Tim's head on a pillow on her lap. Throughout the bumpy journey to the hospital, Marianne saw there were few people walking in the streets, and the shops were closed. Everyone was wearing black. The sky was overcast and threatened rain.

Tim, quieter now, was barely conscious, but he had moments of clarity. First, he seemed to awake brightly and asked Marianne where they were going. She said, "To the hospital. We can find Dr Kingsley. He'll know what to do."

"We should go to New Zealand," said Tim then, with his eyes wide open. "There's land, Marianne, and... good water. Opportunity. Money... in the bag. Just need to get my... strength back."

"Yes, yes. We'll go to New Zealand. I'll go anywhere with you, Tim," she said.

Within seconds he went back into deep sleep. Marianne wiped the tears away with her sleeve. The wind got up, and as her eyes cleared she saw a body being carried out on a board to the undertakers' carriage. The corpse was just a small girl, aged six or seven, uncovered, dressed in a simple white nightgown, with little bare feet. Around her waist was a rag doll and her hair was tied into a neat bun on the crown of her head. She could have been sleeping apart from the death pallor of her skin. Her mother was nowhere to be seen. Just a group of men, one of whom was paying money to other men in black hats, as you'd see in any business transaction.

Marianne had a sudden memory of her mother's burial, the clanging bell at St. Mary's churchyard, the men in black suits. As they rounded the corner to the hospital, Tim woke again, looked up at Marianne and said, haltingly, "Fancy... you walking there... beauty. Face as sad as the... gallows." He closed his eyes, unconscious again.

"No, wake up," said Marianne, close to his face. "Wake up."

Billy drew the cart in front of the fine stone building of the hospital and quickly tied the horse, running around then to pull Tim over one shoulder. "Other side, lift him up," he instructed, and the two of them hauled the big man, slippery with sweat, out of the sheep cart and upright over the dirt path up to the main doors. A couple of green parrots shrieked and darted. Tim, woken by this noise, asserted concentration with all his might and strained to use his legs, but he could barely move them.

"No blacks in here," was the first thing Marianne heard as they entered the building. A sharp male voice. It was like a gun shot.

She wasn't sure what happened then, because suddenly she was falling over, with Tim on top of her. Billy Muster was gone.

There were people scrambling around. Alarmed, prostrate, and trying to roll Tim, who was unconscious again, she shouted out that she'd come to see Dr Kingsley. He was a friend and she needed to see him right now! Her husband was the master of a ship and very sick. She didn't care what commotion she caused. Her voice seemed not to come from her but from some trumpet blasting louder than she had ever spoken before, like she was a warrior crying in battle.

There was a chaos of arms and legs, and people speaking. Tim was lifted up to lie on a trolley, and she was left to struggle to her feet. She dashed behind, as they pushed the trolley down into a high hall full of beds, with people everywhere. "Mind your backs!" they shouted as they took Tim to a bed beside a big open window.

They placed something under Tim's nose with a strong aroma that even made Marianne gasp, but Tim stayed fast asleep. A young doctor took his pulse and made some noise of concern. "He's been very ill with it for ten days," said Marianne. She had some feeling of *déjà-vu*. "He's not usually one to be sick, but... he's been very hot, and dreaming things. I couldn't get his temperature down."

"We need salicylic acid," an attendant shouted from another bed. "The fever is too high."

Then Dr Kingsley was there, with his well-tended shiny hair and air of order: the sensible physician. It seemed a good omen to see him. He'd been a godsend when she'd needed him on the ship, and surely he could work some magic now. Dr Kingsley greeted her quickly and went to Tim with a careful and concerned focus, re-checking everything the younger doctor had determined, as the two medics spoke in hushed voices together.

Marianne stood there, not shifting. She felt she could barely breathe. The people in this great hall were like the sea breaking around a boat that carried only her, Tim, and the doctors who tended him. They were sailing through some currents, holding on, keeping straight, and they just had to wait and everything would be all right.

She remembered her mother before she died. She'd stood like this, beside her mother's bed. That was the feeling: uselessness.

Oh no, not again. No.

They seemed to be trying to wake Tim. They were rough with him now, slapping him around, pushing his chest, pumping.

They were messing with him, doing things.

She just stood.

And after some time they stopped. Dr Kingsley turned around to her. "Marianne, he's not breathing. There's no pulse. There's nothing we can do."

"Is he going to die?" asked Marianne, in utter horror, each word almost impossible to form in her mouth.

Dr Kingsley pursed his lips a little, apologetically, and then said, "I mean, Marianne... he's gone."

Marianne felt as if her boat had capsized. She had to dive away and swim. She turned towards the window for air to breathe and went to it, to hold on to the ledge like a piece of wood on the surface of the sea.

For a long time all she could do was hold on to the ledge. It became the side of the wooden bunk she held on to during the storm. She just tried to breathe, and stay on her feet. She couldn't look at Tim. She couldn't move from that place. Dr Kingsley was there, right behind her, she could feel it. She could hear him saying things, consoling, offering condolences. But there was nothing she could say back. She felt his hand on her forehead, checking her own temperature, and then on her arm. "Let me get you some water, Marianne."

Then there was a cup of water being offered to her – a part of her wanted to take it – but she felt as if she was fused to the window. She wasn't even looking through it, only at the painted ledge where a huge black ant was carefully inspecting the surface. At last she swallowed, and knew she had to function. This was no good, behaving like a madwoman.

Shakily, Marianne straightened up and raised her eyes. Outside, just before her, was a huge green willow.

She fainted.

7
Beslon

Returning to Beslon, François' home village, was always like stepping back into a past; not only his own past but a past of thousands
of people, a past that stretched centuries into a dim history where
generations after generations of forebears had maintained their short
lives in this region as well as they could, planting crops in these
fields, picking apples and husbanding animals in low, long houses built of stone, where their livestock lived in one half and families lived in the other, and the wind blew down wide chimneys into
rooms with cold stone floors. The land here could have some charm
in summer, when everyone was out of doors in the fields, when the
flowers bloomed – hollyhocks and roses, daisies and poppies – but
once the cold came and everyone was shut indoors, the Basse-Nor-
mandie was not a region he particularly liked to call home. There
had been no one very wealthy in Beslon, or the other nearby villages: no great patron, no grand farmer to spread his beneficence. There
were just old farmsteads, old houses, stuck on to an old road that
was not much travelled, far away from anywhere important.

It was January, 1840, and he was again on his way to Rochefort.
It had taken two days to reach Beslon overland from Le Havre on
muddy roads where snow was sprinkled everywhere like salt and
the brown, icy puddles had cracked as wheels turned. He couldn't
afford a closed carriage and had sat for hours with whirls of snow-
dust finding every means to get into his eyes and under his scarf.
Now, approaching Beslon after a six-kilometre walk from the town
of Villedieu, he felt he'd become some kind of snail, squelching along
and bent down under a great load. He trudged on below the weight
of the heavy bag, full of his iron tools, hammers and equipment: all
he would take with him to the southern seas, to a new life. His hot
breath shot out into the air in a white cloud. The fields, where wheat
would soon begin to spring tentatively green into this frosty atmosphere, were commandeered by black crows. Everything was grey

and sepia: the trees leafless, the earth paled by snow. The branches of apple trees alongside the way were black veins against the sky.

François saw in the distance the house in which he was born, in which his father and his older sister Marianne had died, where now his mother lived with his older brother Guillaume and his family. Pushed through the door of his own history by the sight of it, as usual, he reflected on everything that had taken him away from this village. Gardeners and labourers, the family had been pleased to see that François was technically-minded, and at thirteen he'd been apprenticed to a locksmith in Villedieu. That had been a great success for the entire clan, to see their youngest son in such a promising position. His father had been proud, and even more so when he'd gone off to Paris to be a locksmith there. No more the backward village of Beslon, the rural poverty of lower Normandy, the life of the simple cultivators of the earth. He would be a city man – a *Parisien*. But his mother had thought of him as soft. He could tell. She hadn't brought him up to aspire to the life of the bourgeoisie. The look in his mother's eyes as he'd gone away had said it all.

It was as if she'd cursed him, because his time in Paris had soon seemed like a prison sentence. His life fitting locks on doors, or mending them, had brought him face to face with everyone who had something worth stealing, or anyone who feared for their security. But he realised as he made perfect locks for them that he had more sympathy with the potential thieves, the destitute who would rob the rich of their treasures. In Paris he saw first-hand the terrible ravine between those who had and those who hadn't: the women in their lace and silk, on one side, and the wine-swilling street-girls hoisting up their ragged skirts on the other. He couldn't bear it. He couldn't stand to see the Revolution turn to slime and the memory of Napoleon – the Code – smashed like a bottle on walls of the Seine.

His mother had been drumming it into him, after all, from his boyhood. Napoleon's Civil Code of 1804 had banned privileges of birth and championed the principles of liberty, equality and brotherhood for all the people of France, together. Those who excelled would be rewarded for their excellence, and advancement would not be based on status and inherited privileges. There were new values: education, human rights, freedom to set your own destiny. It was one rule of law for all, for the rich counts and countesses

75

in their palaces to the poor farmers of Beslon. But, with the end of Napoleon – thanks to the English – the old order had risen up under fat-arsed Bourbon Charles V, and those decent values had been swept into ditches. But he was damned if he was going to live his life placing locks on treasures that should be flung to the people.

At 19 he'd become a Bonapartist, sitting with men secretively in bars, planning a better world. He'd lost his nervous quietness and detachment and found a voice. He discovered he could speak with as much eloquence as Danton, they said, when he got going.

To his father's dismay, he'd abandoned the finicky life of a locksmith and had become a coach driver between Paris and Versailles. Then success – the uprising of 1830 and the end of the reign of Charles. But what for? A constitutional monarchy under the Duke of Orleans, the bourgeois king Louis-Philippe! Puh!

A revolt. 1836. Failure. Then the fear: gossip, betrayal, people being dragged off for interrogation, or worse. He'd come home then, back to Beslon, walking up this very same road to find his mother proud of her son at last: he was now a revolutionary.

It was her who'd told him he should get out of France for a time, on a ship, for his own safety. With his poor father now dead, of sudden heart failure, and his mother under the care of Guillaume and his wife Marie, who had taken over their smallholding, there were at least no paternal lectures anymore on the importance of gaining a good, secure job for a better life. He was his own master. He went to a blacksmith down the road in St.-Maur-des-Bois and learnt this trade so as to be necessary as a crewman. He'd returned to announce his departure, and his mother had given him a painted box with her most precious herbs: the greatest treasure. He'd set sail on a summer's day in 1837 from Le Havre, on the *Nil*.

There was a golden glow through the windows. An oil lamp was burning inside the house this afternoon and smoke rose from the fire in the hearth. François quickly opened and closed the door, shutting out his journey behind him. He dropped his bag to the floor.

His little mother, Jeanne, stood up from the stool by the fire, where she was mending, letting her work slip. "My God," she said, as if horrified. "François. Another visit so soon?"

"You didn't get my letter?" He'd written a letter. He'd seen it go in the postal carriage at Le Havre.

She made a face and came to him, locking her arms around her son in a tight embrace. Her grey head only came as far as his chest, and he was not a very tall man.

She didn't get my letter, he thought. She doesn't know of my decision.

How many hours it had taken him to write those pages, with decent spelling.

"Are you safe?" she asked.

"I'm not in trouble," he affirmed. "I wanted to come and see you..." Suddenly he couldn't tell her – not the very moment he'd arrived – that he was going on a ship again. He couldn't tell her about Captain Langlois and the possibility he would never return to France, not immediately. As his mother hugged him he felt only a childhood wish to be loved and cared for. He felt a prick of deep loneliness. Why had it been his lot to be cast out for the sake of better opportunities? If only he'd been the older son who could have stayed, taking over the house and the fields, being with his mother. If only he'd never been sent off to advance himself in the world, just because he had technical flair.

"Your brother is away in Avranches. We are a house of women and children," said his mother, coughing into his clothes.

François then looked around, as there was movement, and saw pretty Marie, his sister-in-law, at the doorway to the bedroom with a tiny baby in her arms.

As François' mother released him, he saw that his mother's eyes were softened by tears. This was a strange thing, for she hardly ever cried. It must have been because his appearance was so unexpected. She cleared her throat and wiped her cheeks quickly. "Yes, yes, look here, François. You have another niece. Marianne."

Marianne. He stopped himself from flinching at the name of his dead sister. As François went to greet Marie, he understood why his mother was particularly emotional. At the age of ten, suddenly one night his sister Marianne had died of something even his mother hadn't recognised. Marianne hadn't been ill. It was spring. She'd been playing happily with kittens in the yard, and then complained of a headache. Over the past months she'd had an increasing number of headaches and was not seeing so well. They'd thought she'd needed glasses. François had been eight-years-old and was awoken very early in the morning by a terrible shrieking, a sound coming from his mother.

He couldn't really remember his mother extremely well before Marianne died. He had a memory of her laughing endlessly at some joke at a wedding when he was quite young, and he remembered her by his bedside feeding him potions when he was ill, giggling about a story told to cheer him up, so much that she could hardly speak to finish it. But after Marianne died he remembered feeling that his mother did not laugh very much and when she did it was in a different way than before. She only sang at sickbeds. He thought of her as one who toiled: in the fields, in the house, selling their produce at the market, delivering babies.

A new baby, after two stillbirths and a miscarriage, was very good news for Marie. When he'd come to visit after his return from the southern seas no one had even told him Marie was pregnant, clearly not to tempt fate; he recognised now that her clothing had hidden it. This must be a great joy to Guillaume. He congratulated Marie and looked at the baby's small, peaceful face. He looked to his mother. She folded her arms.

Marianne. There was something else, of course. Marianne was the name of France, the spirit of France that was everything good and strong, ideal and victorious. Marianne was the Republic. She was freedom. She was the revolution. At his sister's funeral, after the ceremony, sombre and hard, the priest said that she was like France herself: a glowing, beautiful girl with everything to live for. That was in 1818, three years after Napoleon had been sent to St. Helena's island by the English.

After that, François had to fill the shoes of Marianne in a very important task, in helping his mother with the deliveries of babies. To his shame, he was an honorary girl, compelled by need to do as his sister had done. He had no other sisters. His mother, so talented at enabling the safe deliveries of children, and so fervent in maintaining maternal lives, was not blessed with much fertility herself. Marianne was going to be her successor in the mysterious arts of the midwife. Instead, robbed of her daughter, Jeanne had made do with François, at least until his puberty. He learnt to be detached and quiet when his friends called his mother a witch, and him a girlie. No wonder he grew up to be a man with anxieties.

Such was the past. Now, after a good wash, François felt the calm of familiarity in his old home. His young nephews, aged eight and nine, once they came back from their afternoon jobs at a local farm, were happy to see him and hear stories again of his time hunting great whales. His mother's food was fresh and tasty, and the soup was full of the herbs she grew for strength, vitality and resistance to illness. The heavy sense of the past lifted and he felt instead the comfort of patterns and familiar people. He saw that his mother was a kind of second mother to his young nephews, directing them to do this and that, chiding and chastising, amused when they were cheeky. François could see that Jeanne, despite her life's sorrows, was at this time content. She could surely bear losing him to another life. In New Zealand, if Napoleon's willow grew, he would build another France, better than anything ever before. Perhaps, if this took place, his entire family could re-establish itself there on the other side of the world. He could convince them. Miracles might happen.

When he went to sleep on a mattress in the big main room of the house he felt snug, warm. When again would he feel the safe enclosure of such a home? He was glad to know it once more, to take this memory with him on to the ocean.

*

There was just a slight shine of light through the gaps in the window shutters, which could have been that of the full moon, but the sound of a few birds and a rooster indicated that it was morning. François was not quite sure what it was that had woken him, but then understood that it was the sound of loud banging. There was someone calling, urgently, shrill: 'Madame Lelièvre, Madame Lelièvre...'

François jumped to his feet and ran to the door, unbolting the heavy iron bar and swinging it wide. In front of him stood the cold, panting figure of a boy aged no more than eight, perhaps younger. He pulled him inside.

"What is it? You want the midwife?"

This was a familiar scenario, but the age of the messenger was striking. Why hadn't his father come?

The boy nodded. "My mother– " Then he stopped, unable to complete the sentence.

Jeanne came out of the bedroom pulling a shawl around her nightwear, rubbing her face. "Who is it? Oh, it's... no, Daniel! Your mother is not due. What has happened? Is she starting?"

"Yes," said the boy, miserably, politely swiping off his cap.

Jeanne scrutinised Daniel's face for a second and then became like the captain of a ship. "I will get my clothes on. François, give the boy some water and then get the mule ready, and a kid. We must go immediately. His mother gives birth too fast. She bled too much last time. And she's a widow now."

François did as he was told, suddenly transported back to his days of childhood when he was his mother's helper, gathering the necessaries for her duties. She had a bag always standing ready with all the medicines she made herself and various implements that François could only guess about: weird things that were designed to go inside a woman and pull a baby out when it was stuck, forceps, scissors, clamps and knives. Then there were blankets, towels, lotions, bandages, a large canister of spring water, pans and pots.

As a boy he was rarely allowed to see exactly how everything was used; he had usually been on the margins, within earshot, ready to hear and do and fetch and carry, but never privy to the mysteries of childbirth, which were not for men or children. The only times he'd ever seen anything was when there was an emergency and all the rules collapsed under the requirements of need.

His mother had had no formal training in these arts; they were passed down to her from her mother and grandmother, and on back into some very distant times. Jeanne would now pass them on to baby Marianne, her granddaughter, eventually; that was good. But doctors in the area were actively discouraging traditions of midwives. Their ways were not scientific, they said. Only the poor kept going to her because she did not charge. There was only the assurance of reciprocity; when they could, they would do something in return. That way Jeanne knew she would always be looked after by the community she served, with vegetables left at the door, a loaf, an apple tart or some wine.

François went to the animals and got the mule ready, pulling him out and harnessing him up, with young Daniel silently assisting. He then took a kid and tied it, bleating, in the cart. The sun came up red as a cherry in the east, painting the stone walls pink before being swallowed by cloud. But there was no time to look around at the familiar landscape and houses. Everything was done quickly.

François put the bag in the cart with Jeanne reciting a list of things he had to have.

"Take that box I gave you, before you went away," said Jeanne at last. "And do you still have some of the bark from Napoleon's willow?"

"Yes," he said, stunned to hear this mentioned at such a time.

"I've used up what you gave me, but it's good. If she gets a fever it will bring the heat down very quickly, because Napoleon's soul is inside it and his soul is cool."

Now it was François who couldn't utter a response. He quickly extracted the mended painted box from his bag indoors and put it with the rest of the equipment to be taken. He checked what they had. It was all there. They then set off with François driving the mule as rapidly as the animal would go, along through fields, orchards and woods to the outskirts of the village of St.-Aubin des-Bois, along a winding road of four kilometres.

Despite this mission, François decided he had to say something about the reason for his visit. As he sat beside the huddled, well-wrapped form of his mother, he explained as briefly as he could about the chance meeting in Le Havre with Captain Langlois. Like before, his mother said nothing. She stared at the road ahead with barely a nod or a sound to indicate she was listening. The boy, Daniel, sitting on the other side, was the one transfixed. It made François smile a little, remembering when he was as a lad with no knowledge of the world, never going any further afield than Villedieu. François told her everything that Captain Langlois had said, and that he wanted to go to New Zealand again to see if Napoleon's willow had grown there. Surely she would understand this.

He finished his explanation with their destination in sight. "I must make the voyage to New Zealand again, *Maman*. I feel... I'm being called there. At Longwood, on the island of St. Helena, I felt something. There is nothing for me in France anymore, not now. But perhaps there is something for me in that other land."

Then, finally, his mother spoke. Her voice was sad and tight. "I know what's there for you, François. What's there is hope, and, for hope, people will do anything."

81

François sighed, pulled at the reins and directed the mule to stop. "I'm sorry," he said. What else could he say?

Then there was a sudden shift of things as if a huge wave had broken on a ship. A slim woman emerged from the doorway of the house, running, waving, shouting something incomprehensible. Daniel started to breathe fast in panic. François jumped down, helped his mother and the boy off the cart, took hold of the bag and gave it to his mother. Jeanne hurried to the house with Daniel, as François tied up the mule. François then turned and ran too through the entrance into the open room where only the pale morning light was illuminating the interior, and the fire had almost gone out.

The woman neighbour was speaking in a chatter about being called to help, but by that time the baby was born and there was no way to stop the bleeding, She'd got Daniel to get Jeanne because surely she would know what to do. "But he shouldn't be here!" she shouted with alarm, holding up her hand in front of François. "This is no place for a man!"

"No," retorted Jeanne, equally fiercely. "He is my son. He knows about such things."

François stared at the scene. To one side were two children – a girl aged about five and a boy of about two. The little boy was gripping his sister's skirt. The crying girl held a newborn infant swaddled in her arms, delivered by the helpful neighbour. The umbilical cord also had been cut and was lying in a bowl with the placenta – things François recognised from tidying up as a boy: things he as a man should never see.

But the mother... this was bad. The neighbour was explaining that she'd not tried to move her, for fear of making things worse.

The woman was covered in a blanket on the stone floor not far from the embers of the fire. But the truly awful thing was the blood. François was suddenly reminded of a whale pulled up on to the ship when all the men came out to do their jobs of cutting, and the massive floods of blood that poured out of the great beast all over the decks. The children and the swaddling clothes were smeared with it, and so was the neighbour. It was a great pool in which the mother lay.

Jeanne got to work immediately, issuing orders as she knelt down beside the unconscious woman: the neighbour had to take the children to her house, get them warm and give them something to eat; she would be alone with François. As they scuffled off, Jeanne was all action, checking, speaking to herself. "It has stopped already," she concluded. "Her bleeding has stopped by itself. She's alive. François, make the fire, get another blanket."

François half wanted to comment that the bleeding had stopped only because every last drop of blood had seeped out of the woman, but he held his tongue. He got the fire going quickly, though there was little wood to keep it alight for very long. In the background he knew his mother was doing things he should have no knowledge about, muttering to herself that the birth was too quick. She was binding towels, ripping up cloth. Then she started singing one of her songs. She had songs for healings and she had songs for bleedings. François knew he should not turn to see anything. Indeed, he should not even have looked down at this woman on the floor. He should not really be in the same room.

"François–!" Jeanne called, interrupting herself. "The kid."

He then ran out of the door to the cart where the young goat was tied, still bleating. He never liked this, but he'd seen it work before and there was no alternative. He untied the kid and took it inside. His frowning mother had brought out a ceramic bowl with a spout, some bottles of medicine, a pan, some smelling salts and another large bowl, and was kneeling next to the woman on a pile of towels that had absorbed much of the blood. The fire was going well and Jeanne had several blankets wrapped around the woman now.

François went behind the woman's head and lifted her up a little more. Jeanne opened the jar of sharp smelling-salts below the woman's nose as he turned his head away so as not to feel their sting. The woman gave a start, jerking and gasping. She opened her eyes. "Quick," said Jeanne. "I've got her." She slid another rolled-up towel under the woman's head to prop her up.

François released her, grabbed the bowl, went to the kid that had taken refuge under the table, pulled it out, took his sharp knife from its scabbard, pinioned the struggling animal between his knees, lifted its head and cut its throat, turning the neck so that the blood was caught in the bowl. Throughout, his mother was talking quietly to the woman, reassuring her that her baby was safely delivered and alive, that everything was fine, but she had to drink urgently.

Then Jeanne quickly replaced the bowl with a pan that continued to catch the kid's blood. She took the first bowl, poured two of the medicines into it and then transferred the liquid to the ceramic bowl with the spout. This she put to the lips of the woman, who seemed more like a corpse than a living being, such was her pallor. "Drink," said Jeanne.

It was Jeanne's belief that the blood had to be very fresh, living blood to replace the blood that had been lost, and as much should be drunk as quickly as possible, while the life was strong in it. One of the potions she added was designed to avoid the woman being sick. There was something else with sugar and salt. But the idea of drinking warm blood from an animal that might still be alive was one reason some people called Jeanne a witch. There used to be talk of women who sacrificed goats and copulated with the Devil. Perhaps that was one reason Jeanne championed Napoleon so much: in the Civil Code, the crime of Satanic witchcraft was no longer recognised. It was a bogus thing from the world of stupid superstition. The witches of people's fears and imaginations did not exist.

Jeanne was not superstitious. She was suspicious of the Church and had brought up her children to be equally cynical. Her ways were not ones that involved incantations, prayers or invocations of ecclesiastical entities; they were based on old knowledge of medicines found in plants, minerals, roots and berries, some of which she could grow herself. She sang to the souls of the living and the dead. It was a knowledge she'd passed on to François, who kept the choice remedies in the painted wooden box his mother had given him. Jeanne was practical and methodical, down-to-earth, not easily flustered. And she was resilient. She'd stay with her patients as long as needed.

*

Daniel's mother, Louise, lived. François went to the neighbour's house and back, bringing news to the frightened boy and his siblings. The newborn infant cried and another nursing mother in the village was called upon for feeding. The children went to sleep after breakfast, on some blankets. A gift of firewood was presented, which François used immediately. Jeanne boiled water and cleaned up Louise, singing to her, and when she stopped her songs she told François snippets of Louise's story. François heard how her husband, someone he vaguely remembered, had died after an accident with a saw; he'd lost his hand and his blood became infected.

Around midday Jeanne and François carried Louise, cleaned and tidied and bandaged up, to rest in her own bed. François brought fresh buckets of water from the village pump. Jeanne scrubbed down the floor and put the linen in buckets to soak. François butchered the kid ready for cooking and saved the skin for fine leather. They said almost nothing to each other about anything except practicalities, even when eating some bread and cheese.

By mid-afternoon a strange normality settled, with Jeanne still ensuring that the very weak and pale Louise was given blood to drink at every opportunity. She was now mixing it with meal and some dried powders she had, and later she gave her boiled potatoes and apple. At last the distraught children were allowed to visit their mother with the new baby, and François stared at a scene that couldn't have been more lovely – the pale, sick woman in her bed, with her youngsters leaning close to her, holding on to her hands. Jeanne stood beside him, and then – unusually – clutched his arm.

"Look, François, you're seeing another future before you. She is a widow and needs a husband."

François said nothing. His pleasure at the scene vanished. He shifted a little at his mother's grip. No. This was not his future.

"Ha!" said Jeanne, stepping away and then hitting him on the chest. "I'm teasing you."

François looked at his mother's lined, worn face and the glimmer in her eyes. He did not like his mother's teases. They were jests in the teeth of calamity: the teases of the poor.

"Louise does not need a husband," said Jeanne, scoffing. "She couldn't have another child and live. The next baby will come out of her in an instant and take half of her with it."

François scowled. It was not right to think of these things.

"I've decided, if she lives, that I will train her up," said Jeanne, folding her arms. "She can make her way as a midwife. There needs to be someone else than me around here until little Marianne grows up, and I'm getting tired. You need to have strength and not worry about getting a full night's sleep. I like my sleep. I'm old." She looked at François with resolution.

François looked back at her sadly. She was past sixty, yes, but he did not think of her as old, even with deep wrinkles and grey hair tending to white. She was always more like a young woman to him, a woman with verve and determination who would meet anything with a feisty spirit. He wished he could meet someone like that to be his wife, whom his mother would think of as a sound daughter. But also someone who was different, who would not make such teases.

He sighed.

"Ah," said Jeanne. "François, you must go now."

"Go back to Marie?" he asked, confused.

"No. Go. You must go to your ship in Rochefort. You must go to Napoleon's willow in New Zealand." She turned away from him, speaking to the white-washed wall.

"But... I thought I would spend a few days here with all of -"

"Why?" Jeanne turned to look back at her son sharply. "You left this life a long time ago, François. We sent you out to make your way. And you've chosen where to be. And something has chosen you."

"But I can-"

"Let me be busy," said Jeanne, emphatically, her face suddenly pained. "Go now, when I'm looking after Louise, when I have something to take my mind away from you. I don't want to say goodbye and then sit in my chair by the fire mending Guillaume's trousers."

François was shocked. Their past hours together had been close and intense.

But he could see the sorrow in his mother's eyes and knew he would be doing the right thing if he made it as easy for her as possible. What right did he have to be warm in a little Beslon home for a few days, only to turn away and never see his loved ones again?

"Maman, I may come back if the willow does not – "

"Ah." Jeanne slapped him again. "Hope," she said.

"Hope of a better France... you could come there, to New Zealand." He had to say it.

Jeanne put her hand up and shook her head. "The only hope of a better France is here."

There was no alternative. François realised he must actually go, back to Marie, and then away. But he waited in silence for some time. Only after this, after a lull in the centre of a storm, did he say goodbye, formally, to pale Louise and the children, shaking Daniel's hand, and then he walked through to the main room where his mother had gone to stand by the front door. He picked up his bag.

He went to Jeanne.

François hugged his mother and kissed the top of her head. Then he opened the door and walked outside with tears tumbling down his cheeks, and she closed the door behind him.

8
The Wands

From her fainting at the hospital through to the funeral in November, 1838, Marianne was tended by the efficient Dr Kingsley, from the *Albatross*, who then insisted she stay with him and his new wife, Kitty. Marianne was not in a robust state of mind, and was even less well when she learnt of the death of her maid, Flora, from the same illness that had killed Tim. She walked down by herself to the docks, to the government boatsheds in Circular Quay, to ask the blackfellas camped in their crowded destitution about Billy Muster, and was told by them that he too had died. Dr Kingsley found her there late in the day, hauled her back to his home to be tended by Kitty, and did not speak a word of it.

Kitty, a slim newcomer from Ireland, assured her husband that Marianne would recover, and had suffered hard from grief. Thanks to the Kingsley's discretion no one important knew of her visit to Circular Quay. They helped her sort out Tim's belongings and resources, and her entitlement, and kept her in a fair state with a mind to her future throughout the remainder of the year. She did not tell them about the bag, with Tim's savings, but took it with her.

Marianne became a thin, black-clad figure at the edge of rooms. She didn't cry. She became inconspicuous, without liveliness or passion for anything, without laughter, tears or ambition. She felt as if she'd become a doll in the hands of others, who could put her in any place they wished. Marianne stayed with the Kingsleys in a new stone house near the hospital until she was ready to work, and then they arranged her future life as a governess to a throng of children, one of whom was Betty, her former pupil, who had survived the influenza. Betty's father was Charles Wand, a well-regarded merchant and importer, who counted among his friends Governor Sir George Gipps.

Marianne went to live with the Wand family on January 16, 1839. They lived in a very fine house near Darling Point, and she believed she would live out the rest of her life quietly as a governess whose only concern would be the children under her care. Ironically, she would have the independence she'd wanted, making her own money and setting her own course, though it gave her now no pleasure or sense of safety.

Betty was at first thrilled to have her former teacher as a governess, and was lively and talkative, but Marianne made it clear by her manner when she arrived that she was changed, to Betty's disappointment. She surveyed the four Wand children she would teach dispassionately: Betty, the eldest, aged fourteen; George, aged eleven; Clarence, aged nine and Charlotte, aged seven. There were two others, Anne and William, aged three years and one year respectively, under the care of a nurse, Eliza.

Fair-haired Mrs Felicity Wand, built like a ballerina, and plump Eliza Duncan, built like a stuffed toy, were very talkative and anxious women, always fussing about one thing or another. This meant that for Marianne her role in their company was to be an audience, which suited her well. She did not wish to be involved with this mode of nervous attention to every tiny detail. With the children, she was quiet and firm, overall, in maintaining their studies and duties. They had bright, happy faces, but she couldn't delight in their antics and kept them in firm check. She was fond of them nevertheless, especially Betty, who had a real talent for French and a quick intelligence. But she'd come to see children in the light of the girl carried out on a board to the undertakers' carriage, as potential victims of the great forces of death, and their present laughter seemed only to sharpen her sense of the cruelty and temporality of everything.

When the children were asleep or otherwise engaged Marianne would sit in the shady garden, or in her small attic room, and read, or write long letters to Uncle, who became her confidant in all things as her mind turned over both the present and the past. He would write as well as he could in return, though by the time she got his letters ten months later she was hardly able to remember what he was responding to. He was, more than anything, 'concerned'. 'I am concerned about what society you are keeping and whether you are too much alone.' 'It is of grave concern to me that you have suffered loss and trials of mental strife.' 'I am concerned about your future given the weight of your thoughts.' He even noted that 'it is not un-thinkable, surely, that you should come home.'

Home? She did not, in fact, think of returning to Wivenhoe. In dreams she was very frequently back there in the little town, watching the silvery river, listening to the fishwives tell some story, hurrying to teach her classes, walking out to take Uncle some dinner at the shipyard. Sometimes she was under the willow tree, at which point she would wake in a shock, as if she'd been gripped by a great green hand from the reaches of Hell.

She did, however, take some interest again in newspapers and journals. Charles Wand imported these, and books, among other things, and there were items that she found to be worth reading, largely about new acquisitions to the British Empire. She still wondered at all the mysterious places of the world, but they did not move her deeply. Nothing moved her.

Marianne did not change out of her mourning clothes into ordinary daywear, and in doing so announced her unavailability for courting. When Marianne smiled, it was at irony. The most ironic thing was that Charles Wand announced one hot day a year after her employment began, in January, 1840, that the family would be departing for New Zealand, and he would be most obliged if she would accompany them on this new venture to continue her excellent work as a most diligent and disciplined governess.

This announcement took place at the polished walnut dining table at Sunday family luncheon, with all the children gathered, and the nurse Eliza. The characteristic chattiness of Mrs Wand and Eliza was muted, which told of grave doubts on their parts, but they expressed nothing openly. Charles Wand gave a kind of formal declaration of family enterprise over a meal of cold chicken, potatoes, and cider.

"In the past months there has been much activity in regard to the country of New Zealand. Mrs Wand and I have recently had the pleasure of meeting the newly-appointed Lieutenant-Governor William Hobson and his wife before his departure to those islands, where he is instructed to read a proclamation extending the boundaries of New South Wales to the territory he can acquire for the Queen." He took a mouthful of potato and chewed thoughtfully, while everyone waited for him to continue. "It is agreed by the

Secretary of State for the Colonies that in this case the land cannot be acquired as *terra nullius*, as here, but that the native population there hold the title to the soil and their own sovereignty." He raised an eyebrow to George, now twelve, as if he should take note for the future. "Such land must properly be bought, but at something of a bargain rate." At this, Charles Wand grinned and lifted his glass.

There was a moment of uncomfortable silence punctuated by silverware clinking on green-rimmed porcelain, as those around the table attempted to eat, rather than raise their glasses back. Charles Wand – tall, finely dressed and well-spoken – appeared to be voicing aloud his positive thinking, regardless of how it struck his listeners.

Marianne felt a peculiar sense of slight engagement. Tim had looked to New Zealand, and now also Charles Wand. What would he propose?

"The soil is remarkably fertile, but to buy in absentia, not knowing whether one purchases swamp or desert, is the downfall of many speculators. The best purchases are made by those who live proximate. This is why it's essential that the Wand family as a whole embark on this venture as a collective entity. We will, in short, emigrate and be founders of what will become the capital city of New Zealand."

The announcement completed, Mrs Wand then cleared her throat and spoke, rather worriedly, her blonde ringlets bobbing about like springs, as if to amplify the nervousness in her words. "Of course, we did agree yesterday, Charles, that a cautious approach would be most advisable until the results of Mr Hobson's endeavours become clear."

Charles Wand found this guarded protestation amusing. "Always the same, my dear Felicity. Always the one to stay the hand. But when have I ever been wrong? Would you have all this," he gestured to the surroundings, "had I failed to throw the dice?"

Felicity Wand glanced to Eliza and Marianne, embarrassed. The children froze. It was at this point that Marianne smiled. It was at the irony of the fact that Charles Wand seemed to have everything you could possibly want right here in Sydney Town, and yet wanted more. His many children were in robust health. His beautiful home, like a grand English vicarage, was large and well-appointed, and his garden was the envy of all. He had a pretty and amenable wife, even if she was prone to continual minor worries. Charles Wand was a successful entrepreneur who had a large income. He had status, reputation and the ear of men in the highest places. He himself was a man of physical stature and handsomeness. Why risk everything for a new challenge?

Charles Wand leant back and pronounced slogans suited to politicians. "New Zealand is ripe for the taking. Time is of the essence. We must strike when the iron is hot. Miss Duncan and Mrs Blake, let me ask you, will you join the Wands?"

Eliza, her rosy cheeks pinker than usual, then affirmed her willingness to partake in the adventure. "I wouldn't leave the babies," she concluded. "You may count on my company." She looked meaningfully at Mrs Wand and, under her breath, quoted the Book of Ruth, "Wither thou goest, I will go."

Marianne bristled at the sentimentality that passed between the two women and looked at the tight faces of her pupils, especially Betty and George, who were being asked to leave friends she knew counted for much with them. There was no lively playfulness now in the midst of this adult conversation. What would their life be? George and Clarence would surely soon be posted to England for education: another hard break.

Would she go with them to New Zealand? The babies growing up would mean a new batch of students, and her own security as a governess could be guaranteed in this fertile family. It might be a risk to go further afield than the town she'd come to know, but as a lone woman she was better off with the Wands. She had no yearning for another man. She'd done with men. She couldn't bear to love again. She was resigned to this family and their lot.

"I would not leave my pupils either," said Marianne. That was all. She was not prone to much talking these days, or shows of emotion, though she glanced a little anxiously at Betty.

Charles Wand then looked to her with the same teasing expression that could at other times be found on the faces of the children. "I'm very glad to hear it, Mrs Blake, though may I ask you for one thing as a favour?"

"Of course."

"The black must go. A year has passed and you're no longer officially in mourning. In the days that Betty came to your school I recall you wore something blue, which well-suited your eyes. I remember finding a young woman with a fresh shine about her, especially as she taught the girls French with such gusto and relish for the language. It was quite understandable that the light would be dimmed for a time, given your loss, but that the light should stay so dusky is... a shame, wouldn't you say, especially in our warm climate?" He smiled brazenly. Marianne noticed how curiously sharp his teeth were.

Marianne looked then to the others at the table. The children bit their lips, like they might giggle with nervousness. Mrs Wand and Eliza seemed even more embarrassed.

"We could make a special commission for you... a New Zealand dress, couldn't we Felicity?" Charles Wand smiled broadly and poured himself another cider. "Not one of the flax mats the New Zealanders wear, of course!" He laughed at his own joke. "I mean something elegant and suitable to the times. Mrs Wand will be ordering a new wardrobe for our adventure, especially as I've just unpacked a number of fashion volumes in the last boxes."

Mrs Wand audibly gasped with glee.

"We will have you made ready for a new life, Marianne... and you too Eliza," he added paternally, to the nurse.

Marianne did not say a word of gratitude. The black of mourning was more than a colour choice; it was a sign of her continuing connection with Tim, and her unavailability. In black she was a block of land with a 'no trespassing' notice in bold letters.

She wanted to ask to be left alone to wear whatever she liked, but as an employee she couldn't protest. She smiled, but it was simply her usual smile of irony, that she would be stripped of the one thing that gave her some comfort: the sombre darkness of her clothes, her protection. She felt a strange sense of being re-arranged by the will of Charles Wand, and dressed up in a manner that seemed more appealing to him. He was, indeed, a man who valued appearances in all things. He was proud of his family in that they appeared to look so well and finely-dressed. She'd obviously been an eyesore in the general picture of his female household and children.

But so be it, she thought. There is nothing to be done.

*

93

After a voyage of two weeks from Sydney Town, Marianne Blake stepped off the boat on to the main jetty at the settlement of Kororare-ka in the Bay of Islands, north in the Northern Island. It was a hot, sunny day: Saturday, March 14, 1840. She was dressed in a flowery blue dress with sleeves according to the London fashion, with new petticoats and a whalebone corset. The Wand family indeed looked like a grand self-advertisement as they streamed down smartly and each placed their feet upon the rich soil of New Zealand.

It was all supposed to be an excellent celebration. They had anchored in the Bay in Mr Wand's own chartered vessel, the *Stag*, full of supplies and the best of his imports to enable Lieutenant-Governor Hobson, his officials and the wealthier residents of this place to enjoy more of home and improve their style of living. Charles Wand's aim was to exude confidence and thereby attract confidence: commissions to procure artefacts and provisions, links with traders, the interest of anyone with something to sell.

But the small welcoming party at the quay lacked one very vital component: the Lieutenant-Governor himself. A buoyant man of about thirty years of age, who introduced himself as 'Captain William Symonds', came forward in a friendly fashion. He shook the hand of Charles Wand, saying, "It is my great pleasure to meet you in person at last, Mr Wand," and bowed amiably to the ladies.

Captain Symonds quickly snapped away from pleasantries and spoke close to Mr Wand, informing him that Captain Hobson was indisposed and regrettably couldn't welcome him in person, on account of the unfortunate circumstance that, after beginning with such great success, he'd suffered a stroke while at Waitemata Harbour and was lying in bed on the other side of the Bay, at the Reverend Williams' Mission in Paihia, with his right arm and leg paralysed, unable to speak properly. Messages had been sent to Sydney and it was firmly hoped that Major Thomas Bunbury would shortly arrive with Mrs Hobson and the children, and not a small force of soldiers, to ensure that the steps taken to secure New Zealand for the Queen were not immediately undone.

Marianne heard this clearly and saw Charles Wand's eyes flicker with consternation. The two men turned sharply and walked ahead to where Captain Symonds led the Wand family. They marched in the direction of a new house that had been taken for their rental. There was no carriage. Marianne strained to hear more of their conversation above the children's chatter.

Mrs Wand lagged behind and gazed with foreboding at her new surroundings, which consisted of about fifty poorly-maintained houses and random tents, but Marianne walked close to Charles Wand and Captain Symonds while holding the hands of Clarence and Charlotte, hardly looking at the people staring. She was, in this activity of listening, not detached at all, but heartily engaged.

In truth she started to feel a little different here. She'd found from the very moment they'd reached sight of the clouds of New Zealand that something very strange had happened. It was a painful feeling in the pit of her stomach that stretched up to her throat and unlocked something there. She realised that a weight had been sitting on her chest, compressing her lungs, and a fuller breath caused a change. She'd found herself staring at the new land with tears in her eyes, breathing very deeply, almost gasping in the corset, and she'd wanted to shout some angry obscenity, like a sailor. As the seagulls flew with the boat and they'd skirted the plush hills, she thought of Tim. "I've come here, Tim," she said to the wind. "I've bloody well done what you hoped for."

Was his spirit coming with her, relishing the journey at sea, laughing to see a fresh world? Her new dress, the sea voyage, her new experience, this land, left her feeling a kind of feistiness she'd not felt for a long time.

"Ow, you're squeezing my hand, Mrs Blake," said Charlotte, plaintively, as they walked.

"Oh sorry my dear, but let's keep up," said Marianne, primly, stepping faster behind the two men, who were leading the family troupe up a street with neater wooden cottages. She feared there would not be another opportunity to eavesdrop on men's conversation, since her world was so much the world of women and children. Such men as Charles Wand talked of important things only with each other, unless they had to issue instructions. But it was extraordinary information, to think that the man who was their leader, who had made the announcement of New Zealand's inclusion within the territory of New South Wales, should be ill in bed, with a tiny team of officials left to follow up his significant claim for Queen and country. There had been no military force sent to New Zealand to put down any possible native hostility, apart from those aboard the *Herald*, the ship that had brought Hobson.

"But the land is secure, is it not? The natives accept our government?" she heard Charles Wand say. His was the louder voice.

"A treaty was signed on February the 6th by some forty chiefs of the Northern Island, who are now mainly Christian, but we need to secure agreement from many more. The missions are doing their best for the Crown and we're giving gifts to any chief who puts his name on paper. We are secure in the Bay, but the treaty indicates nothing of the Middle Island, or even Port Nicholson, where there are British settlers already."

"I have to say that there was a clear despatch about this treaty received before we left," said Charles Wand. "Had the announcement been less confident we might have delayed. Sovereignty was ceded on February the 6th, by consent, as we were told." Mr Wand had assumed an air of authority over the younger Captain Symonds, as if he were a headmaster questioning a prefect about school order.

"The Northern Island has been ceded, by consent, and the treaty acknowledges the New Zealanders' ownership of their land, Thus, proper sales can proceed under the sovereignty of the Crown."

"Then all is well," said Wand.

"But I must say," said Captain Symonds, "you cannot imagine the complexity of the situation of land sales, Mr Wand. I've been an agent in acquiring property here for some time and... while there are excellent opportunities, it's not an easy process to negotiate a sale. I myself have just returned from the River Thames, so-called, and Tamaki, and return to Manukau presently. Where negotiations are too quickly concluded, no end of trouble can arise."

"That is why I've put such faith in you, Captain Symonds."

"Already there have been seizures of land without contract, and violence done to defend such seizures. The British Resident, Mr Busby, was supposed to administer criminal matters for those of British nationality, but there are at times far more French or American ships in the Bay than British, and Kororareka is an assortment of every nation under the sun, even Chinese." As if to prove it, a couple of blond men walked past, speaking Dutch, and lifted their hats.

Marianne lost some of the conversation as she struggled to walk in new shoes over the uneven, muddy road, and when she caught it again they were speaking of the New Zealanders. She caught Charles Wand saying "... accountable to civilised laws. I understand they love war, since it provides fresh meat."

Captain Symonds made a noise of disagreement. "The New Zealanders are governed by their tribal custom, which is certainly not our law, but it is a kind of law."

"A kind of law that permits atrocities, and the savages are everywhere here. They are far more numerous than you indicated, Captain Symonds. We saw them as we came in. Their encampments are in every cove. Their canoes followed the ship." This was indeed the case. The Wands had commented on the great number of natives they saw as they came in to the harbour. "Can they not be placed further away from civilisation?"

"In truth, they say they are much depleted in population, Mr Wand," said Captain Symonds. "Smallpox, measles and influenza make them amenable to the missions. And, Mr Wand, please understand that they have many fine attributes, and that it's imperative to honour the responsibility we have in this country. The Aborigines' Protection Society – who have the ear of men in the highest places in London – have been urging us to avoid repetition of the virtual extinction of the native population of Port Jackson. Additionally, there are many New Zealanders who have heard of what has happened across the Tasman. They are natural seafarers, and some of them have gone in ships to trade and seen the situation for themselves."

"You don't think them dangerous?" asked Wand.

"No. The hundreds of ships we bring here every year to whale are astonishing to them. They are cautious with us because they know our strength. There are some who urge the chiefs to get rid of us completely, but most are more interested in a middle way."

"Most?"

"Not all. And some are more favourable to the French than to ourselves. There are Catholic Missions, whose loyalty is to France, and who instil such loyalty in their converts. They are led by one Bishop Pompallier, who is most displeased about the treaty. Unless we extend the treaty very soon and make it hold, there is every chance that the French will undermine our plans."

"The French conquest of New Zealand proceeds by conversion of the natives! How Bonaparte would be turning in his grave."

"They have been very successful. But our missions are winning, and our missions turn the natives towards England."

"But land, Captain Symonds," said Wand, with impatience, "I'm here for land. You yourself have told me that it can be bought cheap, and now is the time. In two years, if the cession of New Zealand holds, then it will be worth ten times as much, or twenty. You see what's trailing behind us, Captain Stanley." The two men turned to look back at the Wand family, and looked straight into Marianne's eye, walking too closely behind with Clarence and Charlotte. "I've risked everything, my family and my business, to pick the fruits of this young country. Your letters have given me cause to trust you. I'm very sorry to hear of the state of the Lieutenant-Governor, and I can appreciate this has caused much vexation to all. But can you assure me as we walk to our new home that I've not come in vain?"

At this point the men strode on too quickly for Marianne to keep up, while holding on to the hands of the children and stepping on the difficult earth road. She dropped back with the other women and children and watched native youths carry their bags and boxes past them as if they were made of air.

She was intrigued by Captain Symonds' words, and he had a vitality and openness about him that was appealing. He was somewhat careless about his appearance: despite the occasion, he was wearing an old shirt and heavy boots, with his hair unruly, befitting a man of outdoor pursuits. How different he seemed to the debonair Charles Wand, who kept himself so immaculate.

Marianne was fascinated too by the appearance of the native lads, quite different to Billy or Flora; they were a more muscular, broader and taller people. They wore European clothing, but their feet were bare and thick-soled.

Then she was surprised. Captain Symonds turned to the lads and, in their own language, issued them with what appeared to be instructions. He pointed to the road up ahead and then to the right.

Even Tim would never speak the language of the blackfellas in public. Perhaps this was a very different place.

9
The *Comte de Paris*

François and an assortment of sailors and colonists – most of whom were so poor their family possessions amounted to only a couple of boxes – arrived in Rochefort in January, 1840, and waited.

Hidden away down the River Charante, Rochefort was laid out like a giant game of chess with a grid pattern of perfect right-angled streets and grand houses, and it felt that everyone, even outside the naval barracks, was ordered and organised. François was awed by the grandeur of the Arsenal and the huge size of the dry dock, with a great ship being built. Everything was wide and spacious, monumental, reminiscent of palaces and classical splendour.

As he lodged in the town in the damp winter of this flat landscape, François could sense excitement everywhere, muffled with secrecy, and a fascination about what this enterprise might do to any colonising plans of the British.

On Wednesday, February 19, 1840, the naval frigate, the *Aube*, set sail under the distinguished officer Commandant Charles-François Lavaud, who was under orders to keep a naval ship in port and be Royal Commissioner in Port Louis-Philippe, protecting the colonists and being a governor to them, aiming to arrive first in Akaroa Harbour and make ready to welcome the settlers.

As for the colonists, the French people had not responded with overwhelming enthusiasm. There were not in fact enough French people willing to be settlers, so a group of pro-French Germans were brought in to make up the numbers to sixty-one in total. They were largely poor couples with young children, ready to take a risk in the absence of little hope at home.

On Friday, February 28, 1840, the *Comte de Paris*, with its load of settlers and sailors, was issued with official clearance from the port of Rochefort.

But there were omens. Perhaps it was a cold dreariness of winter that caused these things to happen. No one knew.

They began with a suicide. The pretty young wife of a prospective colonist drowned herself. They were already installed on board ship at the main quay. While François had looked around with a sense of satisfaction at the ship's newness and its relative space, this young woman's face, seeing the same things, had reflected the nullity of the winter sky. While everyone was looking in other directions, she'd taken her opportunity and jumped into the flat river.

"Éloise!" screamed her husband, Victor. However, unable to swim, he'd only grasped hold of the railings and shouted hysterically for help. Swimming not being one of François' strengths either, he too had watched helplessly as a couple of other sailors jumped into the freezing water to try to salvage the woman, whose form was swallowed up instantly. The point at which she descended was shown only by ripples radiating calmly out towards the quay, brushing against the hull, causing floating bits of wood to bobble.

"Rather death than never see France again!" gasped Emeri de Malmanche, one of the colonists, to François. "My wife would do the same, but for the baby she carries. She would count it too great a sin to kill the child. I've promised her we will return to France again, and I will not cut my beard until we do so."

"She doesn't know how beautiful it is in New Zealand," murmured François, staring down as the sailors frantically diving for Éloise came up empty-handed. "She doesn't understand."

But no matter how worriedly he looked down on the scene and hoped that the sailors would recover the young woman, this riverbed of France seemed determined to clasp onto her. Éloise's body was not recovered till the next day, and her death ended the enthusiasm of Victor to make the journey. Sobbing like a child, he went away with his dead wife in the back of a cart rattling on the cobblestones, to the undertakers, while the ship was towed smoothly down the River Charante. The hubbub on shore of people waving and shouting *bon voyage* soon dimmed. The colonists left as sombre as if they were marching behind a hearse, and everything was grey, brown, beige. Men on piers, in front of little boating huts, waited with their huge nets until the ship had passed, and stared, like the cows stared chewing the cud.

Their progress down the narrow, brown river was slow and quiet. It was foggy and cold. The trees were skeletal and grey, swallowed by white in the distance, and the sun shone weaker than the moon through mist. The boats with hefty rowers heaved and cut the water, and the thick ropes were taut. The river reeds stood upright like a guard of honour watching impassively as the ship looped in a great 'U' from the port of Rochefort, south and around the town and up to the north to the Port-de-Barques, where the *Comte de Paris'* sails were set.

There, finally, the huge canvas sheets pounded out in the wind. The fog lifted, the bow rose and dropped. They glided quickly through the wide mouth of the river and out to the slate-grey sea, where islands were revealed. Passengers looked sadly at the last houses of the mainland, the last buoys. As they sailed between austere Fort Boyard and the island of Aix François peered out, wondering at that lonely house where the emperor Napoleon had gone after Waterloo.

The British had tried to blockade Napoleon at Aix, coming up around him like a gang, but everyone knew he could have escaped. There were so many fishermen that could navigate the waters, even in the starless night. Napoleon decided that he would turn himself over to the Prince Regent of Britain. The emperor had written the prince a letter, now so famous, from that very house. Faced with the factions that divided France and the great powers of Europe, he'd decided to end his political career and come to seat himself at the hearth of the people of Britain: "I put myself under the protection of her laws."

As if the British could behave with honour! On July 15, 1815, just at this time in the morning, Napoleon had climbed up on to the bridge of the British ship *Bellerophon*, without the faintest idea that he was considered an arch-criminal, who would be immediately rendered into an exile, without trial, by enemies he'd esteemed.

Was it a sign, that he, François Lelièvre, would leave France at the very point that Napoleon left France? Napoleon was a captive, and he a free man. Aix was the last place Napoleon had slept on French soil. The passengers of the *Comte de Paris* sighed to see it, knowing they too would not sleep in France again.

He felt a crush of emotion in his chest: the recollection of the English betrayal fused with the shock of the suicide, and the mewing of the colonist women's suppressed sobs, was almost too much.

The ship went on towards open sea, with a pilot on board giving guidance.

And then there was the second omen.

The local pilot did something very peculiar. It was as if this stretch of sea gave out not only fog but some confounding ether that affected one's power to make sound decisions.

It was getting dark. Frightened when the boat that was supposed to take him back to Rochefort failed to appear, this local pilot decided to stop the only way he could imagine: by ramming the *Comte de Paris* onto a mudbank. Captain Langlois made a furious, doubtful concession at the pilot's insistence and shouted every expletive known to France. Passengers and crew together lurched as the tall ship came to a mighty halt. The sails were quickly drawn down. The pilot assured Captain Langlois that the ship could easily be refloated in the morning, once his missing boat was found to take him home.

But the *Comte de Paris*, loaded with fifty-nine colonists and their belongings, some thirty-six crew, a huge quantity of building materials, food, trees, plants, horses, cattle, dogs, rabbits, pigeons, poultry, ducks, geese, and everything else, was a heavy ship. For ten days the *Comte de Paris* was stuck in the mud, in the rain, while Captain Langlois ordered the expulsion of all heavy items that could be lowered down to waiting boats. Finally, she was free, but only to limp back to the road of Aix, where most of the items had to be reloaded, in full sight of Napoleon's house, the windows of which seemed to glare amazed at the embarrassment of it all.

The ship did not reach the open ocean until Friday, March 20.

*

The third omen was not really one at all. It was a feud.

Everyone knew that gruff Captain Langlois was in charge. He had the manner of a commander, and it was he who had made the deal and organised the entire venture. He was touched by the aura of kingship.

But, in its wisdom, the Nanto-Bordelaise Company, headed by men of better breeding that Captain Langlois, had chosen for its official representative an aristocratic intellectual whose main passion was botany: Pierre Joseph St.-Croix Crocquet de Belligny, nephew of the renowned Baron Alleye de Cyprey, the ambassador to Mexico. Belligny, it was said, had long been the protegé of Duke Decazes. He was about thirty, around the same age as Langlois, but tall and superior with a long neck, a kind of giraffe looking down at the barking dog that was Langlois. He was a fastidious and pedantic man perfectly suited to a life of scholarly pursuits at the *Musée d'Histoire Naturelle* in Paris. Belligny's interest in New Zealand was ostensibly to collect interesting, unknown, specimens of native flora. But he was also clearly determined to ensure that the best wishes of the Company were scrupulously maintained, and that no embarrassment ensued in regard to his patron.

Langlois considered the appointment of Belligny a total insult. At his worst moments, he ruminated aloud on how he'd brought land and opportunity to Duke Decazes, and instead of being honoured, thanked, and appreciated, he was being used and undermined. This "upper-class, academic, arrogant, soft, insulated, inexperienced prig" was the last thing the Captain wanted on board.

Langlois had strongly objected to any ultimate authority being invested in Belligny rather than himself, and had managed to engineer a final agreement just before departure that had officially placed Belligny below Captain Langlois in the company pecking order. With that established, Langlois had repaid his rival with a kick in the teeth: he'd completely refused to load all his personal effects on board ship. "The ship is overladen," he'd said, in his blunt manner. There was no apology, no cordial commiseration. Belligny, flustered and offended, faced the plain fact that a captain on board ship was king. With the mudflat incident, the captain was proven entirely right regarding the weight of the vessel, and Belligny was made to feel he should thank Captain Langlois for no further loss of his precious belongings. After all, Captain Langlois was so angry with the local pilot it seemed quite possible that he might go completely haywire and seize all Belligny's private possessions to toss them into the mud.

The squabble about who was truly in command, and the issues of Belligny's baggage, set up a deep mistrust between the two leaders of the company venture. They would work together only with gritted teeth. That was obvious to everyone.

*

Once they were on their way, rolling over the turbulent seas of the Atlantic Ocean, the settlers wanted to disregard these shadows. What mattered now was their future. They marked out their days and their rations with work, eating, and occasionally even drinking. One Sunday night the men were allowed some wine, and stood around the barrels on the lower deck enjoying every drop.

"We should call the town the New Marianne," suggested Jean-Pierre Éteveneaux, a mellow sawyer in his forties from the Jura, and father of three children. "That would be a fitting name... the name of France herself."

"Yes, for sure, that's better than Port Louise-Philippe, named after the king of the bourgeoisie," said François, feeling the personal weight of the name. He liked to be around the settlers and found himself talking quite convivially with them, in a way he'd never talked to whalers. The more he sat with them, the more they accepted him as one of them, if not a kind of authority among them. They would ply him with questions about the land, the water, the types of vegetation.

'Shshshsh," interrupted Joseph Libeau, a diminutive but feisty Rochefort gardener whose wife was pregnant, glancing around morosely. "You don't know... one of them could be a spy, and Belligny is hardly a Republican. You don't know what he might write back to France about our conversations, if he overhears."

"Well, there are more of us than of them!" said Emeri Malmanche, whose beard was starting to grow. He was a deep-thinking man who had left a smallholding with his pregnant wife and two surviving children, determined to start a new life away from the memory of those children he lost, despite his wife's misgivings.

"On the other side of the world, miracles can happen," said François, thinking of his willow.

"Then let us drink a toast to it," said little Joseph Libeau, solemnly. "Let us carry the Republic with us."

At that, a quieter member of the company, François Rousselot, a slow-speaking stocky man from Jallaucourt in the Lorraine Plateau, said, "I haven't drunk such a toast since Waterloo."

At that everyone fell silent and stared at him.

"You fought with Napoleon at Waterloo?" asked Libeau, amazed.

Rousselot looked hesitant, as if he was not sure he should have spoken. "I was fourteen. There were a lot of us that age, or younger. The armies of Wellington and Blücker were made of trained soldiers, but we... so many of us... were boys, or old men. Our strength was in our hearts, in our souls, and we almost won the battle. David almost slew Goliath." He stopped then, sadly, remembering.

No one could speak for a moment. Everyone sat, recalling what they knew of that fateful battle in the summer of 1815. They had all grown up with the events of Waterloo engrained through countless tellings, reminiscences and speeches.

Then François broke the silence. "I've often imagined what it was like, to fight with Napoleon at Waterloo."

Rousselot looked at the blacksmith blankly, as if he were watching something in his mind's eye from long ago, and his voice cracked as he said: "A lot of noise, and smoke. We couldn't see anything."

This was not really what François had wanted to hear about the battle. It did not sound heroic. Was it just a cacophonous fog?

"So it was, I'm sure," said Emeri Malmanche, who was a boy when the battle was fought. Malmanche looked sympathetically towards the sensitive eyes of Rousselot, and touched François cautiously on the arm, as if to hold him back from saying anything critical. "To France," he toasted, diplomatically, and every man drank to his own dream.

10
Kororareka

From March, 1840, home for the Wand family in the small township of Kororareka was a two-storied wooden structure painted white, with an iron roof and a picket fence all around a naked plot of land in which native shrubs were growing, and where a couple of bright blue swamp-hens with long red legs were wandering. Beside it were some wooden stables, and close on the other side was a small cottage in a neighbouring plot, also rented by the Wands. Marianne was assigned one of the rooms in the cottage, because of the much smaller proportions of their house. Betty Wand, now fifteen – and turning sixteen in September – was her companion there, with an old German stable-master and workman, Holger, in an adjacent shed. He was also a kind of guardian, and slept with his rifle. The word 'temporary' was mentioned rather frequently. There were plans to build a grand home suited to their needs in the new capital, which everyone agreed couldn't be Kororareka, being tarnished on account of all the drunken sailors.

The cottage was new. Marianne's room was spacious and fresh, smelling of whitewash and wood. She felt some sense of liberation, being removed a little from the main house and the daily problems of the Wands. Betty – who was already more of a young woman than a girl – was also very pleased. Together they looked through the back door. Lying at the back of the small town, comprised by all varieties of wooden houses, the prospect looked out on the undulating spread of tree ferns, and other strange trees and bushes, and then to blue water.

How extraordinarily empty it all seemed here, after the city of Sydney. It was quiet, with only the calls of birds and sounds of people talking or hammering in the distance. Marianne had no idea this land would be so devoid of civilisation. It was like a spread of new cloth, waiting to be cut and formed, full of promise.

To Mrs Wand, however, it was terrifying. Two days after their arrival, she went into a kind of madness, and would not emerge from her bedroom, where Eliza tended to her as well as to the babies, so that Betty and Marianne had to take over the administration of all domestic arrangements, including caring for the children, the hiring of female servants, organising the buying of food, administering cleaning and laundry, and the arranging of household furniture and effects. Betty and Marianne were therefore usually in the main house, rather than the cottage, except for sleeping. When visited upstairs, Felicity Wand remained almost motionless in bed, and could hardly be tempted to eat. When she was alone she could be heard, through the thin wooden walls, sobbing miserably, and asking, "When will the troops arrive?" as if they were under siege.

Despite their concerns for the welfare of Mrs Wand, new responsibilities welded Marianne and Betty into a tighter bond, so that the old relationship of teacher and student broke down into one of friendship and co-operation. They were both practical-minded and quick. Betty clearly felt the weight of standing in for her mother acutely, but relied on Marianne's guidance. Charles Wand, being preoccupied with business and the peculiar political circumstances, was often going on day trips by boat with Captain Symonds and others to Paihia and beyond. He clearly trusted that his daughter and governess between them would manage everything at home perfectly well.

Their independence and responsibility led to more sojourns out and about than they would otherwise have made, sometimes with the lumbering Holger, but as time went by quite often on their own. Marianne was fascinated by Kororareka, which in many ways reminded her of Wivenhoe. The houses were more spaced out, with larger yards and gardens interspersed, but the size of the population seemed not so different; she'd heard it said there were eight hundred permanent inhabitants in Kororareka, but that number seemed not to count some two hundred or more New Zealanders or the transient people. While Wivenhoe lay on the Colne River, Kororareka lay on the wide Bay of Islands, with higher hills around. The vegetation was completely different, as were the birds, but the overall feeling of the place was familiar. The whalers and sailors whose reputation was so regrettable seemed not unlike the sailors and shipbuilders of Wivenhoe, who were equally irreverent and suspicious of organised religion, and equally prone to fall out of a public house. The ratio of public houses to the population in both Wivenhoe and Kororareka was about the same: one did not have to walk far before there was a place for a convivial drink. If a cheeky sailor hailed her with a word or a whistle then that was no different to what she'd grown up with, and if it hadn't been for such a sailor she'd never have met Tim. The difference was, however, that a large number of men in Kororareka were just passing through. The ships swept in tides of sailors and swept them out again, much more than in Wivenhoe or the Hythe at Colchester. There were, naturally, the whore-houses too; in Wivenhoe everyone knew the girls at Nancy's place, and Milly's. In Kororareka there were so many establishments it seemed that half the women were on the game.

Of the settled population of the town, the New Zealanders seemed to feel no compunction to move off into land further away, and sold vegetables, flax-ware, fish and all kinds of artefacts down on the quay. Many of them were working with the traders and businessmen of the town, or as servants and workmen, and there were native women married to settlers, with fairer-faced babies tied on their backs. Such intermarriage was not much found in New South Wales, except among the men who had gone to the bush.

The native women were clearly sought-after as wives, since marriageable European women were scarce. There were even fewer settler women to each man than in Sydney, and those not working in the brothels were more like the oyster women and fishwives of home, largely ex-convicts from Australia who were able to drink as hard as the men. There were a few wives of merchants and farmers, mainly from Britain, but also from other European lands, but they had a slightly hounded, preoccupied look about them. Then there were the mission women, who arrived occasionally in the town, looking piously superior. No wonder Betty and Marianne elicited so much attention when they went to the stores. It was quite amusing, and Marianne saw that Betty rather liked it, despite her blushes.

In the house there was some male attention also, in the form of Captain Symonds, who came to visit Charles Wand on three occasions at home before Symonds' departure south. With Mrs Wand indisposed, Betty and Marianne played hostess over morning tea for the Captain, who seemed rather delighted to be in their company, before having to engage in serious discussion with Mr Wand the moment the ladies departed. Betty was very much taken with Captain Symonds. Charles Wand, however, seemed to find the obvious pleasure shown by the captain to be irritating, and could be a little cutting as a result over things Captain Symonds said, though Marianne supposed that was natural for a father when he saw his daughter being viewed as a woman rather than as a little girl.

Captain Symonds' departure to his base in Manukau filled Betty with yearning. She expressed this in French, for fear that anyone important would overhear. This was rather excellent, thought Marianne, in terms of motivating Betty to greater proficiency in the language. Betty confessed that in truth she couldn't stop thinking about Captain Symonds for one minute. She lay awake at night dreaming about him. She fretted about his journeys inland to dangerous places and thought he was the bravest and most accomplished man alive. She gathered information about him: he was on extended leave, having risen very quickly in his regiment. He was adept at surveying, and a brilliant negotiator, well-bred, well-liked by everyone and highly regarded by Captain Hobson. She wondered if Marianne had heard anything at all about his marital circumstances. Had he left a wife behind in England? Did Marianne feel that Captain Symonds had any regard for her, Betty, or did she come across as young and silly?

Marianne tried to be reassuring and hoped that Captain Symonds would, on his return, make some proper request to court Betty, properly, as was fitting for a girl of Betty's social status, despite her very young age, though she was a bit afraid that in Kororareka such formalities were not quite the done thing, as they rarely were in Wivenhoe unless you belonged to the group who could be invited to a party at Wivenhoe Hall.

Then, on Thursday, April 16, one month after the Wands' arrival, the troops Mrs Wand had hoped for finally arrived. On this day, the magnificent ship *HMS Buffalo* anchored in the Bay, carrying Major Thomas Bunbury, sent from Governor George Gipps to take over operations in New Zealand if necessary, with eight British officers and eighty soldiers. With them, travelled Mrs Eliza Hobson and her children, who proceeded with Major Bunbury straight to Paihia to tend to the mysterious invalid, Lieutenant-Governor Hobson, whom most people still called 'Captain' Hobson, since his official title seemed rather grand given the peculiar circumstances.

There was apparently an immediate riot, of sorts, with New Zealanders and Europeans shouting against each other, and the first action of the military was to quell it, which they did largely by blowing bugles and threatening. More New Zealanders and farmers were in town than usual in the days that followed. Mr Wand was very preoccupied.

On Friday, April 17, Betty and Marianne found it necessary to take a walk to try to see for themselves, as Holger said there would be an announcement. He accompanied them at a distance, alert to their safety. Marianne's purpose was to catch a glimpse of Bunbury, since for once in her life she was in a situation that might well be written about in the *Times*. She actually felt interested. Betty's purpose was simply to see whether this event might possibly coincide with Captain Symonds' return from his visit to the Waikato, made to urge more chiefs to sign the treaty. They joined a small gathering of settlers outside the General Store, in front of where a large number of soldiers were assembling on the quayside, and Betty started articulating a stream of thoughts, in quite good French.

"Mama told me that Mrs Hobson married Captain Hobson when she was sixteen and he was thirty-four," said Betty. "Mama met her several times in Sydney and Mrs Hobson told her. And Captain Hobson adores her very much. I'll be sixteen on September 30."

"Of course, age is not what matters in a marriage... you're quite right," said Marianne, distractedly, also in French, thinking she saw a man in a major's uniform standing with other officers. There were people everywhere. The soldiers looked very impressive in their red and white, with muskets and knives and polished boots. The little town had come awake, alert to watch this, and most people appeared to be sober. Around her different accents and languages signalled the mixed population of the Bay. There were American and Canadian voices, and the tongues of Chinese, German and others Marianne could not recognise, as well as the New Zealand speech. It seemed remarkable that the British could be so confident of success, when the proportion of British people here was barely a majority.

Betty sighed. "He's been away for very long."

"Well, that is his work, to travel and secure land. Your father depends on it."

"Papa says he always sends regards to us in his letters, to you and to me, as well as to Mama."

"Really?" Such salutations hadn't been passed on to Marianne.

"I tell Papa to send our regards back. Do you think... given this... that I can write to him myself?"

"I don't know... it's– "

Then Betty suddenly turned to Marianne with emotion and said, "Madame Blake, do you think perhaps that Captain Symonds has feelings for me?"

At this point there was an intrusion into their conversation, from behind. In very good French, a male voice said, "Good day, ladies. I'm very pleased to hear the French language spoken by two such elegant additions to these shores. We must surely be introduced?"

Marianne spun around to find herself and Betty face to face with a bishop, with a shy-looking priest beside him and a group of European-styled New Zealanders. The bishop was tall, long-nosed, dark-haired and finely-attired in ecclesiastical clothing, which created the impression of great superiority, but he had a kindly face. Betty blushed, clearly flustered to think of the conversation these priests may have overheard.

There was courteous nodding and bowing from the men, while Marianne and Betty curtsied awkwardly. Marianne realised that this must be Bishop Pompallier, first mentioned by Captain Symonds on the walk to their house on that first day, and much discussed – as a trouble-maker – ever since.

Bishop Pompallier smiled a little, quite warmly. There was in the bishop a kindliness and intelligence, and air of insularity that was so much like Uncle, Marianne almost felt he was familiar. Even the twinkle in his eye, that revealed he'd heard a little of the conversation, was the same as what she knew.

She felt it was difficult to speak. Between recognition of Betty's embarrassment, the memory of Uncle and her own surprise she was not particularly able to think. Nevertheless, she gathered herself together and introduced herself. "Your excellency, Bishop Pompallier," she began, unsure whether *excellence* was the right form of address, "my name is Marianne Blake, and I'm governess for the Wand family. May I introduce to you my companion, Miss Betty Wand, the eldest child of Mr Charles Wand."

"Ah, so you know of me already, by name, and I know of you, at least of the family Wand. I understand that Madame Wand has suffered ill health since her arrival in Kororareka. I'm very sorry to hear of this effect of the town on a sensitive disposition. Please forgive me my impertinence in speaking to you so forthrightly on this occasion. The custom here is to be very bold in making the acquaintance of newcomers, whether gentlemen or ladies. The manners of Europe are not at all the manners of the southern seas." The priest beside the bishop appeared to make concurring noises.

"Not at all, your excellency," said Marianne, glancing at Betty's downcast eyes. "We are very pleased to make your acquaintance."

"And I would like to introduce to you Father Petit." The shy-looking priest with the bishop nodded respectfully. Marianne curtsied again.

"May I also I commend you on your command of the French language, Madame Blake. You speak as a Frenchwoman." The bishop seemed intrigued.

"My mother was French," said Marianne. "She came from La Rochelle, where she met my father, who was in the British Navy, just after the capture of Napoleon. When my father was decommissioned, he brought my mother to England." She then stopped herself. She noticed how the bishop looked right into her, as if he knew instantly that she'd been baptised a Catholic. This was significant for him. Then she thought she heard a clap of hands and turned away to look.

Bishop Pompallier and his companions also looked in the same direction. Crates were being thrown together to make a platform, and a crowd was assembling around it. The straight-backed man in a red major's uniform, with a resplendent crested cap like that of a bird, was shaking men's hands.

"How lucky it is for the British that their uniforms are the colour of *tapu*," said Pompallier, to Father Petit. "Blood red."

"*Tapu*?" asked Marianne.

"An item painted red, in the world of the New Zealanders,

indicates that something cannot be touched. The untouchables are the ones with the power. "

Marianne looked to the faces of New Zealanders around her. They did not seem to be in awe. Rather, some appeared amused; others were suspicious and solemn.

"We are going to have an announcement, as predicted," said Bishop Pompallier to Father Petit again, with a trace of consternation. "At least this time it's not in their church, designed to exclude us." Then he turned back to Marianne. "We will go closer and introduce ourselves, for this business, but please ladies, do take the opportunity to call upon us at any time. Our door is always open. Perhaps as a teacher yourself you may wish to see our school, Madame Blake?"

Marianne was touched by the bishop's hospitality. "Thank you. That would be very nice."

After cordial goodbyes, Bishop Pompallier's party strode off towards the major, with people parting to allow his passage, like the sea around Moses.

Betty rolled her eyes. "He heard every word I said!" She spoke in English now.

"Oh no... it's all right," assured Marianne, distractedly, looking after the party with interest. "It's not as if Bishop Pompallier would ever sit down with your father, or Captain Symonds, and drop a hint."

"No, indeed. They would run a mile from him. Didn't you hear Captain Symonds say that he sowed seeds of discontent about the treaty? He didn't want the natives to sign, to permit the sovereignty of the Queen. He told the chiefs that if they signed they'd end up breaking up rocks to make roads, ruled by us as slaves. So there were some important chiefs, who are Catholic converts, who have not agreed to it. Captain Symonds does not approve of him at all."

Marianne was even more intrigued. She watched dignified greetings between the bishop and the major, and the keen observation of the British officers standing nearby.

Finally, on the quayside, Major Bunbury stood up on the crates to make a few announcements to the hushed crowd. He was no public speaker and these were mainly clarifications of the British position in regard to the extension of the colony of New South Wales to the Northern Island of New Zealand, and Major Bunbury's position as acting for Hobson, but it was all very brief. The main point of it all seemed to be ensure everyone knew who was in charge and how many soldiers were there now, standing beside, to make the point.

*

In the days that followed – with the arrival of Bunbury and the British troops, along with Mrs Hobson – Mrs Wand reappeared. She was thinner and very pale, but she now ate downstairs with either the children, Eliza and Marianne, or else alone with Mr Wand in the dining room.

The arrival of military provided more authority to the officials around Captain Hobson and there was a definite sense of purpose. There were endless meetings in which Charles Wand was an active participant, both in terms of colonial administration and of land sales. The seat of government seemed to take root in land beyond Pomare Bay at Okiato, called Russell, where the Hobsons migrated; the officials eschewing Kororareka on the advice of the missionaries. Mr and Mrs Wand went across the Bay to visit the Hobsons, and Felicity Wand came back looking better each time she was able to talk privately with Eliza Hobson about the matters that concerned her.

After one such trip across the Bay, Mrs Wand was positively bright with the children at tea. She announced that they would be moving to the 'new capital' very soon. She stayed up a little talking with Marianne about household concerns, before retiring with Betty, whom she asked to read to her. Betty did not come down, and Marianne assumed she must have fallen asleep at her mother's bedside. As it was their custom to go to the cottage together when evening fell, she waited for her downstairs in the drawing room, reading some old newspapers by the light of a whale-oil lamp. Eliza had gone to bed at the same time as the children.

Charles Wand, out at a business meeting, then came back with a driver and cart containing two crates. Holger helped to lift them in and they were placed in the dining room. Then Charles Wand came into the quiet house, into the front room. He greeted

Marianne secretively, in a hushed voice, though with a slightly wobbling manner that suggested he'd been drinking.

"Mrs Blake, are you all alone?"

"Yes, I think Betty must have dropped off upstairs," said Marianne. "I'll just wait." In fact, she was greatly enjoying her reading and turned back to an article on Aden.

"Oh, well, while you're waiting, come and see something. Hush hush." He put his finger to his lips and beckoned her to follow. Reluctantly, she picked up the lamp and they went through to the dining room, where he closed the door. He picked up a crowbar on one of the crates and gently prised open the top. Marianne placed the lamp on the table and waited, wrapping her shawl close around her, as the air felt a little chilled, and watched him uncomfortably.

Pulling off wrapping and stuffing, Wand found what he was looking for. He carefully removed a fine porcelain plate that shone with blue images in the lamp-light. "I thought this would cheer up Felicity a little. She's always wanted the willow pattern. What do you think?"

Marianne's stomach lurched. "The what?"

"Ah, you may well ask, when it's hard to see a willow. But look, there it is." Charles Wand moved close to Marianne and held up the plate in front of the lamp, and they both looked closely, together. It was a white plate very heavily coloured with blue, with a strong lattice border all around and a picture in the centre. Wand pointed to the image of a tree with a curving trunk with long tendrils in three clumps. It was surrounded by other trees and little Chinese pagodas.

"It's a story," he said. "I don't suppose you know it, do you?" Marianne could smell whisky on his breath.

"No." She stepped away slightly. The room, this situation, felt oppressive. Was this proper?

"It's an ancient tale," said Wand. "You see, there was a wealthy Mandarin, who had a pretty daughter, who fell in love with this fellow who worked for the Mandarin, who was nothing much, and so the Mandarin threw him out and built a fence around the house to keep him away. See the fence there."

Marianne peered at the picture. There was the wooden fence at the bottom.

"The Mandarin arranged for his daughter to marry a powerful Duke, and the day the Duke arrived with a casket of jewels, blossom fell from the willow tree – so that is why the tree there is in the middle. The Duke's boat is here. But the young fellow found his way in, disguised as a servant, and took the girl off with the box of jewels. The lovers ran over the bridge, chased by the Mandarin, and got to this island."

Marianne looked closer, obediently, identifying each part of the story in accordance with Wand's indications.

"One day the Mandarin heard about their island and sent soldiers, who murdered them. The compassionate gods, however, transformed them into a pair of doves to live forever... just there. And they flew away. So it goes, a romance of forbidden love."

Charles Wand then put the fine china plate on the table. He reached into the breast pocket of his jacket, extracting a letter. "Speaking of love, this came for you today, from Captain Symonds. He sent me a companion piece, explaining the contents."

"For me?" Marianne felt as if she'd just been slapped.

"Yes." Charles Wand put the letter on the table next to the plate. Marianne did not pick it up. She saw the captain had sealed it with a red stamp.

"You've been corresponding with Captain Symonds?" asked Wand.

"No, not at all. I haven't written to him. I have no intention. But... it's not for Betty?" Marianne stopped herself. Oh, how terrible.

"Ah." Charles Wand appeared to ruminate for a moment, and then he sighed again. "I know very well that Betty has a childish infatuation. It's impossible for the poor girl to disguise. But I hope surely that you're not tolerating it, especially given that it must have been clear to you that Captain Symond's interests lie elsewhere."

"I... thought he enjoyed our company, but..."

"But that the Captain is enamoured of you... you had no idea." There was something a little sarcastic in Wand's tone. He raised an eyebrow. "The man has lived an austere existence with savages for months and comes into town to find a pretty widow arriving off a ship. Well."

"There was no... encouragement." Marianne stepped back. This conversation was highly inappropriate.

116

"But Captain Symonds is, I'm sure, one of the most eligible bachelors of New Zealand, and you would do very well in accepting his advances. Your position would be elevated no end."

"Oh no. That is not my interest." She did not like the tone in Wand's voice.

Charles Wand stared hard at Marianne. "That is not your interest." Wand suddenly stepped closer, as if she'd given him an invitation. "I have to say, that... to my mind, to be absolutely frank with you, it's just as well he is called to travel so much, and stay away. I don't feel disposed to losing my children's governess. And, I don't feel disposed to... losing... you."

Marianne's jaw dropped with shock.

Charles Wand stared at her. "This little tale on the plate is one I can relate to. I suspect that forbidden love has no happy outcome."

Marianne instinctively stepped back again, and Charles Wand caught her arm.

"I'm frightening you," he said, with feeling.

"Mr Wand, I... "

"Do you not have any... ? I would never... force you." But, despite that, suddenly Marianne found herself pulled towards Charles Wand, with his lips on hers, and unable to prise herself away until he released her.

Marianne gasped and stood still, looking with alarm at Charles Wand's crestfallen face. "Mr Wand," she said, breathlessly. "I wish to remain in your employ, for the benefit of the children, and especially for the sake of Betty, and I have no intention of responding favourably to any amorous letter from Captain Symonds, whose attentions I wish could firmly be directed to Betty. But no... no. And I would ask you, please, to refrain from... out of respect for Mrs Wand... for everyone... for me. I will take this incident as a result of your... drinking, and I will say nothing. You have my word."

"Oh." Charles Wand let her go and put his hand to his forehead, as if amazed.

Marianne heard then the creaking of the stairs. Betty was returning. She took the lamp and whisked out of the room, leaving the letter on the table and Charles Wand staring into the darkness.

*

All through the night, Marianne lay awake, feeling it was impossible to re-enter the main house to collect the letter, in case Charles Wand was still downstairs. She was afraid he would see her re-entry as a sign of interest. It had certainly been impossible to leave the room with the letter, with Betty there outside. She resolved that the moment it was dawn, before Betty was awake, when the servants came in to make the fire for breakfast, she would rush into the house and collect it. She did not think for a moment that she'd sleep, after what had happened. Entering into the world of the willow-patterned plate, walking over the bridge, falling into the water, she did not think of as sleep; it was an extension of reality to find that in the neighbouring cove of the bay there was a blue pagoda, and an island offshore. Therefore, when she jumped from this at the sound of the rooster crowing outside her window and the light streaming on to the floorboards, she was horrified. Alarmed, she got up to find Betty had already washed and dressed and gone.

She dressed as quickly as she could and dashed to the house and through the front door.

"There's a letter on the table with Captain Symond's seal, addressed to you!" said Betty, running out of the dining room as breakfast was being laid, flushed with excitement.

Marianne stood in the hall and tried to control her breathing. "A letter from Captain Symonds?" said Marianne, as if surprised.

"Why would he write to you?" said Betty, wide-eyed, worried. Betty sped back into the dining room and returned with the letter, which she proffered to Marianne. "Do open it and see what it says!"

Marianne swallowed, her head swimming, and took the letter doubtfully. She looked to Betty. Her pupil's eyes were fearful. Had she already suspected that the Captain's interests were directed towards her teacher and friend? Oh, why had she been so stupid not to guess? Was it simply that she couldn't think of either the Captain or Mr Wand in that way? Did she still think of herself as wearing black? Shouldn't she have been more alert?

"I'll get a letter knife," said Betty, and was soon in and out of the front room, handing it to Marianne, who remained stock still.

There was nothing to be done. Marianne took the knife and prised the seal, feeling as if she'd just plunged a knife into Betty. She opened out the thick piece of paper and read it quickly, feeling sick.

"What does it say?" asked Betty.

So Marianne read it aloud, without emotion:

Mrs Blake,

I write having returned to Manukau from the Church Mission station at the Waikato Heads, where I was received by the Reverend R. Maunsell on April 3rd. We have successfully obtained more signatures to the treaty, upon the chiefs' receipt of presents of the same nature as supplied at Waitangi on February 6th. Tonight the stars shine with extraordinary brightness and my mind turns to thoughts of Kororareka, and the pleasant society I enjoyed at the Wand house prior to this journey. I wish only to ask, if I may, whether it would be acceptable to you if I were to have your company on a short walk in the town. I have written separately to Mr Wand, concerning this matter, and hope I can be assured of his approval. I await your written response, which may safely be left at the offices of the Waitemata and Manukau Land Company.

My cordial and most respectful regards,
W. C. Symonds

Marianne looked at her pupil, who had gone pale. "Oh Betty, I have no intention at all of granting his request. I had no idea – "

Betty's fierce young emotions got the better of her. She burst into tears and ran up the stairs to her mother's room, almost knocking over Clarence and Charlotte, who were coming down. Marianne felt as if she had been squeezed of life and was left like a damp rag flapping on a line. How could this happen?

The remainder of the day was horrible. Betty was closeted with her mother – who had clearly replaced Marianne as confidante. Mr Wand was nowhere to be seen. Marianne took the opportunity to focus on lessons for the children, which served to take her own mind off the cyclone of emotions that had hit the household.

Then, to make things worse, Mrs Wand appeared, nicely dressed and quite cheerful, and ordered the table to be laid for dinner with the new plates. The table was soon well-presented with a white tablecloth, silverware and rows of blue plates, each with a calamitous willow in the centre. The women and children ate their meals from this fine porcelain, as a special treat, except for Betty – who had been excused and was sleeping in her mother's room, having come down with an unspecified malady – and Mr Wand, who was still absent on business. Marianne sat at the table stoically and ate like a puppet, while Eliza and Mrs Wand talked much as before, and then she went out to her room, where she vomited her entire meal into a chamber pot.

That night Marianne was exhausted, but once more she lay awake, now alone in the cottage. Fortunately, she had not seen Charles Wand since the incident, but she surely would see him the next day, and the next. What would happen then? Would he take hold of her again? Would there be something worse? Would he enter her chamber now, in the middle of the night? How could she sleep?

If only Captain Symonds hadn't written that letter – not that he was guilty of any malicious intent. He was just ignorant of the havoc he was causing.

Betty's disappointment with Captain Symonds was one thing, but what would Betty think if she knew her father were also contemplating a dalliance beyond her mother's bed? In truth, it was unlikely he'd slept with Mrs Wand since their arrival in Kororareka. It seemed to Marianne that the Wands had separate existences, with Mr Wand in a room designated the 'smoking room', where he had his papers and desk, as well as a narrow couch, and Mrs Wand in the main bedroom, which had turned into her special sanctuary, where Betty was now ensconced, perhaps never wishing to share accommodation with the teacher who had taken the heart of her beloved.

What if Betty found out about her father's desires? Betty could never know. But how could Betty never know? Betty would find out; she'd be watching Marianne closely all the time, for signs of any interest in Captain Symonds. She'd notice instead there was some intrigue with her father. Mrs Wand might know already, or even Eliza. Had that knowledge contributed to Mrs Wand's illness?

She'd been forcibly kissed by Charles Wand! It was repugnant, a disgusting violation. She felt contaminated by it.

How could he have thought this was acceptable behaviour? A governess was not a serving maid. Was it her social class? She did not speak with the vowels of the best citizens of England. Did

Charles Wand assume she would eventually give way, as women like her invariably gave way to their well-bred employers?

Yet it was true what he said. She could marry Captain Symonds, she thought, and everything would settle. Captain Symonds' star was rising, and she could be the wife of a high official in a new colony – what could be better? He was an attractive and likeable fellow. Surely she could grow to love him. He would rescue her from this mess, and the Wands would grow used to the new circumstances. Betty would marry someone else. Mr Wand would come to his senses. Captain Symonds would make a very decent husband. She had not been sure of Tim, at first, with her head full of James Placard, and then look what had happened.

Oh Tim, no, no... Captain Symonds was not Tim.

And the plates, the willow plates?

They were a sign of evil.

For the second night, Marianne did not sleep except for fitful dozes. As the thin light of dawn brought her white-washed room with its heavy furniture into view again, she got up and scrambled to pull out her carpet bag, opened the false base and counted out her money. She decided it was impossible for her to stay in a house and eat from plates bearing the willow pattern.

*

Marianne stood at the front door of Bishop Pompallier's Mission, dressed in her old black, with her valuable carpet bag and possessions within it. Was this the right thing to do? In the Bible, there was sanctuary, holding on to the horns of an altar. She'd heard it all in Bible lessons at school. Could she cling on to an altar now?

She'd left two letters in the cottage, one addressed to Betty and another to the Mr and Mrs Wand, stating with profuse apologies that she had gone to the Mission on pressing matters of religious conviction. It was a pathetic excuse, but the only one she could think of. She asked Betty to visit her there at her earliest convenience.

As the sun rose, she'd made her escape around the back of the cottage, away from Holger's shed beside the stables, and had skirted the town towards the Catholic Mission, which was some way out of the centre at the foot of a hill. A French flag flew within the grounds, beside a long driveway that led towards the house.

The garden of the Mission was a haven, very well-tended, with a proper lawn and all kinds of European flowers, particularly roses, and fruit trees: apple, plum, pears, with oranges and lemons, figs and grapes. Everything seemed to be bursting with ripe invitation in this southern autumn that hardly showed, given all the evergreen trees.

The front door was opened by a New Zealand housekeeper, a big woman with grey curly hair, and Marianne asked in French if Bishop Pompallier was available, or Father Petit.

"Yes, of course," said the housekeeper, likewise in French. "Bishop Pompallier is in the church for his morning prayers, but you can wait." She took Marianne through the central hall of the house to a garden at the back, where there was a wooden garden seat under climbing roses. Marianne was astounded. She could be back in Wivenhoe, or some other corner of Europe. She sat down, not sure though if she could keep herself calm and unemotional under the circumstances. She did not want to appear weak.

She waited about twenty minutes, steadying herself and rehearsing what she should say, before Bishop Pompallier came through the back doorway and greeted her gently. He was dressed simply in black. His dark eyes were kind.

"*Madame* Blake, you come to visit so soon." He immediately spotted her bag. "Is there a problem?"

Marianne jumped to her feet as the bishop came towards her, but then felt slightly light-headed and immediately sat down, like a bag of potatoes being dumped on the floor.

"Are you quite well?" asked the bishop, with concern. His voice was soft, mellow and yet strong.

Marianne felt dizzy. Perhaps it was lack of food and sleep. She commanded herself to say something to Bishop Pompallier, but found herself unable to do so. Sounds became slightly fuzzy and distant, but she was aware of the housekeeper returning, and a drink of lemonade being offered, which she drank gratefully. She felt constricted and took short, sharp intakes of air. Eventually, the housekeeper went inside and closed the garden door.

"When you're ready," said the bishop, quietly, "please tell me why you've come." He sat down close to her, on a bench beside a high flowerbed, and leaned with concerned attentiveness towards her. "You have my utmost discretion."

"I was baptised a Catholic," said Marianne, eventually.

"I thought perhaps this was the case, since you have a French mother," said the bishop. "You've not practised your religion?"

Marianne concentrated on breathing for a moment and tried to think. She should try to be honest. She said, "I don't practise any religion, anymore, or believe anything. I go to church with the Wands, because everyone goes to church. But I don't understand how a good God can make the world so very hard. Everywhere the good and the innocent die, and the cruel triumph. God doesn't answer prayers. Every time I hope, I'm crushed."

"Ah." Bishop Pompallier seemed thoughtful and pressed his fingers together. "You're confused by Protestant notions of providence and prosperity, which are to us of course a heresy. I will not explore this with you now, but will only say that you've forgotten about the Fall. We do not live in the Garden of Eden, though we may try to make our small corner resemble it. Paradise is our hope for the future."

Marianne looked quizzically at the bishop. He had the same twinkle in his eye she'd seen before. The Fall. Adam and Eve sinned by disobeying God in the Garden of Eden, and so humanity could never again live in the perfect world; from then on life would be hard. Even with Christ's atoning sacrifice, salvation would be for the future; being a Christian gave you hope, not a guarantee or a good luck charm. She knew this, theoretically. She knew also what the bishop meant about 'Protestant notions of providence and prosperity': that God would, even so, reward the hard-working, decent people of faith, here and now.

The bishop continued, "I believe God suffers with us, weeps with us, as we see in Christ, and also in the sorrow of Our Lady. God answers prayers. But you must learn to pray correctly, for the right things. And I do not believe you can do this outside the embrace of the true Church."

Marianne suddenly thought of her mother. On her deathbed, she'd asked Uncle to try to find a priest, but he couldn't procure one. Even though Britain had allied itself with the Holy See against Napoleon and there had been Catholic emancipation, tolerance of

Catholics was minimal. There was no priest in Colchester, as there hadn't been when she was baptised. She'd been taken to London. Her mother had died without absolution, and confessed her sins to Uncle instead, such as they were.

"May I stay here?" asked Marianne, bluntly. She couldn't bear to explain her circumstances. "Do you need help with the school? I've been teaching children in all subjects."

"You want to run away from the Wand household?"

Marianne looked down at her trembling hands. She must appear such a sight. What was she doing? Mr Wand would be furious to lose his governess to the Catholic Mission. Everyone would talk about this, and gossip him into the ale house. What about his reputation? And what about Betty? She was abandoning her and the other children.

No. How could she be in the same house as a man that had forcibly kissed her, who might do this again, or more? She would rather risk everything and leave, for her own security, than cling to loyalty and stay. Again the thought of the willow plates came to her mind, and she felt sick.

There was a long pause and then the bishop asked, "Do you want refuge? You don't need to explain why, but if you seek it then it's yours."

"I have some money to give... and I can work."

"Ah well, you may need your money, but we all work here and we need a female teacher for the girls. The girls are very important, because they will be mothers, and a mother is vital for the spiritual growth of a child. But you cannot teach unless you're again within the Church, and I ask you first to rest. You look very tired."

Tears ran down Marianne's cheeks. "Thank you," she said.

The bishop let her cry without interrupting, but she felt his presence alongside her.

"Marianne, I see there are many things that trouble you," he said then, with concern. "I will be pleased to discuss these matters at any time, for this is my role. I'm here for the sake of the inhabitants of the islands of the South Pacific, but also for anyone who seeks. Don't be afraid to think. A loss of faith may be because the faith was misunderstood. Now, you've come to me for help, and as long as you need my help I am here."

*

Unfortunately, Charles Wand had no intention of losing his governess and arrived alone later that afternoon. Having spent hours sitting in the small, carefully dusted church, not so much at prayer but in a state of exhaustion, Marianne was called by the housekeeper, whose Christian name was Susanne – though it was pronounced 'Tutanna' – to come to Bishop Pompallier's library, a large room at the front of the house where he met visitors. Outside the door, Marianne paused and listened, and heard Mr Wand's voice.

"It was a quarrel between my daughter and Mrs Blake, nothing more. You know what women are like. It's ridiculous for you to be enmeshed in the affairs of girlish romances, especially at such a time. It would hardly do your reputation any good to be laughed at over such a thing, *Monsieur* Pompallier. My daughter is beside herself with remorse for driving away her governess. I ask you then to return her. Once this is done, you have my word I will say nothing of your unfortunate involvement in this trivial matter."

He was speaking English. Did the bishop understand? Would he believe him? Marianne waited to hear his reply. She felt an ache of guilt about Betty.

After a long pause, Marianne heard the words of Bishop Pompallier, heavily accented, in response. "I give her refuge, because she asks, *Monsieur* Wand. You know, perhaps, that Madame Blake is baptised a Catholic?"

Mr Wand made some noise of surprise. "Ah... her mother was French. Though I understand she has taught in a Congregationalist school. She is very much an Englishwoman."

"Is she?"

At this, Marianne opened the door slowly and came in, glad that she was wearing the black that Charles Wand had explicitly asked her to remove. In black she matched the bishop, and the other Marist priests. She was an ink blot on his blue and white world.

Bishop Pompallier and Charles Wand both stood up and let her sit down on a red leather chair before they reseated themselves, but neither of them said anything. She felt as if she'd entered a court of law. The beautiful room full of cases of leather-bound tomes smelt of furniture polish. Her heart thumped powerfully.

125

Wand barely looked at her. Bishop Pompallier, using all the force of his natural bearing, stared at Marianne with something of a knowing manner. He said to her, in English, "*Monsieur* Wand comes here and asks that you will return to his house. Will you do this?"

Marianne had a sudden, overwhelming sense of revulsion. "Mr Wand," she said, in a rather small voice. "I'm very sorry but, as my letter explained, I must ask to be dismissed. I do not wish for any payment for days worked since my last remuneration. I can assure you that I will make it known to everyone that this is purely a spiritual decision."

Oh God, could he see she was lying?

"A spiritual decision? What? Are you going to become a nun?" said Charles Wand, who seemed to be containing, through a manner of derision, an urge to jump up and shout.

"What I choose to do as regards spiritual matters is my business, Mr Wand," said Marianne. "But I trust that Betty received the letter I left for her, and very much look forward to seeing her here at the Mission as soon as possible. I would also appreciate it if you would tell Betty that my decision to leave the Wand household has nothing whatsoever to do with her. Please send her my fondest love and my deepest apologies for the suddenness of my departure."

Mr Wand coughed. "Well indeed... Mrs Blake," he said, "I think you could have given us all fair warning. The children are most distressed, as is Mrs Wand."

Marianne noted his ability to look like the injured party in front of the bishop, and cast aspersions on her reliability, compassion and dutifulness. But what could she say? The truth? 'You forced me to kiss you!' Better to lie and be believed, than tell the truth and be branded as a liar. "I'm so sorry," she said.

Bishop Pompallier indicated by a nod that Marianne could now leave, and she walked out trying to hold her head up, saying "Good day, Mr Wand," formally. She went to the door, put her hand on the handle, and then Wand said, coldly, "And don't think that Betty, or any of the children, will visit you here, Mrs Blake. This is something I could not possibly permit."

She turned and stared at him for a moment. Did he want her to beg, or agree to visit the house regularly? Was he trying to force her to return, knowing that never seeing Betty, or the children, again would be too hard for her? She said nothing, opened up the door, went through and closed it behind her, paced quickly down the hallway and around the corner. There she stayed, with her back to the wall, listening.

She heard Mr Wand speaking quite angrily, but while the door was closed, she couldn't distinguish the words. Finally though, after some minutes, the door creaked open and the two men went out to the front door.

Then Mr Wand's voice: "Well, Mr Pompallier, you can trust that you've made a firm enemy of Captain Symonds. This will also sit very badly with others, at a sensitive time of negotiations with the natives when your... behaviour... has been noted as exceedingly unhelpful."

There was then the sound of the front door opening and slamming shut.

Bishop Pompallier walked down the hallway and found Marianne listening around the corner. He seemed troubled now. Mr Wand's words had stung.

"I'm so sorry, Monsignor," she said in French, plaintively. "Forgive me. I've caused you these new difficulties, and... "

"There is a much bigger business here, with very great consequences," said Bishop Pompallier, trying to smile a little. "We must be careful."

11
Banks Peninsula

All through March and April, 1840, the *Comte de Paris* sailed south-wards, stopping only at the island of Palma in the Canary Islands. Passengers and crew went on shore to buy fruit and vegetables, and swarmed around the markets of this exotic place in hot amazement. Then the ship continued its course far away from the coast of Africa, though not so far west as to reach St. Helena. Through May and June they went on, rounding the Cape of Good Hope, through the Indian Ocean and south of Australia, without any storm or great incident. One baby was born, to the Libeaus, and one child died, from the Gendrot family. Celebrations and grievings took their course and the settlers stood together more resilient and determined to find their promised land in New Zealand.

This was, however, a very different experience to being on board a whaler. François found himself in a group of trusted friends, with Malmanche, Libeau, Éteveneaux around him. For the first time in his life, he felt no longer alone. He shared his thoughts, but he did not share his dreams. He did not tell them of Napoleon's willow.

However, when July came – near Van Dieman's Land – a great storm clenched the *Comte de Paris* in a mighty fist of winds, thunder, lightning, rain and crashing waves. The argument between Belligny and Captain Langlois, which provided a running ship-board drama of two foes locked in mortal combat, led to disaster. Belligny had warned Captain Langlois a dozen times about the dangers of not having an earthed lightning conductor on the main mast. Since the warning came from Belligny, Langlois ignored it. The first flash of electricity shot down from the depths of a black cloud to the alien poles sticking out of the violent sea. The ship was struck by lightning twice within three hours, setting fire to the sails, bolting through everything on board and turning the ship almost on its side. The foremast was cracked in two. Emeri Malmanche's desperate wife, seven months pregnant, almost lost her baby. The settlers vomited, prayed and moaned as the sailors fought the elements. Two young men, already sick with scurvy, died. François helped the sailors as a seaman, and was left with hands raw from pulling ropes, wet through, pummelled by rain, cold as a fish for hours on end.

Afterwards there was grave fear. They spent weeks progressing like a limping man, relying on Captain Langlois' expertise to sail the damaged ship through chilly, rougher waters. Belligny fell silent and there were no arguments. François worked every hour he could mending broken fittings, re-fixing, melting, smelting, forging iron. All the colonists laboured with the sailors on repairs. Women helped sew the sails. François healed their sores with herbs.

Then, dry land was sighted. Women wept, men laughed and Libeau sang a song. On Sunday, August 9, they finally managed to reach Banks Peninsula, as Captain Langlois deftly manoeuvred the ship by means of a jury sail. The blasting winds made this difficult and the Captain managed only to aim the ship to anchor in Pigeon Bay, a deep bay on the outer north side of the Banks Peninsula, since it was impossible to sail south and then turn at a right angle north into the narrow mouth of Akaroa Harbour.

The colonists gathered on deck and stared out gratefully at the vivid green hills that embraced them on three sides, and the grey waves flashing with white as they broke on the pale sand. They had arrived in New Zealand. "New France," said Libeau, quietly. "New Marianne."

A whaleboat was sent off from the ship with rowers to look for the naval ship, the *Aube*. Langlois announced to everyone that the official naval frigate, which had departed just before them from Rochefort under the command of Commandant Lavaud, was one of the best ships of the French navy with a capacity to make astonishing progress across the seas. The *Aube* surely had to be at their destination in Paka Ariki Bay already, and would make everything ready for their arrival. The French Navy would send a navigator to help them into Akaroa Harbour. They were almost there. Everyone, even Belligny, applauded him loudly. His negligence over the lightning conductor was forgotten; his expertise in sailing a damaged ship to a safe anchorage was not. Langlois was their saviour.

After the boat departed, there was nothing else to do but wait. The sailors, with François among them, went ashore on boats to the green, forested hills, watched by the colonists who had decided not to leave the ship until disembarking at their new home. It was freezing and threatened rain.

The purpose of the sailors was to fill up tanks of water from the fast-flowing stream that ran out of the forested valley, and to bury the two young men who had died. François walked up and down on the sand as the sailors dug the graves. How he wanted to get back to his little *whare* to see his willow planting! Everything, for him, depended upon it. He wished he could set off over the great bush-encrusted hills on foot, but he had no clear sense of direction. There were no New Zealanders here to ask about Matthieu Le Bon. There was nothing to hear, just the rustle and songs of birds in the forest, the calling seagulls, the crashing of the waves, the noise of digging and familiar voices.

It was beyond all frustration! If only they all knew how badly they needed to see the sign of Napoleon's willow. If it was withered and dead, this would be an evil omen above all others. It struck François too that the first thing the sailors of the *Comte de Paris* were planting in the ground of New Zealand were corpses.

Back on board after the burial ceremony, presided over by Captain Langlois, François went back to his fixing, screwing in an iron block on the starboard side, and overheard a conversation just outside the midships door. The aristocratic scholar Belligny and Normandy sea-captain Langlois were returning to one of their arguments, now they had arrived, which were more like sword-fought duels, each antithetical man prodding the other with words. Belligny said he knew from Duke Decazes that Captain Langlois had express instructions to confirm the 1838 deed, to ensure that the land deal was absolutely secure. This must be the first priority.

"Trust me, Belligny. I have it all in hand," said Langlois.

Belligny walked away muttering as he passed François that this man was a complete imbecile in matters of diplomacy and would run everything into the ground.

Confirm the deed? François watched the two men as he worked during the course of the day: Belligny's unsure glances to the Captain, and the Captain's indefatigable steeliness. Something was going on. Eventually François couldn't contain himself, and stood up as Captain Langlois passed him, stating, "Captain, excuse me, but I must tell you that it is absolutely essential that a certain New Zealander be found by the name of Manako-uri, called Matthieu Le Bon. He speaks good French and can act as an interpreter in any discussions."

Langlois looked slightly curious and made a face. "Ah, Matthieu Le Bon, I've heard of him. He earned his name because he was so sure and reliable with a harpoon."

François was taken aback. That was the reason for his name, 'the Good'?

"Yes," continued Captain Langlois, recalling. "Why should I find him? I heard he was a murderer. He killed an Englishman... knocked him dead and burnt his body. For this reason, he keeps clear of the English and only spends time on French ships."

François stammered, "I... I don't know... but Matthieu is the man you need."

But Captain Langlois bristled. "Need for what?"

"To talk to the New Zealanders."

The Captain walked away gruffly and then turned back to François, annoyed, and shouted: "I... myself... talk to the New Zealanders."

François then said nothing further to the Captain. Matthieu a murderer? He would not believe that. Whalers' stories were seldom the whole truth.

Anxiously, everyone waited. The next day, Belligny decided to set foot in New Zealand and spent time on shore collecting botanical samples and distracting himself with science. How naive he seemed, to François, discovering 'new' species and pressing them carefully between large sheets of white paper. He too needed to talk to Matthieu Le Bon, who could tell him everything about these plants.

White paper: both Belligny and Langlois believed they would capture this place by it.

Then something very disappointing happened. The boat sent off to contact the *Aube* arrived back from Akaroa Harbour late on Monday, August 10, with news: they'd met with Captain Billiard of the French ship the *Pauline*, but the *Aube* had not yet arrived.

Captain Langlois, impatient, then immediately went by boat to Port Cooper to confer with his old associates and sort matters out as he saw fit. The rowers took him off to the west and the *Comte de Paris* waited inside Pigeon Bay. Belligny continued his research. Sailors swam and fished. All on board ate well and drank fresh water as if it were an elixir of life.

*

Less than twenty-four hours later, on the afternoon of Tuesday, August 11, Captain Langlois returned, accompanied by a magnificent flotilla of New Zealanders. The colonists, on seeing this, feared a war party and locked themselves in their cabins in sheer fright. François waited on deck with the sailors, scanning the long, carved canoes for the face of Matthieu Le Bon, or anyone he recognised. Belligny gripped the rail close to him, white-knuckled, staring at the New Zealanders rigidly. The canoes rounded the ship several times as Captain Langlois came on board and announced he would assemble on the *Comte de Paris* all the chiefs in the region, in order to verify the agreement he'd made in 1838. "Does this meet with your approval, Monsieur Belligny?" he asked, and walked off.

"My God, that man is a full of confidence tricks," said Belligny, to François. "This is a performance, designed to intimidate me. To think anyone has trusted him."

François, Belligny and the sailors then became the audience to what may well have been a strange piece of theatre. More canoes arrived, each one full of tattooed New Zealanders carrying muskets. Langlois proclaimed that there were in all twenty-eight chiefs and notables with authority over the land, and another one hundred and sixty other people whose permission was essential. The settlers remained below, keeping themselves apart out of sheer terror.

Despite François feeling more affinity with Captain Langlois than the arrogant Belligny, François couldn't help feeling disappointed with him. Langlois made no attempt to find Matthieu Le Bon. Instead he chose a man named Tomi, who said he could translate to English. Langlois prided himself on his English. Belligny, who also spoke English, was not permitted to engage in the negotiations. Langlois insisted it was only he that could speak for France.

All through the night the flotilla was there, with encampments on land and meetings on the ship. The colonists did not sleep at all in their cabins, deeply afraid, asking one another questions. Where was the *Aube*? Why this assembly of fearsome savages on the ship? Was the original deed not sound? Had Belligny made problems that good Captain Langlois now had to sort out? François went down and gave them updates, but nothing calmed their fears.

François had other questions. He asked many of the New Zealanders, in what he knew of their tongue, if they knew the whereabouts of Manako-uri, and was only told he had gone far away on a ship, and no one knew where he was.

Langlois gave the assembly of New Zealanders gifts of blankets, flour, tobacco and wine, and sat with them drinking, talking to them in English through the interpreter, and they affirmed their signs on the contract. Additionally another contract was determined, with further signatures. They drew again the same designs on new, loose, completely blank pieces of paper, relying on Captain Langlois to write up the agreement, much to the surprise of Belligny when it was shown to him after the departure of the deputation later that day. The paper was presented to Belligny by Captain Langlois in front of some of the ship's officers, and also François – now assembled in the Captain's cabin.

"It's confirmed. The chiefs have sold all of Banks Peninsula and more. This is France!" said Captain Langlois.

"There is nothing written on this paper, Captain Langlois," said Belligny, observing the large space of blankness it as if he was looking for errors in spelling.

"This is their way," insisted Langlois to Belligny. "It's the oral agreements that matter to them. The written documents are just for our records."

"If you say so, Captain Langlois, I'm sure that is true," said Belligny doubtfully. "Though to speak in English about these complicated matters is surely unreliable. Are you sure that your words were translated accurately in the ears of the chiefs? They have absolutely agreed to the sale of the peninsula?"

"Absolutely." Langlois stared Belligny hard in the eye.

"They have agreed that this land is now subject to French law? They have ceded sovereignty?"

"It has all been agreed, Monsieur Belligny, as Duke Decazes wished."

Belligny looked at Langlois with mistrust. "But was it also necessary to give these natives so much of the cargo of the Company to make this validation?" he queried.

"What could I do? Our position must be secure. Look at all these settlers waiting to go ashore! They are my responsibility, and I will make sure that they are safe."

"Are you sure it's secure?"

François looked to the other men, who glanced to one another and back at him worriedly. Yet another argument between the Captain and the aristocrat! The officers were on the side of the Captain. François wanted to be, but his doubt was a lead weight inside him.

"Listen, *Monsieur* Belligny," said the Captain, "you leave me the job of ensuring France is soundly placed in ownership of the land, and the natives placed under French law, and you look after the business of the Company and the settlers when we take up our place here."

Belligny bristled at the rude way Langlois always addressed him, especially given the audience, but bowed punctiliously, so as not to escalate the captain's fury. This was clearly done because these were the rules on board ship. Captain Langlois, here, was in charge, though François sensed that it would be different on land.

Then, suddenly, in the midst of this conversation, there was a shout from one of the sailors and a knock on the door. A boat was spotted, a European boat, with men rowing towards them from the harbour mouth. Those who were in the Captain's cabin rushed up on deck and saw a new boat coming towards them. As it came alongside the *Comte de Paris*, they greeted some French whaling captains from Port Cooper, and an American captain. They were brought on board with great celebration, as all the colonists now emerged from their cabins, and drinks were poured, with the tone completely turning to festivity. Even without the *Aube* there was much to celebrate. Captain Langlois was the hero of the hour. Everyone ate pork and potatoes bought from the New Zealanders. On Friday, August 14, the captains too signed their names to the blank paper, as witnesses to the agreement between France and the chiefs of Banks Peninsula. The ship became the centre of partying and congratulations. Preparations were made to hoist the French tricolour flag at Pigeon Bay, and for one hundred and one canon shots to salute it. This would be a ceremony of momentous significance.

But then, as preparations were in progress, the *Pauline* passed by Pigeon Bay on its way back to Port Cooper from Akaroa Harbour and shot cannon, indicating there was a message. A whaleboat was quickly dispatched to make contact with a boat sent from the ship. Meeting, and returning with news, the sailors tried to shout from the distance even before they reached the *Comte de Paris*. "The *Aube* is here!"

Climbing on deck they spoke rapidly and excitedly to Captain Langlois. The captain of the *Pauline* had boarded the *Aube* at the heads of Akaroa Harbour on Wednesday, August 12 – three days earlier when the flotilla was in Pigeon Bay – but the *Aube* had gone back out to sea because of the winds. Not only that, but there was something mysterious: a British sloop, the *HMS Britomart*, had arrived at Paka Ariki Bay.

A British ship? After hearing this news, Langlois ordered that the *Comte de Paris* be made ready for departure right away, which took place the next day. He decided that the French tricolour would not be hoisted on the land of Banks Peninsula at Pigeon Bay, because it would be hoisted at the place where the colonists disembarked to found the colony. There was no formal declaration of French sovereignty, on the basis of the new agreement made with the local chiefs, because a better declaration would be made in the presence of the French Navy, with all that it represented, regardless of the presence of the British ship, clearly sent to observe them.

The *Comte de Paris* sailed to the entrance of Akaroa Harbour on Sunday, and a whaleboat was sent to search for the *Aube* further in. Returning, the sailors reported that the corvette was indeed sighted and hailed, and was anchored next to the British ship. In the evening, despite its damage, Captain Langlois managed to turn the *Comte de Paris* into Akaroa Harbour through the dangerous, rocky heads, and anchored ship safely.

On Monday, August 17, the colonists stared out as they sailed down the long harbour and the hills closed all around them, shutting off sight of the Pacific Ocean and the great seas they had crossed.

François, not prone to gaiety, burst into a shining smile as he saw the white-flippered penguins on shore and great swathes of nikau palms. It felt as if he'd come home. He pushed his worries aside. He felt a sudden hope.

*

They were almost there, at Paka Ariki Bay, which cut a deep dent into the curving harbour on the starboard, to the right, so François quickly ran below decks to sort out a few tools to take ashore. He wanted to be the first off the ship, ready for the boat.

Then, suddenly, he was stunned. Shaking the ship and making a great noise, two of their cannon shots went off, one after another. Was Langlois sending a signal? François went up on deck again, where Langlois was peering through a telescope in the direction of what looked like a dinghy, which was coming directly towards them, though he couldn't see the ship from which this boat had come. The settlers were looking outraged. Belligny appeared distraut.

"The British are coming to meet us!" said Captain Langlois scornfully.

A dinghy carrying an English naval officer and two well-attired Englishmen speedily approached and arrived at the starboard side. Without great courtesy, they demanded – in French – to come on board. Langlois obliged, truculently. He faced the delegation with sharpness, speaking a terse welcome in English – actually only the word 'gentlemen' – and seemed reluctant to take them below. Prompted by Belligny, who urged the utmost politeness, he acquiesced, and thumped down ahead of them. François was called to follow, along with officers again to act as witnesses. It seemed that the more French men in the small room, the more the British would feel uncomfortable, which is what the Captain intended.

There were quick introductions made in English. The naval officer spoke, and apparently identified himself as coming from the *Britomart*. The two others were introduced as 'magistrates': Michael Murphy and Charles Barrington Robinson. Langlois boomed out some more sentences in English, which made Belligny visibly squirm, until Robinson explained in fluent French that perhaps it was best they spoke in the language of France on board a French ship. This might have been a diplomatic gesture, but Robinson's tone was superior. He was a dark-haired man with a sharp nose and a wily, fox-like manner that made Langlois look even more like a barking dog.

"We almost thought... you were firing at us," said Robinson, in French, a little affronted. "But I assume that the cannon shots were to signal that you required us on board, sir? What are you going to use such fine cannons for?"

"For a French fort, eventually, of course, *monsieur*. And I would like to know your business in the territory belonging to France," said Captain Langlois, folding his arms.

Robinson let out a victorious chuckle. "France, Captain. I have to tell you that New Zealand in its entirety belongs to Queen Victoria, on the basis of the British declaration of May 21, made while you were at sea. We do understand you have a land claim, which I can assure you will be very reasonably considered. I'm pleased to inform you that our Governor George Gipps of New South Wales did not go forward with a bill that would have made all land deals hitherto conducted in New Zealand null and void."

Langlois looked up and down at this Englishman and stated bluntly, "If any foreign power has the right to proclaim sovereignty over the Middle Island of New Zealand, it is France! I made an agreement with the natives and they have sold me... and to the Nanto-Bordelaise Company... the entirety of Banks Peninsula, in August, 1838. The French Government is protecting this expedition, and our warship the *Aube*, under Commandant Lavaud, is under orders from the King to aid the establishment of this colony, and will surely put here at this place a battery to defend it. I have sixty settlers waiting to go ashore and take possession of the land. You can go back and tell Queen Victoria." The last sentence was said in English.

Belligny inhaled sharply.

Somewhat taken aback by the loudness of the Captain's voice and his fury, if not a declaration of war, Robinson drew himself up and said, "Captain Langlois, I do not know which chiefs signed your paper. In June of this year, the significant chiefs of Banks Peninsula, Iwikau and Tikao... called John Love... ratified a British treaty originally signed on February the 6th in the Bay of Islands by the northern chiefs. They are thus content to authorise the sovereignty of the British Crown. As for the declaration of British sovereignty, the Middle Island is proclaimed British by right of discovery."

"Discovery!" exploded Captain Langlois. "This is an independent country belonging to the New Zealand natives, who have the right to sell property. It's they who discovered it. Ask any one of them. Only they have the right to cede it, as your treaty supposes. Does British arrogance have no limits at all?"

"Yes, discovery?" interjected Belligny, heightening his long neck and peering down at Robinson, united with Langlois now in common incredulity. "You impose the right of sovereignty on the basis of discovery, which, I think, may I say, is at least contestable. Even if it's European discovery you mean, this would place you in some discussion with the Dutch. Didn't their Abel Tasman reach this island in 1642, exactly... one hundred and twenty-seven years ahead of Captain Cook?"

Robinson, though clearly grateful to Belligny for his restraint, was unprepared for a debate about history. He tried to raise himself higher. "I don't believe so, *Monsieur*."

"Yes, Abel Tasman drew a chart depicting the north-western part of the Middle Island. It's quite well known." Belligny smiled winningly.

"Not to me. I think you'll find that our Captain Cook discovered this island. I'm sure Governor Hobson researched this point thoroughly before the declaration was made."

"Governor Hobson!" exploded Langlois.

"As I mentioned, the Middle, or South, Island, has been declared British since May 21. You may contest discovery, *messieurs*, but our declaration was followed by another at Cloudy Bay on June 21, through the offices of Captain Nias of the *HMS Herald*, who fired twenty-one guns, since sovereignty was ceded by the chiefs there in accordance with the treaty." Robinson produced a scroll that he unfurled on the table. Langlois and Belligny bent down together and looked at the date as if it were impossible.

"Such declarations mean nothing," said Langlois, stepping away to gaze, unseeing and furious, at a naval chart on the wall.

The officer from the *Britomart* at this point interjected in whispers to his companions, apparently advising Robinson what to say. Robinson duly announced, smugly: "Commandant Lavaud made no contrary statements to our claim when he met Governor Hobson at the Bay of Islands very recently. We will now depart and discuss the matter with Captain Stanley of the *Britomart. Messieurs,* goodbye."

With that the British party turned and exited, leaving Langlois and Belligny momentarily united in outrage.

One of the sailors was brusquely instructed by Langlois to accompany the British off the ship; Langlois would not provide that courtesy himself.

*

François left this room with the witnesses, Belligny and Langlois, and went up to where the settlers were assembled like a flock of worried sheep, bleating to each other.

"There is absolutely nothing to worry about," announced Captain Langlois.

While the meeting below had taken place, the ship had now rounded the point. On their left, in all its glory, was the resplendent French man-of-war, the *Aube,* carrying precious cargo, French priests, and also Langlois' brother, Aimable, who was to be in charge of the Nanto-Bordelaise Company store. On the right was anchored the smaller British naval ship, the *Britomart.* The French and British flags flew proudly on each ship, but only one was planted on land, at a promontory, and it was not the French Tricolour.

Everyone stared at the Union Jack as if they were looking at a monstrous boil.

"It's nothing," affirmed Langlois to the baffled colonists. "There are some British who have come here for whaling. These visitors came only to greet us. Their flag is for some ceremony of the whalers. The native chiefs have sold this land to us and confirmed it only a few days ago. They would have told me if there was any problem."

Belligny turned to François and others who had been below, and put his finger to his lips. They would let the Captain get away with the lie, for the time being, so as not to promote hysteria among a group of people who had risked everything, over so many months at sea, and who were exhausted.

The *Comte de Paris* now sailed close enough to the *Aube* to see the sailors and some priests waving on deck. They waved back.

Some of the women cried. Dropping anchor at Paka Ariki Bay, past the point where the Union Jack was flying, a signal of cannon fire was sent to the *Aube*. It was half-past-three in the afternoon.

The colonists remained fretful and even questioned Belligny what this visit from the British meant, but Belligny reassured them. "Everything will be fine," he said. "There are some small problems to be overcome with the British, but it's not serious. A misunderstanding... about the past."

Captain Langlois heard, and nodded to Belligny, indicating a rapprochement in the face of a mutual enemy.

*

François had to wait for an entire day, watching toing and froing from ship to ship as frantic diplomacy took place. He was not permitted to be one of the first to disembark; that was the privilege of the French navy. Sailors from the *Aube* went on shore and erected two sail-cloth tents so that the colonists could sleep comfortably under canvas on land. Two young Marist priests from the *Aube* boarded the *Comte de Paris* and spent all day with the colonists on necessary religious matters.

It was Wednesday, August 19, when the French colonists finally went down into a whaleboat, carefully carrying children. Sailors rowed them to the shore singing French songs. Libeau jumped out first, laughing and singing, even before they drew up on shore and splashed into the beach.

"We are home!" cried Éteveneaux, his arms up in the air.

But mostly the colonists were too much amazed by their new surroundings to exclaim. All around great forests rose up to high rocky peaks. The harbour here was like a lake, with high forested hills all around, sheltering the water. New Zealanders in canoes paddled close by, and were there waiting on shore with food for them to barter. Bare-footed women dressed in shabby European clothing offered them pigs, potatoes and cabbages to trade for blankets, needles, fabric and tobacco. The settlers looked worriedly at the New Zealanders, yet traded a few buttons and trinkets for what they offered. There were things to be done, fires to be lit, shelter in the tents to be defined and organised.

Among the Onuku people with foodstuffs were those François recognised and greeted, though they seemed slightly reserved and showed no special enthusiasm about seeing him again. He asked them keenly about Manako-uri, Matthieu Le Bon, but they were diffident and told him only that he'd gone away. Everyone seemed to tell the same story.

This was disappointing, but for now François had only one particular purpose. Receiving permission from the second officer, he left the busy shore party. Quickly, he found the stream. His excitement and anticipation were overwhelming as he walked the distance inland through the trees to find the *whare* he'd constructed two and a half years earlier with Matthieu Le Bon.

This would be the sign, to see whether the French would prosper in the new land. Did Napoleon's willow grow? His heart beat like a drum, pounding out as he made his way.

Had any of the people of Onuku cut it down? Had it died?

Everything on the thin track seemed to be the same. The stream tumbled, fresh and cold, just as it had done before. The birds called. It was as if everything that had happened in the intervening time was a dream, and this place was eternal. As he neared his *whare*, he could hardly walk. He started to feel afraid. What if this entire enterprise was doomed? What if his hope was vapour? How would he tell his friends, the settlers? What would he do?

At the place where the hill rose up on the left, he went up, away from the stream and trod the path up towards the *whare*. A dancing bird dipped around him, as it had done when he had first come here all those years ago, when he was so afraid that he would be killed. Nothing had changed, except for the feeling inside him. Or perhaps not even that. Then he was scared. Now he was scared.

And there, all at once, he saw it. There it was. The tree. Napoleon's willow.

It lived.

François let out a noise of sheer amazement.

The willow he'd planted was indeed still growing. Its tiny sprouting leaves were bright and fresh, bursting into life at the end of the winter, different in colour to the evergreen leaves all around. It was the colour of European spring: bright lime green and luminous.

The tree looked as if it were shining.

There was still a pole beside it painted with red-ochre, placed by Matthieu Le Bon to mark the tree as *tapu*. Beyond it his *whare* still stood, though some of the wood of the roof had sprouted, growing leaves like a wig.

He was home.

"My God! You are alive!" he said to the willow, touching it. How fast it had shot up, faster than he would have believed possible. It was thriving, over three metres in height and already with bark! How incredible! It was not just growing, it was a giant. The willow had three main boughs hanging down, like three strings of a necklace covered with emeralds. Nowhere in France would it grow so quickly, so vigorously, and be so mature in such a short time.

François grinned and nodded, and then he kissed its leaves like he was kissing a baby.

That was the sign. It was still growing. Napoleon's spirit was here.

France had chosen to plant a settlement just where he'd planted his tree, exactly where the willow grew. Could that be mere coincidence? Surely not.

How could he explain to anyone what this meant? He thought he would cry, or then that he would laugh. He bent over and lent his hands against knees, and breathed in and out, overcome with emotion. He looked to the earth, the rich brown earth that had nurtured this tree, and then reached down and dug his fingers into the ground. He closed them around a clod and picked it up in his hand, and then he smeared it over his cheeks. This was his earth. This was France. This was more the earth of France than France itself had become! If only his mother could see this!

And then he straightened and stepped back again and, all on his own, in the middle of the New Zealand bush, he sung the banned song of the Republic, *Veillons au Salut de l'Empire*, with its rousing chorus:

Liberty, liberty, that all mortals would honour you!
Tyrants, tremble - you are going to pay for your crimes.
'Rather death than slavery' -
This is the motto of the French!

François dropped to his knees and lay down prostrate. Of all the people that had arrived at Paka Ariki Bay that August, François Le-lièvre was the happiest. Whatever became of negotiations with the British, Napoleon's soul was planted in this earth.

12
The *Aube*

The months from April to August of 1840 were for Marianne the beginning of a new life, yet again. She threw herself into challenges of work, learning and thinking. Despite her experience and expertise, Marianne was not allowed to teach girls at the Mission until she completed a programme set by Bishop Pompallier that would lead her – he hoped – back to the Church she'd never known. He gave her books to read, and pamphlets, and talked to her at times about matters of theology that bothered her. She read everything, while working with Tutanna in household duties; there were no servants in the Mission and everyone did their bit.

In a tiny room upstairs, Marianne wrote many letters to Betty Wand, apologising and explaining her need to pursue a different course in life. She indicated she very much hoped that her departure would, nevertheless, loosen Captain Symonds' interests in her, so that they might be directed to Betty. Finally, she did receive a letter, in French, received secretively via a very embarrassed Father Petit, who had encountered Betty in an assembly on the quay. Betty stated that her father did not allow her to see or write to Marianne, and, if Marianne had written to her, she should know that no letters had been received. Betty was full of remorse for reacting with mortification at the letter, and understood that the contents had been a surprise to both of them. Captain Symonds had visited and been very attentive to her recently, and she was prepared to be patient. The Wand family were now departing, however, to the new capital at Okiato, or Russell, where all the government and military personnel had been established, because the people of Kororareka were, according to her mother, "very coarse and hardly British at all".

Marianne also wrote to Uncle, explaining things honestly and giving her address at the Mission. There was no point in hiding anything from him. In fact, she did not think he would be disapproving of her decision to come to the Mission. While, like her father, he professed no particular religious faith, he was perfectly content with any and all. She imagined he could just as well sit comfortably in some holy gathering of Turks as Congregationalists. Her father and Uncle were true sailors, at heart, having seen the world and all its infinite variety. He would understand why she could not possibly have stayed at the Wands', given Mr Wand's abominable behaviour.

Marianne spent long hours kneeling in the church, in silence. She learnt or relearnt prayers that were more like chants, the words dancing off from some deep past. She liked going to mass, especially with Bishop Pompallier officiating, though he travelled often to other missions he'd established. She liked peering at the faces of the New Zealanders gathered in the pews, with their green tattoos, so deeply devoted and intent as this sacred drama unfolded, at times, in the New Zealand language the bishop called Maori. The liturgy of the mass felt like a deep mystery no one could possibly entirely understand, and the terrible death of the Son of God seemed now to Marianne to represent God's deep compassion for the suffering of the world, even her own. It was all there, hung up on a type of tree.

She was lulled into a world of symbols, and symbols turning on symbols that did altogether have meaning, though not one that was neatly explained in the books she read. She began to believe in God, though not quite the God she'd disbelieved in before. The God she believed in now seemed more mysterious and remote. Her protectors were intermediate figures, saints, who had human foibles, whose lives stretched back over centuries of the Church's struggle in the world. There was a grand network. The greatest of all was the Blessed Virgin, Mary: all the priests were especially devoted to her, hence 'Marists'.

Meanwhile, the important matters referred to by Bishop Pompallier when Wand departed on the first day of her time of refuge rested heavily and pressed into the Mission, though Marianne never went beyond its gate. As the weeks went on, the British move to join New Zealand territory to that of New South Wales became absolute. Major Bunbury, in his ship the *Herald*, was often off travelling to urge chiefs to cede their territory to the British crown. Then, on May 21, there were two proclamations, one regarding the cession of the Northern Island and another the southern islands. Bishop Pompallier read them both aloud to everyone who lived at the Mission, along with certain eminent Catholic New Zealanders assembled in his library. He read these short pieces first in English, and then translated them into French and Maori. The second one read:

Whereas I have it in command from Her Majesty Queen Victoria, through her Principal Secretary of State for the Colonies, to assert the sovereign rights of Her Majesty over the southern islands of New Zealand, commonly called 'The Middle Island' and 'Stewart's Island,' and also the island commonly called 'The Northern Island,' the same having been ceded in sovereignty to Her Majesty: Now therefore, I, William Hobson, Lieutenant-Governor of New Zealand, do hereby proclaim and declare to all men that, from and after the date of these presents, the full sovereignty of the islands of New Zealand, extending from 34° 30' north to 47° 10' south latitude, and between 166° 5' to 179° of east longitude, vests in Her Majesty Queen Victoria, her heirs and successors, for ever.
Given under my hand at Government House, Russell, Bay of Islands, this 21st day of May, in the year of our Lord, 1840.

After this, he said, gravely, "I believe that the British have learnt of certain plans, of which we have recently been informed, to establish a colony of France in the Middle Island, in the Horomaka, called Banks Peninsula, an initiative of the Duke Decazes." Everyone gasped. "We must await the decisions in Paris. In the meantime, we can only pray that the French settlers will not travel months on the seas only to be met by British guns."

Marianne recognised that her loyalties had shifted. As she moved closer to Catholicism she did indeed move further away from the national cause of Britain. After the reading of the proclamation, and discussion, with both New Zealanders and French talking heatedly, the bishop gave her a pamphlet to see, written by the Wesleyan missionary Henry Williams and his associates, who had acquired vast tracts of land from the New Zealanders and had strongly encouraged all the chiefs they had converted to sign the treaty of 6 February. It denounced Catholicism as "the Antichrist".

Marianne then felt even less inclined to venture out of the Mission grounds.

She made her confession, to Bishop Pompallier, finally, on Friday, July 3, and he absolved her with little penance, as if nothing surprised him at all. On Sunday, July 5, she was confirmed and had her first mass as a full participant, receiving the body and blood of the mystical Christ and thereby joining herself to Christ's body, the Catholic Church. She felt she'd become part of a great family, with an overwhelming sense that this was her destiny. There would be a path for her, an independent path, one that would lead her somewhere important. In the meantime, she began to teach literacy and numeracy to the daughters of New Zealanders that had converted, in French and in English, learning too some Maori herself, and still continued her menial duties as well. In this new regimen, something began to settle, on the surface of the day, though at night she had strange dreams, of being back in the ship with Tim, with green leafy boughs coming up like fingers from the depths of the sea. In one she saw Betty, entwined in willow.

In the middle of the night of Friday, July 10, in the midst of one of these nightmares, Marianne was woken by cannon salutes. These were not completely uncommon when a ship came into the Bay of Islands, but they were noisier than ever before and insistent, going on from one ship to another like neighbours having an argument over the fence. They quietened and she slept again. Then, she was woken before dawn by Tutanna, who told her she had to get up. "There's a French warship in the harbour," she said, anxiously.

Marianne quickly washed herself with cold water and tar soap, and rushed into the austere dining room where it was usual for the bishop to have a cup of coffee before prayers. He was not there, though Father Petit was. "I've just come from Monsignor at the quay," he said, flustered. "We must make ready for the visit of the French commandant. It is unbelievable. The great naval ship, the *Aube*, is anchored now next to the British ship, the *Britomart*. And there are war canoes, all ceremonial, but... no one has seen anything like it before!"

Then there was a furious flurry as Tutanna went and bought provisions, while Marianne and others cleaned and dusted. When Tutanna returned they cooked, set things out and made sure everything was ready. Finally, a dignified deputation arrived with Bishop Pompallier in his purple robes walking up the pathway into the Mission, with the resplendent figure of Commandant Charles François Lavaud – a white-haired, wide-shouldered man who stood upright, powerful like a rooster in a farmyard, alert and elegant, distinguished and authoritative. Marianne and Tutanna curtsied as they were introduced and, once the party went into the dining room, they rushed to prepare food for serving, helped by others, even the gardeners.

Dressed in an apron and with a scarf over her head, Marianne helped to wheel a trolley with a large tureen of seafood soup down the hallway to the dining room, where Commandant Lavaud, the imposing officers of the *Aube* and four new Marist brothers were sitting at the table with Bishop Pompallier and Father Petit. Marianne served the soup with a large ladle, without comment, not wishing to draw attention to herself as the bishop explained the local delicacies: *pipi, paua, toheroa*. Despite her main concern being the serving of soup without it dripping all over the white tablecloth, she was, at the same time, privy to snippets of conversation. The question of the French colony was being discussed.

The imposing naval officer was open in expressing his views and clearly not entirely surprised by the British declaration.

"I must tell you, Monsignor, that I had a feeling that this could happen," he went on. "The waters of New Zealand are full of treasure. The whale oil makes us mad with the lust for riches, and it is only France and Britain who dive together to seize them. Yet, the British are nearer than we are, in New South Wales. They can act more quickly. I was told to proceed directly to Akaroa Harbour, but when I heard of Captain Hobson's departure for New Zealand I thought it wise to investigate this situation in the Bay of Islands. Extraordinary! What if I'd arrived in Banks Peninsula without knowing of the British declaration, or Hobson's treaty? The British would have declared war to defend their economic interests."

"I'm so pleased to hear that Captain Hobson was cordial and in fair health," said the bishop, who seemed to respect Lavaud, though his manner was cautious. He glanced at Marianne and nodded with thanks for the soup.

"Indeed, *Monsieur* Hobson was most polite. In body he is weak, but he is firm in his insistence of British sovereignty, which of course I couldn't affirm, having no orders on the subject. It's not up to me to recognise this claim, no matter how loudly they say it. But Hobson has agreed there will be no objection to the French colony."

Bishop Pompallier seemed unable to eat. "You have this agreement written on paper?"

"No, no, but I trust the word of a gentleman. Surely we can still shake hands and understand each other? Captain Stanley, of the *Britomart*, was there to witness, and others."

There was some general conversation, while Lavaud ate voraciously. "Very good soup," he said.

"And so you await further orders from France," asked Bishop Pompallier, at last. "And in the meantime there will be no declaration of war because of our colony?"

"I will write immediately to our government, for intervention with the British. Meanwhile, here, yes, France is in my hands. In this changed situation, my official instructions cannot be followed. We may establish a settlement, with neither an acceptance nor a denial of the British claims."

Pompallier cleared his throat and then said, "Might it be that we can convince the New Zealanders of the Middle Island not to give up their sovereignty, despite the British proclamation, but rather to keep it for themselves and their descendants under the patronage of France?"

Marianne looked at the bishop, amazed. This could be an independent country of New Zealanders? She almost forgot it was her role to offer more soup.

"French patronage of an independent state of the New Zealanders," continued Bishop Pompallier, "is... in my view... best for the Church. But, of course, in matters of politics we at the Mission must remain entirely neutral."

"Of course," said the Commandant. "Though an independent state of New Zealand would be welcomed by neither London nor Paris. Whatever happens now, we must emphasise agreements that have been made, upon which we act without guile, awaiting our orders. There is no need for aggression, or subterfuge."

Marianne thought of Mr Wand. What would he make of news of a French colony in the Middle Island? Would he – or others like him – think there was no need for aggression to forestall it?

When soup was done, Marianne collected plates and wheeled them out on the trolley. She then helped to serve the main course of pork, cabbage, potatoes and sweet potatoes, before withdrawing.

Another Mission worker was the server on duty at the table; though Marianne still heard snatches when she entered to clear. Bishop Pompallier praised Captain Hobson as being a decent man who genuinely wished to protect the New Zealanders and their rights, in contrast to the British missionaries and the property speculators. He described the assembly at Waitangi on February 6, recounting the debate among the chiefs and highlighting the objections of a chief named Rewa. "Even in the Bay," he said, "not all the New Zealanders are convinced, and I do not believe that all those that have signed the treaty understand its deeper meaning."

Lavaud smiled and said, "Ah, for the men of the Church everything must have a deeper meaning." He meant this as a joke, and everyone laughed politely. Yet the bishop glanced up at Marianne and she saw his eyes held no joy.

*

Later, after coffee and sugary sweets, when the party from the *Aube* had finally gone and Marianne was helping to wash and tidy in the kitchen, Bishop Pompallier suddenly appeared. He was still wearing his formal attire and looked very regal in purple, which was incongruous in the environment of pots and pans. "Marianne," he beckoned, and went out.

Marianne looked to Tutanna and then followed the bishop dutifully along the hallway.

"You listened very carefully to the conversation at the table," the bishop observed, as they walked towards the library.

"Yes."

He opened the door and they went inside. "Please sit down."

She sat on the leather chair. He sat down on his chair behind the desk, reflecting pensively. Bishop Pompallier seemed tired. "How strange everything is now," he said. "This world in New Zealand is upside down in more respects than one. We must take risks and behave in unexpected ways."

Marianne nodded, wondering what he meant.

He pressed his fingers together. "I have been thinking about you Marianne. You have particular skills that at this time may be useful. Your fluency in both English and French is rare. There are French people who know some English, like me, and there are English people who know some French, like Captain Stanley, who translated for Commandant Lavaud with Captain Hobson. But you are fluent in both languages. At this time of delicate diplomacy, this is very helpful."

"Thank you," said Marianne, wondering where this was leading.

"My priests have very little English. I would like to send one of them with Commandant Lavaud, since he knows the language of Maori well and can work with the New Zealanders. You've met Father Jean-Baptiste Comte?"

"No."

"He's been at our mission in Hokianga. He has learnt Maori very quickly and can surely learn English soon, with close instruction. You saw tonight at the table two priests and two lay-brothers, but none of them speak Maori. I will retain three of them here and send Father Comte with a young New Zealander, Jerôme, who shows a great deal of promise." Bishop Pompallier paused, and then said, "I will send only the fourth newcomer, Father Jean Pezant, as well as Brother Florentin from the Hokianga as a helper, but I would like you to go with Commandant Lavaud to Banks Peninsula also as a helper."

"Oh," said Marianne, astonished.

"You see my problem and my reservations because you are a woman, and so recently confirmed. You are not mine, within the Marist order. How can I send you?"

Marianne flinched. Her immediate feeling was that she never wanted to leave the Mission, or Monsignor. 'Please don't ask me,' she wanted to say. 'I never want to leave the Mission here.' Instead, she asked, "What's it like there?"

Bishop Pompallier leaned back. "What's it like?" he repeated, and then said, "The one thing I know is that the British will not leave a French colony in the Middle Island alone. No one must trust them. And it's far away from my protection. It's nearly nine-hundred kilometres to the south."

Marianne's jaw dropped open. She had no idea New Zealand was so big. Nine-hundred kilometres? What was that in miles?

Six hundred? The full impact of the British proclamation sank in. The coastline and the whaling waters were vast. Such treasures indeed.

"There will be nothing there at all but a few new houses of French settlers, a Maori village or two, and whaling stations, though of course the *Aube* will be anchored in the harbour for some time, for help and protection. But it's not at all certain how this matter will resolve itself." Pompallier frowned.

Marianne looked glumly down at her feet. She wore sensible boots here, made in the Mission from cattle hides processed in the tannery. They were good for outdoors or inside and kept her feet from getting wet very well. You needed that here, since in winter it was not so much cold but rainy. Seven-hundred miles south it would be more like the climate she'd left behind; not that this was bad, but she would need warm clothing. She was aware then of her own thoughts. Had she already decided to go, that she should be thinking of such practical matters? "Do you want me to be a housekeeper for the mission there?" she asked.

Bishop Pompallier smiled a little and said, "I'm thinking of some role for you like this, yes. But also I would like you to teach the girls as you do here, and to teach the brothers to speak English, because they must be able to talk to the English and defend themselves."

Marianne looked at the bishop's eyes. She felt he wished she'd been a man.

"But I'm afraid... if I do this... I would be sending you into the mouth of the lion," said the bishop.

"How?" she asked.

He looked away. "Or perhaps the better image is that I cast my pearls before swine. I don't know. I've seen a role for you here, but I'm aware also that since you have taken refuge, you never leave this place to go into the town of Kororareka. You are afraid of what's outside the perimeter. You cannot live like this. Now, I'm sending you to the wilds." He looked to her again.

"Do you want me to have more courage?" asked Marianne. She was aware asking such a direct question of a bishop was not usual practice, but she had a slightly irregular relationship with this man. For her, he had stepped into the shoes of Uncle. He reciprocated in the same familiar way, though at the age of around forty he was not quite old enough to be a replacement. It was as if he wanted at least one female companion in this world of male priests and that he'd come to take some delight in her presence, educating her in the faith, watching his attention bear fruit. She saw it on his face. He felt some genuine affection. He himself did not want to lose her, but he thought of the benefits of having her with the colony; it was a kind of personal selflessness.

There was nothing unwelcome, however, in this recognition. She liked it that he liked her, that he seemed to care about her.

"It's good to have courage," said the bishop, and smiled, as if to himself. "But it's not good to be stupid about danger. I don't know if this is too dangerous for you. To begin a new mission anywhere involves taking some risks. And there are particular risks for you, as you know, because to be a beautiful young woman in a world of men - where there are not so many women, and not many that are beautiful – is ... especially dangerous, as you've seen already in your life."

There was a short silence. Marianne stared down at the patterns on the carpet rug. "There will be women among the colonists?" asked Marianne, finally, not wishing to show any reaction.

"Yes," said the bishop. Then he put his hands together again. "Don't decide now," he said, after a moment. "Sleep, pray and think about it tomorrow. We can talk more."

This was a cue for her to leave. She got up.

The bishop seemed weary. She wanted to say, 'Don't worry, it will be all right. I will be fine.' But she only said, "Good-night."

"Good-night," he said, and his sad expression said it all.

*

The tension of having two warships in the harbour, French and British, side by side, set everyone in the Bay on edge. There was talk of how many hours it would take for the French, with their massively superior cannon, to overthrow the British military: six hours, two days, a week? The New Zealanders would be loyal to whoever was the strongest, despite the treaty. Bishop Pompallier silenced all such talk whenever he heard it.

Then, suddenly, the *Britomart*, under Captain Stanley, departed for Port Nicholson, where there was another British colony recently established, apparently to reassure the settlers there and take some magistrates to the growing town. This was on Thursday, July 23. The *Aube* was left on its own to rule the waves of the Bay of Islands, making some people talk of a deal. Had it seen off the British ship? The *Aube* took on supplies and prepared for its onward voyage to Banks Peninsula, to Akaroa Harbour where the French colony would be established.

Marianne boarded the *Aube* on July 30, having said a restrained goodbye to people at the Mission, including Bishop Pompallier, since everything was in public and she wanted to be very controlled about her emotions. She left another letter for Betty with Tutanna, asking her to deliver it into her hand, and then hugged Tutanna tightly. She picked up her carpet bag of belongings and money, some of which she had given to the Mission, and went on to the rowing boat to the ship looking forwards rather than backwards. She felt the same pain she'd felt leaving Wivenhoe and Uncle. How did this happen, that life played the same music over again?

As she stepped up from the ladder on to the deck she looked to the immense, gleaming grandeur of the French corvette, with its huge masts, ropes and immaculate decks. She was still wearing black, with a black scarf covering her dark hair rather than a bonnet, hoping to appear as nun-like as possible. She stood next to Father Comte and young Jerôme – who seemed no more than seventeen – without speaking, because she couldn't speak. The two men talked together in Maori, and it was clear that Jerôme – or rather Hiromi – did not speak much French. This made it easier for her to close off.

They were shown to three cabins for passengers. One, Father Comte shared with an older, rather stolid priest who had sailed from France on the *Aube*, Father Pezant; the other, Hiromi shared with a muscular lay-brother, Florentin; the third was entirely hers. She shut the door soon and was strongly hit by a memory of the *Albatross*. The same narrow bed. The same chest of drawers. The same port-hole. But no Tim Blake.

This was too much. She felt desperately low. She sat down on the bed. But she did not weep. Another familiar feeling returned: that of detachment. There it goes, and all because of the fruit of the forbidden tree.

They left the Bay in the evening, guided by the stars.

*

Over the hundreds of miles southwards their journey was unremarkable. Marianne kept herself distant, writing to Uncle, not knowing when she would even be able to send off this letter. She started sewing a better dress from some fabric she'd bought from a trader visiting the Mission. It was grey wool, rather than black, and thicker than the Sydney daywear she had retained. She also worked on a heavy crocheted shawl out of brown wool. Most of the time she stayed in her cabin, since there was nothing much to see but sea and occasional dolphins. With the Marist brothers and Hiromi she undertook devotions and taught them some English, as well as doing some mending for them. She had a few good conversations with Father Comte, a young faired-haired man who seemed brotherly and was willing to talk to her as something of an equal. They sailed wide of land and turned in to the coast on Tuesday, August 11, their journey slow because of head winds. They sighted land and reached the entrance to Akaroa Harbour on Wednesday, August 12. Commandant Lavaud's expertise in navigation was clear to all.

At this point there was excitement when they drew alongside a French whaler, the *Pauline*, and its master, Captain Billiard, came on board to act as a pilot. The passengers all went up on deck to greet him, and heard him say that he'd just met with sailors from the colonists' ship, the *Comte de Paris*, which was badly damaged and anchored in Pigeon Bay. The next news he gave was grave. He said that the *HMS Britomart*, the British warship that had been in the Bay of Islands, was now in Akaroa Harbour.

Commandant Lavaud was stunned. "What?" he exclaimed. "Stanley is here. They told me that the *Britomart* was going to Port Nicholson! They said that there would be no objection to our colony." As his face clouded, so did the sky. The weather and sea soon turned against them. The wind dropped and the current swept them dangerously towards land. A northerly pushed them further. The *Aube* had to turn around and go back out to sea, and so Captain Billiard returned to his own ship in a whaleboat.

As if the wind was conjured by the British, the *Aube* couldn't sail into Akaroa Harbour until the evening of Saturday, August 15. Then, finally, favoured by a slight breeze from the south-east, Lavaud advanced the ship and anchored it beyond the heads. The priests worried about the colonists, praying they would have strength and hope, and celebrated the feast of the Assumption to commemorate the Blessed Virgin Mary's place in Heaven.

There a whaleboat arrived with Captain Stanley, of all people, who came on board to offer his assistance. Marianne stood with the Marists and watched from a distance a cautious and gentlemanly exchange between the two captains, in French, since Stanley was clearly a well-educated man. Neither of them would lose their tempers. He told Lavaud that he had been given last minute orders to sail for Akaroa Harbour with two British magistrates.

But Commandant Lavaud showed no indication of being ruffled. There were careful smiles on both sides. He agreed to let Stanley's boats tow the *Aube*, because of the winds, and on Sunday, August 16, the French and British warships were anchored side by side in Paka Ariki Bay, where – shockingly – a Union Jack was already flying at the point.

The two ships side by side were like floating pieces of Europe – similar, elegant and modern – no matter how much their two countries fought. Outside, everything was alien and ancient. Marianne looked around at thickly forested hills where birds seemed not so much to twitter but shout, and at the wooden canoes of the local people, who were fascinated by such a huge ship as the *Aube*. Father Comte and Hiromi greeted the rowers in Maori, but they seemed suspicious. The setting sun behind the western hills lit whispery clouds with a fantastical array of red, orange and pink. The bright greens of the landscape turned to purple and grey, beside this great swathe of fiery hues in the sky and in the water. Despite the wind, Marianne stared up at it until bright stars shot through and the scene turned dark. It gave her hope. It was simply so very beautiful.

Marianne waited all the next day, hopeful that the colonists' ship would arrive without harm. She talked a little with young Hiromi, learning some Maori from him, and did some needlework. There was cannon fire, perhaps an announcement, and then, mid-afternoon, the battered *Comte de Paris* sailed past them. It seemed small, next to the *Aube*, and on deck there was a crowd of people, staring anxiously. There was no cheering. Marianne stared out and tried to distinguish the faces, and felt the settlers' worry. What must it have been like for them, together at sea all those months? What would it be like for them now? These French settlers were people she would have to get to know. These were her future. She waved, and saw arms waving back like seaweed in a swell.

She looked at boat parties going backwards and forwards from ship to ship as matters in the world of men played out in the cabins of European captains: great matters of diplomacy and trade, economics and empires, nations and government, all being decided while they floated on the water, in suspension, watched by the people of the land.

13
Manako-uri

The talk François Lelièvre heard everywhere was of land: who owned what, and when they bought it; what sales had been complete; where were the boundaries? In the midst of this, the dream of France holding Banks Peninsula in its entirety seemed to blow away.

It turned out that an Englishman, James Robinson Clough, was living at Onuku with his Maori wife Puai, who was the cousin of chief Iwikau. Another chief Tuauau had 'sold' the whole of Banks Peninsula to a Sydney whaler, Captain Clayton, who had established at shore whaling station at Peraki – a big operation run by a man called George Hempelman, who employed a number of New Zealanders. A man named William Rhodes had bought land from a Captain Leathart in Sydney, who claimed he'd bought the whole of Banks Peninsula from a chief called Taiaroa. Rhodes had left a farmer, William Green, with a wife and child, to establish a cattle station in November, 1839, and they had a well-built house where the Union Jack flew. They'd burnt off scrub and allegedly cleared a mass of human bones from Takapuneke, and were now grazing cattle on grass they'd planted there. The people of Onuku were very unhappy about this; they claimed this land was not to be touched and the bones were not to be disturbed, as it was the site of a massacre. Green's grazing stock surely couldn't have been what Chief Taiaroa agreed to. François knew very well, from Matthieu Le Bon, why this land was out of bounds.

After his discovery that Napoleon's willow was thriving, François had walked along to the next bay to the north, Takamatua, where he first encountered Matthieu Le Bon. He found that the willow planted there had died. This confirmed to him even more that the French should be at Paka Ariki Bay. In fact, the Germans who had come along on board the ship chose to make their camp at Takamatua; the French came to the place where his first willow had grown. All of this was coincidental.

He decided that now he would tell his closest friends the entire story, and brought Malmanche, Éteveneaux and Libeau to witness the growth of the willow themselves. He recounted the entire history, from its beginning on St. Helena's Island, and all three men wiped tears from their eyes.

"Napoleon is here," said Libeau. "He is with us here, and nothing the British will do can drive his soul away from us."

Malmanche told Captain Langlois about it, and Langlois then was fired with new zeal to finalise the Pigeon Bay contracts, by including the signatures now of Tuauau and other local chiefs who hadn't signed, giving further gifts, and writing up the exact wording on the basis of draft contracts he'd received from the Nanto-Bordelaise Company. He himself came to visit the willow, and he too wiped away tears. He even hugged François.

Meanwhile, Belligny cultivated now a close relationship with Commandant Lavaud. With his support, he seemed to tower over Langlois, whose rule was on the *Comte de Paris*, but not on land. It was rumoured that Lavaud and Belligny, who were treading a fine line between Langlois and the British claims, could concede that the colony would be a French settlement with only limited autonomy in a British island, not France proper, and such a compromise seemed like a betrayal. They might well accept the declaration of British sovereignty that everyone was discussing.

Lauvaud and Belligny also walked a real line. On Thursday, August 20, they marked out agreed areas of settlement with Captain Stanley and the magistrate Robinson, as well as the chiefs Tuauau and his associates, with the Marist priest, Father Comte, translating Maori, creating boundaries that stretched all the way up the stream to François' *whare*, which became at times significant, and was used profitably in discussions as an indication of previous French residency. The willow was noted by Belligny, and its state of remarkable growth commented upon, but its association with Napoleon was of no interest to him. According to Langlois, he dubbed faith in the willow a 'superstition of the ignorant'. One by one, all the colonists came to visit it, nevertheless, knowing its significance, and proclaimed it a miracle. Yet, they kept it as something of a colonists' secret, their own private sign to those that understood. They feared if they talked too much the British might cut it down.

The official discussions led to an agreement. There would be a divided town, which started to be called, informally, Akaroa. The French settlement would go no further than the Paka Ariki stream, though it would sweep around north to the promontory of Onawe. Captain Stanley, apparently by order of Hobson, could not accept the French had a right to any more than three thousand acres, but Langlois continued to claim thirty thousand, which he believed was the whole of Banks Peninsula.

Despite everything, François had hope and took pride in Napoleon's willow. He was considered a hero now. The tree brought such hope everywhere, the settlers started to work hard and with enthusiasm, planting other trees, including willows. The objections were to be expected of the British foe; but France would win.

When the rain stopped, sailors of the *Comte de Paris* unloaded wood and other materials, so that work could progress on houses, but there was not enough dry wood because so much had been burnt on board ship to supply the needs of cooking. The wood left over was initially employed in constructing the large Nanto-Bordelaise Company headquarters, comprising a shop, a hospital, and the office of Belligny, which all became known as the Magasin, the 'Store', for short. Aimable Langlois, the captain's brother, was in charge of the store, and François set up his workshop opposite. He was allowed to transfer his employment from Captain Langlois to Belligny, to work as a blacksmith for the Nanto-Bordelaise Company on shore. He sold seeds of French plants.

The Germans in the next bay, who were knowledgeable about logging, unpacked all of the tree-felling equipment and set to work cutting down trees and sawing them into planks. The sailors of the *Aube* were like a well-organised swarm of ants. They quickly started to build a naval establishment out of prefabricated walls, and other materials, and a fine residence for Commandant Lavaud.

On Sunday, August 23, there was a ceremony within the precincts of this establishment. After the first mass celebrated on the foreshore by Fathers Comte and Pezant, everyone gathered inside this official zone and the French Navy hoisted the Tricolour. Port Louis Philippe was established as a French commune, run according to the laws of France, under the direction of Belligny as Mayor, and militarily supervised and protected by Commandant Lavaud as

Royal Commissioner. There was no role for Captain Langlois, and he was heard shouting that this went directly against the Nanto-Bordelaise Company instructions.

It was an emotional moment and many tears were shed by the colonists. Everyone had their private grief and hope, and seeing the French flag flying on New Zealand soil seemed to summon up everything that had been suppressed through the long voyage, and all the days of hard work and anxiety since their arrival.

During this ceremony, François noted there was among the missionary priests a woman, apparently a lay-sister, who stood beside a brawny lay-brother. She was young and pretty, but seemed sad and removed. Her eyes did not catch his eyes, or anyone else's. He thought it a remarkable thing for her to be here, with the Marist priests in this faraway place, and when he asked it was said she was the housekeeper, and also that she would teach girls in a school.

It bothered him a little, that the Church should claim a young woman like that, when the colony so needed unmarried young women. This was more a matter of principle than personal affection. As the days passed, he watched her come and go, carrying wood, making food for the priests on a fire she built separately by a makeshift oratory. The Marists always slept on board the *Aube*, however, waiting until their house and the chapel could be finished, mainly through the diligent labour of the burly lay-brother who seemed to be a carpenter. They worked in the meantime, like everyone else, on planting vegetables and European trees in the plot they had been allocated on a rise to the north of the centre. Father Pezant, a plump man who seemed unsuited to outdoor activity, was usually either on board ship or talking with the colonists. Fresh-faced Father Comte appeared more concerned with the Maori, and spoke to them fluently. François talked with him a little and asked the name of the woman that was with them. He was told her name was Marianne Blake.

That made him laugh, not dismissively, but more in a kind of wonder. Marianne. The name of his sister and his niece. The name of France. That seemed a sign. But 'Blake' was not a French name. He asked Father Comte about that too, and was told that she'd been married to an Australian before coming to New Zealand, but she was a widow. She was very dedicated to the Mission, and a very pious and dutiful woman who was a great asset.

"Such a waste," François said. He couldn't help himself.

From the moment the demarcations of land were established, the whole group of some two hundred and twenty sailors and colonists were busy, making repairs to ships, erecting buildings, organising rations, planting. François planted, finally, after waiting so long. He was allowed a parcel of his own land, around his *whare*, on a lease – since he was not a colonist – with the understanding that he would buy it from the Nanto-Bordelaise Company in due course. With that agreement, he cut down native bush and put all his precious, special seeds in the ground everywhere: a great sweep of herbs, bushes and vegetables. While sleeping in his *whare*, he worked hard on making it into a proper cottage, as well as doing his blacksmith work. Like all the other settlers, he went to bed early, exhausted.

*

Marianne kept busy. She felt she was almost continually running around, backwards and forwards on the boat to the land. She bought potatoes and fish with the little money the priests had, and also her own, cooking such food – with some rations begged from the Commandant – cleaning up, washing clothing, occasionally translating. On Wednesday, August 26, the *Britomart* departed, leaving the British magistrate, Charles Barrington Robinson, behind to exercise authority over the British residents of Banks Peninsula. Such was the agreement: Robinson would apply British law to the British, Commandant Lavaud had authority over the French, and the New Zealanders would exercise their own customary laws: a tripartite legal division in which everyone was content, in the absence of any clear settlement about who owned what overall, and sovereignty.

Marianne respected Commandant Lavaud; no matter how discouraged he felt, he maintained an air of polite amiability to the British. He even offered Robinson accommodation on board the *Aube* after the departure of the British ship, until his own accommodation was built on land. Robinson spoke quite good French, having lived in Paris for a time, but his manner to Marianne was abrupt.

So there was the strange circumstance: a French naval frigate playing host to a British magistrate placed there to spy on it, all in the interests of diplomacy.

As for the Marists, Marianne heard from Father Comte about the permutations of land claims and sales, and the history of things in the Hokianga, and the grievances of everyone, and fears. His concern was with the New Zealanders. Father Pezant spent a great deal of time talking to the colonists. Father Comte confided in Marianne more than in Father Pezant, who, when not gossiping with the colonists, preferred to be reading religious books. Brother Florentin and Hiromi, on the other hand, were mainly occupied with cutting and construction and had formed their own bond of friendship over this work. Father Comte seemed quite enthusiastic, though troubled by the fact that the people of the village Onuku had recently been partly evangelised by Wesleyans, who had warned them against the French, insisting that the British Government would protect them against British criminals.

Everything was complicated and fraught. Communication was clearly a key issue. They all needed skills in Maori and – with the new interests of the British in the Middle Island – they had to learn English. While Brother Florentin and Hiromi laboured and learnt each other's tongue simultaneously, Marianne gave Father Comte English classes daily. Father Pezant could only learn one language at a time, this being Maori, from Father Comte. Therefore, Father Comte taught both Father Pezant and Marianne Maori, or at least tried to. It was clear that Father Pezant had no skills in learning any language, and kept saying how much he preferred Latin.

Marianne soaked up these classes eagerly, finally getting a better sense of the speech she'd tried to learn at the Mission. She loved learning things. Father Comte explained, for example, that 'Maori' was not the term the New Zealanders themselves used for their language, since until the arrival of the Europeans they had no idea of there being a different speech. Instead it meant 'ordinary': they called themselves *tangata māori*, 'ordinary people', or *tangata whenua*, 'people of the land', as opposed to *pākehā*, 'pale ones', since *keha* meant 'light' in colour, or 'pale', though the *pā* he was not sure about, since it could mean a 'fortified village', or a 'dam', but it could also mean 'group', and he thought perhaps originally then the term designated the 'pale group' of people. He mentioned beliefs of there being pale beings in the ocean, that fish could turn into such *pākehā*, and that they could summon up ships out of reeds.

Father Comte said that for missionary work it was important to use the terms the New Zealanders used for themselves, and for others, and therefore he referred to them as they referred to themselves, as 'ordinaries', Māori, while Europeans were Pākehā. More than that, it was important to understand tribal divisions. Hiromi was Ngapuhi, and felt himself to be as different from the Ngāi Tahu of Akaroa as a Provençal from a Normand. He found this climate cold and the language peculiar. They said, for example, 'l' for 'r', so that Akaroa was pronounced Akaloa.

Father Comte and Marianne, discussing such interesting things, became firm friends, and they soon said the familiar 'tu' with each other. He became Jean-Baptiste to her. She liked that his attitude was pragmatic, despite the difficulties, and he worked hard, never complaining about their limited food, thanking her always for her labour, especially the simple meals, and praying very devotedly to Mary. Father Pezant, on the other hand, was clearly dissatisfied, especially with the food that she daily tried to prepare as well as possible. After all, there were only so many ways of cooking potatoes.

Over the next weeks, Marianne watched as what was formerly bush-clad lowland beyond a slim foreshore became completely transformed. Trees of the forest were cut down and sawn for timber, and houses erected, the sailors of the Aube becoming instantaneously a huge force of builders, carpenters and labourers. This was despite the weather turning bitterly cold. However, the cold had nothing of the greyness and darkness of the winter in Wivenhoe. The sky was still a shining blue when the clouds cleared, and the forest a vivid green, since the leaves stayed on the trees. Powdery snow might fall and settle, but it just added white to the strong colours. Marianne felt a growing contentment. She looked forward to the mission house and church being built, so that she could create a place that was homely and welcoming, with a garden of flowers, vegetables and fruit trees.

She got quite used to being the only woman when on board the Aube, and roamed around the ship more, as far as she was allowed. She made the acquaintance of the amusing and clever medic, Dr Raoul, who frequently went off with Mayor Belligny, investigating native trees and plants.

However, one day she'd just come from a rather pleasant conversation with Dr Raoul when she ran into the British magistrate, Mr Robinson, as she rounded a corner from the starboard passage of the second deck.

She did not particularly care for what she'd seen of Mr Robinson. He had the airs and graces of the superior class of British society, akin to those of Charles Wand. His French was actually spoken inelegantly with a strong English accent. He'd been allocated a large swathe of land for his private use in the southern turn of Paka Ariki Bay, and seemed rather pleased with himself.

"Oh, I beg your pardon," she said quickly, in English, as she encountered him. She stepped aside and went to move on.

"I beg your pardon?" replied Robinson, intrigued. "You speak English, Sister... er... "

"Mrs Blake," she responded, instinctively.

"Mrs Blake," he said, with emphasis, as if surprised, and then chuckled. "Well, well. My word."

Marianne immediately regretted letting her guard slip, softened by the conversation with Dr Raoul. She should not have spoken English, without thinking. His chuckle was more of a snigger, she felt.

"I'm sorry," she said, cordially, trying to keep her composure. With all the careful diplomacy she'd witnessed recently, she could surely apply lessons she'd learnt to this predicament.

"Ah, excuse me, Mrs Blake, but your name is familiar to me, though perhaps that does not surprise you." He seemed very knowing.

Marianne pulled her new, thick shawl around her tightly and drew herself up. She was glad that Mr Robinson was not very tall.

"The Bay of Islands is a place where people talk idly of many things, Mr Robinson," she said, "and often there's barely a scrap of true information to go on."

Robinson smirked, and said, "Oh, excuse me if I speak very frankly, but I think there is quite a bit of sound information circulated about you, Mrs Blake, don't you think? Or would you accuse such reputable men as Mr Wand of spreading lies?"

Marianne held herself strong. Think. What would Commandant Lavaud do, faced with such personal accusations?

"If they insinuate anything against my character, Mr Robinson, I do indeed accuse such men of spreading lies."

Robinson seemed to be enjoying this, like it was a sudden flash of sport, a little entertainment in a day full of heavy business. "Indeed, perhaps I should correct myself to say that there is another who is mentioned with greater... force. I mean to refer to your benefactor, Mrs Blake. It is true to say that the blame is most commonly laid at his feet."

"My benefactor, Mr Robinson?"

"You do know of whom I speak, I'm sure," said Robinson.

Marianne remembered Charles Wand's words at leaving the Mission, after his request that Marianne be returned. She stared at Robinson defiantly.

"Having failed to manipulate the bulk of the native chiefs, he must have needed a little solace, apart from the fine wine he most usually enjoys. Tongues do wag, I must say."

It was only at this point that Marianne realised that Robinson had been drinking. The smell of whisky on his breath brought back the claustrophobic moment of Charles Wand's kiss. No wonder he was speaking in such an overt, offensive tone, when a gentleman such as he would normally be far more subtle. And how ironic to accuse Bishop Pompallier of his own vice. "A little solace, sir?" Marianne kept herself absolutely rigid and firm. She kept fixing this man with a sharp glare.

"Now, if I were a strategist, I could explain your appearance here in Akaroa very neatly," continued Robinson, slightly slurring and spitting his words. "Mr Pompallier, aiming to whiten his reputation, sends you away to the farthest corner of New Zealand, thus showing the world that he can rid himself of certain pleasures inconsistent with his vows. Having stolen an English governess, and indoctrinated her into his superstition, he casts her off and renounces her entirely. How very noble of him."

"You know nothing," Marianne said, calmly, though her insides churned. "My reasons for coming to the Mission were spiritual. Bishop Pompallier did not indoctrinate me anew. I was born a Catholic. My mother was French. I would be very grateful, Mr Robinson, if you would never speak in this way, either to insult me, or my religion, or the reputation of Bishop Pompallier, or I shall readily inform Commandant Lavaud of the slander. I assure you, sir, that his investigations of the matter will vindicate every word I say."

She turned and started to walk away, but then heard behind her silken words, as if Robinson was a fox in an old tale. "Oh no but you are mine, Mrs Blake. You are not under the jurisdiction of Commandant Lavaud. You are assuredly a British subject, and therefore under my authority here in Akaroa."

She did not pause. She kept walking in the direction she was going, until she reached her cabin, which she entered in a state of fury. She closed her eyes, and kicked the floor. Poor Monsignor! So that was Charles Wand's revenge.

Did Bishop Pompallier know what they said?

Somehow she felt sure he did. And that was the worst thing. That was awful.

Did he send her away to quell the rumours? Would he do that to her? No, no, he was fond of her. The look on his face that evening he made his request was clear – he cared about her.

And Robinson claimed her now in the grossest way imaginable, given his inebriation, as the man she should consider her leader, her legal authority, since she was a British subject. There was no fighting that one. The nationality of her mother couldn't define her, when her mother had left France, married a British subject and given birth to her in England. She herself had married a British subject in New South Wales. Lavaud's neat and tidy deal with the British had failed to account for the fact that her circumstances were not neat and tidy.

*

The colonists discussed agreements and divisions, over and over, until François felt he could hardly hear another word on these matters. The only man who seemed true to the original vision of the enterprise, Captain Langlois, had been excluded by the alliance of Lavaud and Belligny, who had now made friends with the British magistrate Robinson. Langlois went from family to family, giving them moral support, but his morose aura was worrying, and he indicated straightforwardly that Lavaud and Belligny were busily selling out completely to Captain Hobson. A defiant, uncompromising position was the only one Langlois could accept: it was a simple case of win or lose, and it seemed to him that everything was going the way of a terrible loss, without drastic intervention from Paris. While Langlois shared his thoughts with the settlers, Commandant Lavaud and Belligny, as gentlemen of a higher social status, seemed to have decided that the best policy was to keep the common colonists totally in the dark.

There were many clandestine meetings. Éteveneaux, Libeau and Malmanche urged Captain Langlois to keep writing to the Nanto-Bordelaise Company and any other French dignitaries that might be able to help, to promote the French cause. The colonists were in no mood to compromise and be diplomatic. They had a dream, confirmed by Napoleon's willow, and they felt threatened by Lavaud and Belligny, who seemed to be able to give that dream away so easily, as far as they could understand from Langlois, their true leader.

The colonists accepted no compromises or social interactions with the British. This was French territory – Banks Peninsula as a whole and much more – no matter what the British told them. It had been bought legitimately from the New Zealanders, with whom they were already on reasonably friendly terms, after the initial fear and coolness. There was now a striking difference between the authorities – represented by Lavaud and Belligny – who remained warmly ensconced on board the *Aube* (hosting Robinson), and the colonists, who huddled closely together in the tents as freezing rain fell on land. The *Comte de Paris* and the huge, resplendent *Aube*, became two different political networks fiercely opposed to each other, with only the Marists going to and fro, neutral.

Finally, Commandant Lavaud announced that he needed a sound document, and the one at Pigeon Bay was useless to him, given that it was agreed after the British declaration of sovereignty on May 21. He made it clear to Captain Langlois that he had to have an endorsement of the original agreement – dated to the original time – between the Port Cooper chiefs and Langlois. He needed one with the date of August 2, 1838, and no other. It would not be a fabrication, it would be a kind of reiteration, expanded to include more chiefs, most importantly those who lived closest to the French settlement – their neighbours at Onuku, Tuauau and his men – whose absence in the original contract was simply incredible.

"How many contracts must I make before one of these can hold?" fumed Langlois.

But Lavaud was finally able to gain Captain Langlois' acceptance of this odd procedure and Langlois went off once more to contact all the relevant parties, and any others who may have been missed out of his previous contracts.

On September 4, making use of the British magistrate Robinson's convenient absence at a nearby whaling station, which people said was in fact to procure liquor, Captain Langlois managed to gather together on the *Comte de Paris* all the chiefs of repute who had some claim to the territory, accompanied by many others – men, women and children – a much larger assembly than Langlois had ever put together before. Belligny was overtly astonished at how many were there, and made swift calculations aloud of how much land would be retained by the New Zealanders given Langlois' promises.

The colonists themselves were not permitted to participate, but since François was not officially a colonist, he was there, promising them all a full report. The size of the assembly made it clear to François that Langlois had bought land originally off a very small handful of chiefs at Port Cooper in 1838, when far more were needed to make a secure deed of sale. Whether they had claimed sole authority over areas in which they needed agreement from other chiefs remained unknown. Or perhaps they had actually originally agreed to sell a much smaller section of Banks Peninsula than Langlois had thought. Langlois may have misunderstood. The possibilities of misunderstanding seemed to grow exponentially every time François thought about it. And yet here there were sixty adult settlers and their children who believed they were creating a little France in this chilly corner of the South Pacific.

As with the Pigeon Bay assembly, many New Zealanders arrived, but now in bigger canoes, some with extraordinary carvings. They came aboard and massed all over the *Comte de Paris*. Some of them spoke a little French, some of them English, or smatterings of other languages like Danish, or German.

New Zealanders had come from north and south of Banks Peninsula and from further afield, to constitute a great gathering of chiefs from the tribe of the Ngāi Tahu. Langlois had worked extremely hard to find anyone with land rights. He strode up and down speaking in English, French and a little Maori himself, asserting his own authority as a kind of chief, despite the presence of Commandant Lavaud and Belligny. Captain Langlois seemed to use English especially with certain chiefs, when he did not want the monolingual Commandant to understand.

Fortunately, discussions now proceeded with the more competent interpretation of Father Comte. François was able again to look at the young woman Marist there, standing straight and subdued in a grey dress in between the priests and Commandant Lavaud himself. It seemed as if she was more engaged this time. More than that, as the proceedings went on, he realised that she was talking. When there was any part in English, whether on the mouth of Captain Langlois, or in a speech from one of the chiefs, she spoke quietly in Commandant Lavaud's ear, so that he did not miss a thing. Captain Langlois seemed not to notice this, his attention being totally focused on the chiefs. Despite the great drama of these speeches and the presence of so many eminent chiefs, François couldn't help looking at this woman. She wore a grey scarf in the same material as her dress, and a brown woollen shawl, but even with such plain clothing and no adornment, she was so beautiful. Her eyes were blue and he could see that her hair was dark as the wind lifted her scarf up and undid the pinning.

The speeches went on and on. All the chiefs insisted that it was not the whole of Banks Peninsula that had been sold, but only part of it, without the properties belonging to the English, or land retained for their own purposes, including *tapu* land. The whole of Banks Peninsula had never been sold to Langlois, not even at Pigeon Bay. Langlois hadn't understood them correctly. They had only permitted occupation.

Captain Langlois interjected then and said to François, standing nearby, as if talking aloud to himself: "They overrule their own agreement. We will end up giving everything we have! We will insist on what's been sold."

"Perhaps the New Zealanders are only now beginning to understand what we mean by a sale, Captain," said François.

Langlois snorted. "Lavaud has made some deal with Hobson, I'm sure of it. Those who come in the name of the king are the people who betrayed the Emperor Napoleon. They do not believe in liberty, equality and fraternity. They believe in power."

This was the kind of thing Langlois often said to the colonists now, and it endeared him to them, but François could not completely put his trust in Langlois, whose interests seemed, to him, also self-serving. Was he not aiming to be paid in shares?

Then a young Chief Iwikau of the Ngāti Rangiāmoa sub-tribe came forward to speak. He was a powerful man, wearing a French jacket. Father Comte translated, and said he was paramount in Port Levy and Pigeon Bay. Iwikau recited a list of where there would be no sale: "the bays on the northern and eastern side towards the sea are not the property of the French." The names of these bays were recited, ending with "… all the other bays toward Putakoro, including Katawahu, which is the place where Manako-uri has planted his vegetables and lives apart with his *whānau*".

François, after so many hours of listening, hardly caught this statement, but the name of his friend crashed out like a cannon shot. "What… what did he say, Captain Langlois?" he asked.

"He claims we do not own the northern and eastern bays towards the ocean, for example Pigeon Bay, where Jotereau and Chardin are buried. Their graves are not in French soil!" replied Langlois. "With all these exclusions, we own nothing."

"No, Captain – " François grabbed hold of Langlois' arm, forgetting his place. "The name Manako-uri is Matthieu Le Bon."

The Captain looked at him with vexation, trying to understand the significance of his words, and his inappropriate conduct.

When Iwikau had finished, François could not stop himself. He suddenly stepped forward, blurting out a question as if he had been permitted to take the floor. "Where is this place where Manako-uri has planted vegetables?" he asked, "And where is he?" The questions burst out of him like a great spout of a whale coming up from the deep.

Langlois, alarmed, said to François under his breath, "Idiotic imbecile, you have no right to speak." But he said nothing to counter François directly before the chiefs, afraid perhaps that it would not seem good for the French to show disunity.

It felt as if everything fell quiet, even the sound of the sea and the breeze, and everyone there on deck was staring at him. So

François continued, with Father Comte worriedly translating. "You said, sir chief, that there was a bay on the peninsula where Manako-uri grows his vegetables. Then surely Manako-uri should be here. Is this not the man who has served on French whaling ships, who used to grow vegetables here in Akaroa Harbour and goes by the name of Matthieu Le Bon?"

The chief drew himself up and looked at François with seriousness. His reply was brief and, translated, was simply, "Manako-uri, of my *hapū*, has gone away, but I... Iwikau... will protect his plantations, and I... Iwikau... will protect his honour. The place called Katawahu is not for the French and not for the English, and not for the people of Onuku. It is for Manako-uri and his *whānau* to grow what they want to grow and to live apart, undisturbed."

"Manako-uri is a friend of France," said François, loudly, to everyone. "And France is a friend of Manako-uri, and everyone who trusts him. What happened to his people, your people, here in Akaroa Harbour, will never happen again as long as we are here with our ships and cannon. No matter what you've been promised by the British, it's we, the French, who are here in this bay at this time. It's we who will care for this earth and these waters, and we are your friends, as Manako-uri is my friend. Allow us to live here and you will be protected."

François felt the ship dip and the wind blow, and he could almost touch the amazement of all the French deputation on the *Comte de Paris*, that he – the blacksmith François Lelièvre – who had always been so quiet and detached, a man they had probably not even noticed, would suddenly open his mouth and speak like a warrior in the middle of this assembly of chiefs, in front of Commandant Lavaud and the officers of the *Aube*, in front of Captain Langlois and Belligny. This was his moment. He heard the sound of the priest translating. He looked at Father Comte for a few seconds as he spoke, and then he looked at the woman in grey who stood there, who looked back at him now, with those blue eyes, in a manner that seemed to him to be admiring. He could hardly look away.

The chiefs began to talk among themselves. His utterance caused a discussion, which led to an agreement. There was a new piece of paper signed. It was agreed that an area of land on the southern side of the peninsula – around Peraki and Hoiho bays, but excluding the whaling stations – would be retained by the New Zealanders, as well as land in the easternmost of the northern bays. Other *Pākehā*-occupied and *tapu* land was also excluded, though the issue of the *tapu* land in Takapuneke they would take up with the British, since a British farmer was occupying it. There was sale of land within Pigeon Bay and other places, though from the oral pronouncements it seemed unclear to François, and it felt to him that Father Comte and Hiromi were struggling at times to understand the dialect of these southern Maori.

Langlois and Belligny affirmed to each other that this clearly meant the sale of thirty thousand acres of Banks Peninsula and shook on it. The area of the French colony in Paka Ariki Bay would belong to the French. The total price was now six thousand francs. More items from the *Comte de Paris* were distributed. The documents were written prior to anyone's signature being added this time. It was read out in French and in Maori. It was agreed to and signed by the chiefs, including Tuauau. Since it was conceived as an endorsement, it was dated by Lavaud to August 2, 1838, to ensure that under scrutiny from the British it would hold as a prior deed, before the time the British declared their sovereignty over the island. It was a case of making good a previous agreement that was somehow not quite right as a whole. It was not a completely new arrangement.

Despite the celebration, Langlois hit François on the arm.

"Fool, you could have wrecked everything. Never do that again. If you were still my blacksmith I'd have you lashed for insolence."

*

Marianne was fascinated by the man who spoke so passionately of his friendship with a Maori of this place. Who was he? How had he become friends with a New Zealander who did not appear in the assembly? She was struck by the fact too that the man had looked at her, while Father Comte translated, and noticed her.

"Who was that, Jean-Baptiste?" she asked Father Comte, as they waited their turn to leave the ship. "Who was the man next to Captain Langlois that spoke to Iwikau? Him, over there."

He seemed to be loitering, talking a little with Captain Langlois, who was hitting him on the arm. He was well-built and quite good-looking, though with heavy eye-lids that made him look as if he'd just woken from a nap.

"Ah, you must be careful of him," Jean-Baptiste replied. "François Lelièvre is not a colonist. He's a blacksmith, and a Bonapartist. The colonists like him, but many of them also have Bonapartist sympathies. He has shown no interest in the Church."

"How has he come to be friends with a Maori?"

"I've heard he worked with the whalers and came here two years ago. He knows this place better than anyone, and has a little hut up the stream somewhere. He's a curious man, something of a loner, they say. He's never really been one to speak very much before, at least not to me."

Marianne glanced away as she noticed this man returning an interested gaze back at her. She kept close to Jean-Baptiste Comte and left the ship by the ladder to the boat trying not to look at him again.

The next day the Marists made a decision to leave the *Aube*. In order to ally themselves more closely with their Catholic flock, as well as to make better progress talking with the Maori, they could no longer live on the naval ship, which was still associated with compromise with the British.

This was a relief to Marianne, since her life on board the *Aube*, after her conversation with Robinson, was fraught. She was continually vigilant, fearful she would run into the British magistrate. They met only fleetingly, fortunately, but every time he looked at her she felt a stab of fear. It felt as if he was indicating, by his manner, a certain knowledge about her. It was as if he was saying, 'I know what you are, and you are not what you seem.'

14
Charles Barrington Robinson

The Marists' transfer to live on land was completed easily, and – after the blessings – they entered two sleeping huts made out of timber posts and latticed *toitoi*, with branches and rushes forming the roof. This hybrid construction was the result of the careful collaboration between Hiromi and Brother Florentin. In one hut, built high enough to stand in though the door was low, the four men arranged themselves around a central hearth, and in a smaller, low hut beside it, which was more like a wooden tent, Marianne crawled through the doorway into a dark, windowless space where there was a woven flax mat, to serve as a mattress, on the beaten earth floor. She felt as if she'd become a Maori, living in a *whare*. In addition, there was a small oratory and a large communal house to serve as a dining hall and a school room, though it was not quite finished.

Jean-Baptiste gave hearty congratulations to Brother Florentin and Hiromi for their clearing of this land and the construction of such excellent housing, though Father Pezant asked him later how long they would have to live in houses made of 'grass'. Father Pezant exuded a manner of growing discontent. He was concerned about the political situation and settlement, feeling that the Commandant was acting against the interests of France. He became more disgruntled, and voiced political statements that Jean-Baptiste felt were not as disengaged as Bishop Pompallier would have wanted. The priests should show impartiality. "Blessed are the peacemakers," he said to Father Pezant. In Jean-Baptiste's dealings with the Malmanche family he'd worked hard to stress the good faith and hopes of their leaders. Father Pezant did not dispute this, but simply insisted that if they needed further protection from the elements – in the event of a storm against which the huts provided scanty shelter – they would take refuge in the *Comte de Paris*, not the *Aube*.

On Sunday, September 13, about a month after their arrival, there were the baptisms of baby Isidore Libeau, born at sea, and

– surprisingly – of Abner and Mary, the two children of James Robinson Clough and Puai, the cousin of Iwikau, as well as two other babies born of unions between Englishmen and New Zealand women. One named Thomas, after his father, and the other, a girl named Mary Anne, taking the name from Marianne, who had held the baby without a thought that this would be the consequence. Jean-Baptiste Comte was heartened by the eagerness and friendliness of these English-Maori couples, though slightly concerned about the ecclesiastical issues, recording in the register that he'd baptised them as Catholic – despite their parents being 'of the Protestant heresy' – simply and without ceremony, 'because of the recognised danger of death to small children'.

With these auspicious deeds the weather turned warm. It switched from cold to heat with no in between. A warm northerly melted away the snow, and yellow *kowhai* flowers blossomed. This change had an immediate effect on everyone, and on the soil. Seedlings were sprouting everywhere. In the days that followed, the tents dried out, more wood became usable, the oratory became less make-shift, and the priests made good progress on the school room.

As the last whaling ships began to leave at the end of the whaling season, the priests received a letter, delivered by means of a French whaler. It was from Bishop Pompallier, replying to letters they had written that had been sent back with Captain Stanley. While there was only so much they could trust to paper in the circumstances, they had communicated the main thrust of the extraordinary stand-off that had taken place. Bishop Pompallier replied that he was very happy to receive news, and thanked God that they were all well. He would come to visit them at the beginning of October.

"So soon!" exclaimed Jean-Baptiste. "We have hardly begun!" He'd wanted to make much better progress with conversions, and constructions, before the bishop made an inspection. Father Pezant, on the other hand, was pleased, as he wanted to give the bishop a full account of the political situation. "And this is also wonderful," he said, "because Monsignor can consecrate the cemetery, and encourage the building of the church. Perhaps he can convince Commandant Lavaud that some sailors can be spared for the task."

Marianne was sent into a spin of fear, given what she now knew of Wand's story. Robinson would have told Belligny, and Belligny would have told Commandant Lavaud.

What would it look like to Robinson, and his allies on the British side of the town, when Bishop Pompallier came here? They would scoff and say that the bishop couldn't live without his little plaything.

She felt desperately sorry for Jean-Baptiste, who worked so earnestly and in such good faith, daily making visits now to the people of Onuku and elsewhere, labouring, planning. She felt personally responsible for tarnishing Bishop Pompallier's name, and of limiting the effectiveness of the whole task of spreading the message of Christ to the Maori.

It seemed she'd come down to earth, as if she'd been in some way floating above it, caught up in the lightness of Heaven, a sheltered haven within the Mission. The hut smelt of earth. It made her wonder about herself and what she was doing. Did she really belong to the Mission? Earthly feelings surfaced too, as she woke from dreams in which François Lelièvre would play a carnal part. Over the following days she lay awake at night, worrying. She longed to see the kind bishop, but the thought of Robinson's sneering was the serpent in this Eden of reunion.

In the end, out in the real garden planting seedlings in the ground, she straightened up and told Jean-Baptiste of her predicament: every word that Robinson had said, and her experience at the Wand household. It was not a confession, simply a sharing between two friends.

Jean-Baptiste was disturbed. He said he'd learnt nothing of this, but, after all, he'd been in the Hokianga, where there were several French Catholics, and what passed around the Bay among the British was unknown to him.

"But Monsignor surely knows what people say," said Marianne.

Jean-Baptiste accepted that he knew there were many slurs on the good name of the bishop. If his enemies could attack his propriety in any way, they would. "And he has chosen to come here, to Port Louis-Philippe, despite this," affirmed Jean-Baptiste, "so you must not be alarmed. Monsignor will have decided to spend no time thinking of the malicious things people say about him. If it bothered him he would not have decided to visit us so soon."

"And you, Jean-Baptiste? If I'm a temptress, do you worry what people might say of you?"

At this the fair-haired young priest hesitated. Indeed, his whole life was dedicated to love and personal sacrifice, in order to be a true servant of God. Marianne watched a shadow fall on his face. For him, to be successful in his mission was everything. He wanted to tell her such rumours were of no consequence, but in the struggle for the hearts and minds of the Maori, the reputation of the Mission and its honour – its *mana*, as he called it – was very significant indeed. How could a Mission flourish if it was said to be tainted by immorality? He couldn't hide that fleeting cloud, though he said, "I'm not worried."

Marianne stepped away and looked up at the hill behind the mission house, now called Aube Hill, to where the cemetery had been designated further up. Oh God, how long before this weary life was over and she would be put down to lie forever there in peace?

"Really, Marianne," said Jean-Baptiste, "Don't think about these things." Jean-Baptiste walked away and flung his spade hard into the ground.

She turned back to planting some sprouting bulbs she'd been given at the Kororareka Mission: daffodils, jonquils, grape hyacinths. Was she being stupid? How could you preserve your reputation? How could someone like her do that? Someone like her! If they only knew! She thought of herself at the weeping willow, with James Placard, two years ago. What a life she'd had since that moment when she'd succumbed, out of love and passion, and fallen like Eve.

But now where was she? She sat back on her haunches as she dug and looked around: her world had become this shoreline, with its narrow beach, the string of little houses under construction, the main building of the naval office and the Magasin. Outside Paka Ariki Bay this world stretched north to Takamatua where the Germans had settled and operated the sawmills, and south to Green's Point, beyond which was the Maori village she'd not visited. She could count twelve houses in her line of vision, though there were others obscured by trees and up the stream. She looked over the Navy garden to see the distant, bent form of Madame Libeau digging up fern roots to clear the Libeau town plot for more planting, with her baby Isidore sitting on a blanket nearby.

And then she got up and hurried after Jean-Baptiste, catching him as he was washing his hands in a bucket. "Perhaps I should go, Jean-Baptiste. I should not live in the same place as you. I could ask to stay with one of the families and help them... the further away I am the better for you, and for the Mission. I could come everyday with water and make lunch, enough for dinner as well, as I do now. I could do the washing. There's not much cleaning to do in these huts, and I could do that. You'd get your own supplies. But if I stay to help you for much longer I'm afraid that in the end I won't help you."

"You would leave the Mission?" he asked, crestfallen. "What about the school?"

Marianne looked away, to the whaling ships in the harbour, the *Aube*, and the *Comte de Paris*: a little city of ships far more populated and sophisticated than anything on shore. They reminded her of the cluster of ships at Wivenhoe, and a world she left behind, the person that she was. 'I want to be an independent teacher,' she wished she could say. 'I need to earn my own living, separately. I need to forge my own life.'

"Jean-Baptiste, how can I be part of the Mission when there are people who think of me as a... ?"

"Listen, this is madness now. You are part of the Mission, because Monsignor has sent you here."

Marianne looked down. The last thing she wanted to do was disappoint Bishop Pompallier.

"Please, Marianne. Wait, and talk to him."

*

During the next weeks something happened among the colonists: they went from worry to anger. They did not understand why the territory of 'France' across the stream should be allocated partly to Britain and British settlers, ostensibly to deal with British settlers and whaling ships. What Lavaud considered a success, and a necessary basis for future negotiations with the British, the colonists saw as another step in the direction of a total sell-out.

In one of the larger tents they assembled with a spirit of revolution. "Lavaud has used Captain Langlois to create a document he can use to sell our land to the British," said Libeau, feistier than ever and seeming taller than his height. "Why has he allowed the British to build their magistrate's office in Akaroa, if he really sees our land as French? It's we who will be betrayed. We will discover we have emigrated to England, not to a new France. We will become subjects of the British Queen!"

The apparent compromise of Commandant Lavaud seemed to be obvious from the fact that not only had he invited the British magistrate to stay on board the *Aube*, but – when Belligny's accommodation was built – he was invited to live there, with Belligny. The clear division between British and French sections on shore was one thing, but Robinson seemed to think he had a perfectly welcome place in the French area, and walked around as if he was joint mayor. He went on botanic expeditions with Belligny and Dr Raoul. Robinson soon had three constables to police the British whalers and settlers around the peninsula effectively, and indeed a number of British settlers had arrived over the past weeks. His office was built well to look imposing and permanent. The cosy relationship between Belligny and Robinson was viewed, not as Lavaud and Belligny doing their best to stay on the right side of a potentially troublesome man, but as a kind of treachery.

"Belligny and Robinson become closer every day. They go off on walks like a couple of newlyweds in the woods!" said Éteveneaux.

In the last week of September another public meeting was called by the colonists, which became a sombre march of protest to the naval headquarters. Captain Langlois stayed on board ship, for diplomatic reasons, and left it to the settlers. They trudged silently from the tents, with determination and a sense of justice resting on their side. They went into the naval compound without asking permission, pushing past the guards by sheer force of numbers – men, women and children together. They marched right through to the building. In the front reception room the key men representing the settlers confronted Commandant Lavaud and Belligny, who came out to meet them, looking astounded.

Standing firm, the colonists made formal complaints to Commandant Lavaud, stated bravely by Joseph Libeau. They expressed their firm support for Captain Langlois. They asked for a representative government through a free election by the French people of the settlement. As French citizens they were landholders entitled to vote for their own leaders. They had rights and they knew it. Libeau then handed their demands to the Royal Commissioner, all written down neatly by Malmanche on a piece of paper.

Standing behind Libeau, François saw the Commandant's face redden with rage as he received it. He could put up with everything except insurrection. The people's marches of Paris would not be replicated here, not on his watch.

Lavaud had been at sea for many years as commander of his ship, in which his word was law, and he had the power to execute offenders. Disobedience was not tolerated for an instant. The settlers' demands, at this stressful time, seemed to him like mutiny. Lavaud was a man who never looked as if he lost his temper. He was dignified, careful and considered. But this was too much.

He left the room, followed by Belligny, closing a door behind him, but the wooden walls were too thin to stop his voice booming through.

"Who do they think they are?" he shouted to Belligny. "Uneducated peasants! They want the right to vote. They should prove they have any rational faculties at all before claiming the right to exercise them! They don't have the foggiest understanding of what I've been through, or what's required to manage a situation like this. Thankless imbeciles! The Nanto-Bordelaise Company should never have permitted this class of people to settle New Zealand."

Then another door was slammed. The colonists turned to each other in a mixture of fear and outrage. "That's what he thinks of us," said Libeau. "Now we know."

The commandant's response was swift. He put Libeau in irons on board the *Aube* for five days as the supposed ringleader of the revolt. Despite Captain Langlois' vociferous protests, curses and threats, Lavaud would not relent on his decision to punish Libeau, or accept any further petitions from the settlers who, from henceforth, so he said, needed to abide by his law or submit to much fiercer punishment than irons.

One moment fired by the spirit of the Republic, the next moment defeated, the colonists were terrified again. Madeleine Libeau was left on her own in their new, partially built dwelling, with two children and a baby, though Marianne came to help her. As if to underline the cruelty of everything, there were sudden hailstorms that damaged tiny seedlings and clattered on wood, as if invisible beings were throwing stones at the settlement. François thought of the old spirits of this land, the gods that Matthieu talked of which protected every rock and stream and tree and vegetable. If Tāne had allowed his willow to grow and the spirit of Napoleon to flourish, what if there were other spirits who wanted to vanquish this? What if all the spirits of this country were at war, like the tribes who lived here? How could there be any guarantee?

François fretted about these things all the days that Libeau was in irons, in his own filth, on board the *Aube*. He knew what this punishment involved, and it made him sick to think of a decent, spirited gardener like Libeau, who had never been toughened by the sailor's life, having to endure this trial. The hail stopped, and started, and then rain swelled the mud. The settlers were silenced. When Libeau was released François went to visit him, while his wife poured water and scrubbed him down, and commented to him that he was lucky he hadn't been lashed. Libeau scoffed at this, but François had only one answer. He lifted his shirt and showed his back.

The settlers felt they had no other course but to submit. Their revenge on Lavaud, and on the British, would be by staying, by building houses and clearing land, by doggedly pulling out the deep fern roots – which they ate for food, like the Maori – by planting and reaping, and having children, and somehow, sometime in the future, there would be a reckoning, and this place would be run the way they wanted it to be run. They would no longer be oppressed.

Nevertheless, there were those who wanted to go back to France right away, and could barely tolerate the circumstances. Anne David could not leave her bed in the flapping tents, even when a little house of sorts was built for her by her husband Guillaume. Their twelve-year-old daughter Marguerite, and eight-year-old son, Jean, sat in vigil with her, until eventually she took some steps out to look at the sea. "We are going to die here," she said, and fainted. It was another four days until she walked out again. This was the first time François had used his box of herbs for other people, crumbling dried valerian root he had into some warm milk from Mr Green's cows, milk being the only thing Anne David seemed to be able to consume, so that day by day this frail woman learnt what it was like to leave the tent without trembling. She went out, walking up and down the foreshore until the colour came back to her cheeks, and then, finally, she went to the house. François saw her drawing water from the stream to wash and cook, like the other women. She did not ask for any further valerian, and no one mentioned her collapse.

It was shocking to François to recognise the hardship suffered all around by his French compatriots. He wished they would still take heart from the willow. If only Matthieu would return to affirm it. Perhaps he would be able to say something. No one knew where he was, but it was curious that his vegetables were growing in a bay on the peninsula. Should he visit and talk to the people there who were part of Matthieu's family? They were not all dead? Had he married again? Once the weather was more reliable and the ground less wet and muddy perhaps he would, he thought. He'd go overland. It would take perhaps two days, allowing for the difficulty of finding out how to get there, and given the steep ascent through the bush. He would have to find his way upstream, through the towering trees called *kahikatea*, *tōtara* and *matai*, through the tree ferns and vines where he and Matthieu had caught wood pigeon together, and onwards, upwards to trees he did not know on the summit of the peaks above seven hundred metres in height, and how far then would he have to walk on the other side to find Matthieu Le Bon's bay?

François was cheered by one thing. During September there had been considerable improvement in relations with the people of Onuku, who provided the settlers with vegetables, fish, pigs, pigeons and all kinds of skills. The settlers came to know the route leading five kilometres south to the *kainga* – the village – pronounced *kaika*, or 'the Kaik' for short. You could walk there in just over an hour. He felt certain that a good relationship between the New Zealanders and the French was necessary for their future; as he and Matthieu had become friends, so other friendships could be forged.

François had his own personal goals: he worked every minute of every day to build single-handedly a one-room house out of his *whare*, with a proper door, windows with shutters to the front and the back, and a proper wooden floor, though the roof was still made of trunks and reeds. He had a purpose. He had in mind a particular invitation.

He watched her, Marianne Blake, going and coming as she came up from Aube Hill to the Magasin, and helping *Madame* Libeau. His blacksmith hut was close to the store on the other side of the road, and when she came out he'd always greet her now, with a respectful "Good-day, Madame", so that she couldn't consider this anything but politeness, though he felt there was always something special in it. In the store she could spend a long time negotiating with Aimable Langlois, the proprietor and brother of Captain Langlois, regarding goods from the Nanto-Bordelaise Company that he kept very careful watch over. Now the sun shone more often and the weather was milder Marianne Blake did not wear her scarf, but wore her head bare like the colonist women. She'd started to teach some of the girls of the settlement in a school house the priests had made, and so greeted mothers and children as she passed in a way that François felt was rather gentle and cautious and sweet.

When he lay down on his mat at night he wondered how he would build a proper bed, with a real mattress, and he thought of Marianne lying on it.

He wondered how on earth he could manage to prise her away from the Mission. How could he, a Bonapartist, a blacksmith with no allocation of land from the Nanto-Bordelaise Company but only a lease he'd have to pay for, have any chance with a pious widow like Marianne Blake? How could he even be thinking of a woman like her?

*

It was on the first warm day of October that Marianne received a summons from the British magistrate, delivered by hand by a huge, boorish constable who swaggered up to the Mission like he was coming into a public house.

"Mrs Blake," he said, with a London accent. "A letter for you from the magistrate."

As Marianne opened the letter she thought how Robinson must have been waiting for just the right time to assert his authority over her.

Mrs Blake,

I am required to inform you in my capacity as magistrate to the British residents of the town of Akaroa, under the terms of my appointment by Lieutenant-Governor Hobson, that your status as a British subject requires you to be registered forthwith at my office at your earliest convenience. I await the prompt presentation of all relevant papers and your attendance in person.

Yours &c,

C. B. Robinson

Despite this being a short and straightforward note, Marianne read it several times, with the constable waiting. She was in the middle of cooking the midday meal, as she always did, under an unwalled shelter where there was a table with stools around it, her iron bucket for water, and a metal tripod with a large single pot hanging from the apex over a fire. She'd hung utensils and equipment, such as they were, from an overhead beam, or rather log. She'd become an expert at single pot cooking: wrapping *weka*, wood pigeon, or fish, in *pūhā* leaves to steam while the potatoes and fern root cooked beneath. While they received ship's biscuit and dried food from the *Aube* supplies, among other things, Jean-Baptiste had brought back information from the Kaik, Onuku, on how the local people cooked and what they ate, and Marianne had found it far better to eat as they did, when Hiromi could catch birds or fish. It was certainly a practical use of fern roots to consume all these pulled out for the sake of planting European vegetation, and they were not totally dissimilar to parsnips, though chewier.

"You can tell Mr Robinson that I'll come right away, this afternoon," said Marianne, matter-of-factly. "I'll feed everyone here and clean up, and then I'll present my papers to him as he has requested."

She went back to the pot, checking the heat, taking a poker and stoking the flame.

"Quite some little establishment you've built here," said the surly constable.

"Everybody's working hard to make the best of things," replied Marianne.

"What're you doing here then, in French Town, when you're English?"

Then she looked at the constable sternly and used her school-mistress voice. "You'd better go and tell Mr Robinson what I've told you. I'll come this afternoon. I'm working now."

He leered at her and stepped too close. "Goodbye then, Mrs Blake," he said, looking at her up and down, before walking off down the slope, on past the French naval headquarters and along the road that led south to what felt like little England, beyond the ditch of the Paka Ariki stream which had become, symbolically, the Channel.

He knows of my reputation too, thought Marianne. Soon, everyone will know.

*

After lunch Marianne tidied and washed up quickly, and spent a long time – relatively speaking – getting ready. The Mission had a privy near some trees and a lean-to behind it where there were two big jugs of water and a bowl shielded by hanging canvas sheets. Keeping this in order was one of her tasks as housekeeper. She went down to the stream for fresh water and spent about half an hour carefully washing herself with tar soap, drying, and making sure her fingernails were clean and short. She combed her long dark hair well, and put it up into a tighter bun. Then she changed into her black dress, and out of the grey, which was at any rate in need of thorough laundering.

She took her bag and marched down the hill, crossing over the stream by the newly-constructed bridge, passing wooden hous-es where she had not gone before. The headquarters of the British magistracy rose like a castle in the centre. In it, there was a reception room where the constable sat polishing a gun. Marianne stood be-fore him, as he did not rise to greet her when she announced that she had come as requested. The constable slowly got up and knocked on a door, said her name to the man within, and cocked his head to indicate she could enter. She walked into a room with an incongru-ously gleaming walnut desk, with bookcases full of green and red legal tomes. Behind the desk sat Charles Barrington Robinson.

He stood as Marianne entered the room and offered her a seat.

Marianne sat down primly and put her carpet bag on her lap. She hoped she looked respectable. Opening her bag, she took out her papers carefully and put them on the desk. Then she sat and waited as the magistrate looked carefully through each one and took notes. She saw her certificate of baptism being scrutinised by his cold eyes. She looked around the room, observing the Union Jack, a painting of Queen Victoria and a small pile of *Times* newspapers which made her yearn to read them.

Finally Robinson spoke. "You were baptised a Catholic in Westminster. But your voice is not a London voice." His tone was laconic. Marianne had to stop herself visibly bristling.

"No, I was born in Wivenhoe, on the Colne, in Essex, and lived there until the year 1837, when I had the opportunity to take a passage to Sydney Town with my fiancé. There's my certificate of immigration, with my marriage certificate from the ship." Marianne tried to seem co-operative and pleasant.

"Why did your parents take you all the way to London for baptism? Do you have relatives there?"

Marianne knew the story well; she'd had to explain it when she'd become a Congregationalist teacher. The Congregationalists didn't mind what she'd been before, as long as she was a dissenter now and was confirmed as such by them. When she was baptised as a baby, there'd been no Catholic priests in Colchester, or even in Chelmsford. For twenty-five years before her birth, Catholics had been able to hold services legally in England, but there were still restrictions. It would have been a hard, clandestine journey with a little baby, by boat from Wivenhoe down the Colne to the Thames, and then inland past Canvey Island to the London docks. That was how much it mattered to her mother that she should be baptised into the Catholic Church, even though she had not pursued her confirmation; there was no mass to attend anywhere close by, and by then her mother was ill. Was she going to explain all that to Robinson?

"No, I don't have relatives in London," she said, simply. He should know the situation for Catholics, she thought.

"I just wondered if your mother had been working there prior to her... marriage."

Marianne tried not to react. Robinson was implying her mother was one of the French prostitutes of Canary Wharf brought back after Napoleon's defeat. The French brothels were a favourite haunt of sailors.

"No," she said. "My mother was a seamstress in La Rochelle. My parents met there, after Waterloo."

Robinson smiled a little knowingly and looked at the death certificates. Then, looking up after a time, he said, "I hear that Mr Pompallier is paying us a visit."

Marianne tried not to look in the least bit bothered by the term 'Mr'. It was one of those English laws, of course, that no Catholic was allowed to take the name 'Bishop'. Only Anglican Bishops were permitted. Robinson, clearly, would not think he was being insulting here; he was just taking recourse to what was correct according to the law.

"Yes," replied Marianne. The less said the better.

"We are to expect him very soon, I understand," said Robinson.

Was this the reason he'd requested her papers now, because he wanted to know more? "I understand he will be coming very soon, yes," said Marianne.

"Now, tell me, Mrs Blake. There is something I would like to know."

"Yes, Mr Robinson?"

"The Marists are an order, are they not, like the Jesuits, or the Franciscans, or any other order of Roman Catholics?"

"I believe that is so, though they are recently founded."

"Indeed. But their evangelism here in New Zealand is not intended to make the natives into Marists, only to make them Roman Catholic. Correct?"

"That is right." Marianne fidgeted with irritation.

"Because of course the deliberate admission of any male British subject into a Roman religious order is of course a punishable offence by British law, and the natives of New Zealand will... if all is approved... become British subjects."

"I'm sure the priests of the Mission in Port Louis-Philippe are well aware of the laws of Great Britain and Ireland, Mr Robinson," said Marianne, tightly. She wondered then if that were so, and thought of Hiromi, and then of Mayor Belligny's position. "I trust *Monsieur* Belligny confirms the same understanding of the situation."

At this Robinson smiled and said, coolly, "Of course. Monsieur Belligny is a most educated and scientific man, a humanist like myself and Dr Raoul, with a sure grasp of all matters relating to Roman Catholics."

Marianne tried not to look at Robinson, or react hotly to his tone. She glanced around the room at the Union Jack, the picture of Queen Victoria on the wall and the large wooden filing cabinet. Do not be provoked, she told herself. She tried not to look uncomfortable. She had to keep calm.

"Tell me, why is Mr Pompallier visiting?" asked Robinson, then, seeing as Marianne was saying nothing.

"I don't know," she said. She looked at Robinson's humourless face. She imagined him smirking as Charles Wand told his tale. "Have you finished with my papers, sir, as I need to return to the Mission?"

"You don't know," said Robinson, as if she was being purposefully idiotic. Then he abruptly scribbled something else down on his piece of paper.

Marianne waited for him to finish, watching him dip his pen in ink and write carefully.

Then Robinson picked up her papers, shuffled them and put them next to a heavy green volume to his right. "I'll keep these for the time being, thank you Mrs Blake. They will be returned in due course."

Marianne hesitated. The idea of Robinson holding on to her precious papers, especially the death certificates of her mother, father and Tim, made her want to throw her bag at him and scream. He was obviously a man who liked to be in control, and for others to know that he was in control. He had every right as magistrate to hold her papers, to make as many checks as he wanted. She was an anomaly, and needed to be investigated.

It was better to obey him, or he would turn nastier. Therefore, she summoned up composure, stood up and said, "Certainly, Mr Robinson. Good afternoon, and... if you happen to write to Mr Wand, do please pass on my regards to Betty."

Robinson did not get up to open the door. He stayed sitting, and leaned back with an expression of slight surprise. "To Betty?"

"Yes."

"Do you not know then?" Robinson's expression was almost serious now.

Marianne felt as if he'd thrown something after her.

He continued: "Betty Wand died of a fever, in August, not long before the *Britomart* departed from Banks Peninsula. Thankfully, the rest of the family were spared."

Marianne swallowed, struggling to retain an impassive exterior. She nodded, as if she had to agree to the shock and let it in. After a moment, when she thought she could control her voice, she said only, "Then please pass on my condolences." She said this to the bare boards of the floor, turned and left.

*

On the shore, Marianne stood looking at the huge ships with their masses of ropes and the curving forms of the forested hills. The birds sung, squawked and called in the distance, hidden by trees all around, while swirls of seagulls cawed nearby. She'd walked along the curving shore all the way from English Town and stopped beyond the French jetty, not far from where the stream, now rather grandly termed Aube River, debouched.

Poor Betty. Little Betty. And her letters to her had never been received. Had the last one been successfully handed to her?

She tried to make her mind think in holy ways, that Betty was now with God and her soul would surely be viewed with all the compassion of Heaven. She was just fifteen, after all, just a girl full of dreams of love and marriage. So much for Captain Symonds. She was too good for him anyway.

But she couldn't make herself think in this way. She felt mainly regret, loss and a guilt that stabbed hard in her gut. She'd preserved herself, in fleeing from the Wands, and left Betty to fend for herself, with a fragile mother and a selfish father, who'd uprooted her from Sydney and transplanted her to the Bay, where she was not strong enough to endure new forms of pestilence. Yet she'd once survived the very thing that had killed Tim.

Marianne berated herself for not thinking enough about Betty while she was at the Mission. She'd just run away from her, and run even further to this point in the world, to this place where the British and the French paced around each other so strangely and sweet-talked the Maori, cagily promising and manipulating and cajoling for their own ends.

She looked along the beach at the dark brown and grey rocks, covered with lichen and whelks, and breathed in the strong smell of seaweed, which lay spread like thin green paper, or red branches, or great brown belts piled in mounds. Little clouds of midges danced around in the air. In this curious auditorium of hills, voices from ships carried far, so that she could hear sailors swearing and someone singing in the *Comte de Paris*, perhaps Captain Langlois, who kept to himself there these days after the failed 'revolution', since it was said Lavaud had threatened to charge him with treason. The sea was still and green, and lapped gently on the foreshore.

She stood, not wanting to walk on and return to the Mission while she was still at risk of sobbing. She must not do that. Everyone suffered loss, because life was full of trials. This was God's way of directing us to eternal truth and everlasting realities. Everything passed. This grief and guilt was to remind her to be careful and live a good Christian life without too much attachment, giving compassion freely, yet remembering that we are all dust. God created from dust, and we will return to dust. We fly as little specks for a time; that is all.

"Madame Blake," came a voice then. "Madame Blake. Are you leaving?"

Marianne turned to see a figure, a man, François Lelièvre coming towards her, crunching along the shore, his hands black from his work, his face anxious.

She felt embarrassed. Leaving? What did he mean? Then she realised: she was standing on the shore with her empty bag. She'd put the papers in it for protection and privacy.

"No, no," she said, trying not to seem so miserable, though the corners of her mouth would not be controlled. "I had to go to the English magistrate with... various things."

"Ah," he seemed concerned. "I thought you might be waiting for a boat to Port Cooper."

"No," she said, looking out to ships, and canoes. Oh, she was going to cry. "I'm just going back to the Mission."

"All right," he said. "That's fine. So... I hope... you are well."

"Yes, thank you. I'm very well." She glanced at him and looked away miserably.

"Why did you go to the English magistrate?" he asked then, perplexed. He seemed to be a man who asked direct questions if necessary.

"I... had to present my papers," she said, "because I'm English."

He seemed baffled to hear this. "I understand that your husband was English."

"He was a British resident of New South Wales, born there," she said, trying to cough away her tears, "but I was born in England. My father was English, though my mother was French. My duty is to obey the regulations set by Mr Robinson for the British residents of Akaroa." Marianne used the term for the whole settlement, rather than 'Port Louis-Philippe'.

"But you live in the French town."

"The French town is not France," said Marianne.

"Yes, yes, it is France," affirmed François Lelièvre, "and a British resident of France is subject to French law, not British law. This is how it is in all the ports of France, when there are sailors from all over the world. If a man transgresses, then he is brought to a French court. If a man is accused, he has rights and privileges under French law. The only difference is that if you are convicted, you may be expelled to your own country. You are here in France under the authority of Commandant Lavaud, not under the authority of Robinson. This is true, no matter what Robinson and Belligny have agreed over their walks together." François Lelièvre seemed exercised about her rights.

His words brought some relief and hope, despite her sorrow for Betty. She liked it that the blacksmith was so protective of her.

"I should go back now," she said.

"No, really. You don't believe me? This is France. If you come to my house, I will show you why this must be France... true France, not the France of King Louis-Philippe. This is a place for freedom and equality, not for oppression, no matter what Commandant Lavaud does to us. Perhaps now it seems that the despots rule, but they will not rule forever here. The people will triumph against them. You don't need to fear our present leaders, whether they come in the name of the royal rulers of France or of England."

Marianne was slightly taken aback now by the zealousness in François Lelièvre's face. But then, he was a Bonapartist, Jean-Baptiste had said. In truth, she did not truly know what this meant. She realised it indicated that he supported Napoleon, who'd wanted to conquer the whole of Europe, but what this meant politically, in France, she had no idea. Her mother and father despised Napoleon. Her father had fought against him. The priests clearly did not like Bonapartists, as they were not favourable to the Catholic religion, as a rule, and the Pope had wanted to overthrow Napoleon. But she liked what François Lelièvre said now about freedom and equality. Perhaps to talk to him at his house would be a way of finding out more for herself. And, at any rate, she couldn't deny there was something fascinating about François Lelièvre, a man who would speak at an assembly, claim a Maori as a friend, and enter her dreams.

"I will make you tea and cake, if you would like to come to visit me," said the blacksmith, as she demurred.

"Tea and cake?"

"Of a kind. You will see." He smiled a little.

Marianne pursed her lips and looked at the sand.

"I can ask the priests for permission," he suggested, worriedly, "if it's improper to ask you, and perhaps Father Comte can accompany you, if it's–"

"No, no, that is not necessary," replied Marianne. "But Bishop Pompallier is coming to visit and arriving any day. There is much to do to prepare, and while he is here I'll be completely occupied. However, perhaps afterwards I can visit you at your house. Thank you for the invitation."

She stepped back and started to walk away. "Goodbye, *Monsieur* Lelièvre."

"Goodbye," he said.

She felt heartened. What a strange thing, to find she had another friend. But Jean-Baptiste and this blacksmith couldn't be more different, and her feelings for each were, likewise, dissimiliar.

15
Bishop Pompallier

Next morning, on Friday, October 2, 1840, Bishop Pompallier arrived in Akaroa Harbour on board his schooner, the *Sancta Maria*.

As the low ship anchored off Paka Ariki Bay, now called French Bay, the priests and Hiromi quickly made ready and rowed out to welcome him. Brother Florentin was at German Bay ordering wood from the sawmillers there. Marianne remained at the Mission doing the usual housework, fetching water, washing towels and undergarments and hanging out linen; it was a relief that she did not need to make a lunch because they had assured her they would eat on board the ship with Monsignor. To her dismay, she'd bled heavily in the night and had now had a bucket of bloodied rags to soak. Only rarely since coming to the southern hemisphere did she have this to deal with. Since losing James Placard's child, it had felt as if her womb had shrivelled up. This blood, a portent of life, indicated to her a readiness for pregnancy, as if it were an earthly warning that her celibate, unmarried state ran counter to nature.

It left her feeling dragged and drained, both mentally and physically, as deep cramps pulled inside. She had to change her rags constantly and was worried she'd have to tear up part of her sheet or a towel if she couldn't soak, scrub and dry her supply in time for re-use. She couldn't remember ever having such a flow.

At the same time she felt left out, and the ache of longing to see Monsignor seemed to be the same in her spirit as the ache in her body. Nevertheless, she resolved that when the bishop was ready and personally asked for her, only then would she see him. There were many more important people for him to talk to, and he couldn't show any particular concern to see her, or her him. She would do what needed to be done in terms of practical matters, leaving the men with men's business. No matter how much she wanted to see Monsignor, she would not indicate to anyone that there was any reason why he should show any particular interest in her.

After the laundry was finished, she gave herself a good wash and then cleaned the wash-house behind the privy. After that, she felt overwhelmed by weariness, and went into the simple school room, now well roofed, with two wide open windows. There was no glass for the windows, or shutters, so every night they placed loose boards in slots over the cavities to stop any wind and rain coming in, and for security. In this bare, airy room there was a long table, on which all the individual Bibles opened out to a reading passage from the Book of Genesis. She laid out paper and pencils for her girls: nine-year old Catherine Libeau, tiny and truculent like her feisty father; Justine Malmanche, a bright eight-year-old; Marguerite David, six years-old, anxious like her mother; Catharina Breitmeyer, aged five, who hardly spoke French at all since the family was part of the German contingent, and Clémence Gendrot, aged five, a sad little girl who'd lost her younger sister on the long voyage. There was also sometimes Marie Judith Éteveneaux, aged fifteen, though she was often helping her mother and already had the basic educational skills for girls. The Éteveneaux family had another daughter, Marie Célestine, aged seventeen, but she was too old for education and, at any rate, rumour had it that she spent most of her spare time with the colonist Louis Veron, continuing a romance that had begun on the *Comte de Paris*, and that they would soon announce their engagement.

The girls came for school on Monday and Friday afternoons, after their household duties were done, the boys likewise on Tuesday, Wednesday and Thursday. They had about three hours, from mid afternoon until the light started to fade, with the older girls reading and writing out a set text, the younger ones learning words and small sentences, copying things.

Marianne looked around her with a feeling of terrible sadness and frustration, thinking again of Betty. Two years earlier, in 1838, she'd been a young, bright pupil with her whole life ahead of her, and at her death she was not so much older than Marie Judith. All Betty's dreams of Captain Symonds! Nothing. If only she'd seen her one last time. She said a little prayer to the Blessed Virgin Mary: "Hold her, tell her that I'm sorry."

She felt a longing for Monsignor, in his ship anchored there in the bay, now come to this place with a cloud of whispers around him. An hour alone with him would make tongues wag. Yet, an hour alone with him was what she craved, simply to talk.

And Robinson! How could he have taken such an instant dislike to her and judged her beforehand as the worst kind of woman, someone that should be punished at every opportunity?

She thought of François Lelièvre, who had touched her by the invitation to come to his house. There was something inherently good about this man. He had a reliable, decent, kind manner about him, and also something valiant and knowing, given that he could speak the way he did at the assembly. She liked his independence, and that he was not a colonist, but rather one who relied on his own personal enterprise. She would most assuredly go to visit him. Perhaps she could (dare she think it?) see him as a husband. He was strong and lithe, with an interesting face.

Sweeping aside these thoughts, she went and looked out of a window to the ships. All the eminent men would be together, deciding on gentlemanly hospitalities and formalities.

She looked back at the table, with the small Bibles ready, open to the reading page. Everything in this school room was religious. A small statue of the Blessed Virgin in prayer was at one end, on a table with candles that would be lit. The Mission was concerned with spreading the faith, after all, and teaching the word of God.

They could do with more science, and mathematics, not just reading and writing from the Bible, Marianne thought. If she moved out to live with one of the colonist families, perhaps she could get a room built for an independent school of her own, as she'd had in Sydney. She could make it open to British settlers too, once more of them arrived, and bring in Maori girls who wanted to learn French and English. It would be a school that espoused no religion or nationality and embraced all; not just Catholic, despite her own convictions, but rather a celebration of every choice, every path, even humanist. It could be a house of integration, so that all the tribes of this place, foreign and local, could come together.

She still had money left in her carpet bag. She could buy a bit of land, pay one of the German sawmillers and carpenters to cut down some trees and get him to build her a little place of her own. She had to have an hour with Monsignor alone to discuss this, and her other thoughts and fears.

She sat down at the table and looked at an open page. She read:

And the Lord God planted a garden eastward in Eden, and there he put the man whom he had made. And out of the ground the Lord God made to grow every tree that is pleasant to the sight, and good for food; the Tree of Life also in the middle of the garden, and the Tree of Knowledge of Good and Evil... And the Lord God took the man, and put him into the Garden of Eden to tend it, and keep it, and the Lord God commanded the man saying, You may eat freely of every tree of the garden, but you shall not eat of the Tree of Knowledge of Good and Evil, because on the day that you eat from it you will surely die.

Marianne decided on how she would use this text in the lesson. After they had read the passage, she would ask the children to draw a picture of the Garden of Eden. Would she ask them to draw Adam, all on his own before the woman was taken out of him, formed from his rib, wandering through looking at all the trees with all their wonderful fruit to eat? No – because he would have to be naked, and that would not be right for children. Instead, they would only draw the trees. She would remind them of what an apple tree looked like, and pear tree, plum tree – and as she thought of these she started to draw on a large piece of paper, remembering the shapes of trees in Wivenhoe: the elderberries of summer, and redcurrants, blackcurrants, raspberries, crab apple trees near the windmill, sloes, blackberries, hawthorn berries, rose hips. She wished her pencils were green, red, yellow, brown, rather than the grey of lead. She was no artist, but she worked hard at defining exactly the shapes of leaves and fruit. And then, after a long time of creating these trees and bushes of every variety around the edges, she drew the two trees of Eden that no one knew the shape of: the Tree of Life – which she made huge and beautiful, with great fat leaves and succulent fruit, with birds in the branches – and then another tree: the Tree of Knowledge of Good and Evil. She drew it like a willow with snake-like fruit hanging down, and placed the wise, tempting serpent hidden there among such tendrils, disguised.

She then paused. That was not really the classic image of the Tree of Knowledge of Good and Evil, which was usually depicted as an apple, but it seemed quite unfair to indicate to these children, who needed reminding about the shape of apple trees, that such good fruit of God's earth should be associated with a bad outcome. Her Tree of Knowledge of Good and Evil truly looked dangerous. She imagined its long fruit as red and purple.

She was so deeply engaged in this drawing, which gained in intricacy and detail the more she worked, that she lost track of the time. She was momentarily conscious of a rat surveying the room, but she was becoming inured to rats, which were everywhere; you just had to hang up or shelve high anything they would eat. She vaguely heard voices in the distance, but then there were often men calling to each other about their labours. She did not notice that a boat had come from the *Sancta Maria* to the French Jetty, and that Fathers Comte and Pezant, with Hiromi, were walking up to the Mission buildings with Bishop Pompallier. She did not hear them coming up the path. She was not in French Town, in Paka Ariki Bay, in Akaroa Harbour; she was in the picture, walking through a perfect garden surrounded by luscious fruit, ripe and ready at the same time, on a warm day.

"Marianne," said Bishop Pompallier, in the doorway.

Marianne jumped to her feet, gasped and dropped the pencil on the table. Monsignor! Here he was! And yet she felt as if someone had just picked her up and flung her from Eden. She was suddenly aware of being constrained and guilty, when in her imaginary world she was free and innocent; and she was simultaneously aware of Monsignor, who was all at once like God, 'walking in the garden in the cool of the day', saying, 'where are you?'

Recognising a tumble of reactions in herself, she was flummoxed and unable to speak. At this moment too, she felt a warm issue of blood between her legs.

"I surprise you, I'm sorry," said Monsignor, who seemed tired. His dark hair was not perfectly swept away from his face as usual, and his eyes seemed clouded. "The brothers wanted to show me what you all have done here. I'm so... impressed by your progress."

Marianne hoped that the rag between her legs was secure and folded thick enough. She tried to pull herself together, and went to Monsignor, knelt down and kissed his ruby ring. But she could hardly take in the various ritualistic sayings that came from her mouth or from his, as her head seemed to swim weirdly, and she felt unsteady. She stood up feeling like she could topple over, and was relieved when Monsignor went forward with Jean-Baptiste Comte to look at the school room so that she could lean back on the door frame for a moment, next to young Hiromi, who alone seemed to notice her lack of balance, and clasped her arm to give her a little support.

Such support was welcome, especially as she saw Monsignor look down, with interest, at the picture she'd been drawing. Marianne realised then that she had to explain, and mumbled something about asking the girls to draw a picture of the Garden of Eden to remind them of all the trees of home that one day would grow here in this land.

She saw Jean-Baptiste turn and look at her then, wonderingly, and she forced herself to stand up straight, firm, away from Hiromi's support. This was silly. She should not be so strangely affected by this shock arrival of Monsignor, or embarrassed by her drawing. Was it loss of blood? She wished now that she could run away to the privy, but this was impossible just as Monsignor had walked into the room. She watched and listened silently as Jean-Baptiste talked of successful conversions, and noted that there would be baptisms and even confirmations very soon. They hoped to begin some morning classes for five or six Maori boys.

"But you need more help with the buildings first," said Monsignor. "I will ask Commandant Lavaud tonight, when we have dinner, to provide manpower for the job, urgently. You've been industrious, clearly, but I'm very disappointed to see that thus far you've been so much on your own. I believe Mayor Belligny is a humanist and not interested in the Mission. I'm sure it must have been very hard on you all. There are no Maori girls to help Marianne?" He glanced to Marianne in a way that made her heart leap, with a corresponding sense of shame.

"The people of Onuku were hostile to our religion, Monsignor, because of the recent indoctrination of the Wesleyans, who stirred up distrust of France, and we needed to establish ourselves."

The three Marists spoke of the difficulties of the settlement further, standing around the table and her work of art, which seemed to idly snag the attention of everyone, perhaps because of the bizarre monstrosity of the Tree of Knowledge of Good and Evil.

Eventually, there was a lull, and Bishop Pompallier said, quite calmly, "Thank you my dear brothers. Your words are very important and require much careful thought. But I ask you now to give me a little time. I would like to beg you for some privacy as I wish to speak with Marianne alone, and then to each one of you confidentially."

Marianne felt she could almost feel the insinuations of Robinson in the air. How much she'd hoped for this time, and how much she now desperately wanted to run away and check on her rags!

Fathers Comte and Pezant nodded obediently and left without looking to Marianne, behind Hiromi, closing the door behind them. And Marianne obediently sat down as bidden, uncomfortably, in the place of Justine Malmanche on the children's bench, looking upside-down at her extraordinary picture. She wished she could ask for a moment, but any mention of a woman's private functions to a bishop was absolutely inconceivable. She would have to endure whatever happened.

She sat alone with Bishop Pompallier. This is what she'd wanted. Her wish had been granted without her specifically praying for it, but it seemed frightening somehow, too loaded with significance or feeling, and coming at the wrong time. And there was too much to say! A part of her wanted to explode with some momentous statement like 'I missed you!' In truth, she missed a feeling of safety she'd felt in the Mission in Kororareka. She missed a sense that he would look after her.

Bishop Pompallier showed nothing but weariness in his expression. He sat in her teacher's chair and sighed, not with dissatisfaction, but with dense tiredness.

"Are you well, Monsignor?" asked Marianne, with concern, seeing this, as it dislodged her self-awareness.

"I... became unwell on the journey from the Bay. It passed, but it has left me a little... fatigued. I'm like the *Sancta Maria*, in need of repair." He smiled a fraction. "The stress of living in Kororareka is perhaps more acute than I'd recognised. The politics continue. The missionary Henry Williams and the industrious Captain Symonds have been successful in convincing Hobson to found his capital not

in the Bay but in the Waitemata Harbour, where land has been purchased for a new city, to be called 'Auckland'. The property speculators are... finally... jubilant." He looked at Marianne sadly. "The
declarations of Britain become stronger every day, and they have
implications for our Mission. It's a relief to be far away, for a time."

This confession of personal feeling sealed for Marianne a tes-
tament of satisfaction, knowing that it was only to her that he would
be so open about his personal sensibilities. Perhaps that, in itself,
was something a bishop should not do. Perhaps they were, in their
relationship, not quite behaving appropriately. But this was the in-
appropriateness of intrinsic familiarity, understanding and trust.

"There are so many difficulties here though. This is not... "

"A Garden of Eden," he said, with irony, glancing at her picture. "I know. I'm bombarded with news." He rubbed his forehead
and eyes. "More than anything, in these circumstances, we must be
very careful about politics. Among us we can discuss and have our
opinions, but to those outside we must show great self-control."

Marianne nodded.

"And self-control is not easy. There are so many difficult lessons... so many ways to fail."

He looked directly at Marianne then. She dropped her eyes.

"I wanted this moment with you, first of all to bring you
some news. Your young friend, Miss Wand, has sadly –"

"Monsignor," said Marianne, holding up her hand. She could
not let him go on if she was to retain her composure. "I know. I've
been told."

"Ah," he said. "I'm very sorry."

Marianne breathed in sharply and tightened herself. Do not
speak of it, she wanted to say. She looked back at him with firmness.

"Tutanna passed your letter to her in the general store," said
the bishop.

Marianne almost broke then, and pulled in her emotions. She
was satisfied to hear that Betty had received her farewell, and learnt
in that note of other letters that had not reached her. But still, she had
abandoned her. There was no denying that.

The bishop, after a moment of observing her distress, went
on, changing the subject. "Now, Marianne, we must speak of pressing matters. May we do so?"

"Yes," said Marianne.

"I would like to ask you if there is anything you want to tell me privately about what has happened here. I must understand as much as possible as soon as possible. You've been able to hear both English and French. I trust your... what shall I call it?... your way of seeing things."

Marianne saw too that Pompallier appeared to pull himself up and become grave. He was asking her to think and explain. But she hadn't explored widely, and put her ear close to what people were saying, especially not in English. So Marianne told him what she knew, but quickly, recounting the entire saga from their arrival to find the *Britomart* waiting, to the hostility between Captain Langlois and Commandant Lavaud and Belligny, to the accommodations, with Belligny and Robinson being particularly close, to the assembly of the chiefs on board the *Comte de Paris* and the endorsement of the original agreement of sale.

"And Commandant Lavaud still believes that there could be a French protectorate in the Middle Island?" asked the bishop.

"I... I don't know, Monsignor. These are matters for... "

"For men." He made a little noise of disapproval. "But the colonists don't trust him."

"No. They demonstrated, and... "

"Yes, I've been told. Thus, it appears I'm called here to mend a rift. I thought I would find the French united against the British, but I find the French disputing with the French. As in France, so here."

And then Marianne saw a twinkle in Bishop Pompallier's eye. He had a certain love of irony.

She felt a renewed devotion to the Mission, which was, she recognised, perhaps more of a devotion to Bishop Pompallier. She realised how much she felt for this man, how much respect she had for him, a deep fondness.

"The brothers are full of admiration for your endless toil, Marianne," said Bishop Pompallier. "Your work for the Mission has been remarkable and I'm very grateful to you. But I fear I may have asked too much. I fear I must let you go."

Marianne folded her arms over her belly and leaned forward. "Has Jean-Baptiste said something to you?"

"Yes, just now as we rowed to shore," replied Bishop Pompallier matter-of-factly. "He says you want to leave the Mission, because of the accusations of Robinson, in order to protect our work."

"You know of these accusations?" Marianne looked away, at the inverted Garden of Eden, and blushed. "It was Charles Wand who –"

"I know of these accusations in Kororareka, and a hundred others, since I am, apparently, the Antichrist. Believe me, Marianne, they are unimportant." His tone was emphatic.

"Robinson doesn't even know me, and yet he's judged me," said Marianne, recognising instantly that she was sounding self-pitying.

Marianne could see this statement amused Monsignor, though only his eyes indicated it. "But this is the way of the world, Marianne. Think of what we say every time we recite the mass. The world is so poor at seeing goodness that it would even crucify our Lord."

'Am I good?' Marianne wanted to say then, stung.

As if he read her question, Bishop Pompallier continued: "There are people who hate me, because of this ring, and this cross, given to me in Rome as Bishop of Maronea, but they don't know me. There are people who hate Hiromi, but they don't know him. Do you know that he was a child slave to the enemies of the Ngapuhi, sold to a ship for sugar, and I found him beaten and violated by whalers on a beach? But Christ said, 'love your enemies, do good to those who hate you, bless those who curse you, pray for those who abuse you.'"

This shocked Marianne. In truth, she'd not asked very much about Hiromi's background. He seemed a nice enough youth, hard working and rather quiet. It hadn't seemed appropriate to ask him many questions, especially as he spoke French only slightly, and she spoke Maori at about the same level, despite Jean-Baptiste's continuing efforts to teach her when he had the time.

"Shall I pray for Mr Robinson?" asked Marianne, chastened. The question was meant to sound genuine, but she heard a sharp edge in her own voice.

Bishop Pompallier smiled. "Prayer is a great solace, Marianne. Robinson has two faces, and it's a friendly one he shows to

Belligny, one that you do not see. There are women who hate men, and men who hate women. For most men, if they feel desire for a woman, they respond with love; for some, the same desire makes them feel hatred. If he is such a one, then yes, pray for him, bless him, do good to him, but keep away as much as you can."

"I don't know if Robinson... desires me," she said, awkwardly. It was immensely disconcerting to hear the bishop speak the word *désir,* and the idea that Robinson could have lustful thoughts was awful. She couldn't help resisting this repugnant suggestion.

The bishop seemed uncomfortable too. "It may be hard to see, but I've found that people accuse me of gaining the thing they don't want to want, and yet crave. For many it is power and influence. For others land, whale oil, money, drink. I am a mirror." At this he looked away, as if recollecting something unfortunate.

"Mr Robinson perhaps wants power," said Marianne, after a moment. "He claims me, Monsignor, as a British subject under his jurisdiction here, in accordance with an agreement with Commandant Lavaud. He has taken all my papers."

The bishop smiled a little. "He clearly wants you to fear him. But your emotions are yours to control. Christ does not say enemies are friends; they are enemies, but they must not succeed in destroying the love we must strive to feel for all humanity."

Marianne looked down at her crossed arms. Clearly, the bishop was a far better person than she. If only he knew half of what went on in her mind.

"Marianne," the bishop then asked. "Do you want to leave the Mission?" His face was very solemn.

She felt heavy-hearted. It reminded her of leaving Uncle. 'I don't want to leave you,' she wanted to say. 'I was always more devoted to you than to the Catholic Church. I'd do whatever you wanted me to do.' But she could not say this. Her heart was bleeding. How could she explain what she'd just thought before, about her own little independent school? She thought again of Betty, and then she realised there was a tear bulging in her left eye. She brushed it away and looked out of the window. She couldn't answer, and simply waited, making sure when she spoke that she would not cry.

"Tell me about the picture you've drawn," the bishop then said, very softly, as if to a child.

Marianne cleared her throat and picked it up, looking at it the right way around. It was a very intricate piece now, with leaves and fruit everywhere. But – most obviously – the Tree of Knowledge of Good and Evil was a very peculiar thing. She pursed her lips and shook her head. "Perhaps it's not so suitable for the girls," she said, finally. How would she explain this monster of a tree? It felt as if so much inside her mind couldn't be articulated to the man she so wished would understand.

"May I have it?" the bishop asked.

At this, Marianne did not look up and passed the picture to the bishop with a deep sense of silly unworthiness and yet honour that he wanted it.

Then she saw out of the corner of her eye a figure walk past the window, and looked up to see Jean-Baptiste. She realised then that she'd been rather greedy with time, despite her bodily discomfort. She stood up.

Bishop Pompallier also stood. "Marianne, you've not asked for letters. I have to confess I've been unsuccessful in gaining anything that has come to you addressed care of the Wand household."

"Oh..." In fact, she hadn't associated Bishop Pompallier with the possibility of any word from Uncle. When she'd first written to Uncle from the Mission it had been April. Uncle would only just have received her letters from there, let alone any sent from Akaroa. He would indeed have written to her care of the Wands, but to a Sydney address. The Wands might well have decided not to forward her mail, in retaliation for her betrayal. Letters from Uncle were one of those things she'd sacrificed in fleeing.

Monsignor continued: "I will make sure that there are some girls from Onuku who will help you, whom you can train. When they are trained, you can do whatever you want. You are not mine. I cannot tell you what to do. I blame myself... "

Marianne was about to object, but he would not let her. "Perhaps you should have stayed in Kororareka," he said. "I've been worried about you."

Marianne wanted to say thank you, or something reassuring, but she felt choked. This was all too difficult. There was too much to express, and things that couldn't be expressed. So the formalities of goodbye were done with hardly a word, and she found herself outside, keeping herself restrained, walking down to the privy at the bottom of the hill, opening and closing the door, unwrapping her sodden bandages in the dark closet feeling as if she was dealing with a deep wound.

*

François enjoyed a sense of happiness he couldn't remember ever feeling before, that Marianne Blake had seemed interested in coming to visit him at his own property, perhaps even alone. He could wait for this anticipated delight. The fact that she'd been open to his invitation was wonderful. He felt a brightness and lightness with everything he did now. His tools seemed to weigh less. His conversations with the pompous Belligny were less abrasive. There was nothing to be anxious about. All would be well.

Everywhere else in French Town, the visit of the respected bishop prompted a celebratory feeling. Even François – despite his reluctance to engage with the Church – was cheered to see the French presence bolstered. At any rate, the Church here now seemed different to him. Father Comte seemed a decent man, earnest in his efforts to disincline the Onuku people from British Wesleyan missionaries, and Father Pezant was with the colonists, virulently opposed to Lavaud and Belligny. And then there was beautiful Marianne, who – though English on the one hand – seemed a flower of France in spirit. François could look kindly towards the cluster of structures at the foot of Aube Hill. He decided he would attend mass officiated by Bishop Pompallier.

Mass was held on Sunday, October 4, in the naval compound, with all the sailors from the *Aube* commanded to be there. There were not only the colonists, but almost all of the populations of Onuku and other villages of New Zealanders nearby. A small orchestra – formed from the naval band – played French hymns, accompanied by a naval choir. Bishop Pompallier had brought with him cuttings and small plants of all kinds from his garden in Kororareka, including an array of flowers in boxes, especially roses and lilies, and these were arranged around a polished wooden travelling altar he set up, where Christ painted on one side and Mary on the other revealed their mystical sacred hearts. Tricolour French flags from the *Aube* were set up proudly. The service proceeded in French and Maori. Some of the people from Onuku were baptised. It was a beautiful spring day.

Pompallier, it seemed, knew all about the theatre of ceremony, which impressed the New Zealanders of the Horomaka who came to the event. They were expectant, having heard something about the bishop beforehand from the fathers at the Mission and from Catholic whalers. A number of whalers and sealers from visiting French ships came, and even deserters who had now settled down with local women, further out in the peninsula, and had children, whom Bishop Pompallier baptised. The bishop's bearing, performance and dignity were impressive, and he obviously made a strong impact on chief Tuauau, and the young chief Iwikau, with others who came to watch this *Pākehā* with great *mana*. He was attired gorgeously in red robes, which stood out against the variegated greens and browns of the landscape like a splash of blood. In all, there were nearly three hundred people who attended the mass he celebrated. François was glad to be one of them, and not just because it gave him sight of the beautiful Marianne. It felt as if it was an announcement to Robinson, and all the British, that the French really did mean business. His only disappointment was that, with all the people there, he couldn't get close enough to Marianne to say 'good-day'.

Afterwards, the New Zealanders who had come to the service were invited to various colonists' houses for a Sunday meal, the settlers here being instructed to make ready for this possibility in advance by the priests. The single men were also to be invited. This was an initiative of the bishop to heal rifts and build community. François Lelièvre went along with a young couple, Mahaka, who was also expecting a child, and Eta, from Ohae – a village under the chief Tikao on the western side of Akaroa Harbour – to eat with the Malmanche family. They arrived at their neat, shuttered cottage where Madame Victoire Malmanche looked ready to give birth to their new baby at any moment and much of the food preparation and service was done by her daughter Justine. Eta and Mahaka were cordial and respectful, observing everything closely, as they sat on the floor. François sat on the floor with them, as did the five-year-old Malmanche son, Pierre, and long-bearded Emeri de Malmanche's brother, also called François.

"Are they really Christians," whispered Victoire Malmanche to her husband. The invitation to share their sparse meal was not exactly done with a spirit of open and trusting hospitality, but as a necessity, because the bishop had decreed it.

Eta had served on French whaling ships and could speak the French language a little; and François, with some grasp of the Maori tongue from his continuing frequent visits to Onuku, could help communication at times, though certain questions Eta asked – like 'Why does the great *tohunga* who serves the French god wear the colour of *tapu*?' – could not be answered in any language.

Fortunately, a great deal of time was spent outside considering the planting of various crops and bushes, and what native species growing nearby could be eaten, which were practical matters of interest to all. A few *kākā* parrots flew around as the New Zealanders noted different practices of vegetable cultivation. Eta and Mahaka were given seeds and cuttings. At the end, the young couple chanted something together, an invocation to certain spirits of the soil. Victoire Malmanche went and sat down indoors, fearing black magic.

Before they left, François took the opportunity to ask where Matthieu – or rather Manako-uri – was, and when he would come back, and this time he was told much more about his friend. With a mix of French and Maori, Eta struggled to tell him what he knew.

He said that Manako-uri was the son of a great *tohunga*, Tomoana, in the family of the wise chief Te Maiharanui, who was defeated by Te Rauparaha of the Ngati Toa who came from the north. Tomoana had over many years saved many people who were ill with *Pākehā* sickness, because of his knowledge of healing plants and incantations. But Tomoana was killed, as were also Manako-uri's wife and children. Then the *Pākehā* sickness grew stronger.

Before the death of his father, Manako-uri cared more about being a warrior, and a whaler, than he did about the arts of the *tohunga*. But after the first massacre Manako-uri was a different man, and had tried to remember all that his father had taught him. Now he was gone for a long time and no one knew where, but it was to do with learning the more powerful arts of healing.

"Did Manako-uri go away because he was accused of killing an English whaler?" asked François.

Eta knew nothing of this accusation.

"And the *whānau* of Manako-uri are living in Katawahu," said François. "Why are they apart from the people of Onuku?"

Eta explained that the *whānau* of Manako-uri were his aunt, three widowed sisters and their children and some cousins, and they lived in the bay of Katawahu because Manako-uri had commanded that they should not make contact with any ships, or other villages, because only if they kept complete isolation from everyone would the sickness leave them alone. If anyone came to their bay and would not stay at a distance, they had to be killed. Even Iwikau, when he went to them, was forced to shout from a distance because they would not allow him to come close.

"A quarantine," said François, understanding, with wonder.

Eta went on, mixing French with the New Zealand language.

"In the days of my *tipuna* here, there were tens of thousands of *māori*, but there was the *Pākehā* sickness. In the days of my *mātua*, out of an *iwi* of thirty thousand, three thousand remain. In a *hapū* of three hundred, thirty remain. In a *whānau* of thirty, there are three. In the days of my *tamariki*, how many? Does the French *Atua* protect us more than the English *Atua*?"

Tipuna – grandparents; *mātua* – parents; *tamariki* – grandchildren. But how could he answer the question? "The French God, the *Atua*… is… I… don't know," said François. What could he say?

Finally, the visitors to the Malmanche home were bidden a cordial goodbye, despite a level of mutual distrust, and agreements were made about exchanges of goods, which included – to François' pleasure – the ingredients necessary to make Maori bread in the way he'd seen it done at the Kaik.

As he walked back to his property François considered how he would make *mānuka* leaf tea and potato bread, *rēwena parāoa*, and bake the young roots of the *tī-kōuka* tree, as he'd seen Matthieu do, to create a sweet, sugary substance. He'd get butter from the Magasin, since Aimable Langlois had a good relationship with the Greens, with their cows at Takapuneke. He would make tea and sweet 'cake', served to Marianne on his own tin plates. He wanted to treat her to pleasure. But when would that be?

Before he got to his home he turned around and looked out to departing canoes, glad to have heard about his friend from Eta, and to be assured that he intended to return, at least to Katawahu.

209

The sun would soon fade in the late afternoon, lost behind the high hills hugging the Maori villages of Ohae, Opukutahi and Wainui, but for now it shed a bright beam directly on to the French settlement, shining into windows and through doorways, and turning it into a little collection of gold.

He looked towards the Mission. He imagined that there the priests and Marianne were engaged in some appropriate activity for the day of rest: reading the Bible, studying, meditating quietly. When would she come to him?

*

The black-clad men of the Catholic Mission at Port Louis-Philippe sat on stools at their table outside. The service at the naval headquarters had been a great success. Now they were sated and slightly inebriated after a good meal Marianne had made from Bishop Pompallier's gifts: dried beef stew, taro, rice, with glasses of Burgundy wine. As the sun shone warmly before its disappearance behind the high hills, Bishop Pompallier talked confidentially and with much insistence. Marianne, boiling coffee, looked at them all with affection.

There was the slightly nervous newcomer, grey-haired Father Jean-André Tripe, a man who had come on the *Aube*, but had been held back in Kororareka for a time to learn a little of New Zealand ways. There was her friend, Jean-Baptiste, fifteen years Tripe's junior, animated and talkative. There was Hiromi, hanging on to the French language where he could, with Jean-Baptiste translating for him. There was heavy-set Brother Florentin, and there Father Pezant, with his manner of concerned truculence. Father Pezant had become possessed of a staunch dislike of Commandant Lavaud, fiercer than ever after the deputation and its consequences, and was at pains to explain to Monsignor just how unfair things were. Their conversation was not without some abrasiveness.

They then passed on to the issue of how soon the *Sancta Maria* could be made ready to sail. Monsignor reminded them all that they were dependent on Commandant Lavaud for repairs done free of charge from the French Navy. Marianne poured out the coffee brought from Kororareka into plain china cups on a tray and placed it on the table in front of the Marists as they discussed their aspirations and plans, with Monsignor appearing to enjoy the enthusiasm he engendered, and the debate, loosened somewhat by wine and full bellies. She relished hearing them discuss matters in the way they did, without any thought for her, as Marist brothers together under the leadership of their beloved Monsignor. She liked listening to men talk about important things and was glad to be included in their circle of trust. It interrupted her sadness about Betty and the routine of her life. It made her feel a part of something important. And she felt so much better today, now that her bleeding had eased and the sun had been so strong.

"As you know," said Monsignor, "our role is to be neutral. But we can, at times, simply seek clarification. And I have a proposal. Once the ship is properly repaired and made sea-worthy, I will go on a voyage further south to meet with the important Ngāi Tahu chief Taiaroa. He has to be consulted regarding the land, since Green's farm is located on Takapuneke as a result of chief Taiaroa apparently selling Banks Peninsula to a Sydney whaler, or so it was understood. Such a misunderstanding can only be rectified by someone going to Taiaroa."

"But that's a long way," objected Jean-Baptiste. "He lives at the very south of the Middle Island, almost at the Southern Island."

"So it's good to have a repaired ship." Bishop Pompallier looked determined. "At any rate, Taiaroa could prove an important friend to the Mission and the interests of Catholicism. Perhaps he may have heard already of certain... discontent in the north."

"What's this discontent, Monsignor?" asked Father Pezant, putting several spoonfuls of sugar into his cup.

"The British are now charging customs duties, of course, and the number of ships coming to the Bay of Islands has reduced as a result, which is affecting Maori trade. I've received deputations from many Maori, as well as Irish, Australian and American settlers and whalers. All those in the embrace of the Church of Rome are more disposed to the notion of French rather than British hegemony, especially the Irish. But this is not our business. We must be neutral. Our interests must always be what serves best the Church and its flock. Yet, as I said, a quest for understanding is our prerogative."

Marianne, sitting outside their circle, looked over at Jean-Baptiste's earnest face.

"Can we hope?" said Jean-Baptiste.

"Hope? Ah, I must tell you that now, for several days I've observed the situation here in Akaroa, and discussed matters at length with the Commandant," said Bishop Pompallier, putting down his cup and looking at the men with him. "This is what I understand."

The faces of his audience were concerned, waiting.

"I can assure you that Commandant Lavaud has not accepted the British claims. It's not his place to do so. This can only be decided by King Louis Philippe himself. Commandant Lavaud has lodged a protest and stated that he would not accept an infringement of the rights of French property. The matter remains unresolved. In his opinion, Hobson's claims should not impede what was already set in motion by the Nanto-Bordelaise Company. But the fact is that the British will be putting considerable pressure on our government to agree to recognise their proclamations, and Lavaud understands politics."

"The British cannot claim the Middle Island by right of discovery," said Father Pezant. "Surely no other nation could accept this."

"No. Now they claim the Middle Island on the basis of the treaty brought here for chiefs to sign, but this remains far less persuasive than in the North. Both chiefs Tikao and Iwikau have signed, but they have also signed the contract agreeing the land sale and French settlement, as you saw. The agreement reached by Commandant Lavaud and Captain Stanley of the *Britomart* was that there would be neutrality between the two nations, here. No one wants war. Both sides are cautious."

"Have the British been cautious?" asked Father Tripe, curiously.

"They are waiting for our government's acceptance of their declaration of sovereignty before they pounce on us," said Father Pezant.

"Perhaps," said Bishop Pompallier, sadly. "But I will do my best. I will write to Duke Decazes praising this settlement and the Mission, and urge him to send more colonists, but we must accept that there is a possibility of the British successfully claiming all of the Middle Island. I suggested to Commandant Lavaud the plan that is dearest to my own heart, of an independent New Zealand under

French protection, and I believed he listened. But now... I must tell you... he is of the opinion that he would like to ship all the colonists to the far north, in order to discharge his duties to the Nanto-Bordelaise Company, to work as labourers for the Baron de Thierry in the Hokianga, and wash his hands of his responsibilities."

Jean-Baptiste put his hands in the air with alarm. "Baron de Thierry is a Protestant madman. He's a disaster, and he's done more to damage the interests of France in New Zealand than any other man!"

"This is what Captain Langlois feared, and exactly what the colonists suspect," said Father Pezant, appalled. "Lavaud will not stand his ground and fight for the rights of the French people."

"Please, I tell you this in strictest confidence," said the bishop, particularly to Father Pezant. "You do not trust Belligny, but it's he who above all has argued against Commandant Lavaud in this matter. The colonists see Commandant Lavaud standing with Belligny, or Belligny with Robinson, and think there is conspiracy, but instead there is diplomacy. Belligny is a curiosity. He keeps himself aloof, as an aristocrat and a man of science, and he is no particular friend of the Church, but he recognises the seriousness of the situation for the Company and Duke Decazes. Captain Langlois has been pushed out of any office and now sits offended in his ship, barely coming on land since the colonists' demands were rejected, and is now planning to go whaling. We attempt to create some rapprochement between Langlois and Belligny. But Langlois is not the hero the colonists believe. He is looking for money, for himself and to pay his men, and he claimed more than he had a right to claim. This is why we must speak with Taiaroa. If the British have their way, they may yet annul all the land agreements made by Captain Langlois."

Father Pezant sighed. "So the colonists are cast adrift by everyone," he said.

"Except by us," said the bishop.

Marianne looked at the honest faces of the Marists. How could she leave them?

Then Monsignor turned and looked back at her. "And there is something closer to us personally we must also discuss. Father Pezant and I have had some conversations concerning Marianne. Tomorrow there will be two girls from Onuku to help her, girls that can be assistants and trained to replace her." His tone was matter-of-fact. Marianne was surprised. This was sudden.

Jean-Baptiste looked glumly at her.

Father Pezant said, "*Madame* Libeau has spoken highly of your help when her husband was taken away, Marianne. Now the Malmanche family have told us that they need help in the house, when *Madame* has her baby."

Monsignor added, "It would be appropriate if you went there, Marianne. But it's your choice, of course."

Marianne saw then in Monsignor's eyes that he was sad, and he'd been disguising his sadness throughout this discussion of important matters of politics and land.

Did he realise now, no matter what he'd said of the unimportance of Robinson's accusations, that the more he distanced himself from her the better it would be for the Mission? Or had Jean-Baptiste said something? She saw Jean-Baptiste shift uncomfortably. He surely had.

"But I would like you to continue to teach the girls," added Monsignor, with some defiance.

"I would like... to do that," she said, "but... it's true... the housework here can be done by others. I'll go to the Malmanche family."

"You will still teach the girls... that's good," affirmed Jean-Baptiste, his face rather pained. She smiled reassuringly at him. It was better he had spoken up. He would still be her friend, even a teaching colleague. She was not going far. The removal was more symbolic than anything. She was no longer an intrinsic part of the Mission. She'd been set free.

Then she looked into the deep eyes of Monsignor, who kept his heart so closed and defended. How opposite he was to the pictures on his altar of Jesus and Mary, where they exposed theirs.

16
The Tree

By means of careful mediation, Bishop Pompallier somehow enabled the colonists to increase their respect for Commandant Lavaud, partly by means of a public handshake at the Magasin between Belligny and Captain Langlois, who then announced his imminent departure to go whaling. On shore, the bishop stayed in Commandant Lavaud's residence in the naval base. It was as if the bishop showed the man of the sea how things should be done, by a careful liaison between different groups. The bishop insisted that there was no surrender to the British, and the Commandant understandably awaited orders from Paris. Everyone must be patient, and all of France in Akaroa must stand together. The New Zealanders also respected Bishop Pompallier as a kind of senior chief of the French, a *tohunga* and chief rolled into one. He made a point of discussing matters of land with chiefs Iwikau, Tikao and Tuauau.

Some two weeks into Bishop Pompallier's visit, on Monday, October 19, Rose Malmanche gave birth to the first French child born in New Zealand. She was under the care of Dr Raoul from the *Aube*, who hadn't delivered many babies. Peculiarly, he made for the birth a private tent outside the Malmanche cottage. Since she went into labour late in the evening, *Madame* Malmanche was concerned not to alarm her children by the event of a birth close to where they were sleeping. Dr Raoul would not have her in the one-room hospital, where he had a couple of sailors still suffering from 'Rochefort fever' – a kind of ague – and the hospital was no place for a lady giving birth, hence the quick erection of the tent. Fortunately, the weather continued warm and Rose Malmanche was comfortable, pleased to be cocooned in her own private place for the event, and accepting of a doctor rather than a midwife. On the site of the tent at the front of their house, once it came down, Emeri Malmanche planted an apple tree.

The baby was baptised by Bishop Pompallier on the *Sancta Maria* on the first day of November, All Saints Day, and the Malmanches – advised by the bishop – made it a moment of reconciliation. Mayor Belligny was designated as godfather. The name 'Charles' was given after Commandant Charles Lavaud. The name 'Joseph' was given after Belligny, and the name 'Maria' after the Blessed Virgin and the ship *Sancta Maria*, in honour of Bishop Pompallier. They would also have called the child Étienne after Dr Raoul, but the doctor was insistent that this baby was weighed down with far too many names already.

At this baptism, François watched the Malmanche family arrive and walk proudly into the assembly: Rose Malmanche holding the baby; Emeri Malmanche with his long beard, since he refused to cut it until he saw France again; little Pierre, and the girl Justine, grasping the hand of Marianne Blake. At this François started. Why was Marianne arriving with the Malmanche family?

They all sat down together on wooden benches in the ship's chapel, which seemed a space of great dignity. Lavaud and Belligny were at their most formal and grave. Dr Raoul was very professional and smart. François watched carefully. Marianne was wearing a blue summery dress he hadn't seen her wear before, appropriate to the warmer weather, and she seemed far less a servant of the missionaries than before. He'd seen her coming and going from the Malmanches, and had heard she was helping them, though she was also still teaching at the Mission. Working in the town centre, he'd thought he'd heard just about everything, especially when it concerned a person as important to him as Marianne.

Since that day on the beach when he'd invited her to visit, François was simply waiting for a sign, some indication that she might be ready to leave her various duties for a short break, to be with him. He was prepared to ask permission of Bishop Pompallier himself if that was needed to allow her to walk with him, have tea with him, and if it meant she had to be chaperoned then that was perfectly understandable. But he so ached to show her what he'd built. He wanted so much to present his garden, and tell her the great miracle of Napoleon's willow that he'd seized on the island of St. Helena. Even though he was not officially a colonist, this is what he'd created here. Look! He imagined showing her, and his pride shone. He hadn't signed papers and received the promise of an allotment of two and a half acres like the other single men, so he would have to buy land from the Nanto-Bordelaise Company, and in order to buy land he sold his services, as a blacksmith and a labourer. He'd do whatever people asked him to do. Look! He'd replaced his *whare* with a small house built in the French style, with wood he himself had bought. He'd done it all himself from start to finish, after observing closely how the other settlers built their houses, and working with them. He'd cleared back the bush and planted any fruit trees and vegetables he could purchase, and herbs he'd brought with him, so that soon he too had a beautiful allotment, in the rich soil close to the stream, in a property now connected to the main settlement by a long road they called the *Chemin Balguerie*. Look, Marianne, he wanted to say. This is your future, with me.

As François watched Bishop Pompallier baptise Charles Malmanche, he thought of the baptism of his own future children, with Marianne as their mother. Marianne seemed to him so lovely it was impossible to think of the ceremony, except to wonder at the smallness of the new-born baby in this great new land. At the con-clusion, as everyone departed, it was difficult to walk away without shouting to Marianne across the throngs, "Visit me! Come with me now!"

And what was he looking for with this sign he needed that he could invite her? He wondered about her blue, flowery dress. Perhaps that was it.

Yes, surely: this was a dress of a woman who was ready to be walked out. He tried to keep himself restrained and sensible as this realisation dawned. He spoke a few quiet words with the Libeau family, who were there only with grave reservations, and then turned to Rose Malmanche and congratulated her on the safe delivery of her child, hardly glancing at the woman who stood next to her. He then turned his eyes to Marianne with great self-control, and said, "I hope you've not forgotten my invitation, *Madame*. It's open for any day you wish to come. I need only three hours notice."

At this there was a whispered discussion between Rose Mal-manche and Marianne, during which François had to wait politely. He could feel his heart pounding in his mouth. They then turned back, with shy smiles.

"In three hours," said Marianne, "you may call for me at the Malmanches'."

*

François was beside himself with nerves. He spent far too much money on buying fifty grams of butter from the fastidious Aimable Langlois, and then practically ran up the *Chemin Balguerie* to his house to make things ready. Preparing and baking the potato bread was a frenetic activity in which he burnt his fingers in the cinders several times, and he managed to coat the crust with a fair amount of charcoal. How often had he rehearsed what he would do? And now, look what was happening! He made some trial *manuka* tea, but it tasted slightly bitter, and even with several spoonfuls of sugar that acridity still remained. Still, perhaps Marianne would appreciate what he'd achieved, and the *tī-kōuka* root was sweet. The main thing was the garden. He surveyed it once again. He'd managed to get excellent grapevine cuttings to take, including what Emeri Malmanche said was a good brandy grape. He had walnuts around, camellia, rhododendron, pear, roses and various daisies. They were all small and insignificant, but surely she would see the potential, especially given what had happened to the willow in the fertility of the soil, in this beautiful, rich earth.

A little down the slope, he stood back and admired the willow tree with pride. This was the most established of all the trees brought from far away, and the most important. And Marianne would be impressed by his story, surely.

In what he estimated was about three hours François made his way down the path from his property to the stream and over it to the *Chemin Balguerie*, feeling his nerves were only just under control. He'd laid things out neatly on a table in front of his house, with a pot full of water ready to boil for tea, and the cake done and placed on a plate, under another pot. He didn't think the rats could climb up high on to the table, and it would be very bad luck if a dog or a pig smelt his cooking, so he felt it was safe to leave it there. He'd spruced himself up into what passed as his best clothing, shaved, washed well in the stream. He was the best he could ever be.

His legs did not feel quite as firm as they usually were as he walked down the road to the town. The Malmanche's house was not far from the Magasin and the main crossroads where he had his blacksmith's premises, located a way back from the street on a slight rise. He walked up the pathway laid with stones and knocked on the door. Almost immediately came the urgent, worrying noise of a tiny baby crying, accompanied by the cooing of Rose Malmanche. The door was opened by Justine, the young girl, who had a wide face like her mother and a low forehead, and a manner of looking surprised.

This look made him feel a little hesitant about asking for Marianne, so he was relieved when she turned up behind Justine, with a book in her hand, saying to the girl that they would continue reading later. She came out buoyantly. Her blue eyes sparkled. He felt perhaps the Malmanches had said good things about him, as she seemed welcoming.

New Zealand demanded uncommon ways of behaving for gaining some privacy. If they had taken a walk along the beach, it would have been as if they were walking on a stage, with all the audience of ships and canoes on one side, and people on shore on the other. Perhaps the Malmanches understood that. Perhaps she did.

At any rate, they set off together up the *Chemin Balguerie* as if they were taking a stroll through a park. They could imagine it in this way: an exotic park with strange birds and lush green vegetation rather than grassy open spaces. They walked along to the sound of the stream and a rustling breeze in the tree tops. The valley was sheltered, and warmer than anywhere else, and it suddenly felt like summer.

François asked her about herself, and she told him her mother was French, from La Rochelle, and her father an English sea-captain. She'd grown up in Wivenhoe, a fishing village on the south-east coast of England, and gone to Australia with her husband, but when he died she'd sailed to New Zealand, in order to help the mission in Kororareka.

Marianne then seemed not to want to talk about herself, and asked him questions, about where he was from and why he was here. He told her about his home village of Beslon, near the town of Villedieu in Normandy, where his mother was a midwife and his father a cultivator with a small-holding. He explained how he went to work as a locksmith in Paris after he'd finished his apprenticeship, though there he experienced the cholera epidemic, and he became aware of politics. He then said how he'd joined with supporters of Napoleon Bonaparte in 1836, and after the uprising was defeated he'd gone to sea with the whalers, because there seemed no hope in France, and he was afraid he might be a marked man.

"And why did you join those people, the Bonapartists?" asked Marianne, seeming genuinely interested. "Napoleon cannot rise from the grave."

"There is an alternative to King Louis-Philippe," said François. "There is a man who comes from the family of Napoleon, and he believes in the values the emperor tried to spread over all Europe: liberty, equality and brotherhood. This man, Louis-Napoleon, would truly improve the conditions of the poor, with schools, housing, health-care, distribution of food, new industry and proper banking. He would bring justice, so that the rich and powerful cannot trample over the destitute. There would be progress and human rights." François stopped himself. He was sounding too passionate.

"Is that what Napoleon stood for?" asked Marianne, sceptically.

François felt a little disheartened by this question. But, of course, she'd grown up in England.

"Of course," he said, "but I know the despots of England, Prussia, Austria and Russia claimed he denounced the Church, and the divinely-ordained rule of the kings. That is why they attacked him. But how can any good God support the oppression of the poor and the weak, which both the Pope and the kings have allowed?"

"Wasn't Napoleon also a despot?" asked Marianne. "He crowned himself emperor and wanted to invade the whole of Europe and turn it into his empire? The English people fought to maintain the freedom of England."

François almost laughed then, incredulously. How disappointing that Marianne should say such things, but then – what had he been thinking she would believe? She'd gone from the world of Britain to the world of Bishop Pompallier. How could she have any other views? He would educate her!

"Napoleon had to be a strong leader, with the same dignity as the other rulers, as our emperor, in order to lead the people in a great army against the despots and overthrow them for the sake of justice in the lands they controlled. Everywhere he went he established structures of liberation, and the Civil Code, which made the people powerful. He wanted them to be educated. The rich, old rulers retaliated by spreading lies, and the King of England, in order to hold on to his own power, convinced the people of England that Napoleon meant harm rather than good, and would destroy their nation. And the Pope did the same, warning that Napoleon would destroy the Church. They wanted to keep the people ignorant of the truth. Alliances were formed against him, and people who should have trusted in what he wanted for the world fought against him as a tyrant, when he wanted to overthrow the tyrants."

He looked at Marianne's face, whose unconvinced expression remained. She said, "My father was on a ship that fought against Napoleon. My French mother saw the English as heroic liberators from his rule. She trusted the Pope."

François felt himself becoming warm, agitated and vexed by this conversation. It truly was a sunny day, a hotter day than he'd ever experienced in New Zealand, and particularly in this breezeless valley. Marianne certainly would take some convincing, but he felt sure he could make her understand, as long as he kept his composure, and did not let his enthusiasm get too much the better of him.

"We have many divisions in France," said François. "You can see them here. Most of the colonists are Bonapartists, more or less, and yet those in charge of the settlement are loyal to King Louis-Philippe. His government has the navy now, to put down any rebellion, and so we are not able to be free, even here. You are a teacher, so you will understand this example... that is, that the last thing the administration talks about is a school. They want the people to be ignorant. But when more colonists come, then we shall see what happens."

"There's a school at the Mission."

"Yes, but for... religion. We need a school for science and history, to train young minds to be free."

Marianne seemed to frown a little, and then she said, "I think so too. But it does not need to be against religion."

François made a non-committal noise.

"Do you want a revolution?" she asked.

"No, no, I'm not saying this. I'm talking about democracy. When more colonists come, then there can be true democracy. At the moment, Commandant Lavaud and Mayor Belligny rule in the name of the King."

He saw Marianne ruminate on this. He recognised that she was an intelligent and thoughtful woman. He liked that.

"When will there be more colonists?" she asked.

"Once they hear that the land sale is secure, and Britain recognises the rights of France here. I know Captain Langlois is confident of his letters being very well received in Paris. You were at the final agreement with the New Zealanders... you saw yourself. It's all secure now. If the letters are swiftly received, then there could be further ships with hundreds of colonists, already by next May."

Marianne's face seemed doubtful again. "You trust the government you want to overthrow?" she asked.

That was a rather stunning question. François felt a little knocked. She was very direct, indeed. Fortunately, rather than replying, he could point and indicate where his house lay up the hill, hidden by bush. They just needed to turn left.

She glanced up at the thick, forested hills, and then walked over the planks he'd laid across the stream as a bridge. She followed him up the path towards the level, flat land where his house and garden lay. He anticipated turning around the bend at the top, and there it would be spread out before them: his small house, with the table and chairs and 'cake' under the pot, the beds with new growth sprouting. But first, before they reached it, he directed her to look at his magnificent willow tree.

*

It had been a strange few days for Marianne, uprooting herself from the Mission and walking with her carpet bag of belongings along to the Malmanche home. The Malmanche house was not large, and other spaces were familiar enough: the kitchen was outside, under a lean-to, with a privy and wash-house at the end of the back garden. The actual cottage consisted of two rooms; a day room with a little comfortable furniture and a table, a rag rug, a few trinkets and cloths, and a bedroom where all the family slept together in two beds: one for the Malmanche parents, and another for Pierre and Justine. She would sleep on a mattress on the floor of the day room and do the housework Rose Malmanche struggled with in the last days of her pregnancy.

While it was hard to make this change, there was hope budding everywhere, singing with the birds, shining in the sun. The birth of baby Charles seemed such a wonder: a sign of good things to come. Accepting the invitation of François Lelièvre seemed appropriate now she was not working as a housekeeper for the priests.

She'd enjoyed the night of Rose's labour. Though she recognised her first duty was to maintain things for the rest of the family and that Dr Raoul was in charge of the delivery, she'd had a number of conversations with the doctor during the hours of darkness that she delighted in, since Raoul was clever, and good company. He told her all about his work collecting specimens for the Museum of Natural History in Paris, work he shared with Belligny, though he made fun of his airs and graces. Marianne had brought Dr Raoul food and drink as he kept in close attendance during the night, and she'd ensured that everyone – especially Rose – had a hearty breakfast when daylight broke and a baby's cries were heard. It was wonderful to be around a time of such happiness, to see the immense joy on Emeri Malmanche's bearded face as he held his newborn son.

Rose Malmanche had been encouraging of François Lelièvre's invitation, and clearly thought highly of him. She said he was well regarded, thoughtful and extremely hard working. He knew how to speak some Maori and had good relations with the people of the Kaik, which she said was a very useful thing given the dangers the natives presented if they turned against the colony.

Marianne had felt reassured, though in truth she was now also rather taken by Dr Raoul, and had noticed that when she'd accepted the invitation in his hearing, at the baptism, he'd seemed bothered. She'd also seen the expression of Bishop Pompallier, which was inscrutable. He had a way of making his face into a blank wall.

Now, as she stood in the garden of François Lelièvre, she tried to replicate the bishop's face. A blank wall.

As she looked at what was in front of her, it felt as if all this budding hope had been an illusion. A feeling of terrible foreboding came upon her.

A willow tree. It was growing vigorously, with pale, thin leaves all over its insipid, hanging boughs. The colour was so different to the rich, dark green hues of the native vegetation. There it was, and it had clearly been planted some years ago, to reach its present size. It was there already, before she came here, with its roots firmly in the soil that she'd been digging.

François was speaking. He was saying, "That is why people call it 'Napoleon's willow'. It grew beside his grave. Napoleon's spirit lives within it. And every tree grown from a cutting of this willow is the same tree. This is not its child, grown from seed; it's the same, like a worm can grow new parts when it's cut. This is Napoleon's willow with new roots, but the same tree."

Unable to hold an impassive expression, Marianne looked at the willow with horror, which François appeared to mistake for awe.

"It's incredible, isn't it? I took a slip from St. Helena's Island when I stopped there in September, 1837. When I first came to this place, I planted the tree here, and you see... it's growing. But it looks more than three-years-old. It looks five. It wants to grow strong here. It's a sign."

Saule de Napoleon, he was saying. *Saule.* Soul. Marianne felt the earth lurch and the birdsong mute, so that the world seemed far away. September, 1837, was when she left Wivenhoe. Her willow. James Placard had pushed her up against the trunk.

François' eyes lit up. "Where it grows, it has his power," he said. "It will affect people. The ideals of Napoleon will live in this land. We will not be controlled by kings and rulers who seek only power and money, or land. This place will not be in subjection. Here we will be free, and the people will decide their own future."

But Marianne couldn't respond. It felt as if she'd been packed into a box, amid thick packing materials, and François' voice was outside it. Inside the box she had only the feeling that terrible things would happen now. What would they be? Death. Illness. Who would it be?

Uncle. She had not received any letters from him, for so long. What if it was not the Wands withholding them. What if he was dead too, like everyone she'd ever loved.

And then all of a sudden she felt a great nausea that seemed to be caused by some kind of invisible poison emanating out of the long green branches of this tree, as if there was not so much a good spirit inside it but something malevolent seeping out towards her, an ether that was puncturing her skin, drawing itself into her by her inhalations, and creating a deep sickness in her belly.

The tree she had drawn in the picture seemed to gain strong colours and come to life. Her nightmares became real.

She turned away, and struggled for air. Feeling herself being choked by something ghastly, pungent, she reeled sideways towards where François had planted new grass, and then back down the pathway. She tried to run, but her legs began to give way. She bent forward as a convulsion shot through her, behind a bush. She vomited violently over and over, hardly able to gasp in air before the next seizure took hold. That was the last thing she knew.

*

Marianne awoke with a start to see a curtain: a white sheet. She was lying on her side and it was in front of her. Immediately she turned and sat up, feeling some intrinsic threat she had to fight against. And there was Dr Raoul, turning towards her, worried. "You are awake, at last. That is good," he said. "How do you feel?"

She looked around. The sheet was one of three hanging from the roof around her bed. Clearly she was in the hospital. She could see through the gaps that there was another patient in the room: a man lying in a bed. She felt sick again. She thought of Tim, in that she thought of him as alive and present. It felt as if he'd only just left the room. She said, peculiarly, "Where's Tim?" in English, before she could correct herself, shifting her mind to the present. He was dead. She was dead. No, he was dead.

"What did you say?" asked Dr Raoul. "François Lelièvre? He has gone to fetch me what he can spare of his willow bark, for one of the men here with a high fever. It's very useful for agues. He knows it, but he has only so much to use. I didn't know he'd grown a willow."

"Willow," repeated Marianne. *Saule.*

"Yes, the bark is known to bring down high fever. I had some salicin crystals with me, but I've used them up already, because of all the Rochefort fever. Salicin is the active ingredient in willow bark.

225

You can get twenty-five grams of salicin from a kilogram of willow bark, but Lelièvre thinks he can only take about two hundred grams, without hurting the tree. Still, it might be enough."

"Not for me, no–" Marianne said, horror-struck, coming to and feeling more alert.

"No, no. You do not have a fever. I think you must have eaten something unusual to cause this reaction. Did you try any of the native berries?"

"No," said Marianne. Her head was swimming. It felt as if Dr Raoul was conspiring with François Lelièvre in some kind of threatening willow pact.

"Can I give you some water?"

"I feel better. I can go now." She wanted him to leave her alone. She had to get out.

Dr Raoul put a hand on her shoulder. "I don't think so. You look very pale. You really must drink some water." He poured out a cup from a jug beside the bed, and handed it to her. "Please, Marianne. See if you can keep this down."

She took the cup and sipped tentatively, anxiously, fearful that some scrap of willow had gone into the mix. How could he speak of it effecting a cure? The tree was an evil thing.

Her mind spun back now to the moment where she saw it growing in the soil of Akaroa, in François Lelièvre's plot of land, that tree responsible for her downfall, or so it felt. It was a dangerous entity, a dark force that had visited her over and over these past years to emphasise that there was some power in the world that would continually foil her chance of happiness. The moment she dared to hope, and relax, that willow came to wreck havoc and destruction. Even here, in the farthest corner of the world, it had followed her, to infect her world with calamity. Something terrible was going to happen.

And someone such as Dr Raoul could be its champion! Someone like François Lelièvre could be its foster-parent! Two men that she'd felt some attraction to had failed her.

Oh God, how she missed Tim!

Then Jean-Baptiste rushed in, red-cheeked and sweating. He bid only a cursory greeting to Dr Raoul before turning to Marianne with much concern. "What happened, Marianne?"

Dr Raoul replied. "She vomited and fainted. She has been unconscious, but I see no sign of a knock to her head. Lelièvre brought her here."

Marianne was satisfied not to speak for herself.

"Lelièvre? Where is he now?" asked Jean-Baptiste.

"I sent him on an errand. He was distressed and needed something to do."

Jean-Baptiste turned back to Marianne. "Is this what happened?" Marianne could feel his protectiveness, and his doubts that François Lelièvre was entirely to be trusted.

"Yes," she said, sipping some more water, though it tasted as if there was soil in it.

Jean-Baptiste seemed to relax a little. "But you cannot stay here, and you cannot go back to the Malmanches while you are not well. Let me take you to the *Sancta Maria*. Monsignor will want to look after you."

"Do not move her now," said Dr Raoul. "Let her rest tonight here. I can look after her."

At this, François Lelièvre returned, even more breathless than Jean-Baptiste, with a small pot of willow bark. "This is all I can take for the health of the tree. Is she awake?" He looked to Marianne with fear in his eyes.

But he seemed to her to be not so much sweaty but covered in mould. The trauma of seeing the tree returned to her, and the sound of his voice reminded her of that moment. She felt her mind drawing away from these men around her, as nausea shook her horribly again. Her intestines tightened and growled, and her breath quickened. She recoiled particularly from François, and the brown flakes he had in the pot, pushing herself back against the wall. Dr Raoul took hold of a bowl and rushed to her side just in time, as she was sick again, though not much came out but water. As she retched she found herself wanting to fight something, as some fierce anger welled up inside her too. How could this be happening?

She felt some pity for François, but it was defeated by a sense of him being in league with an evil thing, as if he was possessed by a demonic power within the tree. She should recite the 'Hail Mary', she thought, to protect herself. She tried to say it. "Hail Mary, full of grace... " she began, and pulled herself upright. "Blessed are you among women... " And then she groaned. It would weave a strong barrier around her, surely. But she felt so desperately nauseous again.

Jean-Baptiste came to the rescue, and completed her prayer, and then said another. As he recited, she heard François say his mother had good herbs for all kinds of sickness, but he had none of them here. It was as if he wanted to run, like a hare, dart here and there in his worry and distress. She wanted him to go.

"What's wrong with Marianne?" François' tone was desperate. "Look at her face."

"She may have eaten something. Did you give her anything to eat?" asked Dr Raoul.

"Nothing. She didn't touch anything."

"This is too violent."

Marianne felt as if she was seized by some devil, as another spasm lashed through her. What was happening? She felt Jean-Baptiste's cool hand on her face, and it soothed her. He kept his hand firmly on her forehead and kept praying aloud. But she also felt his hand trembling. They were all mystified by what monster had gripped her. But she knew. She knew.

"Sit up, Marianne," said Dr Raoul then, calmly, gently. "This may help."

"What is it?" asked Jean-Baptiste, concluding a prayer with a quick 'Amen'.

"A draft of laudanum. It will calm her and act as an anti-spasmodic, as long as she can keep it down."

"Drink, *cherie*," said Jean-Baptiste. "God willing, you will feel better."

*

Dreams, or not dreams. Things slipped over. It was as if the normal world of reality was a page that was turned, and the next page was a jumble, full of misprints, and paragraphs out of sequence, stuck together with snippets from other times and places, old memories, fancies and imaginings. In one place there was Tim, who had seemed to enter the present even before she drank the tincture of opium. Now he was sitting beside her on the bed, but curiously slumped as if he was only half-awake. He was still with her, but like a giant rag doll, paralysed and unable to help. Around her there remained the three men who had taken such a strong interest in her: Jean-François Comte, François Lelièvre and Étienne Raoul. The first one was gradually turning into a statue of a saint, carved in wood and painted, and seemed angelic; the other two had hair that had become twigs, which then grew into branches, so that they changed into trees: two willow trees. These willow trees had fruit: long hanging fruit coloured purple and red. She thought they invited her to taste it, and she emphatically refused. But nothing alarmed her so much now. It was all simply very odd and curious. She observed this absurd world and her place in it with baffled concern, and a certain macabre interest, but she felt no fright anymore. She tried to move Tim, so that he was in front of her, offering her protection, but he was impossible to shift, and then he turned around, but he was Uncle.

She thought she should get up, and walk, but her legs would not move, and it seemed to her that she'd fused with the bed, glued on to sheets and blankets. Oh she was so weary, so tired.

So tired.

She had to sleep.

"What has happened?" That was Monsignor's voice. Where was he? She couldn't see him. The room had turned into a garden full of great bushes covered with fruit. There was no one with her anymore.

The sound of him walking in the garden.

What was that there in the undergrowth? What was that moving?

"Marianne, it will be all right. Sleep now." Monsignor's voice again. But where was he?

"Monsignor, I love you," she said. "Take me home."

So tired. She could sleep forever. Home. She dropped her head down, and she was a child, carried up to sleep in her own little bed at the end of a long day.

*

When Marianne awoke it was day, but different. The sun was not shining through the windows. She awoke not in the least bit groggy

229

or sick, but extremely alert and on edge, as if she was ready to do battle after the hours in which the drug had taken her away into weird hallucinations and sleep. She couldn't stay still. She pulled the sheet curtain away and surveyed the room properly. There were no other men in the hospital but one lying slumbering. There was no sign of Dr Raoul, Jean-Baptiste or François. Good. She would leave.

Instantly, she knew what she had to do.

Still in her blue dress, though her buttons and stays had been loosened, she jumped down from the bed and found her shoes. After quickly putting them on she scraped back her hair into a loose bun and tied it up, and then ran. She rushed out of the hospital and over some cleared ground, to the bush behind the Wai-iti Stream and the *Chemin Balguerie*, avoiding the main route up the valley and the new fields where people would be working, disappearing into the forest like a wingless bird.

She liked it. She liked to feel like a wild thing loose in this bush, climbing over roots and pulling her dress out of snags. Fern fronds curled around her like fists from the ground, and there seemed to be a great urgency in all the vivid life of these ancient trees that spoke to her of the need to struggle your way through this life, like a seed struggling to the light from a bed deep in the ground. She'd been too complacent. She'd let life take her like a piece of wood held by the waves, when she had to be a ship and set her own course. She had to be a spear that flew through the air to a well-defined target. She had to be a warrior, to defend herself, when those who wanted to look after her had their own interests, not hers. She was her own woman.

This would never happen to her again, never. She would never be so weak.

She climbed upwards, on, noting that the rain was beginning to fall, splattering through the upper canopy of leaves and dripping down in huge dollops of water on her head and shoulders.

She slipped on mud and fell, got up, kept going up, trying to gauge the distance she'd gone, and the shape of the hills seen through a few gaps in the trees, until she came to the right place to turn south, and went down the slope towards the stream. She walked for about an hour backwards and forwards, up and down, until she found the perimeter of François Lelièvre's cleared ground.

It was morning. He would be at his blacksmith's shop, sure-ly. She would do what must be done.

After watching, alert, like a fox, she broke through and stood in his garden. He had a nice house. His door was shut. The cooking fire was cool. He was not there, it seemed. This was as she'd hoped.

Now, she felt instead a fierceness inside herself and a will to do battle against this foe.

She hunted, searching around the house for what was usu-ally left propped up against a doorpost, or around the side under cover. It was easy to locate. An axe.

She picked it up as if it was something she'd known a long time. Turning, she walked again down the path to the place where she'd been so affected, as the rain fell, making the willow leaves jig-gle with drops hitting them, so that the tree seemed to shiver.

She wasted no time. There would be no opportunity for the same injury to happen again to her. She would not allow herself to be hurt anymore. This was the end of it all. This tree would feel her rage. It would know the fury she had against everything that had happened to her.

With a natural balance and a strength born of a thousand jour-neys carrying water and wood, laundry and potatoes, she swung the axe up in the air ready to hurl it back on the small, slightly scarred, trunk of this willow tree planted in the earth of this land. It would be her victory against the destructive things that had harmed her. This would be her answer to evil in the world.

But as she started to swing the axe down she felt a shadow behind her and something caught the axe in the air. There was a thud behind her head.

Her hands were knocked off the handle. For a second she was perplexed, half thinking there must have been a bough she hadn't noticed that the axe had become entangled with.

Then, as she twisted to see what had snagged her purpose, the reason was revealed. She stepped away.

She was face to face with a Maori, who held the axe behind her with his right hand. He'd caught it near its head, and was frozen still, staring at her solemnly.

"*Te rākau nei e tapu ana.* This tree is *tapu.*" He said the words in Maori and French.

231

At this she inhaled sharply, and stepped sideways, away. She stared back at this man, who was tall and well-built, clothed in good European clothing and boots. His green tattoos curled around his face like forest vines on bronze. He brought his left hand up to the stick of the axe, to hold it firm and ready to strike. Any moment he would bring it down to fall upon her?

"This tree does not belong here!" she said, furiously. She did not feel afraid.

"It has been permitted by Tāne, and grows under my protection. And it has grown as a sign to the French people that they can live here, under the protection of the Ngāti Rangiāmoa, without war, in our lands. It holds a *wairua*. If you try to harm this tree, I will have to kill you." He was not angry; but simply firm, like a sentinel summoned up from the forests all around.

She wondered at his fluency with French. His words made her feel all the more defiant now. She would never be weak again.

"I will harm this tree. I will harm it, because it's a foul thing... and my father was an Englishman," she said, with vehemence. "So kill me. Keep it and kill me, because I cannot live here with this thing!"

She saw him hesitate, as if intrigued by her statement.

But she was prepared to die. This was it. She would not be fearful of anything at all. "Go on, strike me. Here!" She slapped herself on the chest, hard. He could plunge this axe straight into her heart. "Or I will rip this tree apart with my bare hands."

He looked at her for some time, without moving.

She heard the rain dripping everywhere, felt her breath pull in and push out of her lungs. She thought of Uncle, if he was still alive, and how he might not find out what had happened to her for years, till some report of Robinson was filed. She'd be discovered dead by François Lelièvre's axe, probably by François Lelièvre himself, when he returned. François would be investigated, but he would be all right, if he had an alibi. This Maori would have fled far and away, and no one would be condemned for the murder. There – this was her destiny finally, to go from one willow tree to another, from life to death.

She waited. The Maori shifted the axe a little, and simply stared hard in her eyes, confrontational, as if willing her to run.

Then he let the axe drop on the earth beside his boots. "Something has possessed you," he said, curiously. "This rage is unnatural. It's not the tree you hate, because a tree cannot be hated in this way. If a man or a woman takes an axe and cuts down a tree, without wanting to use it, or to clear the land for planting, or to take it away as an intruder, it's because the tree is a finger that points to the true enemy. Who is it that you hate?"

Marianne was perplexed, and felt her anger turn. He was not going to kill her? What did he mean, that the tree was a pointing finger? Intensely, she looked to this man's face and back to the willow.

Her mind turned back to those moments with James Placard, how she'd felt that surge of something so strong it had made her forget every scrap of caution and morality, and then had lost him. She thought of Charles Wand showing her the willow-patterned plates, as he admitted feelings that he could barely control. She remembered death, the loss of the baby on the ship, the loss of her beloved Tim, the willow tree in the hospital grounds, her dreams, her nightmares, the picture she had drawn in the school room. A wave of nausea struck her again. She stepped back, feeling it well up and grip her all over. But no, she would not let it win this time.

Breathing quickly now, she looked again at the willow. It was just a young tree, with pretty leaves hanging down. It was just a tree. What was she doing?

Then it came back to her again. The hospital where Tim had died. The moment she'd fainted. When she'd recovered after his death, she had not really recovered. She'd gone searching, to the blackfellas, searching for Billy Muster down at Circular Quay, and then she'd been found all loose and unravelled, and she'd been bound and sealed up, put in a box of sensibleness, keeping herself reined in, making sure she did not lose control in some way, not again, making sure she was safe. That was how she was with the news of Betty. She couldn't grieve for her either, because that would have unlocked the box.

She felt her knees buckle and she collapsed down on the ground. Stand up, she told herself. Be strong! She would not be sick. She leant back and closed her eyes, dropping her hands to her thighs. No, no, be still. Stop.

Oh, that was it. She was sad. She was very sad.

And then she didn't feel queasy anymore. She felt lowered into a pool of grief. With her eyes closed, she felt a sense of inward calm in the water of it. She could hear the light rain still falling on the leaves and the ground. She could feel it wet on her hair, face and hands. She knelt like this, feeling these sensations for some time, and the man watching her did not strike her or move her or say anything.

Then she was aware of hot liquid on her face: her own tears, mingling with the rain, dripping down from her cheeks to her chin. Her nose ran. The tears oozed out of her closed lids in a steady stream, accompanied by sobs. She kept breathing in and out, as she felt only the sadness of loss, from her mother and father, to the loss of James, the loss of that growing baby and the loss of Wivenhoe, to the loss of Tim, Flora, Billy Muster, the loss of Betty, the loss of dreams, of security, and – finally – the loss of Uncle. The truth was, dead or alive, she would never see him again.

And after some time, even half an hour, it felt as if she came to herself, to an old self that had been before, with Tim, or even a child self. She could step out of the box, the black box in which she had confined herself. She stepped out here, at the end of the world, in Akaroa, into that deep water of her grief.

She looked up. The Maori was leaning on the axe, staring at her, as if waiting patiently for an answer to his question. The rain was beginning to ease.

"I don't hate anyone." Would this man still kill her? She did not mind if he did. "Everyone I've loved has been taken away from me," she said.

He stared at her. "Either the ones we love are taken from us, or we are taken from them. Love must always end with someone's grief, or it's not love."

Marianne's gazed at him. He seemed strangely knowing.

"You will not harm the tree?" the man asked, after a time.

"I will not harm the tree."

He said something in Maori then, something that seemed to create some sense of finality, of ending this episode. Then he turned to her and asked, "Who is living here now? Is this your house?"

She thought this an odd question. He didn't know?

"François Lelièvre lives here."

At this the New Zealander made some noise of surprise. "He has come back to this place. This is his house, and his cultivation?"

"Yes."

"But you are not his wife?"

"No. He doesn't have a wife."

"Where do you live?" He remained stern.

"With the Malmanche family in French Town."

"Then go back there now. I will not go to your village. Find François Lelièvre and tell him to meet me in Onuku in the afternoon. Tell him that Matthieu Le Bon has returned. Can you do that?"

Marianne got up off the ground, and stood. She did not feel embarrassed by what had taken place. Rather, it felt momentous. Something had changed. She felt light now.

"Yes, I can do that," she said, and walked away.

17
The Kaik

François saw Marianne, completely sodden, walking towards him down the *Chemin Balguerie*, and felt the shout in his throat disappear.

It had been unbearable: to have to pick up Marianne from the ground and fling her over his back like a sack of flour; to carry her to the naval hospital and explain things to Dr Raoul; to hover there uselessly as the doctor failed to bring her back to consciousness; to be told to find willow bark urgently for the fevered, dying whaler in the bed behind them; to run there and back; to return to see the expression of such terror on Marianne's face; to then have to turn away to answer Robinson's enquiries, hearing Marianne tell Bishop Pompallier 'I love you' in her drug-induced stupor; to be interrogated by both Robinson and Belligny in the Magasin, and to inform the Malmanches of the unfortunate events – and on and on – till this morning's shock of discovering, when Dr Raoul and others were outside the hospital discussing the proper disposal of the body of the whaler who had died in the night, that Marianne had disappeared. Robinson had suggested to Belligny that François be arrested, but Joseph Belligny, for once, stood up against the English magistrate and insisted on his authority over the French people. His only decree was that François Lelièvre should not join any search parties and should stay close to the Magasin in his blacksmith workshop or nearby, until further notice. Bloody hell. A man could die of this.

He stood at the crossroads of French Town, with the sea behind him and the new houses around about, staring up the path going along the valley beside the stream, watching Marianne's wet form coming closer. She was walking purposefully, upright, without stumbling. Had she been to see him?

British constables were out searching. Commandant Lavaud had sent off sailors to look along the shore, in case Marianne had gone and drowned herself in the sea and might be washed up, but the sea could take a long time to belch-bloated bodies, as every sailor knew. The priests were looking in the bush, and the colonists too. Everyone suspected people who might have wanted to seize her. People even talked of malevolence.

François recognised he was not the only man to have strong feelings for this woman. He felt that even Belligny, whom she surely hardly knew, had very much noted her. Belligny was deeply upset by her disappearance. Perhaps he felt it was a bad omen and would reflect badly on him, as if he'd been negligent in his duties somehow.

Robinson had then said – with what François saw as feigned regret – that Marianne Blake was known as a trouble-maker in Kororareka. She was a manipulative woman who liked to be the centre of attention. She'd made many men her prey. The truth was she was the mistress of Bishop Pompallier, as her statement of love – coaxed by the laudanum – clearly demonstrated.

François looked at the bedraggled figure of Marianne nearing him with mixed emotions: relief that she was safe, and yet bitter disappointment.

As she came close he saw that her expression was not alarmed. She seemed composed, despite the fact that her hair and clothes were very muddy and wet. She'd been out during the rain.

She came up to him and then clasped her hands together imploringly. "I'm so sorry," she said.

How could she cause this much alarm, and then walk up to him and say 'sorry'? He didn't know how to reply.

"All the world is looking for you," he said flatly. "Are you well again?"

"I hope so. I'm very sorry. Believe me." She seemed plaintive in her concern that he should forgive her, but he was not sure he could. She clearly had no idea how much he'd been through.

"I went to your house," she said.

"I had to remain here close to the Magasin, or I would have been arrested and put in gaol," he said.

She seemed mortified. "They suspect you... of... "

"Your seizure took place when you were with me. You seemed to be afraid of me in the hospital. Then you go missing..."

At this there came a call. It was Belligny, uttering an expression of shock and disbelief, followed by other expressions of relief.

François turned to see his tall, dignified form coming closer, looking from him to Marianne and back again. "What? Where did you...?" Belligny seemed baffled, yet pleased.

"She came walking from the valley," said François. "She went to visit me."

"I'm sorry," said Marianne.

"Ah... the sickness... and the doctor gave you laudanum. You walked away yourself? No one took you?"

"No. I thought I had to... do something. I'm sorry."

"And... your clothes. You are wet."

"I was in the rain, in the forest." She was quite matter-of-fact.

And then men came running from here and there, like flies descending on a sweet preserve. They learned the news and flew away to report to those who were searching.

A boat was dispatched to the *Sancta Maria*, where Bishop Pompallier had recently gone to spend time in private prayer. This bishop, a man of such great reserve and carefulness, had himself seemed very stressed by the whole business. Perhaps that was no wonder, if Marianne Blake really was his mistress, if she loved him.

"I have to tell you something," said Marianne to François, her expression still quite composed despite her dishevelled appearance. "There was a man at your house, a Maori. His name is Matthieu Le Bon, and he wants to see you. He asks you to meet him at the Kaik this afternoon. He won't come into town."

François now felt as if she'd just pushed him over. Matthieu? "What do you mean?" he asked, emphatically. He could have grabbed her. "Matthieu is here? You met him at my house?"

"Yes. I didn't see him at first." Her face clouded.

"What... " he started. What could he ask? He would have seen the willow!

Then Dr Raoul was there, saying all kinds of things to the gathering crowd, and to Belligny, ordering people about and saying that *Madame* Blake was his patient and needed to be returned to the hospital immediately. He took her by the arm and walked her away with him, and she went dutifully, with no sickness or hysteria. She was perfectly herself again, it seemed. Perhaps it was all a mysterious illness, one that François had never seen before, and one he could provide no cure for. He'd been completely ineffectual. He might as well give up thinking of ancient remedies handed down by his mother. Dr Raoul knew everything, and more.

Belligny sighed. "A remarkable business," he said. "This woman is very strange."

"Is it the woman, or everyone who reacts to the woman, who is strange?" asked François.

"You mean she bewitches us, as she has the bishop?"

Us? "No. I mean we do it to ourselves, because we are all fools."

Belligny looked at François, as if with some agreement.

"May I go now?" François asked. "I have an errand in the Kaik."

"Yes, yes. Marianne Blake is found safely, and this matter is closed. There is no charge against you."

"You will tell Robinson?"

"Robinson can be assured that a British woman has suffered no harm in Port Louis-Philippe, though you heard what he said about her." Belligny sighed and walked off.

François went in to his blacksmith's premises, opposite the Magasin, and tried to complete some pressing work – welding back part of a broken hoe before noon. Then he ate the food he'd made the day before for Marianne's tea. It seemed a very miserable thing to be eating it all alone in his workshop, when he'd so wanted it to be for Marianne, but he hadn't eaten anything since the moment of her turn and he was hungry.

He was so tired. But now, of all possible days, Matthieu Le Bon had returned and he would see him. He got up and looked around. He needed to bring something to Onuku, and something to trade with or offer as a gift. Inside, he surveyed his simple equipment and unlocked the cupboard where he kept his tools and some money. He was scrupulous with money, given the importance of making as much as possible, as soon as possible, at any labour he could – not just blacksmith work – so as to pay Belligny for renting his property, and more. The Maori were not so interested in money; they preferred things they could use. What could he spare?

He picked up some nails and screws, and put them in his pocket, then he tidied himself up a little. His sleepless night was probably showing.

Matthieu – Manako-uri – had returned. There was so much to tell him. And what would he think of all of this?

But everything was muted. Weariness and disappointment took his joy away.

*

Marianne changed into her grey dress, putting the soiled one in a bucket to soak, and had a good wash, even her hair. Little Justine Malmanche brought her things, in her bag, with warm greetings and commiserations from the whole family, so she put on everything fresh. She felt cold, renewed, and washing felt like a baptism. She was embarrassed by all the commotion she'd caused, and very sorry about François Lelièvre, but – as Dr Raoul continually insisted – she'd been ill. What Dr Raoul did not know, was that she'd been ill with something within her soul, within her mind, not her body. The body reacted to an inner disturbance, the source of which was beyond his expertise. It now felt as if she'd experienced such a colossal shock that things could never be the same again.

Matthieu Le Bon. Wasn't he the man François had spoken about in the assembly? He could have killed her.

She couldn't wholly remember everything that had taken place the afternoon before, as she'd quaked on the hospital bed. She asked Dr Raoul about the man who'd been there, and been told he'd been brought in all the way from the whaling station at Peraki. He'd been injured by a harpoon rope, and the wound had festered and become infected. Dr Raoul had fought to keep his temperature down so that the body had a chance to fight off the infection, but he'd died in the early morning. The doctor had to be absent then, because there were papers to be signed and discussions about his proper burial, to be done by the priests in the cemetery on Aube Hill. She'd woken beside a dead man.

"Please let me speak to her alone, Dr Raoul," said Bishop Pompallier.

She was left to sit next to her bed, and Dr Raoul gave her some *Journals de Paris* newspapers to read from a year earlier.

Then some hours later Dr Raoul asked her to come to his office, where Monsignor waited, dressed in his plainest priest's clothing: a simple black cassock. The simple room was full of labelled jars of preserved fauna, and flora being pressed, and smelt of chemicals. Dr Raoul closed the door behind him as he went out. Bishop Pompallier simply took Marianne's hand in his and held it to his chest, with tears in his eyes.

"We were all very worried about you, Marianne," he said, quietly. "Jean-Baptiste sat and prayed with you, and so did I, but the problems with Jean Dupont, the whaler who died, took us away. Do you remember?"

"I don't... remember anything," said Marianne, honestly. It felt to her that only snatches of what she remembered might actually be real. She remembered, for example, that Tim was there. It was better to assume that she imagined more than she recalled.

Monsignor patted her hand, and released it. They both sat down. He smiled. "All is well now." It looked as if he wanted to say something else, but he did not. There was a long silence. Marianne felt a sense of shame again, a sense of transgression, that she had brought him into disrepute. 'This tree is *tapu*,' she thought, suddenly: hearing again the sound of Matthieu Le Bon talking. His face and voice had remained with her as she'd gone from the willow, all the way down the *Chemin Balguerie*. He'd carved his form like a tattoo on her mind, his words curling into corners of her memory and brain, making her wonder about everything. How easy it is to transgress. How often there are things that can and cannot be, and how many times one can break something that should not be broken.

"Monsignor," she said, "can I ask you a question?"

He said, "Ask me anything you like."

"The word *tapu* means 'forbidden', yes? For the New Zealanders it's not right to touch something that is *tapu*. It's like the Tree of Knowledge of Good and Evil in the Garden of Eden."

The bishop smiled to himself. He did not immediately answer. "It's difficult to explain what the word *tapu* means," he said, finally, "without explaining very many things about the New Zealanders, and the different way they understand the world. Do you want to talk about what is forbidden... or about *tapu*? Because *tapu* can mean 'forbidden', but it can also mean something close to what we mean by 'sacred' or 'holy'. It can be powerful and dangerous, like blood."

"If you try to destroy something that is *tapu*, what will happen?"

"You may die." Bishop Pompallier looked at Marianne probingly. "You may be killed."

"Then we must honour it, even if it's a concept that is not... ours. It's part of this land."

The bishop observed Marianne with curiosity, but did not ask for explanation.

"Do you think I can return to the Malmanches?" she asked, then, after a moment.

"Yes, of course. Dr Raoul says your condition is not infectious."

"And I can teach at the mission school?"

"Of course. Jean-Baptiste would be very sad if you didn't. You've not transgressed. You speak as if you have." His eyes danced over her lightly, and then he looked away.

Marianne thought about it. No, but surely she was a transgressor in various ways. The moment she moved, it seemed she stepped over boundaries. Unless she kept herself in a box of propriety and suppression, how could she live? How could she live now that she had broken out? She saw Matthieu Le Bon's face again in her mind's eye. She'd nearly been killed today. And what now would he say to François Lelièvre? People would know, and talk, and she'd be known not only as a sinner but as a madwoman.

Indeed, perhaps she was actually still mad, because she didn't know how to behave anymore. Perhaps she just needed to go back to the start, right back to that moment when she stopped in her tracks, when Tim had called to her. She had to believe she could be her own, independent woman, no matter what.

"I would like to continue for a time, but I'm afraid that I'm no asset to the Mission," she said. "You once said to me I might need to keep hold of the money I had. You didn't accept that I would give it all to the Mission, and I so I have some left. I'd like to buy a little land, build a house and have my own school. It was once my dream."

"Your own school?"

"Yes. It can be for the French, but there are British people arriving now, and I would like to teach the children of French and the British together, and the New Zealanders. There are all these divisions... but I carry two nations within myself. I don't fit in anywhere, and yet perhaps I am just what's needed here. You had a sense I would be. If Mayor Belligny allows me to buy land, I could make this school myself, independently. The colonists will accept me, no matter what my reputation is, because... I don't think they really care, to be honest. Reputation and honour are for the high and mighty of this world, and decency is for those who represent the Church, but if I'm just myself, in Akaroa, claiming to be nothing more than who I am, I believe... I trust... that there will be enough people willing to send their children to me for an education."

Bishop Pompallier shook his head. "In French Town, the colonists come from that class of society that is... not so concerned with honour, or the Church. But... this would not be a Catholic school, if you open your doors to anyone..."

"I would like to teach our religion as well, Monsignor, but I want to teach them... geography, and history, and science, and... I want them to learn about the world and politics and trade and all the things that you men talk about that decide the futures of people." Marianne suddenly felt a passion for this.

Bishop Pompallier got up, clearly perturbed, and gazed at the various strange insects Dr Raoul had put in glass jars.

Marianne froze in a moment of anxiety. She had blurted all this out before she had really thought it through. She was thinking aloud, in talking now. Could she do this? Would anyone let her? Would Monsignor find this all deeply offensive?

Finally, the bishop turned to her and nodded, frowning. "I don't know what to say, Marianne. You must choose to live your own life."

"Pray with me, Monsignor," she said. It would make her feel secure. "I don't know what to do either. Pray with me that I will be pointed to the right path."

And so they prayed.

*

The walk to Onuku took about one hour. First François had to go over the Aube bridge, past Robinson's magistracy office and through the small cluster of houses being erected in English Town, and then he went on along the path leading up where there was a sudden flash of European grazing land with Green's barn and his pastures at Takapuneke. He followed the track through where the bush went down to the sea, a dark and muddy road where trees loomed on all sides until the vegetable fields of Clough and Puai opened up the landscape again and the roofs and fences of the village of Onuku came into view in front of the gentle curve of the beach.

Here, coming towards him, was a New Zealander he did not immediately recognise. He was tall, broad, short-haired and smartly dressed in French clothing, with shining boots. As he neared him, he saw that it was Manako-uri: Matthieu Le Bon.

François stopped in his tracks. Matthieu Le Bon came to him, smiling.

François offered him first his right hand, in the style of a European, and then pressed his nose to his. François could not help but react with unrestrained emotion and, after the Maori greeting, he threw his arms around Matthieu Le Bon in an embrace. He then stepped back, grinning. "It's good to see you," he said.

"Napoleon's willow is growing well," said Matthieu. "And so the French have come. And you've returned."

"Yes, yes... " He was so tired; it was hard to know what to say. "I'm not a colonist, because I had to see for myself if the tree would grow. Now I know it's as it should be. It has been... a hard journey." François glanced away, feeling a sting of disappointment.

"There are many hard journeys, François Lelièvre, but your tree is accepted, as you are accepted. This will cause no disruption to the gods at the present time. I've heard of the agreements regarding your settlement in the land. My ship, the *Cygne*, sailed to Whakaraupo, Port Cooper, and I spoke to Iwikau there."

François nodded with some uncertainty. "And you met Marianne? She gave me your message to come here." What had he thought of her?

"Marianne," repeated Matthieu, with some solemnity. "I was waiting for you, and she came to your cultivation." Matthieu did not look at him directly. Then he turned back. "It's good to see you, François Lelièvre. I thought perhaps I would find you in France, but I find you here."

244

"In France?" François was astonished. "You've been to France?"

"To Paris and to Fontainebleau. Does this surprise you? I too can take a ship and travel around the world? Look at my clothes. These boots are from Paris."

François was definitely surprised. He noted how well Matthieu spoke French now, even better than before. He seemed changed: very much more sophisticated. While they had been coming here, he'd gone there! This was incredible.

A dog then rushed past and several chickens made a commotion behind them. François looked around towards the village. He noted the children playing a game, and the mixture of very old and quite new houses; the high food storage hut so that rats would not manage to climb in and eat supplies; the large meeting hut where often the whole village would sleep together; the *whare* and the stick fences, with large fields of vegetables growing all around; the wandering pigs. There were women sitting in a group in the distance, making a large mat. To come from here to Paris!

What was it like for him? He found it hard to know what to ask, what to say. He felt too prone to tears today.

"I have something important to tell you, François Lelièvre," said Matthieu. "It concerns your emperor, Napoleon."

"Napoleon? How?"

"You took the cutting of the willow tree beside his grave, from the island of St. Helena in the Atlantic Ocean."

"Yes."

"The Government of France is doing something else. They are taking the body of Napoleon back to France. By now they will have dug up his remains. They will be returned to the French people, to be placed in a great house near the Seine."

François felt a rush of amazement. "The British have allowed it?"

"It appears so. I left before the ship destined to bring him home departed, but there was talk of it everywhere."

François couldn't speak.

"Napoleon's willow has lost its companion on St. Helena," said Matthieu. "The remains of Napoleon's body are returned to his own country, but his spirit grows here. Tāne has allowed it."

François stared out at the afternoon sun brushing the top of the dark hills to the west. It was all too much. He had to weep. But these were not tears of sadness. They ran down his cheeks like the water was running down cliff faces near the shoreline after heavy rain. Napoleon was returning to France! The king, Louis-Philippe, had relented. The British had allowed it. Whatever the politics of Paris, this outcome was unimaginable five years ago; things turned, things changed. Miracles could happen. That was how life was.

François imagined what an extraordinary sensation this would have been in his homeland; and news only reached New Zealand now, from Matthieu Le Bon! Did Belligny and Lavaud know from official correspondence? Perhaps not, because it was Matthieu who brought such fresh news, from the ship at Port Cooper. François now wanted to run back to French Town and shout it out to everyone. Napoleon was returning to France! It was as if he were resurrected from the dead. He was coming home from exile. The dream of a better society too was coming home.

But Napoleon also was here, in Akaroa, in the willow tree. He knew it.

Napoleon returns to France, and Matthieu – Manako-uri – returns to New Zealand! How long had he hoped that Matthieu would be able to emphasise to the chiefs the legitimacy of French settlement. He'd hoped – well, he didn't know exactly what he'd hoped – just that everything would be made right when Matthieu came back. Matthieu for one completely accepted the French settlement on the basis of the willow tree. Wasn't that the most important thing? Or was it important only to him?

What a day. And what of Marianne, with her name so full of significance? Was everything lost then, with her? Was he just a complete fool like every other single man in French Town? Ah well. With a new ship of colonists there would be some young women. Surely they would come. He was tired of being alone.

Then Matthieu slapped him on the back, with affection and sympathy. "Come with me, François, my friend. Let's eat some food together and we will talk of everything that has happened in these past two years."

*

François did not learn of what Matthieu Le Bon had done in France until late in the evening, when they sat together alone beside the fire after a good meal of roast pork, each man wrapped up in a thick woollen blanket. By this time François could hardly keep his eyes open, and only a keen interest in the adventures of his friend kept him conscious. When he had gone off towards the village with Matthieu's arm over his shoulder, they had immediately been the centre of attention, with Tauwhare, a female elder, insisting on various formalities. Tauwhare showed Matthieu where they had kept his canoe safe while he was away, down by the shore. It was an old one, with carving at the front, and seemed to have some significance. Matthieu spoke mainly in Maori to the people of the village, and there was no opportunity for a confidential discussion.

When he finally told his story to François, it was this. Early in the winter before last, during 1839, there had been a spate of deaths throughout the Maori villages of the Horomaka, on account of the 'coughing sickness'. Old and young succumbed to this disease. All the time there were funerals, wailing, and slashing flesh in grief. There were no plants in the land that could cure this disease, and nothing Matthieu did to invoke the healing blessings of the gods chased away the determination of Whiro – the god of death – to pull away souls from living bodies. After the decimation by Te Rauparaha now they fell to a new invasion, even worse than they had ever had before.

Matthieu had a dream in which he gathered up his remaining *whānau* – his aunt, sisters, cousins and all their children – and placed them on an island that was like a great mother with two huge arms in the middle of the sea, where there was a beautiful tree with red fruit. In the dream there was fire all around the island so that no one could come in, but inside it everyone was safe. He felt from this dream he had to take them all away from Onuku and Akaroa Harbour to a different place, where they would be sustained and remain untouched by the coughing disease.

He took them all in three canoes to Katawahu on the other side of the Horomaka, facing out to the sea, where the land stretches out from the beach in two huge arms and the entrance is narrow. European ships would not call in there, and it was far to walk high over the hills and through the forests from Onuku. He instructed his *whānau* that they should not let anyone come to this place, and should grow their vegetables and hunt in peace here. They went and cleared, built a village and planted fields. They made new canoes. Since the day they established themselves there, no one contracted the coughing sickness, or any other disease.

But it was not his purpose to stay at Katawahu. He thought of the knowledge François had, and the medicines and methods of healing he did not know from his father. He wanted to learn about what skills and knowledge there was in France, so he joined the crew of a French ship, the *Roitelet*, where there was a doctor. This doctor told him that he was not trained; if he really wanted to learn any-thing about medicine he should go to France. So, when the *Roitelet* returned to France with its cargo of whale oil, Matthieu went with it.

On board ship he'd made a little money from cards, and at the port of Nantes he made even more, and won a few fights, so that by the time he came to Paris he had enough money to stay in decent lodgings. He went to the *Jardin des Plantes* where there were great men of science who understood about the healing properties of veg-etation from all over the world. There he caused a sensation, because they had never met a New Zealander before. They were astonished that one such as him would travel so far in search of medicines and expertise, and that he could speak French well, and they introduced him to doctors with whom he trained in surgery and in pharmacy, so that he could better tackle the diseases that caused so many of his people to die. He learnt about the inside of the human body, and all the many and grotesque diseases of the *Pākehā*, so that sometimes he could hardly bear to think of how many things there were that would now come to his people, since the *Pākehā* world was full of the most terrible ailments only a demon could have begun. The doc-tors did not demand payment for teaching him their knowledge. They asked him instead many things, about how people lived in New Zealand, and to repay them he gave some information about secret methods, like the art of the *moko* – the tattoo – and the arts of plants and carvings and making musical instruments, but not too much because it was *tapu*, the special expertise of the *tohunga*, given to him by his father.

In Paris, in the end, he became melancholy, because the light was dim and the colours muted, and everywhere there were so many people and buildings and carriages. The stars were hardly visible, and they were different. He missed the forest. One of the doctors took him to Fontainebleau, which they thought was a great forest, but this was not as great as the forests of New Zealand. It made him feel then he had to return, because walking there where the great trees of Europe still grew he realised that once, long ago, all of the land of the French was covered with forest. The French, no matter how much he liked them, were forest-cutters. He saw it already now in Akaroa. Somehow Tāne had allowed the cutting here, but it filled him with grief.

He'd returned now to use his new expertise to help his people. He'd brought back medicines and implements in a bag he'd left in Katawahu, to visit Onuku and his plantations on Akaroa Harbour. Over the following months he would visit all the villages of the Horomaka, to see if there was anything he could do now with his new skills.

"For example, I've learnt something very important about the properties of the willow," said Matthieu. "You must know this. The tree that I permitted you to plant in the midst of the forest here is a tree that can do wonders. Its bark can take away pain and bring down a high fever."

"Yes, I know this from my mother," François affirmed. "And Dr Raoul, the doctor of the *Aube*, knows this too. In fact, he knows much more than me. He's the man you should be talking to now. I will arrange a meeting. And can I give you some cuttings of the willow? You can grow them yourself, for the medicine. "

He found it hard to sound enthusiastic as he said this. François realised that Matthieu would undoubtedly have surpassed him now. His own expertise from his midwife mother seemed insignificant in relation to that of the naval doctor.

"Thank you. The willow is for you to cut, and only for you, but I will receive what you take from its branches. I will plant the willow at Katawahu and Kakakaiau. What else does Dr Raoul know?"

"Everything," said François, sadly. "Marianne, the woman you met this morning, is being looked after by him."

"This woman, Marianne, is a friend?" asked Matthieu then, curious.

"She's a friend." François sighed deeply.

"She very much needs a husband," said Matthieu.

At this François laughed a little. How peculiar for him to say such a thing. But Matthieu did not say it in jest. His expression, lit brightly by the fire, was serious.

"Do you need a wife, François?" asked Matthieu, after a moment of silence. "If this woman is not suitable for you, then look for a woman here in Onuku."

François shook his head. He would become like the whalers who took Maori wives? Somehow, that was not his dream. What was his dream? Marianne? No – not any more. She loved Bishop Pompallier. And half of French Town loved her. She was the wrong woman for him. He'd imagined her as being someone else, without even knowing who she really was. That conversation with her as they had walked to his property had only clarified their differences.

"I need to work, to pay for my land," he said. "Belligny will sell it to me once I've got the money. I'm sure of it."

"Your land," said Matthieu, with a surprisingly scathing tone.

François wrapped himself more tightly in his blanket. Yes, his land. He wanted to buy his plot, and to be in France, a better France, here in New Zealand. How could he explain that to Matthieu Le Bon? After everything, he felt acutely another sense of difference, this one between himself and his friend. His had to be a French future. And – at any rate – the final agreement he understood was that the chiefs had sold Banks Peninsula to the French. The sign of the willow meant that this had to be.

Then Matthieu rubbed his brow and uttered some string of woeful words in Maori. "François Lelièvre," he said, after this, "your willow grew so that you and the French people who were with you could come to live here. I will defend this. But you cannot take too much. Iwikau has told me everything."

François shook his head. "There must be some misunderstanding. I heard Iwikau and the other chiefs agree to sell all of Banks Peninsula save only certain parts."

"And you believed the exclusions were small."

François tried to remember. How was he to know where exactly the Maori names referred to? The moment lists of Maori names were recited it was as if they were a lullaby to send him to sleep, and probably everyone else felt the same. Who really knew where these places were, or their size? He bit his lip. How was Captain Langlois, or even Commandant Lavaud to know? They did not even have a perfect map. They assumed the exclusions were small.

"You think you've walked into a great house, but you've walked into a small one." Matthieu was looking at him strangely.

"What do you mean?"

"The *tapu* I placed on the tree was a *tapu* I learnt from my father. You do not understand it. But I had to protect this place. It will not last forever, but it will last as long as it needs."

François shook his head again, baffled.

"When I went to your country," said Matthieu, "I wanted to understand why the people of Britain and France come here to settle. Now I've seen your cities and towns. I've seen that there are so very many of you, millions of people. You do not know how to live off the forests anymore. Now you want to come here. You want this place. You do not want to plant your trees among our trees. You want to cut down our trees and graze cows, even when the land is *urupā*. We think we are selling a little land to a few of you. But you think you are claiming all of the land for many of you. What can we do? We can no more protect ourselves from you than we can protect ourselves from your diseases. My cousins here – Iwikau, Tikao and Tuauau – believe that if they give you land then you will bring prosperity and safety to us. But they do not know how many of you there are. They think you will build villages with a hundred people here, and a hundred there, but they do not know you live in cities with thousands and thousands of people in one place. They do not know what the city of Paris is like."

François bristled at this. Truly, he did want to build a town here. This was a great empty country with hardly anyone living in it. It could be filled with millions and still have enough forest. Why should the New Zealanders keep it all to themselves? It would stay backward and undeveloped without Europeans to foster its progress. Under France, it could be a magnificent place: a whole new society where the Civil Code would rule. But he was too tired to make his point, and the last thing he wanted was to start an argument.

"Therefore the *tapu* I placed on the tree is to protect us as well as to welcome you," said Matthieu Le Bon, "and it's a strong *tapu*.

The French people that have come here with you are welcome, and that is all."

"That is all." The words filled François with an unbearable weariness. "You think there will be no more French colonists?"

"There will be no more. The Horomaka will not be a city."

18
Land

One week later, on the morning of Monday, November 9, 1840, Marianne sat in Belligny's office, located at the back of the Magasin. At the front of the building in the store, Aimable Langlois was talking loudly with Joseph Libeau and stating categorically that the prices were set by the Company so that there was nothing he could do, even though he recognised they were exorbitant. Major Belligny, looking superior, sat on a padded armchair behind an oak desk with the French flag behind him, and smiled at Marianne warmly. "You want to establish a school in Port Louis-Philippe?" Belligny was the only person beyond the naval headquarters that used the agreed name of the colony.

"Yes, Monsieur. It would be a private school of my own, here in Akaroa. It would not be a church school." Marianne spoke plainly.

Belligny seemed amused and intrigued. "And what does Bishop Pompallier think of this independent establishment?"

Marianne glanced away. Monsignor had seemed very circumspect and withdrawn as she'd talked it through with him. He seemed, after her illness, to be resigned to letting her go; almost willing her to fly off from his hands, like a captive bird he was releasing into the air. She could do anything she wanted, since it would be a long time until he had the resources to set up a proper Catholic school, with teachers he could send, in association with the chapel that was being constructed by sailors from the *Aube*.

"He values my initiative," affirmed Marianne.

Belligny seemed to stretch up his neck and look down his nose, making Marianne a little uncomfortable, and then he smiled, as if she might have indicated some kind of sexual innuendo. Since Belligny and Robinson had become such friends surely it meant that the French-speaking British magistrate had passed on Wand's slurs.

How little anyone understood her relationship with Monsignor, which was so much more complex than these small-minded men could comprehend. Yet it was hard too, for she recognised now that, with everything that had happened, there was a fundamental alteration in her relationship with him; the bishop was no longer comfortable with her.

Neither was Jean-Baptiste. In fact, he seemed slightly aggrieved. He was not happy about her wish to have a private school, or a solitary and independent existence. His dream had been to keep her forever as a schoolmistress at the Mission, clearly, and her pulling away was a desperate disappointment to him. He had, over the past week, thrown himself into visiting Maori villages, almost to prove to everyone that this was his only concern. He and Monsignor were planning their visit south to Chief Taiaroa and they had several meetings with Commandant Lavaud.

"And you want your own land on which to build this school," affirmed Belligny. "You say you have your own money?" His face was full of disbelief.

"An inheritance. Yes."

"Remarkable."

"Well, would you tell me how much it would be for a small plot, just enough for a house that can have a schoolroom inside and a little garden?"

"I'm selling land on Banks Peninsula at one pound or twenty-five francs an acre... Mr Robinson himself has bought one hundred acres at that sum... but town land is far more expensive, of course. I presume you will want town land?"

"Yes, just a quarter, or even an eighth."

Belligny leaned back. "Though... for you I could make a special arrangement. A lady of independent means is of course to be encouraged, since I too value initiative." He smiled slightly. "But I'm not so sure about the school. The colonists are not very interested in education. They talk more about potatoes and walnuts and where to shoot pigs. They only need to spell to write their names on the bottom of pieces of paper, and they have little money to pay for classes. You may have to gain your income by other means."

Marianne bristled. There was definitely an insinuating tone in Belligny's voice.

Just then there were footsteps on the wooden planks of the floor and Marianne turned to see the black-bearded figure of Robinson trudging into the office from the Magasin, with two constables beside him. One of them she recognised as the man who'd summoned her to see Robinson over a month ago. The other was new: a heavy-set man, fiercer-looking than the first.

"Ah, Mrs Blake," said Robinson to her, in English. "I trust you have recovered from the unfortunate episode that caused such alarm to us all."

Marianne tightened. "Yes, thank you, Mr Robinson."

Robinson then glanced to Belligny, with a questioning look. He clearly wanted to know what their interview was about. He addressed the Mayor. "I would like to introduce you to my new constable, Malcolm Brown."

Belligny got up and walked over to shake the new constable's thick hand. "I am pleased to meet you," he said, in heavily-accented English. "Mr Robinson teaches me English and now I speak better... "

Polite laughter followed his efforts.

Marianne noted that she was not being properly introduced, but it did not bother her. She did not particularly care for this new constable, any more than the other.

Robinson explained then to Belligny in French something of Brown's history. He'd been a whaler at Oashore whaling station, but he'd left there after seeing a friend of his killed and burnt by a native they called Bone as a result of a dispute over cards. He'd gone to the British colony in Port Nicholson, where he'd joined the constabulary there. Now he'd come back to make sure the natives didn't take any liberties again with British whalers, as much as to control the excesses of the whalers in regard to trading women and grog. He was in his youth a wrestler. He was perfectly fair-minded and respectful when it came to the French, assured Robinson.

Marianne wanted then to ask about her papers, but thought better of it. The more unconcerned she seemed, the less Robinson could enjoy his sense of power.

She stood up. There was really no point in staying. "Thank you, Monsieur Belligny. I'm grateful to you for your information."

"Ah, *Madame*," said Belligny, immediately assuming gentlemanly airs to her. "Let me see you out. I want to show you something."

Robinson eyed her suspiciously.

Marianne said cordial goodbyes and walked out of the office beside Belligny, past Aimable Langlois and Joseph Libeau – who were still arguing vociferously in the store – to the front door. There she looked over to where François Lelièvre was clanging a hammer on red-hot iron in his blacksmith's shop. He did not look at her much or give her a pleasant greeting anymore. She assumed he'd heard what she'd intended to do to his willow tree from the Maori who had stopped her, but he hadn't said anything directly. He hadn't formally complained that she'd trespassed or threatened his property.

What new rumours would there be about her now? Raoul might put it all down to her illness, or the medication, and that would help. Nevertheless, the sooner she bought her own property, the sooner she could be truly free. A widow, living alone, was not unknown. As time passed, the colonists would grow used to her state. They would come to her school. Perhaps one day she would marry again, but at the right time, when she stepped out of the pool of grief. For now, it remained. It was not as if it passed away in an instant, as she wept beside the willow in the garden of François Lelièvre. Tears were now all too quick to come.

"Look, *Madame*, come around here." Belligny took her arm and walked to the side of the Magasin building, and then pointed towards the hills up the stream, in the direction of the willow. "Just there on the hill you see some land that would suit you very well, I think. We would be neighbours. For you, I would sell a quarter of an acre, undeveloped, for one hundred francs, or four pounds. We can mark it out whenever you like." Belligny stepped back, as if expecting her applause.

This was tempting: to have her own property. But it felt much too close to Belligny and Robinson, and it was very expensive.

The atmosphere of Belligny's insinuations, the argument in the store, François Lelièvre banging his hammer and Robinson's manner with his tough constables suddenly seemed to create an atmosphere that seemed violent, as if they collectively acted as a forewarning of something dangerous. Marianne inadvertently shivered, despite it being a very warm day. Belligny's pointing up the valley beyond the willow was a sign. She recognised now that the tree created for her a kind of message that could be a useful warning. It was not her enemy anymore. It was a reminder.

She cut the conversation off with a quick 'thank you' to Belligny for his time, assuring him that she would think about this. Then she walked off.

Marianne had just passed the crossroads on the way to the Malmanche house on the *Rue Lavaud* when she saw a figure: the man that she'd dreaded meeting again.

She knew that it would probably not be very long until she ran into the Maori whose form had seared itself into her mind. He was, she assumed, coming to see François Lelièvre. She quickened her step to walk past him as neatly as possible.

She decided that she would simply say a bright, 'good day' and stride longer. But this tall, imposing man seemed to have other ideas. He walked right up to her and stood directly in her path. He was still wearing fine clothes and had an oil-skin rucksack on his back.

"Your name is Marianne," he said, in French.

"Good day, sir," she replied brightly.

"The French call their country by the name 'Marianne', as if the country is a woman."

"Yes. Very strange, isn't it?" She had no idea how to reply to this statement. "But the British have Britannia." She tried to remain impassive in her countenance. He was such a huge, strong man. He could have killed her with that axe. She was suddenly brought back to the moment of her attack, and her sobs.

"But are you English or French?"

"I'm both... but I emigrated to New South Wales, so perhaps I'm an Australian." She watched a green *kākā* swoop nearby, and a *tūī* made a melodious call, as if to ring approval.

The Maori stared at her in the face. There was an uncomfortable silence, while she waited him to say something else, but he did not. He scared her. He looked so formidable. She felt exposed with him. He'd seen her as no one else had seen her, and there was more to it as well. She'd never met anyone like this man before.

"Do you live here, in Onuku?" she asked, then, wondering if it was appropriate to ask him this. But she felt she should not only be the one to answer his questions.

He seemed to find this query slightly amusing. "I live in the Horomaka. The whole of this place is where I live."

She nodded. Then he would find it perhaps a little strange that she hoped so much to purchase a tiny pocket of it. She remembered again the words of François Lelièvre at the shipboard meeting of chiefs, when Iwikau had spoken. This was the same man he called his friend, surely.

"I've been visiting the villages of Akaroa," he continued, "and all the way to Wairewa, but I'm soon returning to my *whānau* on the other side of the mountains, in Katawahu. I'm here in French Town to visit François Lelièvre, and a man named Dr Raoul, before I go back." He glanced around, behind her, towards the Magasin and the new buildings, and his face seemed a little pained.

He looked again at her, curious, and then asked, out of the blue: "Why did you want to destroy the tree?"

"I was confused," she replied, awkwardly. But now she could ask him something. "Please tell me, what did you say to François Lelièvre about it?"

"Nothing. I will not speak of this to him."

Marianne was astonished. "Not speak of it? He doesn't know?"

"No one will know. There is no reason to tell anyone. Why should he learn of something that did not happen? The tree was not damaged."

How perplexing. So François' cool manner towards her was simple disappointment.

"I thought I would see you today," continued Matthieu. Hearing this, Marianne found herself again being overwhelmed by something, as if this forbidding Maori had a curious force that affected her. He hardly seemed entirely human. She could believe he was the child of some forest spirit of an ancient myth. She'd never met anyone more disturbing. The fact that he spoke French well only added to his unreality.

"You thought you would see me?" she repeated.

"I had a dream about you," he said.

She didn't say anything, but was conscious that she might be blushing.

"You were in my *waka*," he said.

"I was in your *waka*... your canoe," she said. *Waka* did mean canoe, didn't it? She must not keep echoing his words! Her heart raced ridiculously. She was not sure whether it was with fear or something else.

"It's over there." He pointed behind to where he'd come from, very near the disembarkation point of the settlers on August 19.

"Oh." What should she say now? "I don't think I would like to sail in a canoe. They are very narrow and I... feel safer in a row-boat." Having said this, she realised that he hadn't actually invited her; he had only talked about it being in a dream.

He seemed to be amused by this. "If a *waka* tips over, it's easy to turn it upright again. If a rowing boat of yours tips over, it's difficult to turn, and people stay in the water and become cold, and drown."

"Well, indeed," said Marianne, feeling she was having an absolutely absurd conversation. Here she was with a man who had caused a sea-change in her life, and she was talking about the design of sailing vessels!

"If you fall into the water, you must get into the boat again," he said, "and row."

She had this peculiar feeling he was not talking about a boat. "I know how to row," she said, with some defiance. "My father was a sea-captain."

"So can you row a *waka* and keep it steady?" He seemed intrigued. But Marianne felt a gathering sense of embarrassment. Surely this Maori thought she was a madwoman after her behaviour by the willow tree.

"I've never tried," she said.

"I can teach you," he said.

She stared into the brown, almond-shaped eyes of this man. Oh God! A part of her very much wanted to go out on the water with him. She must still be mad!

Independence. What did it mean? What was she free to do? There was no man to answer to anymore. There was no one's good name to protect. Couldn't she decide to do anything she wanted? Why care about what people would say, when people could believe any lie they wanted, and her reputation in Akaroa was already ruined? She could buy property and do whatever she wanted.

What was she worried about with this man? If she fell in the water, he looked so powerful he would surely keep her afloat. She could swim anyway, as she had done as a child in the Colne. He would not kill her, or violate her, surely. He'd had that chance already. And, at any rate, there was something about him that made her feel prone to trust him. That itself was absurd. This was all entirely ridiculous! Yes, she was mad.

The realisation felt as if it was truly freedom. Her life had changed. In people's eyes, she had already lost either honour or sanity or both. How much of her previous life was constricted by trying to avoid shame and disrepute; but it had been brought upon her. She'd behaved indecently already, by reputation, and impetuously, madly, by her own decision. What did she have to lose anymore?

"Tomorrow, at dawn," he said, "I'm going out in my *waka* again."

*

After he saw Marianne leave the Magasin, François went back to his work with a heavy heart. In truth, despite the welcome return of Matthieu Le Bon he found it hard to recover from his disappointment about Marianne, and still ruminated all the time of the events of that horrible day, and night. It bothered him to think on what relationship there might be between Bishop Pompallier and Marianne. Of course, every Frenchman knew that bishops could have mistresses, just like any other men, but it seemed uncommonly greedy here, when women were so scarce, that the heart of the fairest one of all should be requisitioned by a cleric. Belligny had told him all he knew from Robinson. Additionally, he felt that Bishop Pompallier did not look after her very well, in having her work her hands raw as a housekeeper, to wash, scrub and clean at the Malmanches, when someone like her deserved so much better. Surely Belligny had the same idea, which was why he was fawning on her now: he'd want her as his mistress the moment the bishop left. François had observed with disgust Belligny's manner as he spoke to Marianne outside the Magasin. As Matthieu had said, she needed a husband; she needed to be properly looked after.

After some time François put down his tools. The sun was sharp and penetrating. He could do with a break. He took a long drink of water, and then went across to the Magasin, not looking again up the road. Inside, Libeau and Aimable Langlois were embroiled in the usual argument about prices. He didn't care so much about the exorbitant charges; he earned good money doing blacksmith work for the whaling ships. But he knew for the colonists who wanted more than basic rations, without any proper income, they were cruel. The sugar and dried peas that Libeau was complaining about were on the counter. François put down some coins and asked for some ship's biscuit, which he was accustomed to eating as a snack during his hours of physical labour. As Aimable Langlois turned, he pressed two coins into Libeau's hand. He couldn't stand seeing the humiliation of a father trying to feed his family. The French settlement should not be like this. Libeau looked at him pitifully, but did not refuse.

"Think of France," he said to both of them. "I have heard news that Napoleon's body is returning to Paris from St. Helena's Island. Things will change."

"Is this true?" asked Libeau, his face lighting up with hope.

At this moment Matthieu Le Bon walked into the store.

François enjoyed sensing both Aimable Langlois and Libeau flinch a little to see the striking figure of his Maori friend arriving.

"Ah, this man has come from Paris and tells me this is so," said François. "Joseph Libeau and Aimable Langlois, I would like to present to you Matthieu Le Bon, who has been studying with doctors at the *Jardin des Plantes*. I'm going to introduce him to Dr Raoul."

There were cordial noises made by Langlois and Libeau, but then, unfortunately, something else happened, hitting the Magasin like a crack of thunder.

From the back room where Belligny had his office, there came three men whose presence in French Town was not much appreciated: Robinson and two constables. One of the constables François had seen before, but one he had not. The new one recognised Matthieu Le Bon, and shouted, "Bone!"

Robinson – and Belligny – reacted with horror.

Matthieu seemed completely unperturbed. The thick-set constable continued to speak, abusively, going red in the face and pointing, with words François recognised as English curses, until Robinson told him to be silent.

François looked from one face to the next. What was this about? The accusation against Matthieu? The murder?

It was Belligny who smoothed things by saying quickly to Robinson, "What passed before we came here is not our business, even if an Englishman was killed. We are not here to judge the natives for their ways. In the current impasse between our governments we have no overarching law. Your role is to ensure the good behaviour of the British, and mine is to ensure the same among the French. We have no power of adjudication over the natives when they behave according to their barbaric natures. To seek redress would cause war with the savages, and we are sorely outnumbered. We can only discuss the matter with Commandant Lavaud."

Robinson scoffed a little. "This is precisely the problem we had in the Bay. The natives get away with murder, and we are to do nothing, for fear of breaking the peace! Under the terms of the treaty the New Zealanders will submit to our law, even if that takes time to implement."

Belligny continued. "Captain Langlois has told me already that this man Lelièvre spoke of in the assembly is both a murderer and a cousin of chiefs. Because of his connections you cannot allow your constable to insult him like this. You must control your men."

François looked at Matthieu's expressionless face. Robinson and Belligny assumed he would not understand what they were saying in French, but he surely understood every word.

So François, summoning up courage, stated outright, "Mayor Belligny, my friend is not a murderer. You cannot assume this man, this English stranger, is telling the truth—" He glared at the constable.

Robinson was insulted. "How dare you speak like this?" he snapped. "You are showing no respect."

"Of course he dares and I'm used to it," said Belligny, with feigned weariness. "These people do not know their place. François Lelièvre is a Bonapartist. He's even grown a piece of Napoleon's willow at the top of the *Chemin Balguerie*, like the ignorant sailors in Le Havre and Rochefort, who believe fairy tales of mermaids and leviathans, and say Bonaparte's spirit lives in a tree!"

"Spoken like a royalist," snapped Libeau. "But Napoleon has returned to France."

"Ridiculous," said Belligny, pulling himself up.

"He's been taken back from St. Helena," affirmed François. "They will have opened his grave and taken him with due honour to the homeland!"

"The people you work for in Paris have bowed to the will of the people," said Libeau. "King Louis Philippe will soon flee before the true ruler of France, the heir of Napoleon."

"Rubbish. Do you want to be tried for treason, Libeau?" retorted Belligny, furious now, and clearly in need of news. "If Commandant Lavaud were here he'd have you back on board the *Aube*, clamped in irons. I'm upholding the law and my duties by the orders of King Louis-Philippe, and I'll have all of you hold your tongues." He pointed his finger at the three Frenchmen. Aimable Langlois crossed his arms. When it came to Belligny, he was on the side of Libeau, despite their argument. He himself was saddled with inflated prices he had to maintain, according to the instructions Belligny insisted on for the sake of the Nanto-Bordelaise Company, but on the matter of Napoleon he was with the colonists.

Robinson made a noise of contempt at the three Frenchmen.

Matthieu Le Bon kept silent and watched this drama with equilibrium. The irate British constable said something else in English, with expletives, pointing his finger in Matthieu's face. Robinson instructed both his men to depart. They trod heavily out of the store.

Belligny then turned to François. "You will instruct your 'friend' to leave the Magasin and not to return to French Town. I will not have such disturbances with the English."

"But I'm taking him to Dr Raoul. He is an expert in—"

"You will take him nowhere. He is not to come here, do you understand?"

With that Belligny turned and marched back to his office, slamming the door behind him.

François and Matthieu bid a quick goodbye to Libeau and Aimable Langlois, who were left to complete their transaction, and François hurried Matthieu over to his blacksmith's premises, shaken by what had taken place. Inside, where it was cool and dark, he closed the door.

"I'm sorry," said François.

"Belligny is your chief now, your leader?"

"He's our Mayor, and close to Commandant Lavaud, who's in charge of the navy in the *Aube*."

"And your leaders care about the English more than you, the French people who live here?"

François rubbed his hands through his hair. What a calamity. "Such is France! We are split in two."

Matthieu remained unflustered by the dispute or accusations. "But this place is for the France of Napoleon. Belligny will not endure here. You will endure. Don't worry."

François laughed then, incredulously. Matthieu was so sure of everything! He would endure, but without further colonists.

"Isn't there another of your chiefs – the bishop?" asked Matthieu. "He has great *mana* in the north. Iwikau respects him. Is he like them, your leaders, or is he like you?"

"No, no, he is not like them or like us," said François, steadying himself and thinking suddenly of Marianne. "He has his own interests. I've heard he is going to visit your chief in the south, Taiaroa, in order to discuss land."

"He has talked to Iwikau about Takapuneke. He understands our grievance."

"Yes, he will talk about that because Taiaroa sold that land and–"

"Taiaroa sold nothing to anyone," said Matthieu, distractedly looking at François' equipment hanging on the wall, and taking down some bellows.

"Well, if he would confirm that to Bishop Pompallier then his voyage south will be of some use," said François, surprised by Matthieu's confidence. "But I don't entirely trust the bishop either. He and his Marist priests have their own objectives, and the Church was no friend to Napoleon." He paused for a moment, and then added, "And Marianne... " Then he stopped himself.

Matthieu turned to him then. "And Marianne?"

"It's said that Marianne is Bishop Pompallier's mistress." François sighed inadvertently.

Matthieu looked at him with interest, after putting back the bellows. "She was?"

"She is –? You think this is past?"

Matthieu smiled a little. "Does he take her to Taiaroa?"

"I...er... I don't think so." François wondered then. Actually, Marianne had accepted his invitation to visit him right in front of the bishop, without any scruples. That clearly didn't tally with the rumour. What if their liaison was indeed in the past? The bishop had cut her adrift?

"So... here it's said that I'm a murderer and Marianne is the mistress of a bishop," said Matthieu.

François watched as Matthieu continued to review his tools, and lifted up a knife. His was a very imposing figure, with his height and strength, and his deeply carved green tattoos in skin that seemed to shine. He could be made of greened copper, not skin and bones and blood. Then, finally, he asked him, "Matthieu, what is it the English think you've done?" This sent a chill down his spine. Could Matthieu have been capable of some terrible crime, in vengeance for Takapuneke, for which he held the English responsible?

"I won at cards. That was my crime. I won at cards against an Englishman, and he went out, to drink alone in front of a fire along the beach. He was so drunk he fell into it and the fire consumed him. This is the truth of what took place. I found him there, but it was too late to save him."

"You didn't set him alight?"

"I did not kill him. And anyone who spreads a lie against a man's *mana* is himself a murderer," said Matthieu. Then after a moment, he spoke to François again, quite softly. "I will not meet Dr Raoul today. But did you bring the willow?"

"Ah, yes, yes," said François. "I have these two slips for you." He picked out willow cuttings from a metal bucket. They were stuck into potatoes and wrapped in wet paper. "I trust they will grow well in Katawahu. But it will take time until you can cut the bark for medicines, and it's hard on the stomach. You boil it, just a handful in a small pot, but it's best drunk with milk and sugar."

"It will lower a fever and take away pain, and can be used on young children?"

"Yes, absolutely."

"I wish I had some yesterday, at Ohae. The newborn baby of my friends Eta and Mahaka died there. They said there was a fire

265

inside Mahaka. They put her in the sea to cool her down, but the fire grew stronger."

François felt a jolt of recognition. "Eta and Mahaka... I met them here, at the Malmanches."

Matthieu had every excuse to hate, mused François. But who was responsible for this illness? You could not put New Zealand in quarantine and keep it separate from the rest of the world.

"François, I need to ask you about the woman, Marianne. I'm going to take her on the water in my *waka* tomorrow. Will the bishop object?"

He looked sharply in François' eyes, as if making a challenge. François was absolutely stunned.

"I... er... Marianne can make up her own mind, as a woman who is independent. Perhaps it's as you say, and their affair is in the past."

Matthieu then asked: "Do you object?"

"No," said François, as his heart sank. "I do not."

19
The *Waka*

Marianne took out her dresses in the Malmanche's little bedroom. What was she thinking? She was definitely mad. She had fundamentally changed from that day she went to destroy the willow. She'd found instead that something else had been destroyed, something that kept her on a path of propriety, of doing what a woman was supposed to do. No one appeared to realise how uprooted she was from her previous existence. Her life helping the Malmanche family continued. Her appearance did not radically alter. Apart from her open determination to buy her own plot, with her own money, to start her own school, there was nothing to indicate she'd become replanted into wholly different soil. This new soil felt as if it was her proper ground, and her roots in this ground were travelling deep and firm. Yet spreading her branches and growing, with this earth, had led her to accept an uncharted course.

A European woman did not go off on the water alone with a Maori man, unless she were paying him for a passage to be transported somewhere. European men might have the freedom to walk, travel, whatever, with the New Zealanders, but European women were surely supposed to keep their distance. And she was a Catholic and he was, as far as she knew, a pagan. She should have nothing whatsoever to do with him.

No one had said this. It was just assumed. Only the loosest European women at Kororareka would give the time of day to Maori men, even when European men would find Maori wives – and then most often they were not 'wives' by law, but by cohabitation.

It was as if the *tapu* attaching to the tree had hit back at her – she had now no restrictions. And in this attitude of freedom she had no ability to restrain herself and follow the course that was decent and proper. She couldn't resist temptation.

She stared at her four dresses, hardly able to think. What on earth could she put on? She had to wear her whalebone corset, or she would not fit into anything, though these days she did not need to tie it tightly, since the hard work and diet of Akaroa had made her thin. She looked at her cotton summer wear and thought it too good, and then she looked at her grey wool dress and felt it would be very heavy when damp, so she chose her black one, which was at any rate now getting worn and she'd had to repair it far too many times. She used to wear this dress as a sign of her widowhood, to make herself unavailable to men who would think of paying her attention, and then she wore it as a sign of her being something like a nun. Now she was wearing it because it could get wet and she wouldn't care.

She hoped that she would not topple off the canoe in a swell. And her boots from the Mission would be heavy if waterlogged, and be ruined. She put on some slippers, since these could be easily thrown off. There was no point in taking a bag. The less the better.

She must have gone mad! But the sense of liberation she felt was exhilarating. Everything had changed now. She'd never felt freer; it was like being a child, rushing down the side of the valley on a sledge over winter snow. It was like being out with her father on the fishing boat when the wind suddenly took the sails and they just let it blow them fast all the way out to Mersea Island.

She explained nothing to the Malmanches, who were resting now after gardening, wearing wide hats to protect themselves from the fierce sun. She decided that she would leave them a note in the morning stating that she had taken out a boat, to inspect some property. Was it so wrong to lie? She would explain afterwards. But she did not expect any trouble, or anything that might stop her.

*

Marianne would not let dawn break around her while she slept, so she did not sleep, and spent all the night hours listening to the lap of waves, the sound of scurrying things, thinking, imagining herself as a teacher in a school for Maori children. As the silvery light of day touched the simple cottage she quietly rose from her mattress and took her clothes to dress outside. She left a note behind on the table.

Hurriedly, she went down to the beach. She looked out at a boat taking sailors from the *Aube* to the shore for the change-over of guards, and hoped they had not seen her.

Ever since she'd come to this bay, her life had been circumscribed, her world had been tiny. She hadn't explored anywhere. Her daily life was all work, prayer, work. She wanted to live. Life itself seemed to be represented by this need to be dangerously on the water with a stranger.

She waited for some time, as the sky turned from grey to pink. She sat down under a *manuka* shrub, not wanting to be seen, until – finally – she saw the shape of Matthieu Le Bon coming along the narrow shore.

This would happen! Marianne was aware she was smiling, and she was unable to push her grin into anything more circumspect. Her sorrow had dried up.

"You're going to learn how to row a *waka*," said Matthieu, with some satisfaction, by way of greeting. He put his oil-skin rucksack in the boat. He was barefoot. "We won't go out towards Onuku and on towards the open harbour. We'll stay in calm water inside the harbour."

Matthieu pushed the canoe out. Marianne found herself unable to speak. This was the most exciting thing she had ever done in her life!

Splashing through the water, Matthieu got into the *waka*, sat down towards the back and held it steady with a paddle against the seabed. Marianne took off her slippers and trod hesitantly over the stones of the shore. She hadn't gone barefoot on sand and pebbles since she was a child, and the soles of her feet were soft, but it was delicious to put her feet in the cool water. She did so lightly, keeping her dress up, aware that she was immodestly showing not only her ankles but her knees, and then she sat down on a narrow ledge at the top of the *waka*. Immediately she felt the different sense of balance in the narrow vessel, as opposed to a wider rowboat. She couldn't help laughing a little, as she toppled slightly. It was hard to know how to sit, as the seat was so high. She positioned her legs carefully. Then, before she knew it, Matthieu had dexterously turned the canoe around and they were heading out.

The shore drew further away. Matthieu did not skirt it, and also kept a large distance from the *Aube*, keeping to a route as far away from any other people as possible, as if he was going towards Ohae on the other side of the harbour. Perhaps he knew too that he

269

should keep a distance from those who might wonder about a Maori man and a European woman together in a boat. They did not speak.

After some time Matthieu passed a paddle and instructed her to use it. "Row," he said.

She held the wooden paddle tightly and plunged it hard into the water, heaving it back, and the canoe rocked. She was told to keep higher, not go down so deep. A wave jumped up at her and flicked water in her face, as if making a joke, and she wiped her cheek with the back of her sleeve, smiling. She kept trying to pull the paddle correctly, but was often told it needed adjustment. Behind her, Matthieu seemed to be trying to fall in with her rhythm, but her rhythm was erratic. The paddle stem was much thicker than in oars of a rowboat and she was worried about letting it go. They kept wobbling. He turned his paddle to keep momentum and balance, passing it over her head.

With Matthieu's sure plunges, and hers working better, they soon made their way, and eventually they started to go evenly. She wanted to cry 'Look at me!' like a child swinging on a rope in the woods. This was the most amazing thing. They were going so fast. She began to feel confident, understanding how to place the paddle in the water, at what angle, and to work with Matthieu to travel lightly over the water, quickly, in this narrow boat. She'd got it.

They turned then to the north. She looked back at the little settlement of French Town, which seemed now to be utterly dwarfed by the massive hills that rose up behind it, forest-covered to the top. The sun was now breaking through huge trees. Birds called and cried, tweeted and hooted, creating an orchestra of a thousand sounds. Then they moved on to see Takamatua – German Bay. Here the forest had been cut back hugely to furnish the saw-milling operation, so that the land was like a giant whose beard had been partly shaved: great patches of bareness lay between the luxuriant growth all around. Towards the beach there, as in French Town and English Town of Akaroa, there were a few small houses and dirt roads. She could barely see the saw-millers working and their fires.

Far out on the water, all this slash of civilisation seemed minute. Even with the *Aube*, the world of Europe in this vast land was tiny, just a little thin strip around the edge of tree-covered mountains and valleys that went on and on for hundreds of miles. How strange it was to come away from that little world and find all of this out here: another much greater world that was wide, wild and vibrant. She felt as if she was being taught something, not just to row but to see.

Her sense of freedom was absolute. She looked up at the red-billed, red-legged seagulls and felt like one of them. The blue sky grew deeper and the forest became a kind of living jewel of every shade of green. The sea was green-blue and deep, but she did not fear it. She'd been out on the waves a hundred times with her father and knew from him that if you fell in the water you had to make yourself like a piece of floating wood, long and wide, with your face turned up, and relax as if the sea was a great bed. She'd seen him and other sailors do it well enough. Wait until there was a calm place for you to swim to shore.

She could believe she was flying in the air, on a cloud. If she dropped now then so be it, for this was better than anything. This is what she'd lived to do. Her sense was careless. There were no consequences she feared anymore.

They kept on going northwards, rounding the shapes of the land but not too close, and went beyond German Bay towards the promontory of Onawe, which was like the peninsula in miniature, a giant teardrop of land jutting out on the northern side of the harbour. They slowed here, as Matthieu did not paddle, so that they floated along until the current seemed to take them. Matthieu turned the *waka* in due course towards the eastern shore again, to a long bay with low, flatter land beyond it on either side of a stream, where there had been some small parts of the forest cut down some time before in places and vegetables planted in plots, with stick fences around them, though these were overgrown.

They reached the shore and Matthieu jumped out of the *waka*, holding it steady as he did so, though Marianne felt the giddy sense of losing balance and clutched the sides, bending forwards. Matthieu waded up to his knees and pulled the *waka* in before he told her she could get out too. As she stepped again into the cool water she realised her knees were shaky, since she'd been holding herself in an awkward position, unaware that her body had been rigid in maintaining balance in this strange vessel. Her hands were shaky too, simply with the thrill of it all. She pulled up her dress – which was wet with the splashing of the waves – picked up her slippers, and stepped uncomfortably on stones through the glass-clear water to the shore. Matthieu pulled the wooden *waka* up single-handed and laid the paddles inside it. He picked up his oil-skin bag.

Matthieu smiled at her, and she felt her heart do something it hadn't done since her time with Tim. My goodness, she thought. I am truly insane.

"You did very well," he said, "for a *Pākehā*. You learnt how to stay balanced."

"And how to row."

He seemed to agree. "You learnt how to row. And the *waka* liked you."

Marianne looked to it. Was it living, in his understanding? It had some carvings on the front. What other strange ideas did he have?

Without further comment he directed her up the slope of the beach towards a stream, and to where the ground changed to old Maori cultivations. She followed him, thinking of pictures she'd seen in books of the aboriginals of the world. They were presented by artists as both barbaric – ignorant and vicious beings – yet as having nobility and dignity besides. There was quite a taste for that kind of image, as if the dissonance was exciting. The native peoples of the newly-discovered lands of the world – outside civilisation – were strange creatures. Their brown skins indicated an inner impurity and inferiority, as if base nature still acted too strongly in their flesh. They were soiled, blackened, darkened by the taint of something low, of the earth and dirt, while white skins meant purity, cleanliness, a nature closer to the pale beings of heaven, the shining brightness of the sky and the spirit world.

But to her Matthieu was something wondrous not because of his race or his strange appearance but because of who he was, and when he'd appeared. She found everything about him intensely alluring.

As they stopped, next to where the stick fence was made, she asked him: "Was it like your dream, when I was in the *waka*?"

"No," he said, and looked away. He seemed not to want to tell her anything else. She wondered if perhaps she was a little disappointing. She wanted then to say she too had dreams. She'd dreamt, for example, about the willow. He would understand. He was far from the image of an ignorant, brutish and stupid savage; he was quite the opposite: someone of superior intellect. She felt it.

"Are you hungry?" Matthieu asked.

Actually some food would be very welcome, she thought, so she nodded. The exercise and the sea air made her feel she could eat anything. But what food? She saw then that in the cultivation there were *kumara* and potatoes, with onions, cabbages and turnips, overgrown with weeds. Matthieu went through an opening into the midst of this and picked up a broad stick that was left there, which he then used to dig in various places, finding decent-sized tubers. He pulled out several long, purple *kumara* of different kinds.

"Are these yours?" Marianne asked, since she could think of no other way of continuing conversation.

"There's a saying we have: *he te toa taua, mate taua; he toa pike pari, mate pari; he toa ngaki kai, mate huhu tena.* It means, 'an energetic warrior dies in battle; an energetic craftsman perishes among his wares, but an energetic cultivator dies of old age.' Once, it was true."

A silence. She felt awkward. His words masked too many terrible things.

"This is very far away from Onuku, or the other villages," commented Marianne, looking around. The sound of cicadas and birds singing was all she heard. There was no one here. There were no boats out in the water to watch them. There were just the ringing insects and the calling of birds, nothing else.

"Out at the *pā* of Onawe, when we moved there for protection, we had cultivations here at Kakakaiou, and also at Kaitouna." He continued his digging. "These places are too far away from the remaining villages now, you are right. There are new cultivations for us."

After he had sufficient, or more than sufficient, vegetables, Matthieu opened up his oil-skin bag and pulled out something wrapped up in paper. Unfurling it, Marianne saw that it was a willow cutting. Marianne almost guffawed, simply with amazement.

"This is from François Lelièvre," Matthieu said. "This soil in the cultivation has been fertilised and lies close to that stream, so I believe it will be a good place for a willow tree. The other one I'll take with me to Katawahu."

Marianne shook her head. This was incredible! The willow again. Why did it follow her? "You really want it?" she asked.

Then he held it out to her. "Here. You plant it."

She took a step away from the piece of willow, and turned. Could she? In truth, she felt differently about the willow now. Yet, it was still a reminder of danger, loss and pain. It was a spectre of death, and love.

Don't be afraid, she told herself. She turned back and cautiously went forward, into the cultivation, where Matthieu was standing, took the willow, with its end embedded in a potato, and put it into the hole that had been dug. Throughout this action, she found that she was crying: the same tears she'd shed before. It was like being at a funeral, burying this body in the ground.

Matthieu then pushed earth around it, and went away to the stream, bringing back water in a small canister to water it, as she stood there, with tears running down her cheeks. Matthieu did not react to this, as if it was all completely normal.

"There are a lot of weeds," said Matthieu then, and started pulling them up.

Marianne wiped her face and watched him for a moment. Then she walked out of the cultivation, still feeling the dragging ache of grief. Since they had met in such appalling circumstances, where only her raw feeling was on view, it seemed impossible to be anything but absolutely natural with this man. She was no longer restraining herself. One moment she could be joyous and the next lamenting. She couldn't take recourse to niceties and politeness; she could only be. A fantail dipped and dived, as if laughing at her.

She looked back at this man pulling up weeds. What had he done to her?

Then she went back to the beach and gazed along it, not really knowing what to do, and noticed something there that seemed to be a wooden post sticking out of the ground beside a tree. She walked along to it, about thirty paces, and saw that it was a new sign, with English writing: a square pole stuck in the ground with a plank nailed to it, forming a cross.

'Land purchased by Charles Robinson, one hundred acres; Nanto-Bordelaise Company lot forty-three. Private Property. Trespassers will be prosecuted'.

It did not take long to read and comprehend, but she kept staring at the sign regardless. It was written in ink: black letters on the plain wood.

She heard then the slight crunch of Matthieu's bare feet stepping closer. Still holding his stick, he stopped. He looked at her and the sign, and asked, "What's this writing?"

Marianne made a face and stated: "The British Magistrate, Robinson, has bought this land from the French Mayor, Belligny. This sign is an announcement of his land title. Robinson... " She wanted to say what she felt about him, but there seemed no words to express it. She felt her face contorting into disgust. *Propriété*, she said, in French. Propriety. Property. In French it was the same word.

Matthieu scrutinised her face for a moment, with interest, and then threw down his digging stick. "*Hie*," he said. He took hold of the post, wrenched it up out of the earth and threw it far with all his might to one side, into some bushes, which seemed to consume it with their tiny leaves, so that only the post stuck out in their midst like a needle.

It made Marianne smile. "Are you not afraid of anything?" asked Marianne.

"Yes, I'm afraid, but not of Robinson," said Matthieu.

Marianne looked up at him then, unable to help herself. His face was magnificent. All those winding tattoos, like curling fern fronds, like a pattern for the growth of trees, curving shells, spiralling currents in the water. His face was life. His eyes seemed to hold such a past... a past that she somehow understood. How could she? What had happened to her? What had happened to her piety?

He took her then, put his arm firmly around her back, and pulled her up to him.

*

Marianne lay looking up at the interlacing leaves of the tree-ferns above her, silhouetted against the strong blue sky, feeling Matthieu's fingers travel around her body, from her face and neck, to her breasts and belly, and beyond. It seemed impossible, but perhaps they would make love even one more time again before the sun went behind the western hills.

She did not want this to stop. It felt as if everything was a dream. Here there was no need for hurried movements, or any thought to keep quiet, or even to stay in one place. The whole of the forest was their bedroom. Their bed was a pile of ferns Matthieu had cut and laid down, their walls the trees, with chairs made out of fallen trunks. She'd frightened birds by her own noises, watched them fly up into the sky squealing. She'd been amazed – almost drunk with pleasure – the first time, after which Matthieu had made a fire, unabashed by his nakedness or hers, and set vegetables to roast. Then the second time had sent her into a rapture. They'd eaten afterwards, talked about how he'd voyaged to France, and laughed about everything he'd seen there. Then the third – it had been so long and sensuous it felt as if time had been erased, and this was eternity. The Garden of Eden. There was no difference between then and now, past and present, earthly and spiritual. She'd entered a state of bliss. How could anything end? How could they return to the town, to all the small-minded pettiness of ordinary life and all the pathetic divisions? She'd wanted to stay this way forever.

He'd asked her many questions about herself then, and had been clearly intrigued and slightly bothered by her English ancestry, as if that side of her was a very unfortunate thing. He'd told her that the English were not to be trusted; he'd learnt that. But she'd told him of her father, a sea-captain, and her uncle, a ship-builder, and the village of Wivenhoe, with such love that he'd seemed to soften, and, as she kept on talking, the love she felt for her father, and Uncle, and her old home town had suddenly overwhelmed her, so that all of a sudden she'd found she was crying again.

He'd held her close then, stroking her hair and saying things softly she could not understand. "This is like my dream," Matthieu said, finally. She was calm again now.

"I thought I was in your *waka*?" said Marianne.

"It began there, but it changed. A *waka* is also something else, not a canoe, but a place of special possessions, *taonga*. The dream told me that you belong to me."

Marianne rolled and looked into the brown eyes of her lover. She put her index fingers onto one of his tattoos, and followed the line around in a circle, and on in smaller circles. She hadn't wanted him to withdraw and protect her from pregnancy. She'd wanted, deeply, to be utterly possessed by him, like ground he was planting in. She didn't care about anything but that moment.

The willow. Was it an omen? Was it a sign of something changing? She did not ask this. Instead, she asked, "In your law, am I your wife now?"

"No," he said.

"So how do you marry?"

"It used to be that the *kaumātua*, the elders, made arrangements. Everything like this was very... serious... very formal. But now things are different. There are not so many elders, because of the sickness that has killed them, and the slayings. The women go to whalers and other *Pākehā* without ceremonies and *karakia*. Do you want to be my wife?"

Marianne couldn't help smiling. It seemed a strange kind of proposal, if it actually was a proposal, made lying naked on a forest floor. But she stopped herself. How would she possibly manage to be with Matthieu? Even if they wed by the laws of France, or England, would this be acceptable? Would she not be shunned from the community of French Town? She would bring the Catholic Mission into complete disrepute, even more than she'd done already. Matthieu was not even a Catholic convert, like Hiromi; he was a pagan.

"I'm a Catholic," she said, emphatically. "Can I convert you?"

He rolled away on to his back. "You're a warrior woman. I saw you with an axe. You're like the wind that breaks down trees. You've blown all the way from the north to the south in your grief and restlessness. You need a man who can hold and satisfy you."

There was no hiding. "How do you know so much?" she asked then.

"For my father and me... this is our... work, our vocation. You have your priest and your scholar. For us, all this is in one man. The *tohunga* must know everything, and understand the world we see and the world we do not see. But now most of the great *tohunga* are dead, and people turn to your religion, because we haven't been able to stop you, or each other, or stop death. I went to France to understand how to stop death. I went to France to run from grief." He did not look at her as he said this; he looked up at the sky.

Marianne rolled over and sat on his belly. "You mean... we are the same? We both blew to the other side of the world?"

"We are the same," he said, "but the Catholic religion is not my religion." He too was emphatic.

She saw Matthieu watch her expression, and then he sat up, pulling her to him with his legs and arms. She put her forehead on his shoulder.

How could they exist together? Surely, only by Matthieu embracing the Catholic religion could there be any slight hope of acceptance in French Town.

"Then what will happen now?" she asked.

"I haven't been with a woman in this way since the death of my wife and children. I believed I couldn't endure such deaths again."

"You told me love always ends in grief."

"Yes, so I thought it was better not to love."

She pulled back and looked at him. His eyes were looking at her, yet behind them she felt he gazed instead at a past: memories of lost moments, lost people, and horrors no one could ever describe. She let him stay there, in the time that had gone, until at last she felt him return to her. His expression shifted, tightened a little, and he pressed his nose to hers and closed his eyes. She breathed in his breath, and he breathed in hers.

And then they were looking at each other again, in a kind of wonder.

Poor Monsignor. She would be such a disappointment.

Matthieu leaned forward and kissed her eyelids.

"Can you come with me, and talk to Bishop Pompallier?" she asked, softly. There had to be hope.

He said something again in his own tongue, as if a little exasperated.

Then he said: "Iwikau is talking the words of your gods, because of what your priest has said to him. But... when I was in France I discussed your gods with many people. I talked with a priest who was going on to Tahiti. It seems to me that you have the same gods that we have, but you know them by different names. All the saints you have for different things, these also are the *atua* we know. Ranginui, the god of the sky, is your great god, for you believe he is in the sky. He is the father, with Papatuanuku, who is your goddess Mary, the earth, and Tāne is their son, who is the god of the forest. This is your god Jesus. In your religion you have only one son and the other *atua* are the angels and saints, but you are mistaken. Whiro is your god Satan. You understand that your Tāne has been murdered, because this is what you have done to Tāne. I see it in your pictures. Your Tāne hangs on a dead tree, cut down, and nailed. This is the symbol of what you do to the forests. You think he was made alive again, but that's not true. He may become alive again, but now, in your lands, he's dead."

"How can our Tāne live again?" asked Marianne, baffled.

"Your Tāne can only be made alive by planting his trees over all the lands where you've cut them down."

Marianne did not know how to respond. If only she had the skills of Monsignor, who would surely know what to say. But she was struck by the fact that Matthieu had been ruminating deeply on such things. Surely, this was a start. Marianne brightened and looked at Matthieu hopefully. "In our religion, Christ will come again and everything will be Paradise. We will return one day to the beautiful garden that God made at the beginning."

"Now... do you make me Catholic, or do I make you Maori?" he asked, smiling.

*

Matthieu agreed in the end that the next morning he would go with Marianne to speak to Bishop Pompallier, but only to ask for advice from a man with great *mana*. He would come to the Malmanche house, early, and they would go to the *Sancta Maria* together.

Marianne recognised that there was no question about their future, either as husband and wife, or not. Their union was fixed, permanent, from this day, and not a matter for negotiation with others. It was a simple destiny. Marianne would never do what James Placard had done to her, and reject Matthieu, for any reason. Her loyalty was absolute. It was true she barely knew him, and yet she knew him. It felt in some way that she'd always known him, that he was a lost part of herself that she'd found, or that she was a part of him: not just a rib taken out and made separate, but a whole side.

When Matthieu and Marianne returned, the sky was flaming red, as if there were fires burning all around the horizon. Perhaps many people were watching, from the ships or from the shore, but the bay was so quiet and peaceful that there seemed no great reason to worry. If anything, Marianne thought how pathetic all forms of social reputation actually were. How absurd it was that she should even be conscious of the need to discuss matters so that she could be with Matthieu, in his own country, where she – and all of those who had come from Europe – were intruders.

They said goodbye lightly. Matthieu went to see François. Marianne returned to the Malmanches, who were extremely relieved to see her. They'd been distressed that she'd been gone so long. Rose Malmanche had been in tears, and Emeri Malmanche had gone and asked François to go and find her. He'd told them that Marianne had gone out with Matthieu Le Bon in a boat, not with a Frenchman. Emeri Malmanche told Libeau, and soon everyone knew.

Marianne made assurances and reassurances, and apologised, but she did not announce her intentions. Only before they blew out the candle to sleep, did she finally add: "In the old country, a man courting a woman may take her out for a walk, or in a boat, or in a carriage. So why not here?"

Emeri Malmanche replied, "Because he cannot court you, Marianne. He's not one of us."

She didn't respond. She thought she would wait until she saw Monsignor.

*

François wished he'd said that he would indeed object to Marianne going out with Matthieu. It was outrageous.

All day, he'd tried to throw himself into his work. He had a job to complete for the whaler *Vaillant*, and he would be well-paid upon its completion, but he gave the hot metal the full force of his anger. When Malmanche came into his workshop in a dither, stating that Marianne was late in returning from a boat trip on the harbour to view property, it filled him with rage. She'd clearly gone out on the canoe with Matthieu already. So he told Malmanche. "She's gone out in a canoe with a New Zealander... Matthieu Le Bon, or so I believe." Then he slammed down his hammer like a god of thunder wrecking havoc on earth.

Many of the male colonists had popped into his workshop during the day and asked variations of the same question: "Is it true that Marianne, from the Mission, has gone out on the water in a canoe with your Maori friend?" Finally, Belligny had arrived with the same question.

He'd simply said that he believed this was so, and left it at that.

"This is unacceptable, and dangerous," said Belligny. "And... I don't understand. I would have taken her. She is a complete mystery. She has been mending socks for the Mission and yet she has her own independent money, and is now looking to buy property. Do you know that? She is not poor! She is a woman who wants to buy land. It's astonishing! And now... what does she do? What kind of example does she set to the women here? Aie! Does the bishop know what she has done today, going off with that native? And no matter what you say, there are men who claim he is a murderer."

Belligny had gone from here to there, talking about how dissatisfied he was, and threatening to tell Robinson, who would want to have a very serious conversation with Madame Blake when she returned.

It was some comfort. Belligny would not allow this, thought François. There would be consequences. François would defend Matthieu from lies, but he would not defend him from truth, not when it hurt him so much.

Now, as evening fell, François looked up to find Matthieu walking into his shop as if nothing had happened. "I planted one of the willows in Kakakaiou," he said. "I'll plant the other in Katawahu."

'What did you do with her?' François wanted to ask.

"When are you going back to Katawahu?" he said instead, hoarsely.

"Not tomorrow, but the day after tomorrow," Matthieu said, pulling his boots out of his oil-skin bag and putting them on.

Then Libeau came rushing in, and stopped sharply, looking at the tall Maori. "Ah, I was just going to tell you that..." François knew he had come to say that Matthieu and Marianne had come back. He changed his tack immediately, and hesitated. "I hear tonight there will be cards played at Green's farm," he said.

This meant drinking and gambling – a chance to take winnings.

François nodded, with some approval, indicating he would join him. He looked to Matthieu, who seemed diffident, more remote somehow, dwelling on things. François felt that he was dwelling on Marianne. Something had happened between them of a personal nature – he sensed that – but nothing was said.

"I'll come for the cards," Matthieu stated.

François felt that everything had become twisted and wrong. There were boundaries marked out not only on land but around communities. These were lines that should not be crossed. And as for himself, his hopes were dashed in so many ways it was hard to keep himself calm and say nothing. He knew he had a debt to Matthieu. If it weren't for Matthieu, who'd let him plant the willow and build his *whare* beside it, then where would he be? He would have deserted the ship, the *Nil*, and gone off into the forest. Then what would he have done? Would he even have survived? He owed him his life.

But Marianne. He should not have her. It was all terrible, upsetting, a total mess. This was not how everything was supposed to have happened. Marianne was supposed to be his wife, and everyone would live happily ever after. What had he been thinking? That this would be Paradise?

This day – Marianne going off in Matthieu's canoe! It was more disturbing than anything. It was all very well that Clough had married Puai, Iwikau's cousin, but it was so wrong of Matthieu to think that he – a Maori man – could have any liaison at all with Marianne, one of their women. And how could she think of him? Was she completely mad? Bishop Pompallier would not allow it. Belligny would not allow it. Robinson would not allow it, especially as he believed his constable about the murder. No one would accept such a thing. Any relationship was absolutely prohibited. Marianne might find Matthieu intriguing, for reasons of her own, but propriety would dictate that she would not transgress decency this much, and lose her place in French Town. She was already odd, in being a woman on her own, somehow both French and English at the same time, and she was the subject of both gossip and desire. She would have to be even more careful than most and ensure she made her place secure. She would know that. No one would allow any romance between her and Matthieu Le Bon, Manako-uri, the son of a *tohunga*.

François felt his hot heart cool to iron hardness.

He would not have Marianne, but Matthieu would not have her either.

A part of him did not want Matthieu to get into trouble, and now a part of him did. He did not want to talk about Belligny's fury or warn him. He thought, as they walked up to Green's farm, that Matthieu would need to deal with everything alone, because it was none of his business. He would step aside so that Matthieu could take Marianne out, fine, and so he would step aside when it came to the repercussions too.

Whatever there was between Matthieu and Marianne would surely be thwarted by social convention and fear, if nothing else. François looked at his friend with unease. How disappointing that Matthieu – of all people – should become a rival.

The veteran of Waterloo, Rousselot, came walking up with them, and said Green's barn would mainly be full of sailors from the *Vaillant*. The single men and Libeau were going there, and Belligny didn't even know about it. Rousselot showed he had some cards.

François was immediately boosted by anticipation. God Almighty, he could do with a drink! The prospect of some alleviation from his mental strife was sheer salvation. Thank God that Green knew about sly grogging, and Robinson turned a blind eye. That was one thing Robinson was good for, at least.

*

William Green's house, beyond English Town, had the Union Jack flying nearby it at a place now known as 'Green's Point'. This was some distance from Takapuneke where his cows and red-painted milkshed caused offence to the people of the Horomaka, and his barn was close enough to Akaroa town to attract colonists, whalers and sailors whenever Green got in enough liquor for an evening of drinking and cards. His main wooden shed beside the house was converted into a public house for the night, and whalers came from all over the peninsula to enjoy the treat, sitting on rough stools and benches and logs. There were also some tough Sydney men from a trading vessel, the *Angel*. Here American, Australian, French and British sailors, as well as a few of the Maori men from the peninsula who worked on whaling stations, lost their divisions in rounds of ale, rum, gin and gambling.

Matthieu Le Bon and François Lelièvre entered the shed together, and each paid for a cup of rum. Matthieu's interest in coming, however, was clearly in cards, and he drank his rum slowly. These were men from the *Vaillant*, and it was their last night on shore. François watched as one by one, they lost their wagers, under the close eye of Matthieu.

François, however, used his remuneration from the *Vaillant* to buy a drink, many drinks, and knocked them back like medicine. He drank so quickly that he barely noticed the arrival of the British constables, who were not wearing their uniforms. Not many men recognised them as the constables, especially since one of them was new anyway. They had clearly come for a drink themselves, though he heard some of the British whalers moan in annoyance. The whalers and the constables were not usually allies, since it was the job of the latter to arrest the former if they became drunk and disorderly.

François looked for Matthieu when the constables came in, but he couldn't see him. *Just as well if he's gone, all things considered,* he thought.

It was quite late in the evening when things turned nasty. A French-speaking American jeered that all of New Zealand was in the hands of Queen Victoria, and that the French settlers should pack their bags and go home, or pledge allegiance to the British crown. The story of the *Britomart* racing to Akaroa and planting the Union Jack on the point ahead of the stupid French, who were dallying in the Bay of Islands, was being told everywhere as a joke, emphasising French humiliation. There would be no more French colonising ships, and the entire settlement was doomed to fail.

At this, Joseph Libeau announced that he happened to know from a number of French sailors that the whole of the country of New Zealand was French already, and the British had no claim to it at all, because of the prior rights made for France by someone named Marion de Fresne. The American whaler translated this into English, and the British then reacted with obscenities.

Libeau seemed to grow more feisty and determined to state this little-known historical case with every cup he emptied.

"Captain Marion du Fresne... Marion du Fresne... " said Libeau, "was a great sailor, who came to the shores of New Zealand seventy years ago!"

"Captain Cook arrived before," retorted a huge British whaler from Peraki, speaking heavily-accented French.

François slapped Libeau on the back, feeling his head swim, and said, "Let it pass. Enough, comrade. Have another drink."

Libeau swilled down another rum. "They buried a bottle on an island with a document claiming the whole of New Zealand for France. And one day we will find it again!"

"Shut up, Libeau," said François, and half-toppled off his chair. He could hear Libeau going on, and see men translating on the other side of the room, their faces looking more and more like Belligny's earlier in the day. Where were the constables? Where was Matthieu? There. No, not there. All these faces were blurring. His head was thick and everything was a fog.

"Marion du Fresne was a fool who was killed. The French murdered the natives of Motorua Island in retaliation!" shouted someone in English, from somewhere, and another whaler translated, and said this in French.

"Why would the natives trust French murderers?" shouted another in English.

Then someone shouted in suit: "You fucking killers. You French just want to take over the world, just like that bastard son of a bitch you called an emperor! Arsehole Bonaparte. You can all rot in pig shit!"

There immediately followed various translations, and mis-translations of what had been said, which resulted in a gathering surge of insults, followed by someone being pushed, and someone having rum thrown into his eyes. A lantern was knocked over and something caught fire. Punches were suddenly thrown everywhere. Clothes were ripped. Kicks thumped out. Tables fell with great crashes and pewter, china and wooden vessels came shattering and tumbling as if an immense wave had hit a ship, so that the room lurched and turned over. Then, finally, the farmer Green got up on a table and shouted out that they were all crazy, *toqués*, stupid, imbeciles! Calm down! There was a pile of men fighting in the corner, and François could see only a monster of legs and arms waving and kicking and flinging. Someone was putting out the fire. Above the hubbub of multilingual swearing and cursing there were equally multilingual pleas for order, not only from Green but from others. Someone shouted for the British constables, but they were nowhere to be seen.

Everyone was fighting, even the Maori, though François still couldn't see Matthieu. Then someone hit him. A powerful knuckle struck him on the side of his nose like a hammer and sent him falling backwards on to a stool, so that his back seemed to break in two with the wood beneath him and he clunked his head hard on a log. François rolled himself over on to the earth floor as blood came pouring out of his nostrils all over the hand he put up to stop it, and he kept lying there as – finally – a shot was fired and French voices were also heard: sailors had been sent from Commandant Lavaud. Then there were voices shouting in English.

It was a sorry night when French and British authorities showed their co-operation in order to curb the drunken excesses of sailors and whalers, but here also settlers were involved. Curses on them all, thought François.

There were further cracks of fired muskets into the air, and warnings that any man who dared to continue to fight would be shot dead.

François thought for a moment he might have been shot and be dead. He suddenly couldn't feel his feet or legs. He thought he would be sick. And then he passed out.

After some time – how long? – he awoke rudely, as he felt himself falling. He hit a surface, and realised then that he lay with his face down on a dirt floor. It was the prison in the naval headquarters. He was surrounded by a thicket of boots and legs, and lanterns were being flashed around. "You will stay here at my pleasure!" boomed the voice of Commandant Lavaud, like God in the Last Judgement, sending them all to Hell. There was then imploring language and apologies, peppered with grumbles, and everything went dark, pitch black. The key was turned in the lock.

Feeling his legs and feet again, François pulled himself together. He scrambled through the legs and was told to be still. He found a space to himself and threw up in total darkness, only to be sworn at.

In truth, this was the worst day of his life.

20
Marianne

Marianne got up at first light after another almost sleepless night in which her memories of the day before turned over and over. She'd been awake through the hours of darkness and listened to heavy rain falling on the roof and splattering on the windows, as the weather turned, and there seemed to be noises of men shouting in the distance, people running: rowdy whalers, she presumed, after a night's drinking. The night had been full of recollections, imaginations, thoughts.

As the sun came up she put on her blue dress. She went about housework during the morning, at first expectant and happy, waiting. She spent some time holding the baby while Rose did her toilet. She and Rose washed nappies, scrubbed pots and cleaned the floors. She baked some corn bread from flour she'd bought from the Magasin to feed the Malmanches at lunch, while Rose nursed the baby, and then made up leftovers into a soup with onions. But keeping herself busy did not alleviate a growing sense of disquiet.

Marianne and Matthieu had decided that he would come to the house early in the day and they would go to see Bishop Pompallier on board the renovated *Sancta Maria*. It was absolutely critical to Marianne that Monsignor knew the whole story, truly, and gave his advice, if not his blessing. She wanted Matthieu to meet Monsignor, for she felt that surely he would be able to convince her lover of the truth of the Catholic religion. She was no model of Christian perfection, given her exceedingly sinful behaviour of the day before, but Monsignor was a far better person who would know what exactly to say. In addition, she wanted to bid a proper goodbye to him before his voyage. He'd been distant ever since her crisis.

At lunchtime, Emeri Malmanche came back from where he was working with Éteveneaux on his land, and announced that he'd heard at the Magasin that Libeau, Rousselot and François Lelièvre, among others, had been put under arrest by Commandant Lavaud in the Naval Headquarters, for behaving in a drunk and disorderly way and causing property damage at Green's farm. There had been a great drinking session there during the night, with dozens of men – up to sixty – which had ended in a brawl. There was no indication when the prisoners would be released, and it was not clear who else was involved. There were sailors from the *Vaillant* who were spending their last night on shore, and the ship's departure was now stalled, so the Captain was negotiating with the Commandant, but the latter was livid that this behaviour had brought France into disrepute. There were Australian and British whalers who claimed the French started the fighting. Robinson and Lavaud had made arrests together, taking all the detainees off – the French to the gaol on shore and the British to the *Aube*, of all places, since Robinson had not yet built a proper gaol on land. Such was Anglo-French co-operation in matters of law and order.

"Were any of the Maori arrested?" asked Marianne, worriedly.

"Lavaud wouldn't take in the New Zealanders, Marianne," said Emeri Malmanche. "He has no authority over them. They can do what they like as long as we have this impasse regarding sovereignty"

Marianne tried to imagine what might have happened. Had Matthieu gone to this makeshift freehouse – but then what?

The sky continued cloudy with threatening rain. Marianne grew frantic. She could hardly think what she was doing. Where was Matthieu? After lunch, she simply announced to Rose that she had to see Bishop Pompallier immediately. Rose was by this time inside, nursing again, and looked up anxiously.

"Don't go," she said. "It's dangerous. Marianne, please."

But Marianne shook her head. "I'm going to the *Sancta Maria*."

She quickly took her shawl and went from the house, rushing down the road towards the centre of French Town. Her first port of call was François Lelièvre's blacksmith's workshop, just in case he'd been released. But it was all locked up and silent. She did not want to visit the Magasin in case she ran into Belligny, so she made straight for the French Jetty, where she could hail a boat to take her out to the schooner.

This she obtained quickly, in the form of Dr Raoul's rowboat. He was coming in from the *Aube*, and was happy to row out to the *Sancta Maria* and to accompany Marianne on the short journey. She tried to make conversation, and he told her the same news about the consequences of the drinking at Green's farm.

He said it was all anyone was talking about today and the gaols on the *Aube* were full of cursing Englishmen. He'd had to stitch some cuts. Robinson was beside himself, as he'd lost a couple of his constables. After all, a great bunch of rough men had turned up at Green's last night, Maori as well. It was just as well Captain Langlois had taken the *Comte de Paris* to Port Cooper to test the new masts, and there were at least no French sailors from there involved. There was talk of rowboats and whaleboats disappearing when Lavaud and his officers came, and the British constables had perhaps gone to make chase, because the naval officers from the *Aube* had made all the arrests. Now it was feared boats may have capsized. The night was rainy, thick with cloud and dark, and it would take days to determine who was missing, given the number of whalers and deserters living around about.

"Are you well, Marianne?" Dr Raoul asked, with some concern, after telling her all this.

"I'm well, thank you," she said.

"I have to say, this incident is lucky for you. Yesterday it was your name that was mentioned a hundred times, for going out alone in a canoe with a New Zealander, without telling anyone. Are you sure you are quite well?"

Marianne noted as he spoke that Dr Raoul's attitude to her had changed. He seemed a little detached and was not so friendly, yet at the same time he emanated a kind of professional concern about her welfare which, under the circumstances, she found bothersome. She felt like screaming, 'Where is Matthieu?' at the top of her lungs.

"Did you tell them that I might be mad?" she asked then. "From what you saw of the illness I had, might I be insane?"

Dr Raoul laughed, nervously. "Do you think you are?"

At this, Jean-Baptiste Comte hailed them from the *Sancta Maria* and pointed to the ladder. They drew up beside it and Marianne dexterously climbed up. At the top Jean-Baptiste greeted her warmly, with kisses on both cheeks, and she sent a quick and grateful goodbye to Dr Raoul, and then mouthed, "Yes."

Marianne was glad to see Jean-Baptiste, who told her instantly, with enthusiasm, about his journey to Port Levy and visits with local Maori, whom he found kind and decent, and highly receptive to the message of Christ, particularly Iwikau. At this, Marianne had a sudden impulse to cry, and had to stop it by simply nodding and smiling at her old colleague. He could not have heard about her escapade. How simple and pure he seemed. His blonde hair almost looked like a halo. It felt like, for her, everything had become so desperately complicated somehow, and she craved simplicity again. Yet she knew also there was no going back. She knew absolutely what her future had to be – even though that thought, that determination, was also sabotaged by the disappearance of her beloved. Where was he?

Then all at once, there was Monsignor. He came out, up the stairs from below, and stood there in his most simple black attire. She went up to him and kissed his ruby ring.

"What is it, Marianne? You are worried." He looked at her face.

Marianne glanced nervously to Jean-Baptiste. "I didn't know when you would be leaving. I wanted to say goodbye."

Jean-Baptiste smiled. "Marianne, we would have told you. We hope to sail in two days."

Marianne looked back to Monsignor, who gazed at her with seriousness.

She wanted then suddenly to say, 'Don't go away!' She had a peculiar feeling that she would never see Bishop Pompallier again.

There was a long pause, and then she said, "Monsignor, can I speak to you about something, in private." Her voice was raspy. Her heart was beating so fast! She looked to Jean-Baptiste with an apology, and he nodded kindly, with concern.

She followed Monsignor down the stairway, and along a corridor to his large cabin, where she stepped over the high threshold and closed the door behind her. The woody smell of the cabin instantly reminded her of her long voyages: to New South Wales, with Tim, in the *Albatross*; to New Zealand, with the Wands across the Tasman Sea; to Akaroa, with the Marist brothers. She'd done so much thinking and feeling in wooden cabins, and it was in one of these a growing life had left her.

"Marianne," said Monsignor, closing the door, "what's wrong?"

It was all Marianne could do not to weep. Oh what was wrong with her, with all this crying? No longer in the box of restraint! She did not speak for a long time, and then she said, "I came here to ask you... about... a marriage."

"A marriage? Whose marriage?" Bishop Pompallier's voice was impatient.

She couldn't look at Monsignor. She felt he was very tense. "Mine," she said.

After a pause, he said, "Sit down... here, with me, please." She saw his arm beckon her to sit on a long, padded bench underneath one of the portholes. She sat down there, and looked across to a neat, narrow bed on the other side, and a small desk in the corner. He sat down at the desk chair.

"Marianne, what are you thinking? To ask about marriage... it should be a thought that brings... happiness. You told me that you wanted to begin a school."

"I would like that. When I was in Sydney, I had a marriage and a school." She still couldn't look at Monsignor's face.

"But what... but... who?" His voice now seemed pained. "Dr Raoul – I saw you come here– "

"No, not Dr Raoul. I wanted to ask you about marriage to someone who is not Catholic... now. I don't know how to convert him." What could she say? She looked at Bishop Pompallier's face, finally. He seemed vulnerable and hurt. "I've met a friend of François Lelièvre. His name is Matthieu Le Bon."

Monsignor's pained horror was palpable. "I was told you went out on the water with this man yesterday. But... "

"He's a relative of Iwikau. His village was Takapuneke, and then Onawe *pā*, but his family was killed by Te Rauparaha. He's been working as a whaler with French ships around the coasts, but over the past years he's been away in France, learning medicine, because he's the son of a *tohunga*. He wants to use his skills to help his people fight our diseases. He lives on the other side of the hills at Katawahu."

"Le Bon's Bay," said Monsignor. "That's what the whalers call it. Jean-Baptiste tried to visit, but was told he couldn't."

"So... Monsignor. What am I to do?" Marianne looked to Bishop Pompallier imploringly.

He looked away, and shook his head. Then he got to his feet, agitated, and walked back and forth as if not knowing where to go.

Marianne sat, breathing fast, trying to take in small gasps and control her heart.

Finally, Bishop Pompallier turned around, and said, quite fiercely, "I should never have asked you to come here. It was a terrible mistake. Marianne, come with me back to the Bay. The British Government are starting a new capital, as I said before. There will be thousands of immigrants coming and you can have your school there. I will help you. You can have everything you want, there in Auckland. It will be a new beginning."

Marianne shook her head. "Monsignor, I have to stay here."

He let out a noise of frustration. "I thought you..."

Oh no! She had disappointed him so much. She felt he stood in lieu of Uncle in her mind. She loved him as a friend, as her protector, and more than that. If he were not in his position in the Church she might even have loved him as a man, despite his being so much older. She'd treasured a personal affection between him and her. And she'd undermined him, by her association with him. Now she was making it worse.

His face had completely lost its usual placid, understanding form. She was causing him pain! "Marianne, return with me to the Bay and have your school there," he said, as if pleading with her.

Marianne felt crushed. She would have to be honest. "I'm not a nun, Monsignor. I can't live a spiritual life of chastity, like you do. I'm tired of being alone. I need a husband, as a close companion, to be with and share life with, and... my body... needs a husband."

"Your body... you mean you wish to have children?"

'Oh much more than that!' she wanted to say. Could he understand that women had desires like men? Had he ever been involved passionately with a woman? Did he have the remotest idea?

"I can't live in the soul alone, not like you can," she said. "You are a much better human being than me. I'm so full of faults and sin."

He seemed flabbergasted. His face was pale.

She said, "Oh please..." She found herself sliding from the bench to the wooden boards of the floor, on her knees. "Monsignor, please forgive me, but I want to marry Matthieu Le Bon. Please talk to him, because unless he becomes a Catholic how can I? How can we live together?"

Bishop Pompallier closed his eyes and rubbed his brow hard, as if tortured by the sight of her. He sat down on his desk.

Finally, he managed to compose himself. He took some deep breaths. And then he said, very flatly: "I will talk to this man, Matthieu Le Bon, about Christ, because I came here to New Zealand to bring this message. I will not talk to him in order to convert him so that he can marry you according to the holy sacrament of the Church, but only because it's my duty and my vocation to urge the Maori people to find firm truth in God and his Son, and to rely on the never-ending compassion and intercession of our blessed Mother Mary."

"Thank you," said Marianne, with some hope. If only this could be. Matthieu and Monsignor could surely talk properly about religious matters, and Matthieu would be convinced!

"But Marianne," continued the bishop, solemnly, "a marriage according to the Church is one thing, but under French law this marriage must be registered as a civil matter, as I'm sure you know. Belligny is registrar of marriages in French Town. Yet... you are not French, and neither is Matthieu, so you will not be registered with him. Your intended marriage is of concern not to Belligny but to Robinson, who administers British law, and who will adopt the usual policies in regard to Catholic marriages. You will need the consent of a guardian. I would need to liaise with Robinson about how to set a precedent here in Banks Peninsula regarding a Catholic marriage within his jurisdiction between an Englishwoman with no local guardian and a New Zealander who is... for the time being... outside his jurisdiction, and who may become a French citizen once matters of sovereignty are settled. What will Robinson do?"

Marianne sat back, still on her knees.

Bishop Pompallier's speech seemed to speed up before this pause. He now slowed it. "Then you have another problem, a much bigger problem." He sighed. "Society."

"There are Englishmen married to Maori women," said Marianne. "You baptised their children."

"Married... no, no, my dear, this is mere cohabitation. And do you think what is possible for men in this world is possible also for women?" His voice was sharp. "Where will you live, Marianne? Where will you have your school? All the things you want to teach, all your ideas, don't you need... civilisation?"

"I can teach the New Zealanders."

He made a noise of despair.

She felt hollow. His words were emptying her completely. She was being erased. He was giving her a choice: a life in Auckland – or else a life outside the European world. Did it have to be like this? He had seen her as someone who could be a bridge between the English and the French, but she had made a different bridge.

There was a long silence. Marianne simply stared at the floor in front of her.

Eventually, Monsignor came to her and took her hand. He pulled her up to her feet, and then held both her cold hands in his. "Marianne, come with me back to the Bay," he said softly. "I will go to Taiaroa now, and you can come with me there if you want. Then, as soon as possible, I will go back to Kororareka." He paused, and pressed her hands tightly. "Come with me. I can look after you. I can protect you."

Tears fell. She couldn't stop them now. It was as if she were planting another willow. She stepped back. She pulled away her hands. "I need... to find... Matthieu," she said. "I must leave you."

She turned, went to the door, and turned back. Bishop Pompallier looked to her and shook his head.

"Monsignor, I thank you. You have been my salvation. Goodbye."

*

On shore, after Jean-Baptiste had rowed her back, Marianne said goodbye to him sadly. She hadn't been able to explain her continual weeping as they left the schooner. Jean-Baptiste had not asked about it, but rather had given her solid kindness and a parting touch on the cheek. He'd helped her to the jetty. It felt hard to leave him.

Nevertheless, she strode off in the direction of the naval compound with determination, without looking back. Tears, tears. Stop now! She shook off her vulnerability. Warrior woman. Be that, she told herself. Be strong.

Outside this large, two-storeyed house, Marianne asked a guard if she could see one of the prisoners, François Lelièvre.

"No visitors," said the guard. "They've been given water, but no food is allowed. Commandant Lavaud has not changed his orders."

She asked the guards about what had happened at Green's farm, and was told a similar story to the one she'd heard from Dr Raoul. Not only were many men in prison, there were others who had gone missing, including the two British constables. Searches were being made everywhere. Commandant Lavaud and Belligny were out in boats. The Maori villages had been visited. Lavaud had talked to each of the prisoners individually to ascertain who was where and when. He considered this all a terrible embarrassment and it was hoped there would be no official reports on the matter.

Marianne then rushed back to the Malmanches. She dashed in, only to get her cloak and bonnet, as the grey sky was beginning to spit a little, but once there she decided to change into black. Suddenly it felt the only thing she could wear. It brought her closer to Matthieu, and to herself, somehow. She felt his skin about the fabric. She smelt his smell. She changed quickly and explained to anxious Rose that she had to go to Onuku. "I'm sorry, Rose, today I will be going to Onuku, but I don't know what will happen after that. Don't worry about me. Please."

Rose was utterly baffled. "The Kaik? Why? It's starting to rain. What's going on?" Rose stood there holding the baby, looking the picture of sweetness. Marianne shook her head. "There's so much I cannot explain. I just need to talk to someone. I think he'll be there."

"But... on your own. No, Marianne. Emeri is still working with Éteveneaux on his land. Ask him to go with you."

"I'm fine... on my own," assured Marianne. "I've been on my own a long time."

Rose seemed crestfallen. But this did not deter Marianne. She made herself ready and put on her good Mission boots, a cloak and a bonnet. Then she walked off from French Town, through the divide behind the beach and on through English Town. She pounded up the hill and then quickly along the track that led to Onuku. She was not afraid to be alone out here, away from the settlement. She felt free. All the clouds of law and religion seemed to be sitting there, behind her, but out here it felt as if the air was open, and that sense of liberation she'd felt the day before returned. The light rain stopped. Grey clouds sat heavily on the hills all around.

Once she skirted Green's farm the track was fairly level, following the curve of the hill behind, and the views were clear where cows grazed, but after the turning beyond Takapuneke the bush cover meant that she walked through a tunnel of trees. She did not hear an approaching party. It was only when she turned around a sharp bend that she saw there were men coming towards her, and she realised who they were too late to hide.

Charles Barrington Robinson was wearing a high black hat and carrying a walking stick. With him were four big men, not in any uniform. They were obviously returning from visiting Onuku, though it was strange to see Robinson on foot like this. He had boatmen and a boat to take him around the harbour villages and beyond, so foot travel was not his usual form of transport. Marianne's heart raced and she quickened her step.

But before she reached the party of men Robinson hailed her.

"Good afternoon, Mrs Blake." Marianne wondered that he could have a snide tone in such a simple greeting.

"Good afternoon, Mr Robinson," she replied. It made her uncomfortable to speak in English to Robinson. Her lower class was advertised so easily through vowels. In French her accent was more neutral. Robinson spoke like the educated London barrister that he was.

"You are off on an afternoon perambulation, I see," he said, as she approached.

"Yes," she said, and made to go through the men ahead, but as she went forward Robinson held out his stick, blocking her path.

She stopped dead.

"I'm most intrigued, Mrs Blake. Why would a lady such as yourself be making this excursion to the Kaik?"

Marianne drew herself up and tried to keep dignified. "I'm

going to... buy eggs and... see what else I might purchase for the Malmanches, and I need to be quick and be back before sunset. *Madame* Malmanche needs more sustenance at this time."

"Oh really, Mrs Blake. You are not interested in making further enquiries concerning matters of property?"

His cynical tone was odious. The men around him seemed to snigger. He lowered his stick, but came closer to her. She tried not to look at him.

"It's such a coincidence. I was just telling these fine fellows from New South Wales about your... interests, Mrs Blake. *Monsieur* Belligny surprised me no end by informing me of the remarkable good fortune you've had in being in receipt of monies, sufficient for payment towards land. Very few ladies are in this position."

Marianne did not answer. It was intimidating to be surrounded by these men here. The Australians reminded her of the types in Sydney that Tim did not much care for, those who would lay into blackfellas like Billy Muster. They were probably from the trading ship, the *Angel*, which was at harbour.

She remembered Monsignor's words about Robinson. He hated her for finding her attractive? What on earth could she do about that? And he would be the man she'd have to go to regarding her proper marriage to Matthieu.

"It's a rather curious matter, I think, that a lady capable of purchasing land would scrub soiled linen for the Catholic Mission, or wash napkins for a family of French colonists. But now I see your real purpose in coming to Banks Peninsula. You are a female land speculator." He laughed out loud.

Marianne then couldn't hold her tongue. "Sir, I went to Monsieur Belligny to ask about the purchase of a small plot of town land so that I could have my own property on which to make a school. I have a small inheritance."

Robinson chortled. "Ah do you now. A wealthy heiress are you? And an explorer too, I'll wager. I understand from *Monsieur* Belligny that yesterday you hired a canoe and went off out of sight. He was, quite rightly, most perturbed at your choice of... ferryman."

Marianne looked Robinson straight in the eye. "Matthieu Le Bon is a very important man, a relative of chief Iwikau and a friend of François Lelièvre."

This was a mistake. Robinson and his men all laughed. One of them whistled.

"He's a murderer, Mrs Blake. We only wish we could bring him to justice, but the current impasse does not allow it. Clearly you are a woman who enjoys a sense of... danger. You do not care for propriety. Whatever is most forbidden is clearly, to you, most attractive. How can I protect you?"

Marianne tried to step forward, but her path was blocked. It was all very well to be protected by British law, but if the custodian of that law might abuse it, then whom would she go to for justice?

"Wearing black does not convince anyone that you are pious, or remain in a state of widow's grief," added Robinson. "Your liaison with the bishop is notorious everywhere. How well your black dress matches the colour of your moral character."

Marianne wanted to hit Robinson. She wanted to pick up his stick and beat him. She couldn't speak for rage.

"Go on a moment, lads," said Robinson, watching her like a fox about to snap at its prey, and the men swaggered off. She heard one of them say, "filthy little whore", and another said something else, and there was laughter.

Oh Lord. She was left alone with Robinson. Maybe she could take that stick now, strike him and run? No – he would shout and they'd all come running after her. This was not a busy lane. No one was here.

"You insult me, Mr Robinson," she said. "And you insult a man you do not know. For what? You took an immediate dislike to me for no reason, on the basis of a malicious rumour. Do you want me to fear you? Is that why you took my papers? Is that your revenge for– "

But she did not finish, as suddenly Robinson pulled her up and around, with his stick-holding arm pressing her neck into his shoulder, so that her back was against his chest, and her rear against his front parts, and he pressed his other hand hard between her legs.

Her breath was constricted. She gasped, and as she did so he said in her ear, "Where is he? Where is he, that murderous savage? Where are my constables and my boat?"

Then, in a sudden sharp movement, Marianne spun from his hold and broke away. She did not know how she did it. It was as if a phenomenal energy took hold of her, of furious anger and strength, and she managed to flick herself out of his grasp in an instant, kicking his shins and turning in a sideways loop. And immediately once she was free she managed to run fast, in her good Mission boots, pounding along the path with all her might. Since her Akaroa thinness meant her corset was only loosely tied, she found she could breathe well enough for running, and she kept on going for nearly a mile until the trees cleared and she saw Maori cultivations. There, as she reached the open *kumara* fields with the village ahead, she stopped. She looked behind her. No one was there. They had not come after her. She drew in breath so hard and so tight that her lungs felt as if they would break. She choked with it. She felt dizzy, and bent over.

"Hello missy, so what's the matter with you?" came a voice, in English, that sounded Bristol in accent. She looked up to see a slim, dark-haired man standing behind a fence to her left, leaning on a fork. Behind him was a small farmhouse, of sorts, rather roughly-built in a form that seemed to be a fusion between a Maori and European building. Beside the main structure was a Maori storehouse on a pole. Large tree-ferns grew around it. There were some pigs and chickens wandering around.

Marianne, still gasping, just stared at this man who seemed friendly. She recognised him as James Robinson Clough, who had come with his wife Puai to have their children baptised by Bishop Pompallier in September, and felt immediate relief. She was safe now, surely. But what would she say? That she was running from the police magistrate? Puai, holding their baby, came out of the house and said something to her husband in Maori, and he replied in suit. Then he said to Marianne again, "You all right? Need some water?"

"Thank you, sir," said Marianne, still breathing hard.

"I remember you from the Mission... Marianne isn't it?" said Clough. "The name's Jimmy, and this is Puai, my wife."

His kind, bluff manner was so completely opposite to that of Robinson's. Marianne felt that she had reached a haven, though she was shaking and panting and hardly able to think straight. Now, here was a proper Englishman.

"Marianne Blake, yes. But I'm not at the Mission anymore," she said, at last.

Marianne tried to walk, but now that she'd stopped running her knees were weak. Jimmy came close with a jug of water and a cup and poured some out. Marianne nodded to Puai. She'd never seen such a huge woman, almost as tall as her husband.

Marianne took the water in her trembling fingers and drank. She wiped her brow and put her bonnet on properly again. She gave back the cup. Jimmy seemed a decent man. He had the gait of a sailor.

"Pleased to meet you again, Marianne. You been running hard. You worried about being alone on the road? There's not so many English here yet, and the man in charge is a git. Did you not just meet him?"

"You don't think much of Robinson?" said Marianne, in reply.

Jimmy made a face. "My namesake. I'm a Robinson, but I don't want anyone thinking we're related. I was all for Iwikau and Tuauau signing the treaty, so our government could come and sort out the whalers round in Oashore and put these people under the Queen's protection for the sake of law and order. That's what the treaty's all about, isn't it? Iwikau's been to Robinson many times to get him to get this problem fixed, and get rid of those cows at Takapuneke. Robinson's supposed to protect the people of Onuku and all the others round about the harbour. But he acts like he's the bloody Prime Minister, and that doesn't go down too well. Now, he's been here today upsetting everyone, as if they know where his constables have gone. I looked in at Green's shed last night... have you heard about last night?"

"Yes," said Marianne, watching Puai rocking her baby. "But you were there? What happened?"

"Well I looked in, and it was a wild thing. It was full of... everyone, and there were the Oashore whalers, who you don't want to know. And there were these sailors from Sydney, who you don't want to know either. I saw the coppers, there in plain clothes. It wasn't like they came down to arrest anyone. They were joining in drinking. They were playing cards with our boys. I left before the fight started, so I don't know what happened, but it was choppy on the water when the wind and the rain came on, so you'd need to be sober to handle the waves."

"Did you see Matthieu Le Bon?" asked Marianne, then, with urgency.

"Matthew? You mean Manako-uri? Back from France?"

"Ah, yes... Manako-uri. I'm looking for him. That's why I've come."

"He's not here," said Jimmy, now a little suspicious.

Marianne's stomach lurched. "So he's not here? No one's seen him?"

"No, Mrs Blake. Now why are you asking? Because that shit-hole Robinson asked the same thing."

Robinson. Yes. But what did Robinson mean by also saying to her: 'Where are my constables and my boat?'

Marianne looked at Jimmy and Puai and answered plainly, using language she never used, "I don't know why that shit-hole asked anything. He's nothing to do with me. I'm Matthieu's... woman. I need to find him. He was going to meet me this morning, but he never came."

At this, Puai and Jimmy started speaking together in Maori, worried. Puai was emphatic about something. Then, eventually, Jimmy turned back to her and said, "Manako-uri was at Green's in the shed playing cards last night. With all the trouble, he might have walked over the hills to his *whānau*. That's a long journey. It's a good twelve miles across the mountains, I'd say, so you won't be seeing him, and no one is allowed to go there."

Marianne stood firm. "Except I need to go there. Just tell me the way."

21
Katawahu

François was released late in the day, and stood blinking outside the naval compound in the dull evening light. All day in the darkness, and now this imminent darkness.

The one thing that had occupied him, distracting him from the stink, the airlessness and his thirst, on top of his own physical discomfort, was the discussion of the others shut in with him, as they all were talking about what they remembered of the events of the night. There were certain mysteries to it. Robinson's constables were, apparently, nowhere to be seen at the end. The British magistrate had arrived with Belligny and Commandant Lavaud's men, with a party of ad hoc assistants he'd commandeered, mainly from the Sydney ship, the *Angel*: a bunch of brutal ex-convicts who took everyone away, with a beating to accompany their seizure. Arrests had been made indiscriminately, though many had disappeared into the very black night. The moon and stars had been hidden by thick clouds, and it had started to pour with rain.

There was something about the appearance and disappearance of the constables that François did not like. It bothered him too that he hadn't seen Matthieu at the end of the evening. Perhaps he'd slipped away after he'd won a few games of cards, since that was what he was there for, not for drinking. But then – if he'd done that – what if the constables had followed him? François dwelt on the angry words in the Magasin. That new constable hated Matthieu. To have them both in the same room spelled trouble. But he, François, by the time the constables arrived, had had at least three cups of rum. He hadn't been worried about anything, and he was not looking out for his friend. He'd been drugged by jealousy.

François walked off, with some difficulty. His back hurt, his right knee was painful, his nose and eye throbbed. He could tell his face was swollen, and he needed badly a decent wash. With that thought paramount, he went to his blacksmith's workshop, took a bucket, a towel and some soap, and then went down to the stream, where he gave himself as thorough a scrub as he could. It felt good to be cleansed of the ordure of the night and his incarceration. The only time he'd been released all day from that reeking room was to have a brief interview with the irate Commandant, who lectured him about bringing the nation of France into disrepute, and let him quickly visit the privy. His guts had been churning. He'd felt nausea come and go, but he'd thought that to vomit again in the gaol might have got him a hiding.

He went back to his workshop and found some clean clothing: old, worn items he used for his labours, but these did not smell at least. He dressed and then had one primary thought. He needed to find out about Matthieu. He'd been stupid telling people about him going out with Marianne, he realised. Belligny would have told Robinson, and Robinson would have told the constables, and they would have thought of him as adding insult to injury. What had he done? He'd been so angry and jealous, he'd wanted Matthieu to be challenged. But the constables did not need much excuse for that.

He went to the Malmanches up the road. Perhaps Matthieu had seen Marianne again today, and she would tell him what had happened.

From the outside the Malmanche house seemed a haven: a cottage with a growing garden and oil lamps lit within, creating a soft warm glow in the gathering gloom. Inside the house, however, there was a whirl of worry. Justine, the girl, was crying. The baby would not settle and was being rocked on the shoulder of Emeri. Emeri's brother, François, was sitting on a chair smoking a pipe, occasionally barking orders for everyone to 'calm down'. The problem was that Marianne had not returned from the Kaik, where she'd gone in the middle of the afternoon. Rose Malmanche told François of her very strange behaviour. She'd seemed cheerful in the morning, but after lunch she'd been removed and upset. She'd rushed off, come back agitated, and rushed off again.

François reassured the Malmanches and said that her disappearance was only that she'd been delayed at the Kaik and couldn't get back before dark. The people of Onuku were friendly and as a friend she'd be treated well. He insisted that he knew the people of Onuku very well and there was no reason for the Malmanches to fear, but at first light tomorrow he would go there and bring her back with him personally. His presence and his reassurances were a balm to the Malmanche family, but in truth he was more disturbed than he let on. He felt sure that Marianne's agitation of the afternoon would have had something to do with Matthieu.

They fussed about his injuries and asked him many questions about what happened at Green's farm. They gave him leftover soup, cold muttonbird and corn bread for supper. It was good to eat, but what he heard about the events of the night before did not settle his anxieties. Men were missing, including Robinson's constables; it worried him intensely. He rued his own drunkenness and envious feelings about Matthieu. He'd never do this ever again.

Afterwards, he walked haltingly up to his own house, along the *Chemin Balguerie*, knowing the way, though the full moon, dipping out of the bright linings of thinning clouds, helped him as he walked along. He half-wondered if, by some miracle, Matthieu might be there, at his property, knowing that he could always find shelter and sanctuary with him, but no. The place was absolutely quiet. In the moonlight, the willow tree stood like a woman with matted tresses of long, grey hair flowing down all around her. He touched the thin leaves.

*

Early the next morning, François ate some leftover potatoes with kouka root for breakfast, and then went again to his willow tree. He looked at the way the bark had been stripped, and touched his fingers over it tenderly. Then he prepared himself and set off for Onuku. He stopped by the Malmanches on the way, and they gave him some food for his journey and some seeds to trade for a chicken, if the Kaik people would agree. He walked out from French Town along the curve of the beach road and through English Town and up the hill. There he looked back at the tiny settlement, where the French flag flew in the naval compound, and then went out to Green's Point, where the Union Jack was flying. Green's farm was deserted. There was no smoke coming out of the chimney. Presumably Green was still imprisoned, and perhaps Mrs Green and their young children had gone to stay with others, for safety.

He turned off the main track that led to the farm, where the shed area was still in a state of disarray. A white dog came to growl and bark at him, until he shouted at it to go away. The big shed door was standing open, and inside there was a mass of broken stools, logs made into seating, rough tables, cards, fallen lanterns, bottles, casks, crockery, and the whole place stank of liquor, tobacco and sweat. Outside the scene of chaos was something the same. There was blood on the shed door. He walked down past the farm building and a sheep pen, towards the southern side where he had a view towards Takapuneke and the red-painted milk-shed in the middle of cow pastures. The small bay beyond Green's Point seemed peaceful. The seagulls called and dived. Apart from this, everything was very quiet.

François walked down the slope to the narrow stony beach. That was where boats came and got pulled up on shore when there was drinking in Green's shed. In various places there were bottles. The waves swished in, and the midges danced, and he was going to walk on. But then his heart went to his mouth. On top of a pile of green seaweed, hardly distinguishable from it, there was a willow cutting – one of his slips from the tree, still adhering to a small piece of sodden paper. A little further on was the potato.

François uttered a string of profanity, as if to undo the profanity of the willow's fate, and – by implication – Matthieu's. He picked it up. It was limp and broken. He looked around him. What had happened? Matthieu would never have left it behind. It was too precious to him.

François then looked around more closely at what else might have been grasped by the seaweed. Eventually, he found a button, but that was no clue. Putting this in his shirt pocket, he walked on, wondering, walking as quickly as he could up to the track again and through the bush, eventually coming out to the other side, past Puai and Clough's farm and the fields, to Onuku.

To his relief, Eta was there. He remembered François from the time he visited the Malmanche family, and greeted him warmly. François gave condolences to him about the loss of his baby, but Eta would not speak of it. So then François told him he was looking for Manako-uri.

"Everyone look for Manako-uri," said Eta, gravely. "I find

waka at Paka Ariki. I wait... All day. No Manako-uri. In night, I come to Onuku."

He had brought the *waka* back to Onuku, without telling anyone in French Town or English Town. He showed François where it was now, on the shore.

He said he could not find Manako-uri when the fight began at Green's farm. He searched for him everywhere, but he was gone.

François struggled with Eta's French, intermixed with Maori, trying to gather what exactly had happened, and when, and who was involved. He himself tried to explain what had taken place at Green's farm, and during his imprisonment. Others in the village gathered around to listen, and there was translation flying off in all directions.

In sum, François learnt this. He found out that no one had seen Matthieu for several days before, because he was visiting villages in his *waka* and on foot. Robinson had come to Onuku yesterday to ask what they knew of Matthieu's whereabouts, but they told him nothing. Marianne had come to Onuku later on, but she was not there now. Eta had shown the *waka* to Puai, Jimmy Clough and Marianne when he had arrived in the night, and told them about losing Matthieu at Green's farm. Puai and Marianne had become very upset.

Eta said that Marianne had gone off now with Jimmy Clough over the hills to Katawahu, but they would not be allowed in there, because no one was allowed unless Manako-uri let them come. They did not go by the way of Paka Ariki and Takamatua, where there was a track over the mountains, because Marianne would not return to Paka Ariki. They went by the old track towards the south, where Rhodes had taken over the tussock land and Green's cows were grazing in the southern bays, and then they would be heading north over the tops of the mountains. Puai had insisted that her husband go with Marianne, while Puai went with the baby on her back in the big *waka*, with three others, to Whakaraupo, Port Cooper, going first to Onawe and then over the hills to Wakaroa, because she needed to talk to Iwikau there.

François tried to grasp all the information, but it was clear that something was very wrong. He did not tell them about the willow, because it was a sign to him, and him alone.

*

Marianne and Jimmy Clough walked up the forested hills behind Onuku. They'd started off just before dawn, as it would be a long journey, after preparing through the night. And what a night! The arrival of Eta with Matthieu's *waka* was a terrible moment. Eta had waited offshore in French Bay, and gone to and fro around the shores all day to see if Manako-uri came down to the beach, but he hadn't appeared, so he'd paddled back to his own village Ohae, to talk to his wife, knowing the way in the moonlit darkness of the night, and then come with the *waka* to Onuku.

Marianne thought of all the times ships and boats had been found without their crew. She had to grieve then, as Puai did, fearfully, but she had to hope too.

They carried packs slung on their shoulders containing gifts from Onuku to the people of Katawahu, food and drink, but they trod quickly. Now Jimmy knew the whole story after their night of talking, Matthieu's disappearance filled him with concern. If Manako-uri had said he would meet her the next day, then he would have met her, he said.

Jimmy, fuelled by a flask of rum he swilled from, liked to talk, and in his long stories he also sometimes mentioned Manako-uri. Marianne started to think of Matthieu's name as this, not as Matthieu Le Bon anymore. 'Manako-uri' seemed so much more ancient and appropriate to the land.

As they walked through the nikau palms and tree ferns and then to high trees that hosted a million singing birds, Jimmy told him about the *hapū* that lived here, about Takapuneke and Onawe, about Manako-uri's father Tomoana, the great *tohunga*, and how Manako-uri's mother was from the Ngāti Māmoe tribe who used to rule over these parts until the Ngāi Tahu came some six generations previously, and about how now the Ngāti Mamoe and Ngāi Tahu were now mostly one people through marriage. He thought perhaps the Europeans and the Maori could do the same, becoming one people through inter-marriage; Maori understood this kind of thing.

He told Marianne he was twenty-seven, and he said that he'd sailed from Bristol and been a whaler until he left his ship when he met Puai, the daughter of Iwikau, the present Iwikau's uncle. He teamed up with Holy Joe Angus, who was anything but holy – and actually a runaway convict from Van Diemen's Land.

He talked about the way Iwikau ended up signing the British treaty, just before the *Aube* had arrived and the French colonists. He'd been with Puai and little Abner in his whaleboat on the way back from the heads when Captain Stanley sailed into the harbour on the *Britomart*. Captain Stanley told them to step on board, and plied them with a big meal with tobacco and grog, which was all right, though Puai had been so nervous she couldn't eat. He'd been asked to cut down a *kahikatea* for a flagpole. Stanley swore him in as 'Her Majesty's Interpreter' and he'd translated the treaty for an assembly of the people on the beach. It was about law and order. The people were afraid because Wesleyans had been saying the French were a danger, but they did not trust the English either. Stanley promised protection, and said he'd make sure no Englishman ever abused them again. They would be looked after by Queen Victoria. It all ended up with 'God Save the Queen' and salute of cannon on the ship, which had frightened the life out of all the people, but they'd got a fair number of gifts and went away happy.

After two long hours of climbing and listening, Marianne was glad to emerge from muddy forest to the windswept landscape of tussock and shrubs at the tops of hills. "Now look, will you," Jimmy said. "Enough to make you feel you're in God's own country."

It was incredible. Marianne, despite everything, couldn't help gasping. She flung her arms out as if she could touch the whole view with the tips of her fingers. You could see far, so very far. The world opened up like a vast tray of treasure. In the east there was the deep blue sea stretching to the horizon: the vast Pacific Ocean. In the distance to the west beyond the hills and more hills, Jimmy pointed out sharp snow-capped peaks emerging out of white clouds. He said these mountains were tens of thousands of feet high, and the coastal area of the country was hilly, with some plains, though inside the heart of it there were hundreds of miles of these impenetrable mountains, where they could find precious greenstone, which gave its name to the whole island in the Maori language.

"We treasure things that sparkle, like diamonds, or gleam, like gold. The people of the land here treasure the colour green, in that stone, in tattoos, and in the colour of trees," said Jimmy.

The day was clearing. They sat on lichen-covered rocks to eat and drink. From the windy height here, you could see how the sea changed at the heads from the rough turbulence of the Pacific to the quieter waves of the protected harbour. The landscape became clear to Marianne, how and where everything was. Jimmy pointed out Peraki and Oashore, and Onawe. Marianne couldn't help but wonder about it all, about how beautiful and rich all this place was, brimming with natural life, full of vibrancy, thick with the treasure of green forest. The European ships in the harbour were tiny, insignificant. This is how we appear to angels, thought Marianne. How pathetic are those aspirations to acquire and possess, our silly comings and goings. This land is forever.

Northwards the rocky peaks of the hills peeped out above the forest cover and patches of cleared land in a majestic row, partitioning the west from the east, with deep valleys dropping away from this high line on both sides. Jimmy said that this was now the way forward for them, following the peaks. It felt as if they would be walking on a high-wire, a narrow ridge thousands of feet above the world.

As they finished eating she was anxious to go. All this wonder at the beauty of everything was sharpened by the thought of her lost lover, the mystery of his disappearance, and a brutality that had struck him down. It made her want to fly out on the wind like a bird and soar down to the bay of Katawahu. If only she could. It felt like the land itself, the trees and the wind were with her in her love and intentions.

And so they went on along the heights, northwards now along the very tops, up and down into valleys where red beech grew, only to emerge on the rocky windblown peaks, for about five miles as the crow flies, but eight miles on foot over the irregular landscape, until they stopped again to eat and rest, and then continued down away from the rocky summits to the forest, the singing birds, following the melody of a stream.

Marianne liked Jimmy Clough and enjoyed all the tales he told. He was like the men she knew at Wivenhoe, easy to talk to and uncomplicated, full of humour and an innate suspicion of those at the top of the social ladder. She'd been completely honest about her feelings for Manako-uri and what had happened, even about the willow – in fact about everything. She'd discovered that she could be completely herself with him and Puai, her rapport with Puai inhibited only by language. On this journey now she found herself relaxing into Englishness again. Combining two worlds, the French and the English, seemed no more difficult than loving her mother and her father equally. They were both part of her, and yet she was something other. What was she? An oddity. Perhaps this was where she belonged, in this strange land.

As the afternoon wore on they quickened their steps. From the peaks down to Katawahu Bay was another five miles, and it was not always easy, with the rain that washed away the track, with the mud and slips, and great roots curling up to trip their feet. But, finally, the valley opened out. They felt the sea wind coming from the north and the lush vegetation thin. There were large areas of marshland where grey herons and bright blue swamp hens walked.

And then, Jimmy held up his hand. "Stop now," he said, "or we might be killed. Stop." He'd reminded Marianne about the *tapu*. No one was to come close to the village at Katawahu. By this means, Manako-uri had protected his remaining *whānau*. Only Manako-uri could lift the restriction.

Jimmy called out in Maori several times. They walked on a little, very cautiously.

He stopped again, listened hard, and called out. A *kākā* squawked and flew from a tree.

He called again.

Then ahead of them they saw a young man running. Marianne thought of Hiromi. But the youth did not appear friendly. He came charging up carrying a spear, and stopped quite far ahead of them on the track, making a face and sticking out his tongue, with loud noises of challenge, and stamping of his feet, followed by a great soliloquy that Jimmy clearly understood, as he assented with much gravity and made affirmative replies.

"Is he here?" asked Marianne, when there seemed to be a pause.

"I... I'm not sure," said Jimmy. "Just wait."

"What's he saying?" Marianne was very weary now, yet stressed and fired with the thought that Manako-uri must surely be here.

"It's about the *tapu*... much of this is according to the tradition of these things, but something has happened. We can't go in."

Jimmy then spoke, for quite some time, recounting why they had come, presumably, and he gestured to Marianne several times.

"Is he here though?" interjected Marianne. "Is Matthieu... Manako-uri... here?"

The youth replied, but seemed very upset. After a few minutes he ran off down the path, leaving them there. Jimmy turned to Marianne. "Manako-uri is here, Marianne, but he is dying."

"What? What?" Marianne leapt forward, as something sprung up inside her, and was about to go tearing down the path behind the youth, but Jimmy grabbed hold of her and wrestled her to the ground. She screamed loudly for him to let her go, but he kept her pinioned down.

"Listen to me," he said, fiercely now. "If you go down that path there will be a party of warriors who will club you to death. Manako-uri's nephews are fighters. Do you understand?"

Marianne, sandwiched between the body of Jimmy Clough and the damp earth, eventually managed to nod her head, as tears rolled down her cheeks. Jimmy, when he'd seen she'd settled, rolled off her and sat himself down, leaning against a rock. "I'm sorry I had to apprehend you, Marianne. That was not a very gentlemanly thing to do to a woman in distress."

Marianne sat up and kept wiping her face, as tears were replaced by more tears. More than anything she felt angry. This could not happen! He was not dying. She would fight and resist this. By sheer force of her will, it could not be. She didn't want to submit to some great force of fate. She just wanted to do battle with something evil out there that could do this. She would not lose every single person that she loved. She would not do that, anymore. She'd only just found Matthieu Le Bon, Manako-uri. He could not be taken away.

"Holy Mother Mary... sweet Jesus... don't let him die!" she cried.

*

After hearing what had happened at Onuku, François knew exactly what his next task was. He rushed back to French Town as fast as he could in his aching state, called in at the anxious Malmanches to report quickly, and then headed back to his cottage up the valley. He took hold of his box of his mother's ancient cures and went to the willow tree. "I'm sorry," he said, aloud. Then he took out a knife and cut off every remaining piece of bark from the slim trunk, apologising to it as he worked. He put the rather green bark in the painted wooden box his mother had given him before his very first voyage. He put the box in his bag, took a few leftover items – some dried eel and biscuit – and walked off quickly down the *Chemin Balguerie*, north past the naval headquarters and the Mission, and up towards Takamatua – German Bay. He'd been given detailed directions and felt sure he would not lose the route. When he came to German Bay, he had to follow the middle stream up to the summit of the hills, keeping a course in between two higher peaks on either side. There was a track that went along there. At the top, where the forest ceased and it was rocky, he would be able to look down and see many bays. The large, deep one that should be a little to the north of him was Katawahu. It would take him about five or six hours to get there from Paka Ariki Bay if all went well.

So he trudged on despite his pain and his swollen face, going on a hunch. Fortunately, today the rain did not fall and it was mild, but the track was muddy and slippery, and following the stream up from German Bay was not easy. Much of the forest around here had now been cleared: cut or just burnt off. This and the rain had obliterated the line of the path, and it took François a good hour to find what seemed to be the right track, and another two hours to get to the rocky spurs of the hills. By this time it was mid-afternoon. His visit to the Kaik and preparations in French Town had taken all of the morning. He'd convinced himself he could do this journey in five hours come what may, but his progress was poor. His knee was desperately sore. He stopped and took out a small piece of willow bark, and sucked and chewed on it as he went. The taste of the willow bark was neutral, yet it was a little rough on his tongue and mouth. He knew this was not the best way of extracting its potency. Perhaps to do this was a comfort as much as anything.

At the peaks he looked down at Akaroa Harbour on one side and the great Pacific on the other. After a walk along the tops to the north, he could see the shape of Matthieu Le Bon's bay, Katawahu, with the sides that seemed to stretch out like two arms, and he made for it. He did not stop long to survey the extraordinary views. The tops of the hills were bleak, with wind-blasted trees and great grey rocks that seemed to be the misshapen forms of ancient giants. The journey down the eastern valley was fairly gloomy, since the sun was below the hills behind him, but the birds kept him company, swooping and diving from tree to tree. A dancing bird, a fantail, seemed to follow him for a good half an hour. He simply followed the stream and trusted it led in the right direction. At last the ground levelled out, and then it was another three or four kilometres until he came to an abrupt halt.

Two people.

He came to an abrupt halt in front of Marianne and a man he recognised as Puai's husband: James Clough. They were sitting on the track against some rocks, and both looked exhausted, but they quickly stood as they saw he came towards them and – in a gesture of guileless affection – Marianne came up and threw her arms around him like he was a brother, and hugged him.

He was immensely moved. He could hardly bear it. It hurt a little, given his aching back and swollen face, but he didn't mind. He was so happy to have Marianne behave like this, despite everything. It suddenly didn't matter anymore that he knew that he would never have her. He knew that she was here because she loved Matthieu. His own disappointment was nothing in comparison with hers. He couldn't be upset about that anymore. He couldn't be jealous. He could only remain Matthieu's friend, and Marianne's friend too, and try to make up for his mistakes.

Then Marianne pulled back and touched his face very lightly, with tenderness. "You were in the fight at Green's shed?"

"Yes."

"Did you see what they did to Matthieu?"

"No. No one I've talked to saw what happened. Is he here?"

Marianne nodded, and her face creased in pain.

François broke away, went to Clough then, and greeted him as best he could in English.

"François," said Marianne, her face tight and drawn. "We can't go any further unless we're given special permission. Matthieu is here, but– "

"He has not given permission?"

"He is alive, but perhaps he can't speak." Marianne looked away.

Clough said something in English and Marianne responded in suit.

Then François told Marianne everything that he'd learned and witnessed the day before at the Magasin, with the new constable, and what Belligny had said after she and Matthieu had gone off in the *waka*. She translated for Clough. "I see now," she said. "When that constable was introduced to Belligny, I was there. Robinson said he was a wrestler. He knows how to fight."

"But Matthieu knows how to fight," said François. "And he is not dead."

"Robinson came to Onuku not only looking for Matthieu," said Marianne. "He was also looking for his boat and his constables."

"His boat?" queried François.

"He went to Onuku on foot."

"So Matthieu is here, but where are the constables?" asked François.

Marianne then quickly translated the French to Clough, but they were now interrupted. A party was coming along the track towards them: the young man who had been there before, an older woman and an older man. They stood in front of them and greeted them, without any challenge. Their faces were distraught. They explained that Matthieu was very sick and couldn't see them.

Then François, with his heart sinking, stepped forward and asked Marianne to translate to English, and for Clough to translate to Maori, because he had to speak properly, so that they truly understood. He greeted them in Maori, and then went on in French, stopping to let this chain of speech take place. He explained that they had come to help, because a terrible thing had happened. They did not know what, but it was such that the *tapu* should surely be lifted for them. He believed that they had been brought here, and that this was meant to be. Then François pulled out the sad little willow slip he'd found on the beach and held it up.

He spoke then, with emotion, and with many pauses, and said: "Three years ago I met Matthieu Le Bon when I ran from my

315

ship. I planted this in the ground. It's just a part of a branch of a willow tree. I wanted to make it grow here. He stopped me and said I had no right to do this. But he noticed something... I don't know what... and it made him change his mind. He let me plant it, and said that he would protect it. He put a *tapu* on my tree, so that no one can destroy it. It still has that. I'm now its protector. I give it to my friends. I gave it to Matthieu, two days ago, to bring to you in Katawahu. But he couldn't bring it to you, because of what happened, something we don't know about. But see... here is the miracle. He dropped it, and I have found it. No one else found it. I did. I too, like Matthieu, know some of the secrets of plants and of medicines. And I'm his friend. The tree asks me to come here."

François stopped. What the hell was he trying to say? This was not a coherent speech, making any kind of clear case. What did he know about *tapu*?

"I don't know what anything means," he said, opening out his arms hopelessly. "Tell me what this means."

*

Marianne did her best to translate into English what François said, and listened to Jimmy's words speaking another translation into Maori. She was, as she spoke out the words, also wondering about them. So François had found one of the cuttings he'd given to Matthieu. She and Matthieu had planted one of the cuttings together at Kakakaiou. There was another willow cutting he was going to plant at Katawahu. He'd brought it back in his bag, and then he'd gone to Green's shed. Her knees felt weak.

After Jimmy had finished his translation, the older woman let out a wail and seemed to recite something long, as if she was mourning. She used gestures. The men stood by. The woman was almost singing, almost chanting. This lasted for some minutes. Then she fell silent. There was a pause. It felt as if something had been unlocked.

Then the woman came forward a little and welcomed them, without smiling, and told them to follow.

The bay of Katawahu, opening out to the vast ocean, was very different from the inland bays of Akaroa Harbour. It was rough, wild, and noisy with the crash of waves, though these were obscured by sand-dunes covered in wild grasses. Now, under the pink sky, the colour of everything was turning from rose to grey.

Inland from the sand-dunes there was a collection of *whare*, a store-house, fencing, pigs, chickens. Only one living being came towards them – a brown dog. It scampered up eagerly, straight to François, and jumped at him, licking his face and yowling. Marianne watched as François smiled a little, and handled the dog with familiarity, scratching and patting until the dog settled. François looked to Marianne sadly. She understood how he would have known this animal. He didn't need to explain. She wished then she could ask him so much of what he'd known of Manako-uri before, when François had come to this country as a stranger in the land of the Maori.

There were further words spoken before they were allowed to go further. After coming into the settlement, they took off their shoes, and the woman and the two men led them through the low entrance door of the biggest *whare*. The dog was left outside.

There he was.

Here, inside, it seemed that all the people of Katawahu had gathered around the unconscious body of Manako-uri, Matthieu. The newcomers entered cautiously, barefoot, and knelt beside the mat on which he lay. There were burning candles, but it was dark in this windowless place. Marianne looked at the unmoving form of her lover, hardly believing it was really him. And it did not look quite like him, there, lying on the ground. He could have been a form cut out of wood, sculpted with skill, laid out like this, like a figure carved to realistic perfection. He was a tree that had been felled and made into this shape by a knife and chisel.

The older woman, who had temporarily removed the restriction on their entry to Katawahu, spoke to the people in the *whare*, who were amazed and worried to see visitors.

Marianne, numb, watched, as if from some distance. Her body had entered this house, but her heart had not. She tried to take in what she was seeing. Manako-uri lay under a blanket that covered him up to his chest. His face showed no pain. But the huge bruises and injuries on his body indicated that he'd suffered. There were some knife wounds on his arms, but these were cleaned out, and not bloodied. The main wound was on his head: a gash mainly on his forehead. Marianne wondered if what he suffered now was from blood loss. But what could anyone do about that? Marianne took his hand. Not wood. His skin was cold and clammy. She grabbed his wrist. There was a fast but weak pulse. She looked to Jimmy and François. What could they do? Reconcile themselves to the fact that he was dying after all?

Emotion was like breath she was holding inside herself. She had only questions. Her mind busied itself. How had he come to be here? What had happened? Who had found him? What could anyone do? François seemed diffident, staring. Jimmy was talking to people, and noting their replies, and Marianne simply watched Manako-uri, noticing his breathing now. Not wood. He was alive.

François did not do anything, or react in any way. He held the willow in his fingers.

Then finally Jimmy spoke. "The Maori, when their warriors lose blood in battle, have methods of treatment. They get their men to drink blood. There's a pig tied outside ready for slaughter for this purpose. But they can't get the blood inside him while he is unconscious. They've tried various pungent roots to wake him, but nothing has worked so far."

"How did he get back here? Did he walk? Where did they find him?" asked Marianne, releasing some of her questions.

"They found him unconscious in a rowing boat, caught on the rocks at the heads of the next bay." Jimmy frowned. "Two of the young men had been setting traps for birds early this morning and saw the boat. There were no oars, so the sea must have taken him from the harbour heads."

Marianne translated all of this to François. And suddenly it was as if he woke up and realised something. François asked, "When he came back from France, he brought a bag with him? It had medicines from Paris."

"Yes," came the reply, after translation.

François put the willow on the mat, asked for the bag, and it was found in a corner of the *whare* and pulled over to him. It was a small case, well made of leather and wood. Marianne watched as François used a knife to unpick the locks dexterously and open it. Inside, it was full of containers with labels. François scrambled through them, excited. Marianne wished Dr Raoul was with them.

She should return immediately to French Town and fetch him. Tomorrow, that was what she should do. But, curiously, François seemed to know what he was doing.

"I have some smelling salts," explained François to Marianne, "but they were not strong enough to wake you when you fainted. Even Dr Raoul's were no good. What these people have among their own medicines will not be powerful enough. Matthieu may have brought something better from Paris."

Finally, he opened a small, wax-sealed tin of a highly pungent mixture that made everyone react with disgust, coughing and wiping their stinging eyes. François closed it again quickly. "Ah," he said. "This will do it. They can kill the pig."

Marianne queried this. "Drinking blood... how can that– ?"

"My mother does the same," he affirmed. "She's a midwife. When a woman has haemorrhaged after childbirth, she'll kill a goat and make the woman drink the blood. It does not always save the life of the woman, but sometimes it does. I'm not a doctor, Marianne. I only know things that my mother showed me. These people know the same things that my mother knows. Ask Jimmy Clough to tell them to kill the pig and collect the blood."

She explained this to him. Jimmy then said in Maori that the pig should be killed. A couple of young men went out. There then followed a horrible shrieking. After some time of silence, a bowl of steaming blood was brought into the *whare*.

"This is nothing different to what my mother does," said François, looking at Marianne's discomfort.

François issued more instructions. A couple of young men lifted Manako-uri into a flopped sitting position, and kept his head up. François put the tin under Manako-uri's nose and opened it, while everyone else in the *whare* covered their mouths and nostrils.

Manako-uri inhaled, flinched and made a noise, but did not wake.

After a minute, François tried again. Again the same thing happened. Marianne felt a colossal sense of frustration. She looked at the bowl of steaming blood. How could he gain any strength when he couldn't drink it?

Such was her frustration the third time, when the tin was opened, that Marianne felt her sense of numb suspension, of holding her heart-breath, release. She was back at Tim's bedside. She was at the bedside of her mother. She was again at every moment in her life when she'd had to hold herself in. Seeing then the dry willow on the mat, she suddenly picked it up, held it before her and uttered a great cry. It felt as if the cry did not come from her, but from outside – through her. She'd never had an experience like it, but it was a sense of being a channel for something other than herself, like an oracle, a medium, and she had no control. "Wake up!" she cried, in French. *Réveille!*

At Marianne's cry Manako-uri opened his eyes and inhaled sharply, pulling back and raising his right arm, as if ready to fight. He hardly seemed to take in what he was seeing, and immediately the older woman, Manako-uri's aunt, whose name Marianne later found out was Tira, leaned forward and the young men pulled back his head. Tira poured blood into his mouth. He swallowed the hot liquid instinctively, with his eyes wide open still, as if his soul had not yet completely returned to his body.

And so this was the process, and it continued for some hours, with Manako-uri roused by smelling salts, without Marianne's cry, and after a while they let him sleep again, a proper sleep. Tira mixed other plants together, and François added to these mixtures certain herbs he had, including the willow leaves. They made infusions. They mixed these with the blood. Tira chanted, sang and said blessings. Marianne prayed aloud. This was their healing, all night long, until it was dawn the next day.

*

The early morning light shone in through the open doorway. The house was full of sleepers, lying on mats, but Marianne and Tira had not slept. François had for some time been away, outside. Jimmy was snoring. Marianne held Manako-uri's hand again. It was warmer. His pulse was slower now.

Tira told Marianne by gesture to go, to have a break, and so she walked out from the *whare* up the dunes and down to the white sand of the beach. The sun was coming up and everything was golden, though the sun itself was not yet visible, obscured by the arms of the bay. The waves broke steadily some distance from the shore after coming through the narrow opening to the Pacific, and fizzed and foamed. Shags flew down to the rocks. Piles of black and brown seaweed littered the beach like huge balls of hair, along with all kinds of shells, bits of pink crab, mussels and driftwood. Away in the south she could see François standing where the stream flowed out to the sea, where a great many birds had collected. She walked to him, and as she walked she spotted a vivid turquoise shell, of huge size, and picked it up.

When she came to François she offered it to him.

He took it. "It's pretty. It's called a *paua*. It matches your eyes."

Marianne smiled. "François, thank you." She didn't mean about the compliment.

"I don't know what did it... the smelling salts from Paris or your scream." François seemed to be controlling emotion. What could she say?

"Will he be all right?"

"I don't know. When my mother has to heal women who have lost blood, it can take some time. The body has to make blood to replace what has gone, and it needs to draw on something strong to do that, something with life in it. But Dr Raoul could do no better than us." François was clearly pleased about this.

Marianne folded her arms. It was a little chilly in the morning. Her cloak was in the *whare*. But she was all right. She felt sure. Matthieu would be all right.

*

François couldn't help himself. He put his arm around Marianne, just to keep her a little warm. Since she'd hugged him, he felt he had licence to do that, to expect physical intimacy, and she did not resist.

"I had a sister named Marianne," he said. François felt an ancient pain. "She died when she was ten-years-old, and I learnt the arts of my mother instead of her, because my mother needed some help. That was when I was just a boy. Men never learn such things."

"And it is the name of France. I think that's why my mother wanted me to have it," said Marianne. "In me, there was a part of France with her too."

It all seemed to François that there was a pattern to everything. All the random, cruel things of life fell into an order – here, now.

They stood there in each other's arms, not speaking.

"I'm not going back to Akaroa," Marianne said, eventually. "Please tell the Malmanches and... everyone. I'm going to stay here."

That now seemed inevitable. What could he do? He accepted it. Perhaps there was even some relief.

"What will Bishop Pompallier say?"

"I think... I've already said goodbye to him," said Marianne.

"Did he let you go?"

"I never belonged to him in the first place."

"But you... loved him."

Marianne stepped away and looked at François quizzically.

"I heard you say that to him, when you had the laudanum. We all heard you," affirmed François.

She looked away at the sea, and then back to François, apparently dumbfounded. "François, there are many kinds of love." Then she became pensive, as if remembering something.

François put his arm around her again. "I'm sorry," he said. "I love you. But now I will love you only as a sister. You are my sister, Marianne, in this place."

Marianne smiled, and tears fell at the same time. She took his hand. "I'm sorry, François."

*

Later that day, Manako-uri woke up enough to see where he was, and who was with him. Two days later, when he was able to speak, he told the story of the night he was lost. At Green's farm he was told by a sailor that there was a man outside who would give him money due to him for winning the card games, away from the crowd in the shed. He thought he should be wary, but he went out there anyway, and was seized before he knew it. They crowded around him and carried him off to the shore before they beat him. No one saw. He shouted, but the crowd in the shed was drunk, noisy and deaf. There were eight men, including the British constables. Three men he could fight against and win. Five men he could fight against and win. But eight men he could not fight.

He fought there in the darkness and injured three of them, so that then there were only five, but by this time he was bleeding from their knives, and wearied by their punches, and – before he knew it – there was a heavy thing that hit him on the head.

He did not completely pass out, but his body dropped away from him. He was conscious a little, but unable to move. They took off his boots and emptied his bag, laughing. They were speaking English, so he didn't understand. They did not knife him anymore. Perhaps they were afraid of there being too much blood, and that would incriminate them, if they couldn't clean it or trust it would be washed away by rain and sea. They didn't want a body either, clearly, and that was why they picked him up and threw him in a boat. Being thrown there woke him up, but he didn't want them to think he was conscious. He pretended to be dead.

As he lay in the boat he began to feel confident, because out on the water he knew he had the advantage, because of his skills. Out in the boat, there were not so many of them. The three men he'd injured stayed behind with two others, so that there were now only three men with him.

They rowed out, further and further towards the heads. They clearly didn't want his body washed up on a shore of any inhabited bays, so they went far, too far for their small boat, because the waves became rough and high, and they should have known they should stay clear of the harbour mouth or you could be sucked out to sea. He heard them pull up their oars and shout, as it began to rain hard.

And then all at once he got to his feet. He shocked them when he stood up, right in the centre of the boat. He was like the mast of a ship. He had his arms to the sides to steady himself, and he rocked the boat hard from side to side on the waves, keeping his balance in the centre, so that they fell, one by one, all three of them, into the deep water. They were swimming though. They were men who could swim, and were trying to come to the boat to grasp hold of it, but the boat was soon out of reach. He left them to Tangaroa, who would do with them as the god saw fit.

But by then he was very weak, as he was bleeding from his head and from the injuries on his body. He tore his shirt to use for bandages, to stop the bleeding from his arms, where the knives had sliced him as he was fighting. But his head wound was worse than those. He felt himself becoming dizzy and sick, and saw that the boat was being carried out further to the heads by the current, being pushed to the northern rocks where the penguins nest.

He tried to pull at the oars to steady the boat so that he could make for land within the harbour, but his arms were too weak now. As he heard the waves of the open sea he lost one oar, and then he lost another, and that was the last thing he knew.

Marianne first heard all this with the others of Manako-uri's *whānau*, in the *whare* where he lay weak and sick. Jimmy translated. Everyone made noises as he told the story, haltingly, but Marianne said nothing. She was too angry.

When Manako-uri and Marianne were left alone, he told it to her again in French. She decided to let her anger stay outside, and heard it now with equilibrium. Why should she cling to rage? Manako-uri was alive and safe. He was the victor, and justice had been done. She whispered a little prayer thanking Mary and Jesus. Or was she thanking Tāne, or Tangaroa, or Papatuanuku? Perhaps Manako-uri was right and they were the same, all these deep forces of the world, these senders of miracles, destiny, salvation.

She took off her clothes, let down her hair, kissed her lover's skin and lay down beside him, as if the touch of her own skin might itself be healing. She pulled up blankets around them both so that they were in one small nest together, and clasped his big warm hand in hers. She then had a need to sing. She sang to him an old song her mother knew about a soldier, caught in exile, who missed his home.

"I love you," she said, at last. "I will stay here if you will have me."

"I love you. This is your home," he said. "I'm lifting the *tapu*."

And then they lay together for a long time – silently, knowing – until they both slept.

*

When Manako-uri became strong again he instructed his *whānau* to destroy the boat that had taken him from Akaroa, and they took it out to sea and sank it. There was then no evidence linking him with the action of the constables. He asked none of his *whānau* to inform the British or French what had taken place. Iwikau, Tikao and Tu-auau said that Robinson knew very well that he had no authority over the *rangatiratanga* of the chiefs, and should have controlled his constables, if he'd known about what they intended. He might now have been informed of certain events from the men who attacked Manako-uri on the shore. He should have taken action against them, if they were still in New Zealand, but there was a strong possibility, from what Marianne said, that they were off the trading vessel, the *Angel*, that departed back to Sydney three days after the events.

Iwikau said that Robinson himself was implicated by association, and by his words to Marianne. But he would not know what had happened on the water, and if he made further enquiries his own possible involvement would surface. The chiefs reasoned that if he was guilty, then once he learned that Manako-uri was alive he would himself drop all questions and try to hide everything. This was indeed the case. Robinson's official conclusion was that the missing constables had taken the boat and gone after some whalers. In the rough seas, the boat had been lost to the waves and they had drowned.

Bishop Pompallier departed on November 14 to Otakou with Fathers Comte and Pezant, in the schooner, the *Sancta Maria*, and arrived back from his journey south on January 12, 1841. Bishop Pompallier and his Marist priests brought with them a letter conveying the words of Chief Taiaroa, at Otakou. They had clarified with Taiaroa that the land in Banks Peninsula could be sold to the French, according to the agreement of the local chiefs. He asked only for compensation for his own *hapū*. The French colonists celebrated this good news with gifts to the bishop. François Lelièvre presented him with two cuttings from Napoleon's willow, which he accepted. "To remember Marianne," said Francois, cryptically, as he passed them into his hands, and the bishop bowed his head to him.

Bishop Pompallier did not remain long in Akaroa, and did not see Marianne again. Just one week later, on January 19, he sailed to the British settlement in Port Nicholson, now named Wellington, along with Mayor Belligny, who was anxious to liaise with the British there, having heard reports of conflict in Palestine that could result in a declaration of war: the British had acted against the Pasha of Egypt, who was under French protection. Events of far off lands were no longer insignificant, and they took the *Aube* away from Akaroa Harbour. On February 12, 1841, Commandant Lavaud set out to sea, since he feared that British warships might attack the *Aube* in Akaroa Harbour. The French settlers were left completely on their own under the supervision of the British magistrate, Robinson.

However, that very day Robinson received a deputation. Alerted to the arrangements made for the departure of the *Aube*, Iwikau took the opportunity to come to Paka Ariki Bay with a hundred fighting men. Despite the reassurances of François Lelièvre, the French settlers believed that the Maori had risen up, now the French naval force was no longer there to protect them, and stayed inside their houses fearful they would all be killed.

But this deputation of fighting men was not concerned to harm settlers. They camped outside the offices of Robinson. Iwikau went in and brought Robinson out, and spoke to him, with Jimmy Clough as translator. Robinson clearly believed he would be killed, fell to his knees and begged for his life, but Iwikau simply said that it was important that Robinson understood that it was his job to protect the people of the Horomaka from the British who would act abusively, by word or deed.

Robinson assured Iwikau that he would do everything in his power to protect the people of Banks Peninsula, and it was his solemn duty as a magistrate to ensure British subjects within this region abided by Her Majesty's laws or suffer the consequences. Upon request, he also delivered to Iwikau official papers belonging to Marianne, now the wife of Manako-uri, and letters from her uncle in Wivenhoe in his possession, which Iwikau passed to her in Katawahu, in a carpet bag delivered to him from the Malmanche family.

Robinson filed no official report of this. Even the incident at Green's farm and the disappearance of the constables was obscured in official records and correspondence. Robinson thereafter trod very warily with the chiefs, and was consistently deferential and careful. It is said that Manako-uri put a curse on his land in Kakakaiou. Robinson never managed to take hold of the land, though it became known as Robinson's Bay. In following years he tried repeatedly but his efforts were foiled by strange accidents. He never farmed it.

François Lelièvre thrived, and eventually found love and marriage with a French woman of the colony, but that is a different story. He became a well-respected leader of the settlement of Akaroa, and had a large family. His willow became famous, and cuttings were planted in the French cemetery on Aube Hill and elsewhere. His descendants remember.

Marianne lived with Manako-uri, called Matthieu Le Bon, in Katawahu, called Le Bon's Bay, and then later in Wairewa, called Little River, never marrying according to the laws of either Britain or France. Marianne bore six children, and five lived to bear children themselves, so that in her lifetime she knew twenty-three grandchildren, and two great-grandchildren. She taught them, and other Maori children, literacy, numeracy and expertise in matters of the world, in her own little school. In a ship bought from the whalers – when there were no longer sufficient whales to warrant the trade – Manako-uri took his skills in both the new medicine and the ancient arts of the *tohunga*, taught to him by his father, to all the villages of the Ngāi Tahu.

In the course of time, the descendants of Marianne and Manako-uri spread out like seeds on the wind, even when the forests of the Horomaka were felled and they no longer possessed the land. They planted themselves everywhere.

And they remember.

Acknowledgements

Firstly, I thank Peter Tremewan, whose finely-researched book, *French Akaroa: An Attempt to Colonise Southern New Zealand* (Christchurch: University of Canterbury Press, 1990, rev. ed. 2010), is invaluable. Peter was very generous in sending me materials, including unpublished French documents and letters, when I first began work on this novel, and I acknowledge a great debt to him.

The writing of this story has involved trips across the world. I am grateful to archivists at the Akaroa Museum, the National Library of New Zealand and the Alexander Turnbull Library in Wellington, the Christchurch City Library, and the librarians of the British Library, London and Wivenhoe Town Library, and the staff of many museums and sites in Paris and Rochefort in France. I thank Jeanette Jacobson at 'Mt Leinster', in Akaroa, for letting me visit her home, to see François Lelièvre's property, and for showing me her records.

I thank my mother and late father, keen gardeners, who cultivated a slip taken from the surviving willow in the French cemetery in Akaroa, which grew into a beautiful tree. Our visit to Akaroa and Le Bons Bay was critical for my research, and a special time for us. They read drafts of this novel and their encouragement was really important for me.

I thank also Jenny King for sending me materials and for comments, as also Michael Gallagher, Murray Darroch, Sandi Sharkey, Florence Leader and Thorunn Bjornsdottir Bacon for their critiques and suggestions.

I am hugely grateful to the wonderful guys at RSVP Publishing for taking on this novel and for bringing it into the world with such care. Thank you so much Stephen Picard and Chris Palmer; you are amazing. I thank Jane Dixon-Smith for her beautiful cover design. Thanks also to Linda Malpas, Ken Johnson and my husband Paul Hunt for their proofreading.

Special thanks to my dear friend Aroha Yates-Smith, to whom this novel is dedicated, who believed in it from the beginning. Her sharing of her deep knowledge of Maori spirituality led me down paths that led to this story, and her grace, courage and compassion are surely an inspiration to all those she touches.

I thank also the late Bob Le Lievre (descendant of François) and Pam Jorgensen (descendant of Kahutia of Otakou, whose great-great grandmother Maria was baptised by Bishop Pompallier, during his visit to Taiaroa in 1841). Finally, I thank again my very supportive and insightful husband and our children, Emily and Robbie, who have accompanied me on my travels and are my treasure.

Historical Note

This novel is based on true events surrounding the birth of New Zealand as a nation, as it took shape under British sovereignty, and what happened regarding the French colony of Akaroa. The ships, the dates, the main players, the issues and the conflicts are described as they are known to have occurred.

The real François Lelièvre, from Beslon (Normandy, France), was born in 1810. He was a blacksmith on the *Nil* and came with the French colonists on the *Comte de Paris*. In due course he became one of the most successful French settlers of Akaroa. He married Justine (Rose) Malmanche on March 4, 1851, when she was almost nineteen, and they had nine children. The French-style bed made for their marriage is now in the Akaroa Museum. François lived to the age of ninety-two, dying in Akaroa on 12 July, 1902.

There are various stories of Napoleon's willow and how it arrived in Akaroa, but the strongest is one told among the direct descendants of François Lelièvre. A fervent Bonapartist, François took cuttings (two or three) of the willow from St. Helena's Island in 1837, when the *Nil* stopped there. He planted these beside a stream in Paka Ariki Bay and in German Bay, and later they were grown in the French Cemetery on Aube Hill. Many people believe that the willows now along the Avon River in Christchurch were taken as cuttings from the willows propagated by François.

Originally François built a *whare* near the willow. In 1845 he built on the section a European-style house: 'a very snug little cottage with three rooms and a loft about half-a-mile from the beach', according to the description of a visitor. (1) Four years later, in 1849, he sold it to John Watson, the new British Resident Magistrate, who was well-liked by all, and during this time it had three willows growing. Much later, Watson leased this property to Howard C. Jacobson (arriving in 1881), who named it 'Mt. Leinster'. In 1909, the original willow was blown down in a storm.

But the memory lingered and willows proliferated. In 1954, the elderly Miss Ada Jacobson, daughter of Howard Jacobson, wrote a letter to Mrs. W. A. Newton, who was a granddaughter of François Lelièvre, recalling a story she heard from him as a girl:

When I was going to school one day, my father and I were standing under the willow tree [on Balguerie Street] and your grandfather [François] rode by. He told us, when he was a boy [actually, a young man], he was apprenticed to a whaler. I have forgotten the name of the boat, but they stopped at St. Helena and he cut a slip of willow from Napoleon's grave and kept it in a tin. Whilst in Akaroa Harbour, he had a row with some of the crew and ran away, taking the slip with him. He hid in the bush and planted the slip in an open space (2).

This is the version of the story, based on what François said, that is re-told in this novel.

Most of the willow trees of the French Cemetery in Akaroa were cut down in 1925. There were complaints about the cemetery's neglected condition, where the old wooden crosses had disappeared, and the roses had become overgrown. The willows apparently had a disease, but there was also a preference for native trees. The land was cleared, and a stark monument erected with inscriptions recording the still-legible names of those buried there. The huge stumps of the old willows can still be seen there.

However, Napoleon's willow was reinstated in Akaroa from a cutting given to Bishop Pompallier. In the *Akaroa Mail* of September 5, 1939, there is a record of its replanting. It seemed appropriate 'when France and England were about to take up arms against a common aggressor in Europe, that the bond between French and English in the settlement of Akaroa should again be recalled in the planting of this willow tree.' François Lelièvre's son placed it in the ground. The *Christchurch Press* of November 2, 1939, reports:

Just recently, Mr E. X. Le Lievre planted on the old French Cemetery site a slip from a willow from Jerusalem, Wanganui River. The slip was taken from a tree planted there by Bishop Pompallier. Bishop Pompallier secured a slip from the first willow brought to Akaroa in 1840 by Mr Francois Le Lievre, one of the original French settlers, and father of Mr E. X. Le Lievre.

Francois Le Lievre secured his willow from Napoleon's grave. It grew in Akaroa for many years in the Balguerie Valley, where this Frenchman built his whare and cut down the bush to clear his section.

Today, in the French Cemetery, there is a small trunk of Napoleon's willow still growing from an old stump, which seems to be from one of the oldest trees.

As for other people in this novel, the colonists in Akaroa are portrayed on the basis of the facts as known. The history of the colony in French Akaroa is fully told by Peter Tremewan, in his book *French Akaroa*, and for those who want to explore actual events further, and find out about this settlement in detail, I highly recommend his work.

Charles Barrington Robinson, with interests in maintaining his property investment in Akaroa Harbour, remained there until 1845, despite not developing his land. Robinson returned in 1850 hoping to farm, and in 1853 married a young woman named Helen Sinclair, twenty years his junior, whom he mistreated violently and she left him, fleeing to her parents in Pigeon Bay with their infant son Aubrey in 1855, and eventually going to Hawaii. He left New Zealand, and died in Surrey, England, in 1900.

Bishop Pompallier moved from Kororareka to the new capital, Auckland. He was a prolific writer of books, pamphlets and letters in French, Maori and English, and he tirelessly travelled both within New Zealand and back and forth to France and elsewhere, seeking to build up the Mission and foster Catholicism in New Zealand. He returned to France for the last time in 1868, because of illness, and died there three years later.

Pierre Joseph St.-Croix Crocquet de Belligny returned to France in 1845, and kept a friendship with Robinson over many years, corresponding by letter. He became the French consul in Zanzibar, in Manilla (Philippines), and in Charleston, South Carolina, where he was at the outbreak of the American Civil War in 1861.

Marginalised by Lavaud, Captain Jean-François Langlois went away whaling in the *Comte de Paris* in December 1840, and, though he did come back to Akaroa, there were further hostile interactions with Lavaud. He returned to France in the ship in 1842 and continued to assert the validity of the agreements he made. He remained in the business of whaling and fishing, but never returned to New Zealand.

Commandant Lavaud was esteemed by the French Government for avoiding conflict with the British in New Zealand. After he returned to France in 1843, he was made an officer of the Legion of Honour for his diplomatic services. He was governor of Tahiti (1846-1849), before being appointed as an admiral in the French Navy.

Jean-Baptiste Comte stayed in Akaroa until 1842, and visited frequently thereafter from his new station in Otaki, north of Wellington, until he returned to France in 1854. He lived a long life.

The chiefs of the Ngāi Tahu are named in various deeds of sale for Banks Peninsula and in records concerning the Maori of the Horomaka. Taiaroa's request for payment for the Horomaka, delivered in good faith by Bishop Pompallier after careful negotiations, was never honoured by the French authorities. A final agreement was forced on Maori in 1845. By this time Iwikau was dead, as well as other important chiefs involved in the 1840 agreements. In 1856, the British authorities asserted full ownership of all the Horomaka. Maori were allowed to keep only three small areas, and little compensation was offered. The Ngāi Tahu were not able to seek redress until recent times, a process which began when a claim was registered in August, 1986, with the Waitangi Tribunal. It comprised 'The Nine Tall Trees of Ngāi Tahu', each representing a loss to the Ngāi Tahu tribe, which resulted in the issuing of the Tribunal's Ngāi Tahu Report in 1991.

As for Manako-uri/ Matthieu Le Bon, he is a fictional character formed out of various strands. He is based on evidence of a healer recorded in the words of Jimmy Robinson Clough:

Drinking rum and working in wet clothes brought on a bad attack of low fever, and for three weeks I was in bed. As a last resort, my wife, who was a powerful big woman, carried me over the hills as far as Wairewa (Little River), where there was a Native doctor supposed to be very clever. Anyhow he cured me with Native herbs... (3).

I have linked this healer to the name Le Bon, and moved him from Waiwera. Katawahu is recorded as 'Le Bons Bay' from at least 1843. There are various theories about how it got its name: one story holds that it came from a mysterious *Monsieur* Le Bon, and another that it was called 'Bones Bay' (as it appears in some English charts), though it was never the site of whaling.

The character of Marianne is also fictional, but she is inspired by real women who came to New Zealand in the mid-19th century. History is so often focused on men, especially those in powerful positions, or on the women of the higher echelons of society who left diaries and letters. For an ordinary woman's life it is harder to find evidence. There were single women who travelled in the ships to New Zealand, and their stories have often been overlooked. In creating Marianne I have been able to explore what it really meant to be a woman like her, because imagination allows us to enter a woman's past experience in a way that we cannot with the slim remaining facts alone.

Joan Norlev Taylor

1) Charlotte Godley, *Letters from Early New Zealand* (Plymouth: Bowering Press, 1936), 252-3.
2. *'The Akaroa Willow,'* The Press, 4 July, 1970. I am grateful to Margaret Harper of Christchurch City Libraries for finding this reference.
3. Howard C. Jacobson, with James Stack, *Akaroa and Banks Peninsula 1840-1940* (Akaroa: Akaroa Mail Company, 1940), 147. Text corrected.

Selected Historical Reading

Baughan, Blanche Edith, *Akaroa* (Auckland: Whitcombe and Tombs, 1918).

Best, Elsdon, *The Maori As He Was: A Brief Account of Life as it was in Pre-European Days* (Wellington: Dominion Museum, 1934).

Binney, Judith, Bassett, Judith and Olsen, Erik, *An Illustrated History of New Zealand 1820-1920* (Wellington: Allen and Unwin, 1990).

Butler, Nicholas, *The Story of Wivenhoe* (Wivenhoe: Quentin Press, 1989).

Buick, A. S., *The French at Akaroa: An Adventure in Colonization* (Wellington: New Zealand Book Depot, 1928).

Dieffenbach, Ernest, *Travels in New Zealand*, 2 vols. (London: John Murray, 1843).

Ell, Sarah, *The Adventures of Pioneer Women in New Zealand: From Their Letters, Diaries, and Reminiscences* (Auckland: Bush Press, 1992).

Godley, Charlotte, *Letters from Early New Zealand* by Charlotte Godley, 1850–1853, ed. John R. Godley (Christchurch: Whitcombe and Tombs, 1951).

Hallett, Ross C., 'Willows in New Zealand', unpubl. M.Sc. thesis, Waikato University (1978).

Hutching, Megan, *Over the Wide and Trackless Sea: The Pioneer Women and Girls of New Zealand* (Auckland: HarperCollins, 2008).

Jacobson, Howard C., *Akaroa and Banks Peninsula, 1840-1940*, with James W. Stack (Akaroa: Akaroa Mail Company, 1940).

Jacobson, Howard C., *Tales of Banks Peninsula*, 3rd ed. (Akaroa: Akaroa Mail Company, 1914).

Keys, Lillian Gladys, *The Life and Times of Bishop Pompallier* (Christchurch: Pegasus, 1957).

King, Michael, *Maori: A Photographic and Social History* (Auckland: Reed, 1983).

King, Michael and Filer, David, *The Penguin History of New Zealand*, Illustrated (Auckland: Penguin, 2007).

Lambourne, Alan, *The Treatymakers of New Zealand: Heralding the Birth of a Nation* (Lewes: The Book Guild, 1988).

Lelièvre, Valerie, *The Lelièvre Family, Akaroa: The Story of Etienne Francois and Justine Rose Lelièvre and their Descendants 1840-1990* (Lelièvre Family Book Committee, 1990).

Locke, Elsie and Paul, Janet, with Christine Tremewan, *Mrs Hobson's Album* (Auckland: Alexander Turnbull Library, 1989).

Macdonald, Charlotte, *A Woman of Good Character: Single Women as Immigrant Settlers in Nineteenth Century New Zealand* (Wellington: Allen and Unwin, 1990/ Bridget Williams, 2015 [e-book]).

Mawer, Granville Adam, *Ahab's Trade: The Saga of South Seas Whaling* (New York: St. Martin's Press, 1999).

Ogilvie, Gordon, *Picturing the Peninsula: Early Days on Banks Peninsula* (Christchurch/ Auckland: Hazard Press, 1992).

Sinclair, Keith, *A History of New Zealand*, rev. ed. (Auckland: Penguin, 1988).

Tremewan, Peter, *French Akaroa: An Attempt to Colonise Southern New Zealand* (Christchurch: Canterbury University Press, 1990, rev. ed. 2010).

Turner, Gwenda, *Akaroa: Banks Peninsula, New Zealand* (Dunedin: John McIndoe, 1977).

Woodhouse, Airini Elizabeth, *Tales of Pioneer Women* (Auckland: Whitcombe and Tombs, 1940).